Praise for

L. A. BANKS
and
The Vampire Huntress Legend

THE DAMNED

"All hell breaks loose—literally—in the complex sixth installment . . . stunning."   —*Publishers Weekly*

"In [*The Damned*], relationships are defined, while a dark energy threatens to destroy the entire squad. Banks' method of bringing Damali and Carlos back together is done with utmost sincerity and integrity. They have a love that can weather any storm, even when dire circumstances seem utterly overwhelming. Fans of this series will love *The Damned* and, no doubt, will eagerly await the next book."   —*Romantic Times BOOKreviews*

THE FORBIDDEN

"Passion, mythology, war and love that lasts till the grave—and beyond . . . fans should relish this new chapter in a promising series."   —*Publishers Weekly*

"Superior vampire fiction."   —*Booklist*

THE BITTEN

"Seductive . . . mixing religion with erotic horror dosed with a funky African-American beat, Banks blithely piles on layer after layer of densely detailed plot . . . will delight established fans. Banks creates smokin' sex scenes that easily out-vamp Laurell K. Hamilton's."
                    —*Publishers Weekly*

"The stakes have never been higher, and the excitement and tension are palpable in this installment of Banks' complex, sexy series." —*Booklist*

"Duties, pain, responsibilities—what this duo does in the name of love is amazing."
—*Romantic Times BOOKreviews*

THE HUNTED
"A terrifying roller-coaster ride of a book."
—Charlaine Harris

"Hip, fresh, and fantastic." —Sherrilyn Kenyon,
New York Times bestselling author
of *Dark Side of the Moon*

THE AWAKENING
"An intriguing portrait of vampiric society, reminiscent of Anne Rice and Laurell K. Hamilton." —*Library Journal*

"Again, Banks brilliantly combines spirituality, vampires, and demons (and hip-hop music) into a fast-paced tale that is sure to leave fans of her first novel, *Minion*, panting for more." —*Columbus Dispatch*

MINION
"[*Minion*] literally rocks the reader into the action-packed underworld power struggle between vampire rivals with a little demon juice thrown in."
—*Philadelphia Sunday Sun*

"[A] tough, sexy new vampire huntress challenges the dominance of Anita Blake and Buffy . . . Damali is an appealing heroine, the concept is intriguing, and the series promising." —*Amazon.com*

Also by
L. A. Banks

BITE THE BULLET

A Crimson Moon Novel

L.A. BANKS

St. Martin's Paperbacks

This is a work of fiction. All of the characters, organizations, and events portrayed in this novel are either products of the author's imagination or are used fictitiously.

BITE THE BULLET

Copyright © 2008 by L. A. Banks.
Excerpt from *Undead on Arrival* copyright © 2008 by L. A. Banks.

Cover photo © Barry David Marcus.

For information address St. Martin's Press, 175 Fifth Avenue, New York, NY 10010.

ISBN: 0-312-94912-X
EAN: 978-0-312-94912-9

Printed in the United States of America

St. Martin's Paperbacks edition / October 2008

St. Martin's Paperbacks are published by St. Martin's Press, 175 Fifth Avenue, New York, NY 10010.

10 9 8 7 6 5 4 3 2 1

For Helena . . . may you know that things are not always what they seem to be, and that life has layers and layers of complexity within it. I hope you can see the magic of it all. Your eyes are beautiful, so is your vision . . . so is your soul.

Special Acknowledgments: To Manie and Monique, the dynamic duo who bring order out of the chaos of my life <laughing>. Admit it, because you know you do. Thank you for going on yet another adventure with me. To the St. Martin's team, and my solid Street Team, thanks for always having my back!

Chapter 1

Northwest wilderness along the Canadian border . . .

A howl tried to climb up her throat but she swallowed it down until her lungs felt like they were going to burst. Her human side refused to give the wolf free rein. Not like this.

Sasha licked her lips, trying to find the Lieutenant Sasha Trudeau that she'd been before the full moon, before the heat. With Max Hunter on her flank, the lines between her wolf and human selves became more blurred. They had to find Fisher and Woods, the last two guys on her ambushed Paranormal Containment Unit squad. Familiars. She hated the term and preferred to call them friends.

Sweat slicked her body beneath layers of clothes. The frigid night air felt good against her face. Hunter had told her what to expect; so had his grandfather, Silver Hawk. As an alpha Shadow wolf mate, Hunter would know; as her lover, he would have warned her. But that was just it—there was no understanding this unless one experienced it. They'd said that, too. Yet, they were males. How could they even attempt to describe transforming from human to wolf during the burn that came with being in a female heat? What they'd conveyed was only secondhand knowledge. The mates had no concept; the insanity that came with this defied definition.

Besides, the moon was a gorgeous, radiating disk above her, impossible to escape. Sasha stopped running for a moment and squeezed her eyes shut, panting. The sensation of an abrupt wolf-change so near the surface of her skin strangled her reason. Suddenly the backpack she carried felt too heavy; it had become an onerous appendage just like her suffocating parka, thermals, boots, and jeans. Thick fabric restricted her being and made her want to scream with frustration. Labored breathing filled her ears. It was hers. Scents from the pristine environment stabbed into her sinuses and caused her to take in gulps of air through her mouth.

"Sasha . . . baby, just let her go," Hunter said in a sensual murmur as he loped to her side.

"No!" she shouted, hugging herself and bending over to pant harder.

"It's natural, a part of—"

Her low, warning growl stopped his words. "I want to be in control of me!" Tears stung her eyes but she refused to let them fall. "Can't you understand that? I'm a goddamned soldier!"

Hunter backed away from her with a nod and leaned against a tree, cloaking his form in the shadow of it. He'd instinctively done so as if he could tell that his mere presence was making her testy, and she appreciated his innate understanding that it had.

Sasha glimpsed where he'd been standing and then released a hard breath of relief that she could no longer see him. It was difficult enough catching his wondrous, earthy male scent when the winds suddenly shifted or hearing his easy footfalls in the snow that made shivers dance up her spine. Seeing his handsome, six-foot-five, muscular body peel out of the shadows had literally sent an irrational jolt through her system.

There was something about the way his long, jet-black ponytail had come loose on the run to spill onyx velvet over his thick shoulders . . . but that was nothing compared to the expression on his rugged face or the lingering question that burned deep within his intense, amber-rimmed irises. When he'd absently licked his lush bottom lip just before shadow-blending, she'd almost gone to him. But no. She would remain in control, would remain focused on the mission. Shadow Wolf or not, she had a job to do.

What she needed was distance and time to pull herself together. Slowly straightening, she lifted her chin and kept her eyes on the horizon, giving him her back. She refused to even look in the direction of where he'd been. What would be the point? It didn't take rocket science to know that he was staring at her. She could almost feel his hot gaze penetrating her back. He'd been looking at her like that all night.

Regardless, she was a military-trained, Special Ops, fighting machine, Sasha reminded herself as she began to pace. Squad leader of the Paranormal Containment Unit—PCU's top gun. The only genetic mistake that had made it out of the moonlight madness alive. Two of her men were still moving under radar behind Shadow Wolf territory lines, and she had to bring them in. The United Council of Entities was having an international meeting in New Orleans during the rare blue moon right after Mardi Gras, and every supernatural species would be in attendance— she had to prepare, be sharp, and gather intel. Demon-infected Werewolf virus was still on the black market. And now that she'd learned how to spot other wolves, plus the Fae, Pixies, Dragons, and other supernaturals, somebody would talk.

Damn the moon and any genetic defect she harbored! Despite the pressures of being what amounted to a double agent, the wolf was controllable, the clan elder had said! Mind over matter. That was the only way her kind had remained concealed for centuries. They were different from the outlawed species of demon-infected Werewolves that they hunted, a breed abomination that fed on human flesh and had no choice but to follow the phases of the moon. The transformation-burn would pass.

Sasha yanked back her hood and raked her fingers through her hair, noting with dismay that it had thickened on the run. She closed her eyes and turned her face up to the luminous disk in the sky and shuddered.

"It's different when you're in heat, baby," a very deep voice murmured from the shadows.

"What would you know about it? Screw you!" she shouted, whirling on the sound of Hunter's voice as it began to circle around her.

"Definitely an option I wish you'd consider."

Sasha snarled. If Max Hunter had laughed, she would have lunged at him and gone for his throat.

"I told you after that last time, no matter what, not until we were out of range of my men, your men, and the whole clan!"

"All right, I'm sorry," Hunter said in an amused tone that irked her to no end. "You ready to run some more or do you want to make camp and eat?"

"I want to get to the Shadow clan base camp tonight, not tomorrow," she snapped.

"Not advisable," he said flatly, coming out of the shadows with his arms folded. "You need to allow your *condition* to . . . mellow."

"My condition?" She felt her hands slowly begin to ball into fists at her side.

He nodded and stared at her hands. "As beautiful as you are, you might make me kill one of my own men in *this condition*."

She flipped him the bird and almost growled when his only response to the rude gesture was a dashing smile.

"Uh, yeah," he said, smirking. "My point, exactly."

"It's only twenty more miles! In a flat-out run, we could make it!"

Total frustration engulfed her as she began to walk back and forth before a stand of trees. "And you've got another thing coming if you think I'm going to enter a Shadow Wolf clan camp that has two of your best friends there, with me smelling like I've been knocking boots on the trail. I have some freakin' pride, Max Hunter. I'm a squad commander, and I will not have my men even remotely think that I delayed a recognizance with them because of some personal bull! Never happen. Not after all they've been through — especially them."

"I hear you," Hunter replied calmly, slipping into another shadow. "Understood."

"Good! I'm glad we've gotten that straight, because if you haven't noticed, every body of water we've passed is frozen solid."

A deep baritone chuckle echoed throughout the glen. "So, at least you've thought about it. Now I feel better. Slightly."

"No, I didn't think about it!" she shouted, her voice carrying against her will.

"Be honest, Sasha. You've weighed the logistics and

come away with a negative conclusion. That I can accept. I told you before I am no liar—and the last person I ever lie to is myself."

"Kiss my ass, Max Hunter."

He stepped out of the shadows with his head tilted and dropped his backpack in the snow. "Gladly."

She drew her nine millimeter on him and he simply smiled, now flashing canines.

"Like I said, I try not to lie to myself, and my condition isn't wholly stable, either."

She stared at him but didn't lower the weapon. He didn't seem the least bit concerned by its presence.

"We need to make camp here. I've gotta eat," he announced and glanced down with a weary sigh. "You're not the only one subject to clan embarrassment; you do realize that, don't you?"

"We keep moving," she said through her teeth.

"Suit yourself," he said, unfazed, and began to unzip his parka. "This is moose country."

"So you aren't coming?"

He smiled a wicked smile. "Not yet."

She turned away from him and holstered her gun again, determined not to allow him to see her hands tremble. Her angry footfalls turned into outright stomps in the snow when she heard him unzip his jeans.

"You need a guide," he called out behind her. "Until you're scented in as a non-hostile clan member, they'll hide from you . . . will also hide your men for their safety."

"Then stop messing with my head and come on!"

She didn't turn around as she'd yelled out her response. The last thing her nerves could stand at the moment was the sight of Hunter's dark, stone-cut body in the buff. They'd never see eye-to-eye on the point, anyway, so what was the use of arguing? He claimed status as a warrior, she was a soldier—the difference being, according to Hunter, warriors chose their own missions and fates, whereas soldiers took orders. Problem was she now had two hierarchies to serve. As the alpha female of their pack, she, too, was a warrior . . . and her pack status was supposed to supersede any military rank any day, according to supernatural law. Blah, blah, blah.

Yeah, so what, she still worked for the brass and he was his own loose cannon leading a local pack and the frickin' North American clan. She doubted they'd see Hunter's point in a military court while being court-martialed for literally getting waylaid while on an important mission to find vials of missing biohazardous materials. Oh, yeah, that would go over big. Like trying to argue with the feds about taxes—losing proposition.

Remembering the philosophical debate made Sasha grind her teeth as she trudged in the snow and tried not to think of Hunter's deliciously naked form hidden by the shadows. His silver and amber amulet was probably stunning against his rock-solid chest, too—but she was *not* going there.

To her way of thinking, some things were a matter of personal ethics; as a soldier, she had a job to do first and foremost. There was no time to be self-indulgent. The military didn't give a rat's ass about things like phases of the moon, natural ebbs and flows of Shadow Wolf menses, thermo-combustion properties within one's bloodstream, or the acute pain involved in repressing a howl. She wasn't even supposed to exist. As far as the brass knew, she didn't—well, not as a Shadow Wolf, anyway. She and the other members of her squad had been a laboratory mistake, and in order to not be added to the most wanted and hunted target list, she had to maintain her human presence at all times.

"Sasha, you have to stop running with all that gear on," Hunter called out, nearer to her than she'd wanted. "You'll drop from heat exhaustion holding back your wolf and pressing on like this bundled in layers under a full moon. It's dangerous!"

"Go to hell!" Had he any idea how much politicking had gone into her and Doc Holland convincing the generals from Special Ops Comm that she needed her own budget, her own Special Forces Paranormal Team, and to keep her so-called informants, like him, off radar?

"I'm not stripping out here or changing!"

"Then slow your pace and walk it off."

"Fine. Are you coming with me, then, or not?"

Sasha slowed her pace to a trot, breathing hard. Cold air knifed her lungs and she hated that Hunter was right; she was burning up. Acute pain made her fight against a whimper. She could tell that Hunter was undecided. He claimed he was going to make camp and needed to eat, but yet he was following her, torn. That was the problem, they were both torn. But she had to remember what was at stake: lives. Human lives. She should have taken the meds Doc had developed, but doing so blinded her to so much of the preternatural world that she needed to see. One week clean and she could see Fae auras. Two weeks clean and she'd been able to see the subtle mesh of scales beneath the skins of those who hailed from the Order of the Dragon. Phantoms announced themselves to her nervous system now even before she saw them, bristling the hairs on the back of her neck. Without meds muddying her perception, she could scent other Werebeings, especially other wolves, a half mile away. And

Vampires made her snarl while still vapor. Meds might have made her survive the heat with less duress, but they definitely wouldn't make her job in New Orleans any easier.

Bottom line was, she had to focus—had to collect her squad members Fisher and Woods from the Canadian border, and then double back to the big shindig in New Orleans, regardless of Hunter's beef with the Werewolf clans or Shogun, the alpha southeast Asian pack leader.

As it was, HQ didn't even know that Fisher and Woods had made it out of Afghanistan alive. Only Doc knew the truth. Flashes of Rod's Werewolf infection going full-blown entered her mind and she briefly closed her eyes as she recalled his death at the barrel of her gun. Captain Rod Butler was more than a fellow soldier—he'd been her closest friend, like a blood brother. The image of dropping her mentor would always haunt her.

Hunter clearly didn't get it. There were also hundreds of decisions to address, like whether or not it was safer to keep Fisher and Woods on the books as dead or let it be known that these two guys with a little natural wolf in their DNA posed no threat to people.

Annoyed that Hunter had neither answered her nor sounded like he was following her, she began to call out to him again, causing her voice to bounce off naked trees and frozen earth.

"My guys have been shifted around the damned globe, and it's been nearly a month since I could shake the brass at the base and get a free pass to handle things my way. Now I'm supposed to show up late and—"

"The time lapse did them good," a low, even voice said, standing close enough to her that she could feel his breath. "They needed time to learn what they were, just like you did. My pack brothers have been educating them to the ways of the Shadow Wolf."

"Oh, great. Just fine, Kung Fu," she said, now picking up her pace to a panting jog. "So they'll really be clued in to my so-called *condition*. Well, ya know what? You're really pissing me off! Maybe I don't want my guys to know all of that. Haven't you ever heard of things being on a need-to-know basis?"

"They won't be able to scent it, only other Shadow Wolves. They're just familiars."

"And knowing that *your* men will know makes me feel better, how?" Sasha began running faster, not sure of the direction but needing to move.

"They know you're my mate. Period. What occurs between a life-mated pair is natural. Known. No shame." His voice had slipped out of the shadows at her side along with a wisp of warm breath against her ear before she'd veered off from the sensation. "There is nothing more for them to know."

"We have been over this already, Hunter! I told you I wasn't ready for the life-mate commitment. We're lovers, true, pack mates, but—"

"Decide under the moon. Making love to me when you need to isn't a sign of weakness or a criminal offense; nor is being my mate. Let the pack, or even the clan, assume what they will. They don't have to know what parameters define our so-called relationship. It is unimportant, as long as you and I know the truth. Period."

"What!" She stopped running and folded her arms over her chest. "That is such a crock. It's about respect. When I meet a new clan, I require that—that's what's *period*, mister. I'm not going down to New Orleans *weak* and waltzing into an international diplomats' meeting under the whispers of foul rumors and—"

"Why would your body following the natural rhythms of ancient Shadow cycles and also having a mate challenge your respect? Now I'm confused."

She turned, following his voice as he circled her. "Because it does—don't try to cloud the issue."

"How? You are trying to layer Western patriarchal concepts about female weaknesses over a culture that does not understand that. A strong she-Shadow is just that—a strong she-Shadow. Her being in heat only makes her stronger, more desirable . . . it doesn't impact her authority. You're my pack alpha, Sasha—even if you have yet to commit to being my life mate. And while I would hate to see you fight for dominance at the clan level to take a lead role as North American clan she-alpha, I have no doubts that you would prevail. I admire that." He paused and she could hear the strain in his voice as it echoed through the trees and she tried to follow it, her ears keen.

Suddenly his voice exited the shadows on what felt like a sonic boom, containing so much force and passion that it gave her a start. "The International Federation of Shadow Clans, even the Werewolf Clans, view a she-alpha in phase with much awe and respect—and screw the flaky Fae Parliament or the lesser voting blocs coming from the Mythics and phantom feudal lords! And *you know* we don't give a damn about the Vampire Cartel. How can I make you understand?"

Sasha closed her eyes and counted to ten as her voice dropped to a disgusted mutter. "Oh, *my God* . . . I cannot *believe* I'm standing out here in the damned forest arguing philosophy with a male *wolf*."

A low growl of discontent made her open her eyes. "I do not believe this conversation, either, Sasha. It makes no sense—especially when the moon is full."

"You think I'm enjoying *this*?" she shouted, suddenly defensive and not sure why. "I didn't ask for this, okay? And it's the first time I've felt so out of control—why now, huh, when I have everything else to contend with? And, so what, I was raised with a Western perspective where we're used to compartmentalizing things!" She was practically stuttering she was so upset and had begun to walk in a tight circle. "Why now? At the most inopportune time— damn!"

"Because of me," a deep voice murmured, stalking her as it resonated between the trees.

"Gimme a break." She leaned against a tree and closed her eyes, beginning to feel fatigue weigh on her.

"How many times do I have to tell you I am no liar?"

If she wasn't so frustrated she would have smiled at his peevish tone. "Yeah, yeah, yeah, all right," she muttered. "Your grandfather said this first time would happen be- cause I had finally been around my own kind."

"Correct," a low rumble ricocheted from nearby. "You and I had been intimate, your senses heightened to male Shadow pheromone . . . now your body has adjusted to no longer only being with humans—each phase will be like this."

"Every time the moon goes full? You have *got* to be kidding me!"

"No . . . like Grandfather told you, just when it's your time . . . and I've taken herbal precautions, as always, so you don't have to worry about a pregnancy before you're ready."

"Glad this shit only happens once a quarter, then," she volleyed back, and was met with eerie silence.

Sasha pushed off the tree and strained to listen for Hunter, and then let out a hard sigh. "All right, I'm sorry—I didn't mean it like that . . . about you or kids. I just hate being out of control, okay?"

Silence met her. Now she had to deal with a wounded wolf, too? Oh, puh-leease! The absolute insanity of being in this predicament made her finally throw her head back and howl.

"You think you're the only one who hates being out of control?" a low, tense voice said behind her.

She glanced over her shoulder and then turned slowly. The most beautiful jet-black specimen had stepped out of the shadows, eyes blazing deep golden fire. He was absolutely breathtaking and stood no less than three feet at the shoulders. A silver chain around his neck dangled with a large hunk of etched amber that matched the one she also wore. All she could do was watch the sinew knead beneath his glossy coat as the moon shone blue-black against him. And then, just as suddenly as he'd appeared to her, he was gone.

Why that made her frantic, she wasn't sure. Why just a glimpse of his wolf had coaxed out her own, she would never truly know. But her backpack hit the snow, and she stripped while running, almost laughing as her wolf broke free to hunt his in the shadows.

Their mission became fuzzy as the primal overtook her human mind. Yes, they had to find the black market sources of demon-infected Werewolf contagion. Yes, they still had to find out if remnants from Guilliaume and Dexter's rogue Shadow Wolf faction had made it out alive after that weasel Dexter did . . . needed to know the real role any Vampires played in all of this going forward. She never trusted the species. Needed to rendezvous with her guys that were operating in the shadows in a way that even her brass at NORAD didn't know about . . . but this thing that had her in its grip was so welded to her DNA that she couldn't have fought it if she'd tried—and she had really, *really* tried.

Hunter headed for a virgin carpet of snow, untouched powder along a lonely slope. Stars winked against midnight as though a thousand diamonds scattered on black velvet. Didn't she understand this was as much a part of who she was as the uniform she wore? More so, as it came from within. And in this form she was so beautiful . . . incredible silver coat that reflected slivers of the moon, just like her clear gray eyes.

Wanting to witness her hunting him, he gave her wide berth, circling her on the slope and hanging back, just so he could face her head-on. Intense joy filled his chest as she lowered her head, growled, and began to stalk him. *Oh, yeah . . . do me.*

Laughing inside, he tilted his head, released a playful yelp, and began running again, loving the chase. He knew what they had to do, knew what was at risk. Their job descriptions were the same—exterminate demon-infected Werewolves and any supernatural threat to humanity.

It was simply a matter of style that created differences between them. Anticipation knotted his stomach as he heard her gaining on him. For centuries his kind hunted according to the natural laws of the universe; she was led and directed by those with no innate understanding or respect of natural ebbs and flows. Perhaps one day she would see the wisdom of the elders, but tonight he really didn't care if she did or not. As long as she kept chasing him . . . as long as her incredible body hunted his . . . as long as she became his mate and gave into an urge that was as basic as breathing, they could square up their differences in the morning.

The sudden absence of sound made him glance over his shoulder just in time to see Sasha go airborne. She collided against him with a thud; willingly her prey, he rolled over on his back and gave her his throat. The sport had gone out of resisting her. Glistening white teeth rested on his Adam's apple, pinning him down. He closed his eyes and released a mournful howl, his man-shape returning naked and shuddering beneath her she-wolf. He wanted her so badly, he didn't care if she got angry and bit him; he'd heal.

Unafraid, his fingers reveled in her thick, soft coat, soon sliding against heat-dampened skin as she shape-shifted right into his arms. The snow at his back began to melt the very second her hot body blanketed him and she took his mouth, coaxing a groan up his throat.

"Just once, like this, out here, tonight," he murmured, stuttering promises into her mouth as his hands traveled over her smooth backside. "Then we'll get back on mission. I swear—I just can't function like this."

The truth finally broke him as he lost his fingers in her thicket of brunette hair, cradling her skull. It was impossible to think, much less remain rational as she dragged her voluptuous five-foot-seven-inch frame up his body in a molten sweep. He was beyond pride. She was in heat. The moan she pulled out of him was damned near a howl.

Skin against skin was making him delirious. Steel-gray eyes pierced his as her silver and amber amulet grazed the similar ward he wore against his chest. His trembling hands soon covered her breasts, his thumbs gently caressing her taut, caramel nipples. She winced with a soft moan, encouraging his fingers to tease her pebbled flesh all the more. Breaths growing shallower, he watched as a combination of agony and pleasure overtook her expression. Beyond articulating, his mind focused on one word: *please*.

She didn't answer him directly, but pulled his bottom lip between her teeth for a second before kissing him harder. He took that as a yes and nearly lost his mind.

Within an instant he'd flip-rolled her so quickly and with so much force that her body left a deep impression in the snow. Melting snow by the second from heat and friction, the slick sound of her, the puddle forming at her back, the sound of her voice, his, all of it echoing off the night, the trees, the very sky itself caused him to enter her on one hard lunge.

Creamy, café au lait skin filled his palms as her breasts pressed against his chest. Her voice fractured the night and his spine, contracting every muscle in his groin with her earthy wail. But it was her scent that had stolen his judgment, just like the feel of her tightening sheath dredged his sac, the all of her demanding recompense for denied release. It wasn't his fault, he'd tried all evening and she wouldn't hear of it—now she was breaking his back . . . and he loved it, loved her, couldn't stop if she'd shot him.

Every hot sweep of her silky hands over his ass caused a shudder, and he cried out when she clutched the halves of it to bring him against her even harder. There was no way to drag enough air into his lungs through his nose. He had to break the suffocating kiss or pass out with a hump in his back. But leaving her mouth, tearing his away from hers, was just as painful. All he could do was throw his head back and cry out her name to the understanding moon.

She released so hard that it felt like her spine might snap from the sudden arch. Her fingers couldn't hold enough of his broad back, nor could her thighs seem to anchor themselves around his waist tightly enough. She needed him inside her but the ache of each contraction that traveled up her canal to devour her womb put jags of his name in her mouth. Every exhale was timed with his deep return to her body. As she thrashed with pleasure, his name was soon broken cries sent forth into the relentless wind.

Tears stung her eyes, his thrusts making her crazy, while the full moon made her entire body wax anything but philosophical. She was still shuddering when he rolled them over with her belly cemented to his, his fingers caressing her back. His large hands sent warmth across her skin. Resting on his hard body was like laying against hot stone on a cool spring day.

Damp, temporarily sated, she could feel his heart slamming against hers through ribs, muscle, and skin. Her amulet was precariously tangled with his, just like their legs were. Both panting, she ran her fingers through his wild spill of hair.

"We need to pitch a tent . . . go back and recover the dropped weapons and supplies," he finally said, gasping. "Hunt down dinner."

She just nodded, hadn't yet caught her breath. He leaned up and suddenly kissed her, forcing her to look into his eyes as he held her face when he pulled back. His gaze was so furtive she thought the man was going to throw his head back and howl.

"I can build a fire, melt snow, make enough water for

you to wash up in the morning . . . but with you in this condition, I'm gonna have to do this again tonight. Especially after we hunt. I'm just being honest."

Sasha simply closed her eyes and nodded again. Some things were just natural. The man was *definitely* no liar.

Chapter 2

Full awareness slowly returned as Sasha opened one eye and squinted against the morning brightness. It felt like she'd been hit in the back of her head with a sledgehammer, but she could only smile at the memory of last night. Sun bounced off the snow and created a reflective glare that made it seem as though headlights were focused in her direction. The last thing she remembered before she'd shuddered and passed out was Hunter's strong arm around her waist as he kissed the back of her skull, mounted her, and repeatedly told her he was sorry. Hell, she wasn't.

Little by little she was able to tolerate the filtered light coming through the tent wall. A cool vacancy at her back told her that Hunter was already up, awake, and on the move. She strained to hear him through her mental haze and then inhaled deeply to pick up his scent. *What a night* . . .

Struggling to sit upright, she pulled the thick sleeping bag around her. It felt like she'd been in a prize fight . . . then she remembered. *Oh yeah, the moose.* She closed her eyes and let her head fall back, taking a moment to relive the joy of it all. The sultry scent of a morning fire teased her nose, and soon the smell of grilling meat drew her out of her private reverie to find her clothes.

She shielded her eyes from the bright sunlight as she opened the tent flap and peeked out. Hunter looked up at her from the sizzling spit with a smile. Hunger made her stomach growl, but the look of him squatting by the flame, jeans drawn taut against his thighs and only a thermal T-shirt hugging his ridiculously chiseled chest and abs, threatened to get her started again. He knew it, she knew it, the situation balanced dangerously on a razor's edge and could be seen smoldering in their eyes.

The issue was, whoever crossed the line first would dictate the next Shadow dance. But as badly as she wanted to just hang out in no-man's-land with him, making love and forgetting about the rest of the world, she couldn't. They both knew they had a mission to complete, even if he'd been right about taking a brief break. She saw that in his eyes, too—the conflict—the same one that must have shone in hers.

Hunter stood slowly, unfurling his fantastic body from the squatting position he'd been in. The sight of him was nearly paralyzing, but her mind seized on the almost eclipsed priority: the mission.

He simply stared at her, meat sizzling on the spit beside him. If he threw back his head and howled, she'd lose it. He seemed to know that and it made his expression become more serious. No. It was only a mental whimper.

They couldn't allow the trail to Dexter to go cold; the brass had already delayed them enough with questions and reports and bureaucratic nonsense. Then again, a general had had his face ripped off in his own home, so a paranormal inquisition was bound to be had. It also didn't matter that she and Hunter had blown away almost all of the offenders involved. The brass wanted everyone and everything involved in "the situation," as it was termed, "cleaned up"—code word for "exterminated"—with vials of missing Werewolf blood toxin returned. The Shadow clans wanted that, too. Yeah. She and Hunter could do that; the exterminating part, without question. It was the returning the missing vials part that was going to be problematic, especially with Hunter in his condition. Ultimately she had to have a conversation with Shogun, but if another male approached her—especially a Werewolf—right now, at least, there'd be bloodshed. For all she knew, he might even snap at one of his own pack brothers.

If only Hunter would stop looking at her like that . . .

They had to remain focused, now that they'd gotten last night out of their systems. He had to understand that the edges of her brain were catching fire with him staring at her as though she were breakfast.

Finding the vials would take time, some diplomatic negotiations between other paranormal species, which often required bargaining chips or deadly force, not that it mattered to her much which way things went. But the process was time-consuming. They had to strategize. She hated that part of the gig, the diplomatic part. Most times diplomacy failed. It didn't work in the same human terms people had come to expect. Working with entities was not like sitting down at a UN summit. She could only imagine what a session at the United Council of Entities would be like. However, on the flip side, the way human-nation negotiations had been going lately, voting at the UCE might actually be a more civilized process.

What the brass would have to begin to accept was that preternatural species were an alien culture to theirs, and each one had their own history, culture, belief systems, abilities, and prejudices. That's where the similarity between those so-called supernaturals and humans stopped. The same rules didn't apply. They took negotiations to a whole different level. Deadly force was acceptable at the bargaining table, which, truth be told, was more effective than sending whole nations to war. Still, she'd have to get used to seeing a supernatural world leader jump across a table to rip someone's heart out. Oh yeah, New Orleans was gonna be interesting.

She was staring at two hundred and twenty pounds of alpha male enforcer. How did one explain this part of her reality to the brass? Clearly one didn't. Sasha swallowed hard and looked away from Hunter as she came close to the fire and warmed her hands over it.

Negotiators were also enforcers—in fact, that was part of the negotiation most times. Entities from the demon realms didn't do things just to be nice or for the greater good. One had to show them how it was in their best interest, or let them know that you could kick their ass, and then had to be prepared to back up the challenge if your bluff got called. Hunter was most definitely a bluff buster, not that she was so shabby herself, but damn.

Opting for humor as an escape clause from the volatile, Sasha dramatically finger-combed her tangled hair away from her face, picking twigs out of it to make them both laugh.

"Good morning. I made breakfast," he finally said, his voice mellow and gracious. He shook his head, chuckling, and walked back to the fire.

She let out a slow breath of relief when he turned his back. The sexual standoff had ended. For a moment she thought he was gonna go straight wolf on her; it was all in his eyes. Instead of imagining the glory of that, she tried to focus on the metal cups on the ground filled with instant black coffee.

"Morning. Thanks," she said, trying to keep her voice as casual as possible as she picked up a steaming cup and cradled it between her palms. The heat felt good in her hands, even if the strong brew was bitter. She glimpsed the moose carcass in the brush fifty yards away and then sent her gaze toward the fire. "Some night, huh?"

He looked up from the fire he'd been poking with a stick and gave her a lopsided grin. "Yeah."

She tilted her head and raised an eyebrow as he tossed her a bowie knife and broke the charred stick in half, offering her a skewered steak. True, it was an obvious lure for her to come closer to him, but she couldn't resist.

Warily she approached him, half expecting that he might pounce on her like he had the night before. However, gentleman that he'd now transformed back into, he exchanged a steak for a quick kiss.

"Okay, you were right. We needed the break before pushing on. Is that what you wanted to hear?"

His smile widened as he walked away from her and pulled another set of thick, crackling steaks out of the flames. He sighed heavily as he rammed the spit into the ground, suspending the meat between them. "No, but I'll take what I can get this morning."

She didn't respond. What could she say? Sometimes silence spoke volumes and she was hoping this would be one of those times.

He didn't look at her as he settled himself on the ground beside her with his coffee and a meat-laden stick, and allowed his voice to bottom out on a mellow, philosophical tone. "I would have preferred to hear—"

"All right, all right, I get it," she said, laughing. She set her coffee down hard, sloshing a bit of the ebony substance on the frozen earth before slicing at the hot, juicy meat. "But we've got to—"

"I know," he said quickly, not looking at her, and then bit into his steak without cutting it, slightly burning his mouth. "Just a passing thought."

She allowed a soft laugh to slip out around the next bite she took, enjoying the companionable silence between them while feasting beside him. Breathing, the sound of meat tearing, chewing, and the natural stillness of the snow-covered landscape, all of it was the way of the wolf. Under any other circumstances she would have fed him and he would have fed her, but that would have definitely started a Shadow dance this morning, something they didn't have time for.

The sad thing was she couldn't stop watching his mouth while he ate. It was totally ridiculous how much that one part of him had become her focus . . . loving the way the muscle in his jaw worked hard . . . the way the natural juices and hot fat from his steak made his mouth glisten—*okay, she just had to stop.*

"I collected some snow in the canteens and let it melt," he finally said in his easy baritone, leaning back on his elbows as he chewed. Using the skewer as a pointer, he motioned toward a pile of heated rocks. "Water should still be warm."

She noted where he'd motioned and tried to keep her voice even as she replied. It was so sweet that he'd remembered and had even gone to the trouble to warm it up for her. "Thanks . . . appreciate it."

He gave her a sidelong glance, then bit into the last of his steak. "So did I. Thanks."

Okay. There was no way to respond to that, so she would just eat the remainder of her breakfast, go clean herself up, and help him break camp. How the hell was this man gonna act this morning if she got naked in the wilderness? For that matter, how was she gonna act under said circumstances?

Sasha stood and stretched. *Enough.* Even with the cold wind whipping, it was a wondrously clear day. An intensely blue, cloudless sky seemed like it was made brighter by the stark white snow beneath it. That's what she'd focus on, the beauty around her, despite the sudden, intense warmth that made her hair damp at the nape of her neck.

Reflex sent her hand there to lift her tousled mass of now too-long curls as she walked, hoping the cool breeze would provide relief. But her fingers collided with raw, sensitive skin that was healing. *Damn, what a night . . .* Then panic seized her as she felt for her silver chain and the amulet she rarely took off, even to shower. When she turned to look at Hunter, his was gone, too.

"Max, last night . . ."

Her voice trailed off as he got up in one very slow but extremely fluid move and threw his stick in the fire.

"Yeah . . . I know."

Her mouth went dry but she pressed on. "The amulets—"

"Were in the way," he said calmly, his eyes beginning to take on a luminous amber hue.

In the way? The question shot through her brain so quickly that it must have shone in her eyes.

"I'm sorry. . . . I popped your chain by accident." He smiled but it somehow didn't reach his eyes.

She didn't back up, didn't move forward, but studied

him very, very hard for a moment. "What happened to yours?" Why she couldn't fully remember troubled her to no end.

"You don't remember?" he asked in a low rumble that made her womb contract. "I don't know whether to be hurt or flattered."

Okay, something was definitely not right about this whole exchange. She glanced at his neck, the place where a thick silver rope should have been and was quickly becoming very, very worried by the deep, almost burnlike rash that she hadn't noticed before. Scavenging for an explanation, she told herself it had to be a friction burn.

"If I pulled it off you like that," she said, quietly alarmed, "I'm so sorry, Max. I didn't mean to . . ."

He held up his hand and came closer, his gaze cornering hers. "Believe me, I'm not complaining." His hands found her shoulders as he gently took her mouth. "Last night was fantastic."

Yeah, okay, no argument there. But when he broke their kiss her eyes were fastened to the wounds around his throat. With trembling fingers she touched the very edges of the gashes, and instant alarm almost made her body go rigid. However, she tried to play it off and act like nothing out of the ordinary was rocketing through her screaming mind.

Shadow Wolves were supposed to be impervious to silver. Unlike the creatures they hunted, it was their ward, their difference, their protection. They were supposed to quickly heal from wounds, and a minor scrape from a popped chain shouldn't have left an oozing sore. In fact, her hands had healers' energy and shouldn't have sent enough pain into the site to make him wince and drop his embrace.

"You okay?" Her eyes sought his.

"It's just a little tender. No big deal."

"Hunter, we have to go get them . . . if we dropped them along the way, ya know? They're too important to just leave out here, especially on our way to a UCE meeting after we go get Woods and Fisher."

He smiled a tense smile. "The chains broke in the tent. I wrapped them up and put them in the backpacks for safekeeping since the clasps are broken—we'll get them fixed when we make camp with the clan. There's always a silversmith around. No problem."

He pecked her forehead with a kiss and she watched him walk away. It was a logical explanation, but his delivery was way too cool for her liking. Clan leaders needed their amulets to be able to hunt beyond demon doors. It denoted not only their rank as being stronger than a local pack leader, but Hunter's signified his high rank as the North American alpha. Their amulets had been handed down within his grandfather's clan for generations upon generations, and now Hunter couldn't wear his? Broken clasp or not, it should have been shoved into his jeans pocket, on his person, in a vest, somewhere easily accessible, and not at the bottom of a backpack. Uh-uh.

Plus, the scent from the wounds that lingered wasn't right at all. Memory stabbed into her brain as she walked toward the canteens completely freaked out. Images of Rod's demon-infected Turn battered her mind as she clumsily retrieved the water Hunter had left. The Werewolf scent she'd also picked up was slight. Maybe she was psyching her own self out. That had to be it, buggin' because her hormones were all over the map. But Rod broke out like that, too, if silver even came near him. What the fuck was happening? Hunter was a Shadow Wolf!

Her hands were shaking so badly that she could barely grab the canteen's straps.

"I'm gonna take a short run while you wash up," Hunter called out. "I think that's best."

The sound of his voice nearly made her jump out of her skin. Any other day, she would have laughed and shot him a sarcastic one-liner. Today all she could do was swallow away anxiety and speak softly. "Okay, baby. See you when you get back."

Nausea made his stomach roil. Sasha had to believe he was just giving her privacy. Terror caused his heart to slam inside his chest as he ran. He always knew this day would come. Fate was a cruel, merciless bitch. Impressions stabbed his mind with each footfall until the cramps made him stop, bend over, and hurl.

Panting, sweating, he kept his eyes squeezed shut. Images collided against one another inside his brain, forcing him to bite his lip to keep from crying out. His mother. Her full womb. A huge predator. The sound of her scream. Flesh tearing. Sudden cold. He was on a blanket of snow, wailing. His grandfather took aim. There was a loud noise. Hunter's body recoiled. He was supposed to be a Shadow Wolf, not this hybrid blend of good and evil.

He pushed himself away from the tree and staggered toward fresh snow and dropped. He had to get the scent off him before he reached his pack brothers. They wouldn't understand. Doc Holland was too far away, so was his grandfather, Silver Hawk. Sasha wouldn't understand. Why was this happening after all these years? What had triggered the dark wolf within?

Only three times before had the battle within his blood occurred. When it did, his grandfather had been there as an ally. Silver Hawk became the wise pack elder, Silver Shadow, and had sweat with him until the purge was complete. So had Doc Holland the first time he'd gone into convulsions as an infant. They'd said it happened the moment the umbilical cord had been severed from his mother's dead body. Doc gave him the antidote as a last-ditch effort that worked. The next one Silver Hawk anticipated in a vision quest, removing him from the pack to take a spirit walk as his body changed from a boy's to a man's. It had been the most humiliating transition in his life but had saved him execution at the hands of his own pack. Then Doc had shot him up with meds just as he'd approached his twenty-fifth birthday, just before his alpha maturity spike . . . and he'd battled from top pack rank to top clan rank . . . all under one full moon—unheard of. They hadn't spoken of the incidents since.

And, yet, the old man had tried to warn him in his very innocuous way, telling him that severe environmental or emotional disturbances could affect the delicate truce within his metabolism. Foolishly, or maybe stubbornly, he'd ignored the warning to let Sasha go out of phase before pushing onward. The old man had been right. He'd never been half of a mated pair, had never experienced the intensity of a she-Shadow heat, because he'd been shunned as a potential mate within the multipack North American clan. Even if Sasha hadn't formally claimed him with words, her body had—they were operating as a single entity, which had been enough.

Absolute defeat seized him as he tried to use handfuls of snow to purge the Were-scent oozing from his pores. But it would be in his hair, his skin, and now his clothes. His mouth tasted horrible; he understood Sasha's previous concern. They needed hot water, soap, clean clothes.

Going into an armed Shadow Wolf pack camp trailing infected Werewolf scent was beyond dangerous—it was a death sentence. Suicide for them both. Pushing ahead past a local pack to find a Shadow Wolf clan encampment made up of many local packs would be no different than putting a nine millimeter to their skulls and simply pulling the trigger.

Hunter stood still and then slowly turned to study his location. That was all there was to it; they'd have to travel through the Rocky Mountains, come out on the Canadian side, borrow real facilities, then and only then try to make contact with his home pack.

As soon as she was sure that Hunter was out of range, Sasha ransacked the backpacks until she found their amulets. He'd shoved them to the bottom, rolled in layers of clothes. The clasps had been broken. She took shallow sips of air, gently trailing her fingers over the tender spot at the nape of her neck and then up the back of her scalp to where a small knot had formed, trying to focus, trying to remember.

They had transformed on a Shadow run. He'd picked up the trail of large game—a bull moose. It was too big; she'd tried to signal him. Hunter was larger than she'd remembered when he'd transformed again; two hands higher at the shoulders, larger jaw, barrel chest. His eyes held something in them that frightened her.

Sasha shoved the amulets back where she'd found them and began to pace inside the tent with her eyes squeezed shut. "Oh . . . God . . ." It was coming back in fits and starts, jags of horror that she wanted to forget.

He'd outstripped her on the run. The animal they hunted turned and lowered its mantle. Hunter went up on his hind legs. Sasha opened her eyes and hugged herself with a start, breathing hard. He hadn't brought it down like a wolf. One powerful swipe from a forepaw had snapped a damned bull moose's neck!

How could she not remember? How could she not remember! *How could she not remember?* She tore around the tent looking for weapons, blood pressure spiking when she couldn't immediately find them.

Cupping the back of her head, she bolted out of the tent. Panic perspiration made everything she wore stick to her skin. Images of Hunter crouched over the carcass, snarling as he devoured the animal's heart and liver, brought her other hand over her mouth to keep from hurling. She could see it all clearly now—blue-black night, steam rising from fresh-kill that had been opened and gutted. Oh, God, oh, God, when did she fall and hit her head?

Backing away . . .

She'd come to a skidding halt. Their eyes had met. She was so stunned that she'd changed back into her human form and stood. He did too, then cried out and yanked the chain from his neck. She'd spun to run, caught a low-hanging branch, and went down. Then she was inside the tent. His arm was anchored around her waist. She squeezed her eyes shut again, remembering his impassioned voice choking out a ragged apology behind her.

Hunter had purposely knocked her unconscious and the reason why broke over her in horrifying clarity.

Hunter was infected.

She felt a scream of rage and grief build in her throat over the thought that something like this was happening. But she swallowed it. There would be time to grieve later.

Survival was imperative and she needed to find her gun.

Chapter 3

Clarissa McGill pulled the unmarked military car to a stop before a dilapidated building in the ninth ward and looked around. The guys with her in the four-door Ford sedan just gaped for a moment, stunned. Even after the cleanup, evidence of Hurricane Katrina still pocked a devastated New Orleans. She dragged her stubby fingers through her short, blond bob, cringing that her hair was damp and oily again. But that was the Big Easy—constantly humid. At least it wasn't summertime when the extra fifty pounds of heft she carried could give a person a heart attack in the shade.

In this environment, one could literally wring the air out and make a puddle from it. Polyester pants and a top were stifling, but jeans on a long drive would have felt like stomach surgery sans anesthesia. To her way of thinking, New Orleans had more things than thick humidity to give a grown man pause, anyway. That was the least of the bioteam's concerns.

She scanned the house again to be sure they were at the right address. The region had primordial stamped all over it . . . she bet the beginning of a lot of species probably came up from the swamps here, the Mississippi Delta, and down into what was now the Everglades. She

and Sasha had to stick together on this as the only females in the PCU, and not follow the guys' lead. Clarissa
squared her shoulders. Female intuition was still more ac-
curate than Bradley's satellites and Winters's databases.

However, no matter what she said, she knew that being
the team's biologist and psychic wouldn't amount to a hill
of beans—she could tell by looking at the guys' expressions that they trusted their own eyes more than her second
sight right now. At forty-three years old, she'd had enough
experience with frightened individuals on paranormal-
monitoring missions to know that. She didn't have to try to
read their minds to know what they were thinking: The
place they were supposed to hole up in and set up a base
station in was a rodent-infested dump.

Mark Winters, their resident computer specialist and
the feisty, youngest member of the team, gave her a glance
of concern. Fear and uncertainty dueled in his hazel eyes
and made his baby face seem even younger. His mousse-
spiked hair now seemed wilder, given his expression, and
she wondered if he'd make it through the night without
jumping out of his skin.

"Okay, maybe it's me," Winters said, his voice hitch-
ing as he glanced around like a nervous rabbit, "but this
looks like downtown Baghdad after Shock and Awe.
There's no sign of even NOPD down here—like, do the
New Orleans cops even drive down these streets? Why
can't we just mosey on down to the French Quarter where
it's been rehabbed?"

Bradley sighed, his normal long tether of patience
clearly wearing thin by the strain. He blotted perspiration
from his forehead with the back of his forearm and then
returned his horn-rimmed glasses to the bridge of his

aristocratic nose with a precise shove. But as he leaned
forward to address Winters from the backseat, he still
looked over the tops of his glasses with steel-blue eyes as
though he were an annoyed professor. A distant streetlight
and the moonbeams danced across his prematurely
graying salt-and-pepper hair. Clarissa stifled a smile and
waited for the cool retort that she knew Bradley would
deliver with perfect British diction.

"Sasha said to go off radar and undercover. *This* is undercover, and probably the best place to get word from
the local warlock community about what's shaking." The
shadow from Bradley's athletic frame and the confident
tone employed by his ten-year-age seniority loomed over
Winters's skittish, lanky build within the vehicle. "Besides," Bradley continued, undaunted when Winters
didn't immediately challenge him, "I need a comm post
where a maid won't accidentally trip over my satellite
gear or, worse, cross a divination circle I've laid."

"Hey, you're the dark arts specialist, not me and
Rissa . . . so if you get a lead, we can just as easily low
jack you and pick you up on a screen from a nice little bed
and breakfast." Mark's voice faltered as he glanced around
at the desolate scene beyond the car windows. His gaze
stayed locked on the mud-stained, dilapidated, leaning
structures and abandoned houses as feral dogs roamed the
shadows with their noses to the ground on the perpetual
hunt for garbage.

Bradley released a weary sigh. "Isn't going to happen.
The power of three, blah, blah, blah, and we were given
express orders not to split up under any circumstances.
So, where I go, you go. Now stop whining and get your
skinny ass out of the car."

"What happened to all the FEMA funds, huh?" Emboldened by fear, Mark crossed his arms over his narrow chest, challenging his older teammate. "I thought they said on the news they were rebuilding this entire area, but it still looks like the storms happened yesterday. Not to mention, we'll probably all walk out of here with some kinda deadly bacterial infection or frickin' cancer from the toxic sludge hanging around. You can't shoot a virus! And what about those dogs? They could have rabies. You can even see their rib bones. Like, what if they're were-wolves too hungry to turn into anything more than mutts? They could still be deadly, ya know—if a bunch of 'em gang up on us."

"Get out of the car, Winters," Clarissa said, smiling. "That's one of the reasons you got cholera shots and they sent a biologist along—*moi*. So, if you start feeling a little queasy . . ."

"Yeah, not to mention, if you start having the yen to howl at the moon, let McGill know, kid," Bradley said, teasing Mark as he opened the back passenger-side door.

"I knew something was wrong when they gave us freaking cholera shots, mosquito nets, and a bunch of crap to ward off malaria. I thought we were going somewhere exotic, like the Amazon—not somewhere in the suppos-edly developed free world! This is the freakin' U. S. of A., are you hearing me? Why does Trudeau get to gallivant off to the pristine wilderness, huh? This shit is for the birds—and need I remind you that the murder rate in New Orleans has jumped like ninety percent since Katrina?"

"Precisely why we're here," Clarissa said, running her fingers through her short, blond hair again and turning her stout frame around in her seat with effort. "So knock it off. We're to feed Trudeau the ground intel she needs. We know that the spike in murders and lawlessness is fueled partially by economic issues, but also something else. The entire graveyard system here was compromised by the flood. Everything that should have been buried floated to new locations and/or was exposed to the sun. Great location to have conversations with the dead, undead, and a few species in between."

"Correct," Bradley said, leaning into the car with his arm draped over the hood. "This is one of the way stations for paranormal black market activities and is still the reigning capital. Between local voodoo priests, warlocks, resident seers, and swamp madams, not to mention the old Vampire aristocracy, and a few zombie kings, we ought to be able to begin to pick up some patterns. But the Big Easy is on the comeback. All statistics aside, it doesn't all look like WWIII here, so relax."

"Or get shot, or eaten, or turned into a zombie," Mark muttered.

Bradley shrugged and rounded the car to open the trunk. "Yeah, one of the above, or you could look on the bright side. Maybe you'll just get bitten by a cute female Vampire and live forever."

A sleek black wolf, slight of build, dashed through the underbrush. He released a rallying howl that made Bear Shadow look up from the card game he'd been engaged in with Woods and Fisher. The massive warrior stood slowly, lifting his nearly three-hundred-pound, muscular frame out of the groaning wooden chair. Woods glanced at Fisher, cards frozen in their hands.

"What is it, dude?" Fisher asked, his voice tight and nervous.

Woods's line of vision studied the way the huge Ute

Indian's ears moved slightly. If something crazy was about to go down, then he and his partner, Fisher, needed ammo. In hand-to-hand, Fisher was good with a knife— tall, lanky, a Kentucky-bred blond who had seen his fair share of trailer park brawls. Add that to the Special Forces training they'd had, and it was all good. But, still, from what he'd seen of the Shadow Wolves, even he wasn't sure he could take one down—and he had a height and weight advantage on Fisher.

Woods raked his fingers through his dark brown hair, which was almost shoulder length now, and a far cry from his once clean-cut, military appearance. Ragged stubble bordered his jawline. It had been a little over a month and a half since the brass thought they'd died in action, and now something was about to pop off that could indeed end their lives. He could tell Fisher was thinking the same thing; it was in the way Fisher had smoothed his palm over his reddish-blond beard. Bear Shadow hadn't answered Fisher's question, but kept tilting his head like a huge hunting dog listening to the forest beyond the cabin window. Something was wrong; it was a killing season— he could feel it.

"Is it your clan contact? Is the lieutenant with him?" Woods pressed, panic bubbling within him.

"Wait here," Bear Shadow commanded in a low rumble. "Trouble. Our lookout picked up Werewolf scent in the territory."

Within an instant he'd opened the cabin door, slid out of his clothes to transform into a massive brown wolf, and then was gone.

Woods and Fisher simply stared at each other for a moment.

"Even though it's more elegant than what we saw Rod go through, it's gonna take a long time for me to get used to seeing them do that," Fisher admitted quietly.

Woods nodded and got up to lock the door. "I just hope I don't have a gun in my hand if I see it at night. Hard to tell who's on our side or not."

Xavier Holland's private cell phone vibrated on his hip. As project header and head geneticist for the PCU, his study subjects had to have twenty-four-hour access to him. But they were more than lab rats to be studied and watched. They were friends . . . family, young people who had been terribly abused by the hand of fate.

As soon as he saw the non-number in the display he walked outside to his backyard. He could never be sure if his Colorado home just outside of the NORAD complex had been bugged again, even though he'd been given the strictest assurances that it hadn't. Supposedly this was a brand-new day, new era of brass after General Donald Wilkerson's death. Sasha Trudeau had proven herself, no less than he'd proven how bad the genetics experiments had gone under Wilkerson's mania.

But he'd been a Special Ops military man too long to believe the hype. Eyes were still everywhere. Old blood samples treated with demon-infected Werewolf toxin that could potentially cause a pandemic outbreak were still missing. On the third ring, he picked up the cell phone that had been procured by underground means. He knew the caller's voice, and this person wasn't generally given to communication by technology or panic. However the strain was clear in his voice the moment he said hello.

"What's wrong?"

"He's had a spike again. Fourth one in many, many

years. You were there for the first three. . . . This may be the last one before we must do what breaks my heart."

"Are you sure?"

Silence.

"Yes. It came in a vision."

"How bad?"

"I don't know, but my sense is bad."

"Have you been in communication with him?"

"No."

This time Xavier Holland was quiet. Sasha was with Hunter. The bond between the elderly men on the phone went all the way back to the beginning of both young warriors' lives. They would have to speak quickly without disclosing names. If Silver Hawk had called him, with his voice tight and rough, his Shadow voice, then his old friend was on the move.

"Do you have some of the antidote left?" Holland waited, worrying, not sure how to do a handoff under the severe scrutiny that followed the general's assassination.

"It is old, possibly expired . . . could do more harm than good," Silver Hawk finally said.

"Perhaps a Silver Shadow could line this cloud of worry?" Xavier said cryptically, inviting the old Ute to come to him in Shadow Wolf form, hopefully undetected.

"Perhaps . . . but where is there no worry, my friend?"

Xavier glanced around his backyard. "I meditate daily out in the yard while gardening . . . to reduce stress, especially by my roses."

"That is a good method—man, nature, and the Great Spirit."

The call connection went dead and Xavier Holland kept his eyes on the horizon. The call had lasted just long enough not to be traced. Now all he had to do was figure out how to get a few filled hypodermic needles out of the labs at NORAD and secreted away beneath his roses.

Sasha looked up quickly, bowie knife in hand. Hunter had returned but hadn't taken any precautions for stealth. Unlike his normal, nearly silent footfalls, he'd simply trudged back through the snow and passed her almost without looking at her to enter the tent. Moments later he emerged with a toothbrush in his mouth and one of the canteens in his grip, and then went to stand before the dying fire to brush his teeth.

"Guns are downwind from the tent by the moose carcass. Just wanted a fighting chance to explain before you opened up a clip of silver shells on me."

His tone was weary, his delivery flat before he spit out foaming toothpaste on the ground. The residue in his mouth made him look rabid and she glanced away to shake the terrible thought.

Sasha sheathed the knife in her back jeans pocket but didn't move toward the weapons stashed by the carcass fifty yards away. "What happened?" she asked more quietly than intended.

Hunter didn't turn around or immediately answer, just kept brushing his teeth, every so often spitting against the embers, which responded with angry hisses. His eyes finally met hers, and the expression in them was a mixture of sadness and defiance.

He lifted the canteen. "I take it you won't be needing this?"

She didn't answer, just stared at him.

"Yeah, thought not," he said in a disgusted tone, then opened it up and doused his hair, face, and shoulders with its crystal-clear contents.

She watched the pure mountain water cascade through his long, jet-black hair, wetting his dark skin till it glistened. Sadness so profound made her lungs feel like they were about to burst within her chest. It just wasn't fair! She couldn't go through this a second time. After having to put down Rod, how did one take out a lover, a friend, someone who'd been her partner, her most trusted companion in life, only six weeks later? Sasha blinked back the tears as she watched the water spill over Hunter's abraded neck, trying to shake the memory of her hands caressing that part of him to travel over his bulk of muscles along his shoulders and down his back.

When she'd had to shoot Rod during his transformation, her heart had shattered. If she'd have to put a bullet in Hunter's skull, she knew she might as well have to put one in her own. As it was right now, she could barely breathe from the grief. She couldn't even get her body to function as a soldier's. Her mind told her to go get the stashed weapons, but she couldn't move. Soon her arms were around her waist and her voice repeated her previous question on a very shaky murmur that sounded like a plea.

"What happened?"

"I got infected," he said, flinging the spent canteen away from him. "Didn't know it at the time, but shit happens."

Paralyzed, she watched him angrily stride away toward the carcass, kick it over, and extract a sack from beneath it. She didn't move as he neared her, flung the weapons in her direction to catch, and began breaking down the campsite.

"When we went after Guilliaume and Dexter . . . through the demon doors in the other realms?" She held the satchel of guns and ammo clips loosely at her side.

"This shit began before I was even born," he said through his teeth with a snarl. "You know how my mother died—you know how Doc saved me with Pop."

"But it's been dormant for all those years!" she suddenly shouted as though arguing with God. Bottled up emotions were making her entire body tremble as she began to talk with her hands and then suddenly cast away the weapons bag. "You're a Shadow Wolf, born naturally, not made in a fucking petri dish like me! We can't get the demon-infected Werewolf virus, and that's why we're the only ones best suited to hunt them. I don't care what happened when you were a baby! Your immune system threw it off. You've lived with it, beat it, the infected Werewolf virus was—"

"*Always* dormant in my system, Sasha! That's why I was a goddamned outcast to the clan, even though I was strong enough to take alpha status!"

She rounded on him, preventing his retreat toward the equipment. "No. This was an aberration. Something had to screw with your metabolism, and we've gotta find out what it was."

He released a hollow laugh. "I already know what it was. I'm staring at the catalyst."

"That is *complete* bullshit," she said, moving with him to shadow his attempts to get away from her. "We've been together for over a month."

Hunter stopped trying to evade her and stared at her head on, counting off the charges with his fingers. "Do the math, Sasha. My mother was savaged while I was in her womb and I got the virus directly into my bloodstream before my grandfather could cut me out and sever the umbilical cord. Contagion hits an infant's system. The only reason I lived through the convulsions or even survived without brain damage is because Doc was there with meds. I spiked in puberty, then again at twenty-five when all wolves spike for dominance battling. Now—"

"But you weren't re-infected for over thirty years," she argued, ignoring his logic.

"Yes, I was. The second incident of close contact happened on the wrong side of a demon door—open wounds, blood and saliva flying as two males battle to the fucking death. I'm still standing."

Hunter stalked away from her, dragging his fingers through his soaked hair and then shook it out wolf-style. "Third contact incident," he said more quietly, as though the reality and emotional fatigue had finally hit him, "was fighting my own infected clan brothers when we went after the rogues up in Delta, Colorado's Uncompahgre National Forest. What's the old saying, baby? Three strikes and you're out?"

"Until I hear that shit from Doc or Silver Hawk . . . until the bloodwork proves it . . ."

"You'll what?" he said, turning to face her, his gaze hard. "Sit with your back against a wall and a gun in your hand? Sleep with one eye open, watching me for signs of transition to the species of abomination?" He stalked away from her and began yanking out tent stakes, now yelling. "I don't even fucking know what I'll do! You think I want my woman around me taking a risk like that?"

"I can defend myself," she said, shouting back and lifting her chin. "Even against you, now that I know. So until we know for sure how far this has gone, or if your system is self-correcting, then—"

"I had blackouts last night!" he shouted, flinging the

stakes away. "Goddamned blackouts! During that time I could've been a beast and wouldn't have even known it!"

Humiliation made him walk away, sucking in huge breaths as he tried to scavenge calm from the surrounding environment. It had never been this bad before. When he'd been with Silver Hawk, he'd never lost full consciousness. His inner Shadow Wolf was always connected to his human, the link unbreakable. Last night, something very fragile in the balance snapped.

"You weren't a beast," her calm, gentle voice said from behind him.

"You were out for twenty minutes. What do you know?"

A firm hand on his shoulder made him flinch away.

"I'm still standing and don't have a mark on me this morning, that's what I know."

He had no answer for her and didn't try to retreat beyond the tree he was now leaning against. Hunter closed his eyes, not wanting to admit that her words offered balm but drenching himself with them nonetheless.

"Let me try to heal the obvious wounds, and I'll keep both amulets on me, not in the backpacks."

When he didn't answer and didn't try to shrug away, she took that as a yes. Slowly and very carefully she touched his shoulder, testing for acceptance, and then stood in front of him.

"I'm not giving up on you," she sad quietly, her gaze searching his until he looked away. "We will use this hand we've been dealt."

"How?" he grumbled, now looking at her with fury in his eyes.

"If you carry a little of the predators' scent, and some of its strength, you might be able to pass yourself off as a transitioning member in human form . . . once the moon is out of full phase."

She waited a beat to allow the concept to sink in. "And you can pass me off as your rogue mate . . . a she-Shadow, just like Shadow Falcon had been, willing to participate in any illicit activities you're involved in. This way maybe we can get those rogues who are immersed in the toxin trade to view what happened up in the Uncompahgre as a territorial battle, not a raid by the preternatural authorities. It's our best lead to Dexter to lure him out of hiding."

"Yeah, well, that would be an airtight plan, except for one variable."

She looked at him, now resting both palms along the broad width of his shoulders. "What variable?"

"Me," he said flatly, his gaze searching hers. "I don't know how this thing inside me is going to affect my mind, ultimately. What if we're out among an infected Werewolf pack and you think my actions are part of the ruse, only to find they're not?" Hunter shook his head no. "Too dangerous, too unpredictable—and for it to work, I'd have to tell my pack brothers to fall back. I'd have to go in submissive, unless I'm prepared to dominance-battle a demon-infected alpha were alone . . . and I'm not."

He hesitated, his gaze boring into hers. "That would be the tipping point, Sasha—if I got cut again. Plus, the other side will only take an infected male and possibly a female at his side, perhaps vice versa, one at a time—not dragging a Shadow pack with them." He looked at Sasha hard and then traced her cheek with the pad of his thumb. "You'd be by yourself with no backup in a den of virally infected male Werewolves . . . not even able to be sure that you could count on me. Think about it, Sasha. What would happen if—"

She closed her eyes and gently stopped his words with her finger against his lips as she laid her head on his shoulder. His loose embrace tightened slowly as he kissed the crown of her head.

"Then I'll be sure to take dead aim and shoot you first," she murmured.

Chapter 4

Hands that had delivered unbelievable pleasure the night before now pulled excruciating pain from Hunter's body as he and Sasha sat facing each other Indian style on the cold ground. It felt like a ring of fire encircled his neck, and he kept his eyes closed and jaw and fists clenched, too proud to cry out.

Sweat coursed down his temples, the bridge of his nose, his chest, and back as Sasha worked, dredging the poison up until his body began to slightly convulse. The stench was something undetectable to a normal human nose, but as a Shadow Wolf it was an offense like none other. Even an average dog might take issue with the infected Werewolf signature leaking from the lacerations left behind from a silver burn.

The whole of it caused nausea to assault his stomach once more, and the only thing he could think of was that the woman had to really, deeply care to even address something as foul as this.

Sasha wiped the perspiration from her forehead on the back of her arm, keeping her face away from her wound-soiled hands or his skin. Seeing her do that tore at his pride; they shouldn't have been swapping spit the night before or anything else for that matter. If only he'd known before it had been too late. Never again. The only saving grace was the fact that her unpolluted Shadow Wolf system would eventually purge it, he hoped.

"I need to get this crap out of your pores . . . get you into a hot tub with Epsom salts, something to help pull it out of your skin."

"I know—we can't do a full purge out here without supplies," he panted, then leaned his head back, taking advantage of the brief rest break she allowed. "I can't carry the backpack or wear my parka . . . the scent will adhere to the fabrics and won't come out. Eventually gotta burn my clothes and get new ones."

"You sound like you've done this before?" Her hands remained on his collarbone like hot coals.

Pain, fatigue, and emotional exhaustion made him confess with a nod. He'd told her as much, but the fact that she was asking again meant that she was unsure if this had been a rarely occurring thing or something that he'd dealt with regularly. Long pauses interwoven with deep inhales accented his bursts of words. "When I was twelve—second seizure. Sweat lodge with Silver Hawk. Third time, just before the onset of alpha maturity . . . he was there, too. I told you that, remember?"

"Then you're sure this is only the fourth seizure?"

Again he nodded, wishing they didn't have to relive the humiliation of his youth. This time she didn't speak but just gave him a curt nod and kept working. When the pads of her fingers traced over the abrasion again, he winced.

"Sorry," she murmured, "but I gotta get as much of it out as possible."

"Do it. Otherwise my pack brothers will attack on sight, no questions asked. You have to also get the scent of me off you and this contagion off your hands . . . just in case they don't understand and rush us."

He stopped talking for a moment and held his breath as she flat-palmed the wounds. Intense, stabbing pain balled his hands into fists. There was so much that he had yet to teach her about the Shadow culture she'd never been raised in. Sasha had to restore not only his normal scent but there could be no significant abnormalities in his aura. Each identifier was used to tell which pack within the clan one hailed from, one's rank, one's history. A change in any of those family markers caused chaos within the wolf pack and then fanned outward to ripple through the entire clan.

"Every pack within the clan has been waiting for this to happen . . . waiting for my grandfather to be wrong. It's why I was shunned as an eligible mate. They wanted to put me to death as an infant, but he was the North American clan's overall alpha male, then, and wouldn't allow it. But the rest tolerated my existence while spreading rumors that I could pass this genetic aberration on to my kids. Now I will finally shame him after all these years."

"Listen, Max," she said, taking her hands away from his wounds for a moment so he could rest. She gripped his shoulders to make him hear her through the pain. "Yeah, okay, your system is going haywire, but up until this point it merged with your Shadow Wolf, created some kind of hybrid that made you incredibly strong, able to go through the demon doors unlike the others, and gave you a battlefield advantage against the enemy."

Sasha waited until Hunter opened his intense, dark brown eyes and stared at her. "Yeah," she said. "You represent an unknown, but up until this point you've been stable within the pack, as well as the clan. Something triggered this spike—it had to be more than me."

When he gave her a half smile she staved off the comment she felt bubbling within him by squeezing his shoulders tighter. "Think about it," she said, cutting him off before he could even say anything. "The first time was when you were a newborn. Toxin hit your system and you began a demon-infected Werewolf transition. Doc shot you up with the same meds he gave me, Rod, Woods, and Fisher to keep the bad wolf at bay. Your system was so new that it needed the outside assistance, something to sway the balance so your brand-new immune system could go against a virulent invader."

She watched him slowly take in her words as his shoulders relaxed under her hands. "Imagine a just-delivered infant being shot up with influenza and nothing to counteract it?"

Hunter nodded and she pressed on, needing to heal his mind and spirit as much as she knew his physical being required a purge.

"The second time, your entire metabolism shifted in puberty—I'm assuming at twelve that's what set it off. Like any normal human's would be at that time, your entire system was in hormonal flux and the recessive strain of this thing wrestled the Shadow Wolf within you for dominance. Twice in a row, the Shadow Wolf in you won. But I bet the second time you didn't need as strong a shot from Doc as you did that first time, did you? Then, when you hit alpha maturity and were ready to battle for your place in the pack and the clan, again your body changed and the recessive trait came forward—but, again, I bet you didn't need as much of the meds as you did when you were an infant. Right?"

"No," Hunter said slowly, his unblinking gaze holding hers. "You're right. I didn't. My grandfather had the needles beside his loaded rifle and told me to make my wolf fight to survive, to make it stronger than the demon-wolf. Somehow I knew he'd rather shoot me himself than allow me to go on out of control. Then he tossed all but one of the needles in the fire and picked up the gun and waited."

"And you won."

For a moment they stared at each other, saying nothing.

"And I won that second and third time."

"And now that you're a man, you're even stronger. Your wolf is unconquerable. You went through it last night and are yourself this morning. That means you're gaining immunity, regardless of whatever might have set it off again."

"You sound like you've been with the shaman." His mouth smiled but his eyes burned with deep appreciation.

"You've lived within a pack, within the clan," she said quietly, her gaze roving over his handsome face. She stroked his cheek with the back of her hand, the side of it that hadn't touched a wound. All she could think of was how he'd stayed with her and had healed the horrible gashes along her torso that would have made her own top brass give the order for her to be shot on sight, not understanding. Then, he'd fed her when she was too weak to eat, gave her a bath to cleanse her wounds. How could she ever forget?

Her voice became a low, thick rumble as she tried to get through his male barriers. "You've scented paired she-Shadows in heat before, and this didn't happen. Don't allow this thing to infect your mind or to rob you of your perception of who you are."

When he looked away, she rested her damp forehead

against his bare chest. "It was a combination of things—
the previous fight, my condition, the full moon, the tum-
ble we took through the demon doors. This will pass,
Hunter. We'll get Doc to look into it, Silver Shadow, too.
But I don't want you to give up on yourself before you've
given yourself a fighting chance."

She lifted her head and stared at him, her voice thick
with emotion as her hands went back to the task of sealing the wounds around his neck. "I won't give up on you.
I can't. I demand that you fight this thing the same way
you fought it—no, harder than you did as a kid. You owe
your grandfather's honor that much."

Finally he nodded, his gaze trapping hers.

The plan had been to come out of the mountains on the
Canadian side and head toward an innocuous little motel,
hotel, B&B, whatever, to restore Hunter to his formerly
dignified scent, but twenty-plus snarls along the tree line
changed all of that. When she felt Hunter bristle she
slowly eased off her backpack and carefully found the
edge of a silver chain inside her jeans pocket with two
fingers.

Extracting one amulet and then the other as though
holding a pair of guns with two fingers, she dangled them
with her arms outstretched from her body.

"We've been battling a demon all night," Sasha called
out, hoping the truth-laced ruse would explain the scent
that had alerted the pack to kill mode. She clearly needed
to tell them something that might buy her and Hunter precious time. If they saw her holding silver, maybe she
could cover for Hunter. It was worth a try. But she had
to do something quickly. He was physically spent but in
a very fragile state of mind—so fragile as to make him

insane enough to lunge into full attack mode if he thought his pack rank was being challenged. His low snarl told her all she needed to know; she had to keep talking.

"We need sanctuary, not attack! Look at the broken clasps on the amulets. He gave them to me to carry to protect his mate, after what we'd been through, and in case we got separated again."

She was no liar, nor was she a fool. Hunter had given her the amulets for her protection, to be sure. The problem now was that she'd openly said she was his mate because the packs dealt in absolutes. Later she'd worry about the fine points of the ruse. Right now they needed a safe haven. That part was no lie. It was all in the wording, though. Shadow Wolves could scent a lie a mile off, so she had to give them something with a rock-solid basis of truth.

Although the threatening snarls had abated, pure silence was often more deadly. She and Hunter turned slowly in unison as they felt the invisible pack circling. Part of her monitored the tension in Hunter's jaw by the pulsing muscle moving beneath his skin; the other part of her monitored the dangerous vibration of the pack that was closing in on them.

Then just as suddenly as they'd been cornered, something indefinable in the very air around them eased and a huge, naked Ute tribesman stepped out of the shadows. It wasn't that he was so tall, but it was his width that made her jaw nearly go slack. The man was built like a small truck. His line of vision locked with Hunter's but held unmistakable relief. He crossed his massive chest with a battle-scarred clenched fist and forearm and she watched Hunter return the gesture.

"Our apologies, brother. We couldn't be sure."

Hunter nodded. "No apologies required, Bear Shadow.

You were doing your job as pack enforcer. We expected no less."

"You know the way to the outpost?"

Hunter nodded. "Yes. By heart, as always."

Bear Shadow glanced at Sasha, who still held the amulets out from her body and hadn't moved. He raised one eyebrow and offered Hunter a sidelong glance with a half smile, not seeming the least bit concerned that he was having this entire conversation in the buff. One by one curious male wolves slipped into plain view from behind trees and out from the shadows, each a magnificent creature in varying hues.

"I would have given her my ward, too. We will clear the way and have eucalyptus water waiting . . . and food. You can then tell us of the battle and we will plan to hunt the creature as one."

In the blink of an eye Bear Shadow had become a massive brown wolf again and he threw his head back and howled. The mournful song was picked up by twenty or more voices coaxing Hunter's call to join theirs, and then they were again a part of the shadows. Gone.

Sasha slowly lowered her arms and then tucked the amulets away into her jeans pockets. It had been the most impressive display of pack cohesion and strength she'd ever witnessed. There would have been no way that a lone Werewolf could have won against such a band of brothers, demon-infected or not. If somehow she and Hunter had been considered the enemy, she now understood his very practical fear for her safety—they might have been able to stop some of them, but certainly not all before being overrun.

Bullets only worked if you could get to your weapon,

and the pack moved like the wind. That, too, would have been very unlikely. One of them would have ripped off her arm before she could've pulled a nine, and if she and Hunter transformed, without a means of ambush, a twenty-plus to two ratio was suicide.

Hunter picked up the backpack without saying a word and hoisted it over one shoulder. In truth, what was there to say? There was no longer the need to keep the scent he trailed off their gear; the pack had temporarily bought the ruse. She'd now finally seen with her own eyes what they were up against. Hunter didn't have to elaborate.

The real question was, however, how long would they buy it, and what would happen under a full moon while the watchful eyes of the interclan pack were on them?

This was some very serious shit, for more reasons than one. Sasha walked quietly beside Hunter, not even glimpsing his profile. Each pack within the regional clan had an alpha male that had sent out their primary enforcers to investigate the wayward Werewolf scent. Those guys weren't even the top wolves! And if Hunter's own strongman, Bear Shadow, had been prepared to take him out for the good of the whole North American clan, then the possibility of serious dissension in the ranks was afoot.

The Uncompahgre incident involved rogue pack members across the clan moving illicit toxic substances in order to change their rank and financial position. Trust was therefore null and void. Hunter had explained the political fallout more times than she'd wanted to remember. All packs had been made vulnerable, thus very touchy and subject to extremes in martial law.

She just hoped that the mini-purge had worked and that Hunter could hold it together while they were around each pack leader. All they'd need was for a bit of the Werewolf virus to surface at an inopportune and deadly time. Then again, what was she saying? If this thing finally took him over, there was only one decision to be made, and it would have to be done in a very detached, unemotional way. There was no sense trying to put one's head in the sand. Hunter needed immediate evaluation.

Sasha kept walking in silence beside Hunter. Maybe that was it; she wanted to know for sure before a permanent, irreversible decision was made. At least that was the partial lie she told herself. If there was ever a time for the Great Spirit to hear prayers it was now. The only other alternative was to get him away from the pack, using a very good explanation . . . but if he was infected, she alone would have a nightmare on her hands.

Sasha chewed her bottom lip as her mind continued to burn with questions. She glimpsed Hunter quickly from the corner of her eye, but his gaze caught and trapped hers as they walked quietly side by side. The same questions she'd had haunted his silent stare and she no longer had to wonder what he was thinking.

"Aw, man, you smell like pure hell!" Crow Shadow laughed as Hunter entered the small clearing in front of the outpost cabin.

"Good to see you, too, brother," Hunter muttered and folded his arms over his chest.

"Drop your gear in the yard, man," Bear Shadow said with a smirk, holding his nose. He motioned toward an old-fashioned tin tub near an outhouse twenty-five yards away that had thick plumes of steam and eucalyptus wafting from it. "We gotta hose you down in the yard before you come inside."

"Trudeau!"

Woods and Fisher burst out of the cabin with a unified shout and bounded across the knotted pine porch and down the steps, practically lifting her off her feet in an excited reunion.

"Shit, Lieutenant! We thought you were a goner!" Woods hugged her tightly and made Fisher wait his turn.

"I thought *we* were goners, dude," Fisher said, laughing and wrestling to join in on the group hug. "What're you talking about?"

"You guys are a sight for sore eyes," Sasha said, slapping them both on the backs and then cuffing their necks to pull their faces against hers.

Family. This was all that remained of her military family, save Doc and the inside team that by now should be in New Orleans. But these guys were in the trenches with her, carried weapons, laid in the mud on missions next to her. There was a different level of bond.

The merry threesome swallowed hard, smiles bright, each one too much of a soldier to let emotion seep all the way out, but it was felt. Relief, joy, sorrow, hard experiences—too much to get out all at once in front of strangers. The stories needed time and several cold beers, if not Wild Turkey, to gain form and substance. For now, just seeing who had made it was enough. Then came the awkward quiet. The moment of silence for the ones who didn't make it.

"Butler," Woods finally said in a reverent tone and shook his head.

"I know," Sasha said.

"Doc told us on sat-phone while we were on the move trying to get back to North America." Fisher's voice dropped to a pained murmur. "Nobody else made it out, either."

Sasha nodded but didn't say more. Memories washed through her like a dirty rain. Fisher's serious blue eyes became moist as he stared at her for a moment, and then just as quickly the unshed tears dried as he dragged his fingers through his unruly blond hair. He was gaunter than she'd remembered, his body more angular. But Woods had oddly seemed to fill out and become broader, heavier. He'd grown a beard and it was hard to tell where his almost shoulder-length brunet hair and the thick growth on his chin began and ended. Stress was an individual thing, affected people differently.

Still, trauma shone in Woods's liquid brown eyes. No telling what horrors these men had seen as their commanding officer transformed into a beast and then turned on the squad. To have that happen, survive it, only to have their own Black Hawk airlift turn the heat on them to try to "clean up the situation" was inexcusable.

Before she could really dwell on it or allow her unspent rage at the brass to make her irrational, she opted for proper pack introductions. Later they could bitch and vent in their beer. There was another, more pressing situation at hand that they all needed to survive. Hunter.

"Guess you guys have met and hung out with Crow Shadow and Bear Shadow long enough to know they're pack lookout and enforcer," she said, giving each Shadow Wolf a nod of utmost respect. "This is the pack's alpha, as well as the North American clan's alpha, Max Hunter. Good man to have at your side in a firefight. Seen him in action."

Woods, the more dominant of the two remaining men on Sasha's squad, stepped forward and extended his hand. "Good to know you."

Hunter stared at Woods's outstretched hand, jaw pulsing. "Tell your familiar I've got toxin on me, but it is good to know him and your other one." Then without another word Hunter spun on his heel and walked away toward the steaming tub, then began to strip.

Sasha opened and closed her mouth and then stepped into the vacant space Hunter had left. "He's really fucked up right now," she said loudly, fury roiling just under her surface as she stared at Hunter's back and then returned her gaze to her stunned men. "After what we went through last night, give him a minute. Generally he's not so rude and is good people."

"It is true," Bear Shadow said, seeming unfazed. "Max Hunter is a man you can count on." He loped away with a smile and motioned toward the thicket with his chin. "Gonna rustle up some steaks—Crow, man, you get the beer and bottles from the locals. But take the truck."

Crow Shadow caught the keys Bear Shadow tossed and winked at Sasha. "Make Hunter refill the tub for you. No offense. You're not as bad as him, but it splattered you. Get Woods and Fisher to bring you both some clean gear from the house when you're done. Burn everything in the yard—damn!" Within the space of a blink, he'd merged into a tree shadow and was gone.

"I still can't get used to this shit, Trudeau," Woods said, glancing around nervously once Crow Shadow had disappeared, his voice almost a low whisper. He kept his eyes on Hunter while speaking to Sasha between his teeth. "Like, what the fuck are we doing here? What's the new mission? Our damned lives are way out of control—there's no more

normal. Half the time I don't even know what the hell
they're talking about."

"Yeah, and what did he mean, 'tell your familiars'? He
meant like family, right?" Fisher asked in a nervous burst
under his breath.

"Yeah," Sasha muttered, glaring in Hunter's direction.
"I'm sure that's what he meant."

Chapter 5

She walked across the yard fighting mad. Yeah, okay, Hunter had some Werewolf shit with him, but that was still no reason to be rude to her men—her family! Not to mention if he couldn't hold it together under non-stressful conditions, he was a dead man walking into a clan council meeting, or whatever kind of powwow the packs were planning for tonight. If he made it past all of that to the United Council of Entities meeting in New Orleans, once Vampires sniffed him out, it'd be all over but the shouting. Seeing him act like this told her everything she needed to know. They had to get out of there stat and down to Doc in Denver somehow, before heading to New Orleans with the rest of her team.

In a few fluid strides, Sasha had reached the tub. Whatever wrangle they were going to get into, it had to happen fast. Woods and Fisher had gone into the house to get clothes and towels, and would be back soon. Rank was still rank, whether military or wolf pack. The last thing her men or Hunter's needed to witness was a shouting match between squad leaders. Although common sense told her that tone and the way she phrased the question would significantly determine the outcome of Hunter's response, he'd plucked her last nerve till it felt like raw meat hanging off a bone.

"And your problem would be?" she asked in a low, lethal tone between her teeth as she rounded the tub. She couldn't have censored herself if her life depended on it. "What gave you the right to—"

"They'd better learn protocol and learn it quick," Hunter snapped and then doused his hair. He came up from the water with eyes flickering amber and his canines elongated. "They're familiars and I'm not their problem. If they address pack leaders so casually during these tense times, their dumb asses will cause a shape-shift and they'll find themselves with their throats between an alpha's teeth."

"You could have suffered their ignorance and told me so I could clue them in. Do you have any idea how freaked out these guys are? I don't even know what the hell protocol is, and I sleep with you! How in the world are they supposed to just *know* all this mysterious crap?" Sasha gripped the edge of the tin tub and stared at Hunter so hard she was practically leaning in the water. "It's not fair!"

"It never is about fair—and you know it. It's about rank. What about any of this is so-called fair? Are you insane?"

He let out a disgusted breath; she snatched the thick, square-cut, homemade bar of soap from him and practically slammed it against his head as she began soaping his hair.

"They aren't telepaths. This culture is brand-new to them and your men should have told them."

"Who said they didn't?" Hunter snarled. "I know Crow Shadow and Bear Shadow; they would have versed them on approach protocol first! What it is, Sasha, is that your men are unpracticed, and at a full clan meeting that can get them severely reprimanded—and if they fight against a reprimand, it could get them killed. The wolf culture is rigid, you know that. My snub was to make them think—just like you would have done in boot camp with new recruits that improperly addressed your rank."

Frustration practically made steam come out of her ears, but the man had a point, even though she wasn't altogether ready to relinquish hers.

"That's all you had to say, Hunter. You could have barked orders at them to address you properly, then told them not to make the same mistake tonight or they'll get jumped. Woods and Fisher aren't stupid. In fact, those guys are the salt of the earth and are solid squad in a firefight. They don't know their roles cold yet. But I'd put money on it that with a little time, they'll be awesome lookouts, will be able to run interference with human forces, courier messages between the shaman, you name it."

"All right. I hear you," Hunter finally said in a grudging tone. "But they have to learn quickly."

"What the fuck were they supposed to do, Max? Genuflect when they saw you? Or do the happy freakin' puppy dance? You tell me—because right now you're being a real ass!"

He turned so quickly in the water to face her that a huge splash sloshed on the ground. "They were supposed to wait for *me* to approach *them*—remain stock still," he said through his teeth. "I scent them, determine if they can pass *my* inspection or not. If they walk forward aggressively toward an alpha that doesn't know them like they did with me, with that G. I. Joe military stare that would bristle even a beta male, they'd get their asses kicked. In the eyes, Sasha? A stare-down?"

"They didn't mean it, they've been military trained all their lives . . . oh . . . shit."

"My point exactly. What is normally the way things are done in one culture is a complete offense in another. You're also a damned diplomat and know what I say to be true."

"I know, I know," she muttered. "You're no liar."

Incredulous that she didn't immediately get it before simply because they were *her men,* people close to her, his voice trailed off into a furious grumble. To his mind, that was all the more reason she should have also been appalled and corrected them on the spot. They were her familiars, not his!

"No damned familiar is to ever look at a pack leader in the eye until he's given them the right to look up—sons-of-bitches needed to lower their heads and look down . . . a direct, in-the-eye stare? Unheard of. A handshake, not chest-cross—one of them, the goddamned dominant male, reached for my swing arm? Bullshit! The alpha from Toronto would have yanked it out of his fucking shoulder socket. We don't play that."

The more Max grumbled the more outraged he became, until he was so indignant that all he could do was turn around and fold his arms over his chest while Sasha angrily began scrubbing his hair.

"*Jesus* . . . What the hell is in this stuff?" she said, making a face and ignoring his diatribe. She needed a moment to recalibrate her emotions and to amp down the fight hormone surging through her. "Smells like Witch Hazel cured in gasoline."

"Yeah, it's got Witch Hazel in it, plus white willow bark, white sage oil, and about twenty-five other herbs to kill the Werewolf stench. Smells like hell in the tub, but once you rinse off, whatever demon splatter you got on you is gone for good. Then your own body chemistry neutralizes it."

"And I've gotta wash my hair with this stuff, too."

A half-smile tugged at Hunter's mouth. "You don't *have* to do anything, Sasha."

"I know one damned thing I have to do," she muttered, rubbing harder to build lather, "is to get my men, along with your ornery, surly ass, out of here with however many other testosterone-pumped alphas. Right about now, New Orleans by way of Denver sounds like a plan. We get out of here before nightfall, hop a plane from Yellowstone Regional Airport to—"

"Why Denver, then New Orleans?"

"Doc is in Denver," she said flatly.

Hunter hesitated. "I don't think, given this unresolved crisis, that now would be a good time for you to go to the U.C.E. meeting. I can take my chances alone, and cannot afford a delay in Denver to—"

"Listen, I've got a squad down there in New Orleans, resources, and my people were from there. I'm going. Period. I can't make you stop in Denver to see Doc; that's your choice. But you damned sure can't stop me from going to the U.C.E. meeting." She yanked his hair back and ignored his smile.

"Then why not Toronto—you don't have to get your intel from a dangerous annual U.C.E. meeting. My grandmother was Haitian and from there—that corridor has a large population of people who know how to access the supernatural realms. Our Shadow Wolf allies are strong along the Canadian—"

"Because *I said so*," she whispered with a quiet, threatening snarl in his ear. "I am *not* going to some highly populated, pristine city in the opposite direction of the action, with you possibly going buck-wild as a demon-infected Werewolf down in a city that has already experienced catastrophic human losses. We clear? I'm a soldier, and it's my job to put my life on the—"

"You're also my mate and I wouldn't be who I am if I didn't care what happens to you."

She looked away from him. The words were right there, climbing up her throat to yell that she wasn't really his mate and had just said it to pass muster—but the words caught in her larynx. She couldn't cough them out. The dynamics of who they were and what they were to each other was changing on the fly and that made her nervous.

"Until we know your contagion is under control," she said in a calmer voice after drawing several breaths, "we head south where I can get to Doc, Silver Hawk, and whatever else we need in a more sparsely populated zone . . . and because the Big Easy *is still* the paranormal black-market Big Apple, and there's also a big Haitian population there, too, if we need to go that route—any questions?"

"Why didn't you just say so?" he said, smiling broadly and teasing her. "You don't have to be so touchy about it."

She ignored him and flung the strong soap into the water, then dug her fingernails into his scalp and scrubbed hard. His change of mood was truly freaking her out. Was it the water that was pulling out the last of the toxin? Was it the fact that his normal Shadow Wolf system had finally absorbed the infection and had quarantined it? Not knowing was the worst. Then again, the niggling thought that by her not challenging the "my mate" comment was viewed as acquiescence gave her pause. But now was just not the time to get into all of that.

"Ow, that hurts," he said, now chuckling and trying to lean away from her.

She wound his long thicket of soapy black hair around her fist, yanked hard and spoke into his ear with a menacing whisper. "If you *ever* treat my guys like they're golden retrievers again, I will promise you it'll get ugly between me and you."

"Okay." His smile widened, and just as suddenly, he reached back, grabbed a handful of her parka, and flipped her into the water. She fell with her arms and legs sprawled over the tub edges, and splashed half of the water out onto the ground. The sound that exited her was a combination of a yelp and a shout. She threw a punch, but he dodged it, making her scream with rage.

Hunter's hard belly laughs only turned her sputtering into a colorful range of expletives. It took her a second to get hold of the side of the tub and push herself up. Completely pissed off, she put a muddy hiking boot in the center of his chest and unsnapped her parka, almost angry enough to draw on him.

"I couldn't resist," he said, laughing harder and dropping his head back. "The need for new clothes and boots, about a hundred-fifty bucks—the look on your face, priceless."

Woods and Fisher were on the porch with fresh towels and clothes in their arms seeming bewildered for a second, and then they slowly began to laugh.

"I owe you," she said, resisting the urge to laugh with them. "And when I come for you, it's gonna be really, really bad, Hunter."

She shoved out of the tub using Hunter's chest for leverage and causing him to release an *uhmph* sound with the forced expelled air.

"Can't wait. Tag, you're it," he called behind her as she stormed away.

Fisher cast his bundle of towels and clothes on top of the pile Woods held and grabbed a huge bucket off the porch, laughing as he headed toward the pump to get more clean water. "Dude, let me warn you that Trudeau has a real bad temper and a very long memory."

"Seen her in battle," Hunter said, unfazed, and stood. "Know that to be true." He jumped out of the tub, using one hand on the edge of it to propel him over the side and then hit the muddy ground with both feet in a gymnast's landing.

"You're still dirty and soapy!" Sasha called over her shoulder, stomping toward the water pump.

"Lucky you didn't get shot, man," Woods said, still laughing, and then heaved his load into the porch rocking chair before grabbing a few logs to put on the fire in order to make more hot water.

Sasha refused to even look at Hunter. There was no way she could, anyway. It was bad enough that she was soaked to the drawers and as angry as a wet hen. Now he'd add insult to injury by letting her men see her facial expression change when she saw his sculpted perfection all soap-slicked and wet? Was he crazy? Oh, and just because he'd used her dousing to break the ice with her men wasn't gonna save his mangy hide, even though judging by the expressions on Woods's and Fisher's faces, all was forgiven. Her men were having a field day.

Fisher held the bucket while she pumped water. It was cold but not freezing like it had been at higher elevations. She blocked out all the sidebar commentary and listened for the huge splashing sound of the tin tub emptying . . .

she could hear Hunter fidgeting about behind her, yucking it up with Woods. Okaaay.

She grabbed the half-filled bucket before Fisher could take a breath, spun into a shadow and came out with an icy splash that sent Hunter's voice booming. She flung the bucket at him and ran.

"You had mud on your chest and soap in your hair!" she shrieked laughing, dodging him. "Tag, you're it . . . and oh, yeah, by the way—payback is a bitch!"

As long as he was eating and drinking and the sun hadn't set yet, Hunter seemed fine. Even his coloring that had gone slightly ashen during the initial healing, was back to its warm, smooth brown with reddish undertones of vitality. On the surface, all was well. Crow Shadow and Bear Shadow seemed oblivious to any anomalies within Hunter. The other Shadow Wolves were still a short ways off, wisely following the dictates of pack life since the beginning of time—namely, replenishing themselves and getting well rested before a hunting full moon. Even her guys seemed relaxed as they bombarded Hunter and his men with questions that she was too distracted to absorb.

Anxiety threaded through her like a C4 trip wire. Her entire system was hotwired and booby-trapped, waiting for the smallest thing to trigger outright panic. She had to get Hunter out of there before true nightfall, but how? Any ruse she came up with would raise suspicion. Then again, what if things had gone too far and she really did need the entire clan force of multiple regional packs to battle a ridiculously strong demon-infected Werewolf on the loose? The fact that she was even hedging her bets was the root source of the distraction.

Everything military within her told her to put down a known threat without blinking. Yet everything else within her told her to give the man—one of the most honorable ones she'd ever known—a fighting chance. It was impossible to make this anything but personal, and by the same token, if an innocent person got killed because she'd failed to act, she'd never forgive herself.

"Isn't that right, Trudeau?"

She looked at Woods with a completely blank stare.

"Earth to Lieutenant, do you read me?" Woods said with a half smile.

"Sorry, guys," Sasha said, her mind still trying to synthesize a hundred different options at once.

"He was explaining how each one of us got different symptoms," Fisher said, dropping his voice low. "Like how I could always hear and smell real sharp, that was the extent of it—like Woodsey, maybe run faster than the average guy, but nothing too out of the norm."

"Other than getting horny as hell during a full moon," Woods said, laughing hard and turning his beer up.

"Hey, no offense, Lieutenant, but goes without saying," Fisher said with a shrug and a huge grin, and flung a bottle cap at Woods as Crow and Bear knocked bottles and laughed.

Although Hunter didn't comment, his smile was impossible to hide as it wrapped around the mouth of his beer bottle when he turned it up.

"But seriously, Trudeau," Woods said, his smile fading a little. "When did you know . . . like, how did you finally find out they'd been screwing with genes in a Petri dish? Or find out that they'd lied to us all, and that whole thing about us being bitten when we were kids, and having that as a fucked-up memory, was all staged bull—sorta leaves a real bad taste in your mouth, pardon the pun." His gaze was intense but within the depths of his eyes there was a haunting sadness. "All this time I thought my people were from West Virginia . . . only to find out the donors, I guess, were."

"Plus coyote or frickin' timber wolf—no offense, guys," Fisher said in a mildly bitter tone before polishing off his brew. "Puts a whole new spin on the word 'kin,' ya know."

"I found out the night Butler died," Sasha said in a quiet voice.

"What, the brass told you what happened in Afghanistan?" Woods looked at her hard and Fisher stopped rocking on the back two legs of his chair to give her his full attention.

All eyes were on Sasha as she glanced at Hunter, his expression unreadable.

"I always knew I could do stuff, was athletic," she said, holding Woods's and Fisher's gazes. "Thought that's what made me a natural for what we did. Also knew I had to take meds because I was given the same story about the Werewolf virus. Like everybody else, I didn't know that I was a part of Special Ops Project Sirius, code name Operation Dog Star." She turned her beer up and then set it down hard on the table, now studying the condensation it made on the wood.

"Butler, rest his soul in peace, went down in the desert . . . then our own choppers fired on us," Fisher said, leaning in, his eyes glancing at each intense pair that met him around the table. "These guys had our backs, thank you much—but I'm not following all the politics."

"Yeah," Woods said in a low, nervous tone. "Like, we only got a chance to talk to Doc in fits and starts—you could tell he was worried about surveillance. Crow and Bear had us laying low; Doc said we had to disappear . . ."

"How about you open up that bottle of Wild Turkey, brother," Bear Shadow said calmly, looking at Hunter.

Hunter nodded and reached for the bottle on the sideboard behind him, along with a fistful of shot glasses.

"Butler didn't die in Afghanistan," Sasha said flatly and then accepted the filled shot glass Hunter slid across the table.

"Well, where the fuck did he die?" Woods said, accepting a shot glass from Crow. "I saw us open half a clip—"

"He died in his townhouse," Sasha muttered, cutting him off and throwing back a shot.

"Whoa . . . How'd—"

"When I went over there to try to find my team, was looking for leads," she said. "He changed on me, transformed—and let's just say he wasn't himself."

Fisher and Woods were out of their chairs, backs against the doors, looking at Sasha wide-eyed. Fisher still had his chair, brandishing it as Woods's line of vision recklessly hunted for a weapon.

"He was strong as an ox, Trudeau. When he turned into that thing there's no way you could have gotten out without getting bitten!" Woods's eyes had become frantic.

"One silver slug in the chest, clean at point-blank range," she said, holding their stares and using a low, modulated tone to ease them off the wall. "I had the one-second hesitation advantage that you guys unfortunately didn't." She belted down another shot and slid refreshed glasses across the table. "Transformed, he wanted me as his lover."

Fisher slowly lowered the chair and both men returned to the table. Fisher turned the chair around backwards and sat down hard.

"Damn," Woods said quietly. "Yeah . . . I can see that."

"That's when I found out that my reflexes were faster than the normal human's, that I could . . . that I could respond better in a firefight against that kind of a target—and believe me, I hate that particular demon more than you'll ever know."

"Tell them the rest," Hunter said quietly, his voice firm but not harsh.

"When they mixed up your test tubes, you were just given a little wolf strain." She chuckled sadly and sipped her shot, then set it down with a wince. "Me, they mixed in the real McCoy—Shadow Wolf. Rod . . . from the beginning, he never stood a chance. He was mixed with demon-infected Werewolf, straight with no chaser."

"Get the hell out . . ." Fisher said, raking his fingers through his hair.

"Yeah," she said with a sigh. "I can transform. But I don't turn into what Rod did."

"Oh, shit," Woods whispered, rubbing his palms down his face.

"I think you can imagine what that was like, finding out under duress and not quite sure of the differences in species . . . ready to put your own weapon in your mouth to save yourself from becoming a cannibalistic beast." She closed her eyes for a moment and pushed back from the table. "If it wasn't for Hunter, Doc . . . Silver Hawk—I don't know what I would have believed."

"This is why we told you as much as we could about our kind," Bear Shadow said, glancing at Hunter and then at Fisher and Woods. "But there were things that were only right for your she-Shadow to disclose. That was not within our right."

Sasha offered Bear Shadow a nod of respect and then returned her attention to her men. "Bottom line is this, gentlemen. Our brass set up this project twenty-five years ago. Rod was the first, and the crazy bastards used bad Werewolf virus trying to create a better soldier, one that could go against whatever slithered out of the supernatural realms. These black holes they were finding within the local atmosphere, and even on the planet's surface, were not solely from erosion due to the effects of global warming, nuclear blasts, or anything else. The portals between worlds have always been here. Our instrumentation just got adept enough to actually see demon doors. Our technology has also made the seals weaker—by how much, we don't know."

"But what gave them the right . . ." Tears stood in Fisher's eyes.

"Nothing," Sasha said flatly. "But don't lay this at Doc's feet. He was a pawn, too, and did what he could— that's why the three of us didn't wind up like Rod."

"What did he do, Trudeau?" Woods said, his gaze going out the window with disgust.

"Doc knew this genetic dabbling was insane," she said without apology in her tone. "So rather than infect a whole team of embryos, creating time bombs waiting to detonate—he did the only humane thing possible within all this madness while the brass was breathing down his neck and swapped out the bad Werewolf toxin for whatever wolf DNA he could get his hands on. Mine happened to come from this pack . . . which is a very long story, one I can tell you guys on the way to New Orleans this afternoon."

"New Orleans? Today, and not tomorrow night?" Crow

Shadow looked at Hunter for a moment, and then he glimpsed Bear Shadow.

Bear Shadow stared at his hands as he spoke to Hunter. "Pack leaders from the entire North American clan are expecting an inter-pack summit tonight, and as overall clan alpha . . . It could be viewed as a significant snub, or worse, a weakness, if you do not open the strategy session under this full moon."

Sasha watched Hunter's expression cloud over as Bear's eyes pleaded for him to reconsider. But she also knew that Hunter couldn't lie without tipping off his pack brothers to the fact that something was seriously wrong. Ransacking her brain for her best diplomatic skills, she dusted them off and put a truth-laced bluff on the table.

"He's gotta go before the trail goes cold . . . has to find out more about this thing that we wrestled with last night, but got away."

Hunter's gaze bored into hers and she couldn't tell whether or not he was pissed off or going along with her.

"That would be the only circumstance that would make sense," Crow Shadow said, glancing between Hunter and Bear Shadow.

"Look, we already know that traitor, Dexter, got away," Sasha said emphatically, holding everyone's line of vision hostage. "Sure, we got Fox Shadow and Guilliaume, and most of their crew of Shadow traitors who stole Werewolf toxin to sell on the black market," she added, pressing on when they didn't cut her off. "But we didn't get all of the vials, that's one issue. That *definitely* doesn't need to be auctioned down in the Big Easy."

Hunter nodded and let out a weary breath and then rubbed his palms down his face. "The other issue is, if there's still any beta Shadows out there who are crazy enough to shoot up with the stuff, and we know from what we saw it do to some pack members that this crap is more addictive than crack."

"What the hell . . ." Woods held his shot glass mid-air as he stared at Sasha and then Hunter.

Fisher shook his head. "Just when you think you've heard it all."

"Oh, here's the best part," Sasha said with a hard gaze on her men and then sent it toward Crow and Bear. "An authentic Shadow Wolf blood transfusion is the only thing that can bring a hyped-up Shadow back down once they've shot up—or they can't control their shape-shifts and begin to lean more and more toward being an infected Werewolf the longer it stays in their system. This isn't like getting bitten by a normal Werewolf. No. When you see this beast, you know something's beyond supernatural about it—it's completely demon." Sasha pushed back in her chair and ran her fingers through her hair. "Pure Shadow blood works like Valium once those rogue wolves who shoot up with it to come down from the toxin."

"Then any Shadow Wolf out there is at risk of being abducted for their blood." Bear Shadow pushed back from the table both incredulous and enraged.

Sasha nodded. "You see, gentlemen, what they stole, and what caused General Wilkerson to get his face ripped off, was virus gene spliced and encoded into human DNA spirals—which is what makes it so potent for the Shadow Wolves. It merges with their human side, and their immune systems can't seem to reject the Werewolf virus that's been so thoroughly encapsulated into the human DNA string."

"That's fucking insane," Woods said, shaking his head. "And betas are shooting up with this shit?"

"You'd be surprised what lesser-ranked beta males would do for a shot at the title," Bear Shadow said with a snarl. "Punk bitches."

"Correct," Sasha said, obliquely monitoring Hunter's poker exterior. "Buyers of this crap don't want the ugly side effects, just the Shadow Wolf-on-steroids instant high and strength. Not to mention that if the sellers decide they can't make enough cash on the remnants of the virus they have left, they could always just sell it to a superpower that wants to replicate the experiments our brass did to create soldiers. Every human military lab around the world wants a little of this stuff that's so hard to get ahold of— simply because the donors aren't exactly cooperative."

"So you think this thing that you fought last night fled to New Orleans?" Crow Shadow's gaze bored into Hunter's.

"I think it might go there," Hunter said coolly, sipping his shot of Wild Turkey.

"If you wanted to unload bad product in a hurry on the supernatural black market, as well as catch Shadow Wolf diplomats unaware and having a good time, heading to the conference site makes sense." What Sasha didn't say was that her team had done some divinations and also had strong leads pointing toward the Big Easy.

"True," Bear Shadow argued, "but my concern is still with the view the clan will have. Many of the brothers from our pack were unfortunately involved. Those misguided assumptions and winds carrying bad rumors must be quelled."

"All the more reason for our pack within the clan to suffer the heaviest casualties and to walk point on the seek-and-destroy mission." Hunter folded his arms over his chest and stared at Bear Shadow until he looked away.

"What about a compromise?" Sasha said, knowing that making Hunter's men suspicious in any way would not be to their advantage. She waited until all eyes were on her. "What if Hunter rallied the alphas, now, before sunset—told them of the New Orleans plan . . . they could fan out, watch for activities in potential pop-up zones where Dexter might function, as well as be on the ready to send in reinforcements in case we got in trouble . . . my guys would go with me to link up with the rest of the paranormal unit already setting up a base of operations down there to recover the stolen vials. Bear Shadow and Crow Shadow could temporarily merge with the packs on patrol to watch the backs of our remaining pack members—but by them helping the regional effort, it shows solidarity . . . and the pre-moon briefing would show that there was no intent to bristle anyone with a diplomacy snub."

For the first time since the sun had come up on this day, she saw Hunter's shoulders completely relax.

Chapter 6

Eighteen million acres of pure wilderness separated him from his grandson's exact location. Yellowstone National Park covered thirty-four hundred square miles in North-west Wyoming alone, but cut through the neighboring states of South Dakota, Montana, Utah, Nebraska, and Idaho, and then folded into the uncharted wilderness of the Canadian border. Individual packs had tracked the remaining rogue members to this region, and then lost the trail here. Therefore, the packs would convene the clan. A hunting party was gathering.

His grandson was at extreme risk, if any irregularities occurred. This was simply the way of the Shadow Wolf.

It had been a long time since the pack, or even the clan, had called him by his warrior name, Silver Shadow. He double-checked the prefilled hypodermic needles tucked within the inside breast pocket of his bear-skin coat and kept walking.

Melancholy filled him. The sharp wind and his memories made his eyes water. There was a time when his howl alone would make the birds go still for miles. However, for many years of retirement now as a clan elder shaman, the other pack leaders referred to him as Silver Hawk. His human name. If they ever pushed him, though, he would prove to them all that he was still to be respected as a formidable alpha. He would stand by his grandson, Max Hunter—pack-named Wolf Shadow—until the very last . . . if Max was not beyond reclamation.

It didn't matter that he was not at the gathering site by his own design. He'd needed the time to collect the medicines and to investigate things for himself without watchful pack eyes. But word still came to him through the murmurs of the trees and carried on the wind and stole into his visions. Once a seasoned warrior, a champion of the hunt, always he would be that.

Silver Hawk squatted by the thick tracks in the snow, mentally sizing up the massive paw prints, and then inhaled the frigid air. The way the bramble was broken and trees scarred, something had ripped through the forest with impunity.

He stopped at a ravaged tree trunk to pinch hair fibers between his thumb and index fingers, judging from their coloring, scent, and coarseness what creature had once owned them. His nose led him the rest of the way, so did the bloodied tracks in the snow that led out of a snow-covered mound.

Warily, he approached the site, his instincts keen, bowie knife drawn as he peered into the dark opening. Squinting with disbelief, he reached in and extracted a severed head.

A thousand-pound male grizzly had been slaughtered within its own hibernation den up at Hoodoo Creek? At least it wasn't human remains. But then, the Great Spirit made no distinction. A life was a life. For this noble animal to be slaughtered for no reason was against the laws of nature. The bear coat he wore was not mere vanity. It had been won and claimed during his early initiation rites, and all of the animal had been both used and revered. The carnage he held in his grip now, however, was pure sacrilege.

Slowly inspecting the gruesome discovery, he saw that the bear's hide had been ripped off at the neck and then pulled inside out over its skull like an eerie hood. The brains and back of the skull were gone.

Crouching low, Silver Hawk reached in and grabbed a huge paw in an attempt to try to drag the heavy carcass out of the den, only to have the paw and the forelimb come away from the shredded body in his hands.

The animal's four-inch claws were broken off, as though the poor creature had done everything it could to back up and defend itself within the small space. The bear never stood a chance.

He didn't need to see more to know what had happened. Something much more powerful than the almighty grizzly had entered the den head first, surprised the hibernating animal in a frontal attack, tore its head off its muscular shoulders, and dismembered the forelimbs that struck out in self-defense. There was only one thing he knew of that was strong enough or insane enough to do that.

The question was why? Was this a territorial marker, for sport, for the rich, fatty protein stored in hibernating bear meat, or all of the above?

And it wasn't the first such attack. A huge black bear had not only been killed but eaten within the Greater Yellowstone Northern Rockies, and natural timber wolf packs had been savaged in Hidden Valley. Silver Hawk more carefully studied the severed limb by his feet and dug into the den with both hands, lugging out what should have been, judging by the paws and skull size, a thousand-pound animal.

Scant viscera and practically no meat left on the bones answered his questions. Something was bulking up on thickly fatted meat supplies that human flesh was too problematic to immediately provide . . . if one were in hiding, a single grizzly already fattened for the winter offered as much meat as four healthy men.

This predator was smart. This predator was in hiding and preparing. There could be more than one, and in all likelihood there was.

The elderly warrior turned his face toward the blustery wind and looked out at the limitless mountain range. It was still technically winter, and the bears wouldn't be on the move for almost a month, awaiting the true spring thaw, so it couldn't have been one of them gone mad. It had to be something unnatural and strong enough to ambush an eight-foot half-ton king grizzly in its prime. There was only one predator that fit the bill.

He just prayed to the Great Spirit that it wasn't Max.

Sasha pulled Woods and Fisher aside before they all reached the clearing. It was important for them to understand what she was just now beginning to fathom.

Huge, aggressive, battle-hungry alphas had come to represent the North American clan, hailing from the Rockies, the Yosemite range, the Sierra Nevada, the Great Lakes region to the Catskills, Poconos, and Appalachians, all the way to the Grand Canyon, and down to the Texas panhandle, as well as the swamplands of the Gulf and back out to the Everglades, with a significant contingent from the Yukon to the Torngat Mountains by the Labrador Sea. Every fierce warrior would be in attendance. There could be no screwups in diplomacy. Even the packs as far north as those from Alaska's Brooks, Alaska, and Aleutian ranges would also be there.

Once Hunter had given her that much to go on, her mind filled in the blanks. Most of these leaders were mated males. That meant she had to be seriously on point to hold the respect of the other strong she-Shadows and not have her rank challenged. The prospect was positively medieval to her mind, but instinctively she knew that to argue was foolish. It was what it was, a culture unto itself. Like it or leave it, she had to put on a good diplomatic show.

The North American clan was massive, as it had been for centuries, richly populated with strategically located and very strong packs hidden among the United States' and Canada's wealth of natural mountain ranges and forests. If the threat spread, it also wouldn't be long before packs from across the Mexican border would enter the fray from the Sierra Madre Occidental.

That couldn't happen—not just because the contagion didn't need to spread, but also because it would bring in the clan leader from another hemisphere, where an alpha challenge could go down between the territories. Hunter's condition was dicey enough without that added complication. Problem was, this was all impromptu. She had about as much of a clue as to what might go on as her bewildered squad. There just hadn't been enough time.

"Okay, guys," she said in a tense whisper, holding Woods's and Fisher's complete attention. "I'm making this up as I go along, never did this in my life. I don't know if Hunter has ever done this full clan thing. But I do know this: Keep your eyes lowered, and only speak when you are spoken to. If you blink wrong at one of these big

SOB's, you could lose your throat and there won't be jack shit I can do about it."

She held their gazes, constantly monitoring the extreme tension within them. "The alphas move like lightning and will not hesitate to make an example of what they perceive as a threat to their rank. Think five-star general on PCP and steroids—keep your distance and give them nonchallenging vibrations at all times. If you trust me, stay cool, don't even flinch like you're going for a weapon, I think I can get you out of here alive."

"You think?" Woods whispered, his gaze on the tree line.

Sasha could literally see the hair standing up on the nape of his and Fisher's necks as Hunter moved forward with Crow and Bear. "Give me your weapons, then," she said, looking at Fisher. "One false move and you could upset the balance of power."

"We should cover you and Hunter," Fisher argued.

Sasha leveled her gaze at him and then at Woods. "No. You shouldn't. That's Crow and Bear's job. You're only on communication today. When you get to New Orleans, you're the squad's early-warning system and muscle while me and Hunter aren't around . . . and I've still gotta figure out how to bring you in to them while explaining that you aren't dead or infected." She pointed to the center of Woods's chest. "But right now, you are stone. A statue," she said in a low warning tone. "Now give me the damn gun."

Grudgingly, Woods and Fisher disarmed, and Sasha shoved a nine millimeter into the front of her waistband, and another in the back. She gave them a look that told them to stay by the big, black F-150 truck, and she walked forward into the clearing to stand six o'clock scout to

Hunter with Crow and Bear flanking them both, sensing multiple shadow presences that she couldn't yet see.

The moment she was in position, Hunter glimpsed her. His eyes suddenly changed and became all wolf. He threw his head back and released a rallying howl that caused the hair on her arms and neck to rise. The tone was so forceful that it felt like it had wrapped around every cell within her to suddenly expand her lungs, climb up her throat, and make her wail join in with his, setting off Crow Shadow and Bear Shadow in a chain reaction.

Chills of anticipation ran through her as another long howl from Hunter jolted her system. Soon the call was answered by a range of vocals echoing through the clearing, calling the meeting to order, calling forth the most primal instincts within her being.

They were magnificent as they stepped out from the shadow line of trees, warriors from every ethnicity and hue, their eyes all wolf, flanked and backed by their most trusted soldiers and their mates.

Hunter stepped forward, yet his rigid carriage told her and his men not to move. Slowly a large, tanned, blond male came forward, a rim of amber surrounding his crystal-blue irises. He and Hunter appraised each other, and then Hunter extended a warrior's forearm handshake. They parted with a smile, crossing their right forearms over their chests.

"Yosemite treats you well, my friend," Hunter said, his smile widening.

The handsome blond wolf chuckled and then inclined his head toward Sasha with a curious grin, as he tipped his cowboy hat. "And the Rockies have been *very* good to you, I see."

"Jason, you are living proof that they can't teach an old dog new tricks."

"Oh, I get it. In front of your woman I'm just Jason, not Lion Shadow. Just disrespect me, why don't you."

"Stop drooling and I'll properly introduce you, then."

Hunter laughed, and the moment he did, fifteen alphas walked forward and a rowdy reunion was on.

Still, Sasha didn't move. It was like watching a fraternity come together to whoop it up at a tailgate party after a March Madness football game . . . but she also knew that the males could go from laughing to a death match in the blink of an eye, depending on how much alcohol and testosterone was in their systems. And although that "your woman" crap thoroughly grated on her, she'd have to address it later—much later. For the sake of diplomacy, now was not the time.

So she waited and watched. She kept a mental catalog of who approached Hunter and in what order, which ones smiled falsely, which ones' voices laughed but where the laugh didn't come from the gut or the heart and only from a political mind. Right off the bat she didn't like the burly brunet from Florida—his good ol' boy tone and shifty eyes made her hackles immediately go up. Fuck Bob. She'd watch him like a hawk.

The brothers from the Aleutian territory, however, put her at ease. They were shorter, stockier, and their low-key approach seemed genuine. Three redwood-sized Canadians just made her gape. They were taller than Hunter by a full head and, like him, seemed to share mixed parentage that was hard to define. But she could tell that they were way more easygoing in manner than Hunter could ever be. Her best guess was that was why Hunter probably seemed more alpha than Jorge, Micah, and Peter in the eyes of the clan.

However, the Shadows from the eastern ranges completely fascinated her with their sophisticated aloofness. She could imagine them walking along the streets of Manhattan or Philadelphia, unnoticed, not a soul aware of what they truly were, slipping between Wall Street and fashion mavens, entering and exiting bars like thieves in the night or disappearing between the tall shadows of towering buildings as easily as disappearing into God's country.

Yeah . . . while she liked Tomas and Anwar's cool style, a style that would fit in well in New Orleans if they needed backup, their politics worried her. Although the alpha from the Appalachian Range seemed like a lean, country tangle of gangly arms and legs, his eyes were honest. She'd seen that kind of soldier before; in fact, Fisher was like that. Misleading, might even say something politically incorrect, but once you were in his bosom, you were family for life. Could probably shoot the eye out of a needle and outrun a NASCAR racer. Okay. Jimmy Ray passed her internal radar inspection.

She collected impressions, layering them to scents, voices, eyes, body types, trying to see their wolf without a transformation taking place. Soon she could envision each magnificent coat—snow white, amber, chocolate brown, mixed timber, gleaming honey, husky markings . . . yes, she would know them in an instant, would know them in a full-out hunt. Would know their familiars, their flanks-men . . . and their mates.

A low growl made the group go still. A tall, voluptuous brunette stepped beside the Everglades contingent, her eyes a narrowed, challenging glare.

"My sister was badly injured at your hands, and that was never fully addressed."

For a moment, Sasha stared at her, an irrational spike

sending more adrenaline through her than was probably necessary. "If your sister is who I think she is, I wouldn't admit that in public. She challenged my rank and then was found to be involved in the betrayal that brings us all to this clearing—so *get out of my face.*"

Sasha had delivered the warning on a low growl as the group parted. The challenger glanced at her husband just enough to quickly draw Sasha's line of vision behind her. Armed familiars were quietly circling. In an instant Sasha had a weapon in both hands outstretched in either direction.

"If you value their lives you'll call them back, or I'll drop 'em the most efficient way without breaking a sweat by calling my wolf." Sasha could feel movement on the periphery cease.

"After the threat to our region is over, we'll finish this."

"No," Sasha said. "We'll finish this shit right here and right now! Either we have a cohesive clan or we do not. If not, then anybody with a problem needs to be rooted out from the core as we speak. That's how it stole in and festered among the Shadow packs before; we're only as strong as our weakest link."

"What would you know about the ways of—"

Sasha had advanced on the female so quickly and had backhanded her so solidly, while still holding a nine millimeter, that it felt like she'd dislocated her shoulder. "I know you didn't see that coming, bitch—that's what I know. Anybody else got a problem?"

A few half smiles greeted Sasha as she took a wide-legged stance and waited for the downed challenger to decide how far things would go. She tossed her weapons to Hunter, whose expression hadn't changed as he easily caught them in each hand and stashed them in his waistband. The female on the ground glared at Sasha but didn't immediately get up as she wiped blood from her mouth and the gash that had opened her cheek.

"Fine," Sasha said as the embarrassed she-Shadow slowly stood and went to her mate's side, still glaring yet humbled, for now. "Then let Hunter do what he's gotta do."

She thought she saw pride burning in Hunter's hard-to-read eyes, but she was still so furious that she'd been disrespected that she couldn't be sure what she actually saw. There were still flecks of light dancing in her peripheral vision like aimless, lit floaters brought on from the sudden burst of rage.

Regardless, there was no mistaking the slightly amused tone of Hunter's voice before the clan got back down to hard business. The only thing that began to de-escalate her from a flat-out field battle was that the other she-Shadows seemed extremely pleased that she'd knocked the snot out of the one named Barbara. In fact, she was oddly looking forward to getting to know those female warriors.

Each she-Shadow had battle-honed expressions and warrior's bodies to match, and there was something very honorable in the depths of their eyes. For once to no longer be the only one of her kind, the lone female in the group, felt really good. Maybe for the first time in her life she wouldn't be an outcast. A band of brothers had been great, but a band of sisters was something she'd always wished for.

Finally calming with that thought, Sasha stepped back and relaxed her shoulders, which seemed to make the rest of the clan reduce their state of readiness for a brawl.

"Well, now that you two have met—Barbara meet Sasha, and vice versa," Hunter said, beginning to walk around the middle of the circle with his hands clasped behind his back. "Glad we got that out of the way, because, as you are all aware, we have a serious threat to address. We have intelligence that the hot trail we lost in the Rockies picks back up in New Orleans—and we need to address the issue before the UCE Conference tomorrow night."

Concerned stares met Hunter's before Jason spoke up.

"What about the recent bear mutilations, dude?" Jason glanced at the Canadian shadows and several members from the Rocky Mountain Range. "As recently as last night what's on the move fed here."

Pure tension coiled itself around Sasha's vertebrae one disk at a time. The Aleutians nodded and the elder of them spoke slowly, his icy gray, huskylike eyes a strange contrast within his native face.

"It feeds with purpose, strengthening like one lone rogue male. To abandon the hunt here would leave the back door wide open."

"Well said, brother," Hunter replied, his voice calm and yet commanding. "This is why we take a point team to New Orleans while keeping the back door tightly guarded. If it becomes suspected that a Shadow Wolf has become demon-infected and is on the loose, then I'm sure the Vampire Cartel can sway the other voting blocs at the United Council of Entities to allow an open wolf hunt."

Jason nodded, his gaze hard. "Our Werewolf cousins could possibly vote with them, given there's been no love lost between our clan and theirs. It would take the heat off of them and redirect it toward us!"

"Word . . ." Anwar said, slowly circling. "In Philly, we call that bullshit foul. That's why I can't stand Vampires.

But I wouldn't put it past those dead mothafuckas to try it—have all the wolf clans at war with each other."

"Yeah, *hombre*," Tomas said with a snarl. "Then the Vamp Cartel gets a vote to do open season on any wolf that's potentially infected, and for the first time in history they can pop us in the streets along with the Werewolves—infected or not."

Jason growled. "If it goes there, we might have to call for a coalition between Shadow Wolves and Werewolves."

"Perish the goddamned thought," Jimmy Ray said, and then spit on the ground. "What's your take, Hunter? How do we play this so we don't get played?"

"We have to set up a containment field for whatever's feeding here, but also keep it from trying to get to the marketplace in New Orleans." Hunter rubbed the tension from the back of his neck as he spoke. "We have to clean up after our own and keep this from hitting the the the Big Easy. That's just as much of a danger as the one potential rogue hunting in North Country, maybe more, because of all the politics involved."

Sasha hadn't breathed nor blinked. Shogun had said the same thing when he'd approached her in South Korea—his clans had sought the courtesy to be able to clean up after their own. Normal Werewolves wanted to be able to capture, execute, and/or contain the demon-infected members of their ranks without a full-scale wolf hunt. Innocent, uninfected Werewolves had been slaughtered in wolf hunts for years, spurred on by the malevolent intent of Vampires. Humans had also been guided by whispers and rumors of where to find these wolves . . . whispers transmitted through Vampire murmurs and phantoms in their employ. Now that could happen to Shadow Wolves.

It also slowly dawned on her, what if all this business with bad blood toxin was a very well-orchestrated plot devised by Vampires to wipe out their most formidable opponents—shape-shifting wolves of any breed? Both Shogun and Hunter had said that if the wolf clans stuck together, their Federations would pose the most significant, allied threat to the Vamps' power structure. The conspiracy theory required time, resources, and proof—something Sasha didn't have the luxury to employ right now, not with a higher priority threat looming.

Random thoughts bounced off her synapses, colliding with both her conscience and common sense. Last night . . . what if the huge predator feeding with purpose was the male beside her . . . the one who'd experienced blackouts? Conversely, what if the pack didn't buy the plan and demanded a hunt prior to heading for New Orleans? Even crazier, what if they went for it? She couldn't have Fisher and Woods travel with her and Hunter.

Until she knew Hunter was stable, she had to get her guys joined up with a safe base of operations that the rest of the team provided. Exponentially complicating matters, how in the world could she get to the isolated team in New Orleans to warn them that Fisher and Woods were no longer MIA, but that the brass couldn't be notified until she had an off the record conversation with Doc? If she broke the airwaves with a sat-phone call, the transmission could be intercepted. Trying to reach Clarissa by shared vision was too sketchy and next to impossible to give her anything beyond impressions that the guys were still alive. The phenomenon wasn't an exact science like a damned telegram!

The variables before her made her head hurt, but she

couldn't even begin to focus on that now. At the moment a tense silence filled the glen as the other alphas considered the change in plans Hunter had put on the table. Finally Tomas gave a curt nod, causing a ripple effect in the group.

"We've got enough muscle here to bring down that bitch, Dexter, no matter what he feeds on or shoots up with. Makes sense to tighten the noose here, flush him out, and intercept any courier he might have sent down to The Big Easy," Anwar said with a rumble.

"Definitely gotta interrupt his cash flow from this shit," Tomas said, pounding Anwar's fist.

The Great Lakes Shadows gave the nod, too. Detroit and Chicago were in. That rippled assent from the Alaskans, Canadians, all the way to the Appalachian Shadows. Jason gave a shrug and a smile to count his vote as a yes. The Everglades grudgingly nodded, but the Texas range Shadows almost seemed as disappointed as Jimmy Ray that they weren't going to New Orleans on the first run.

"We got your back," a barrel-chested Navajo growled, and then slapped five with Jimmy Ray. "You make us second wave—forty-eight hours, two moons, and we'll have a pack in New Orleans. That's definitely our neck of the woods."

"You know what they say," Jimmy Ray added with a sly grin, chewing a twig. "Don't mess with Texas . . . but I can tell ya what we do with people who mess with clan up in the hills where I'm from."

"No, Jimmy Ray," Jason said with a good-natured laugh. "I don't think you need to go into all of that in front of the ladies."

Sasha just looked around the group in complete amazement. They functioned just like a field military tactical unit. There was no long debate, no Congressional-style filibustering. No decision by committee. The way of the wolf was clean and efficient. Just as soon as everything had come to a head and had been discussed, it was decided and over.

Chapter 7

"Can you get these guys some new ID and to a chopper that'll bring them out of the mountains with some plane tix to New Orleans for tomorrow?" Sasha asked Bear Shadow once they'd pulled up to the small cabin and disembarked from the Ford.

Her gaze was intense and she ignored the disgruntled expressions Fisher and Woods had. "I don't want them traveling with me and Hunter during a full moon where we could draw an attack . . . they might have a little wolf in their genes, but if these guys get bitten, it's over. There's nothing in their systems to fight the demon-infected Werewolf virus, and most people don't survive a Werewolf attack, anyway."

"Agreed," Hunter said, looking at the pitch of the dropping sun. "No sense in bringing them this far to have them die on American soil from the same thing they'd been running from."

"Your request is not a problem," Bear Shadow said. "Crow is an excellent lookout and can make sure they get off the mountain with the truck. We'll get your amulets repaired and you both can head out with supplies in the other vehicle. I'll join the hunting party the old-fashioned way." Bear Shadow smiled a very satisfied grin as Hunter pounded his fist.

"You hunt well, old friend."

The two men stared at each other for a brief moment, but soon Woods's and Fisher's complaints broke the calm.

"We don't get a choice in the matter?" Woods argued. "We just found you again, Trudeau."

"And I want to keep you alive and whole, now that we've been reunited," she said in a weary tone. "I don't want to be searching the forest for your body parts. Understood?"

"And we wanna have your back," Fisher said, folding his arms over his chest. "Besides, we don't even know where we're headed, where they are in New Orleans, and I'd put money on it that they're so undercover you don't either."

Hunter looked hard at Woods and Fisher for a moment and then turned his gaze on Sasha. "Home them to the others on your squad."

"Do what?" Sasha stared at Hunter, totally confused.

"They are familiars. Home them. That is how my men could find them so fast. Their minds are a beacon within a pack."

"I am *so* not following you," Sasha said, rubbing her palms down her face in frustration. "My men need an airtight way to rendezvous with my team without getting their heads blown off."

"I'm all for the last part of that," Woods said, pounding Fisher's fist.

"Yeah, dude. Been there, seen it, done that, and ain't trying to have another friendly fire incident again," Fisher said, nervously jamming his hands into his jeans pockets.

Hunter glanced at the two disgruntled soldiers and then turned his intense gaze on Sasha again. "They're rare, only a few born during the life span of the pack's alpha she-Shadow. They are always hers, because she is the one who could be most vulnerable to attack while pregnant and while the pack's Shadow males are on a demon hunt."

"You have got to be shittin' me," Woods said, then hocked and spit. "That's why Doc did this to us?"

"Of all the low-life, twisted—"

"Hold it, fellas," Sasha said, trying to stem a mutiny. "We don't know that." An uneasy feeling slithered through her consciousness. Doc wouldn't have premeditated something like this, would he? She stared at Hunter. Had they both been set up in the ultimate arranged marriage, complete with a pair of familiars? Sasha felt the muscles in her face tighten as she tried to keep shock and horror out of her expression.

All eyes went to Hunter.

"He did you a favor," Hunter said flatly, seeming oblivious to her alarm. "From what I understand, your general Wilkerson wanted every embryo in the experiment infected with Werewolf virus."

"This was a better out, if Doc had to do a bait and switch, guys, trust me. Like I told you, Doc's meds only held the full Werewolf flipout for twenty-five years. Ask yourself, how old was Rod when he really started getting weird?" She was babbling, repeating history for them . . . maybe repeating it for herself so she wouldn't have to think the worst.

Woods and Fisher stared at each other for a moment.

"Right after the birthday party we had for him up at Ronnie's Road Hawg," Woods said, relaxing and his voice becoming sad.

"Seems like it was yesterday," Fisher said quietly.

"A familiar is an honorable position in the pack, and a rare one," Hunter said, lifting his chin. "In the past, legend holds, they were created by the Great Spirit to walk among humans with a wolf's reflexes and savvy, but without alerting the demons—in order to carry visual messages to the shaman. The goal was to always protect the royal offspring from humans, intrapack aggressors, or the demon wolves . . . future leaders depended on this."

"Yeah, well, how come we've never heard about any of this shit?" Woods's voice was strident from emotional fatigue. "Every time I ask a question, you guys say 'legend has it,' but what frickin' legends? I've never heard of any of this stuff!"

"History is replete with legends of these wolf-den-raised human children all the way back to Romulus and Remus," Hunter replied calmly. "But they were hardly the first."

He waited a beat until slow awareness began to dawn within Woods's and Fisher's eyes. Crow Shadow and Bear Shadow simply shrugged as though they didn't understand what the big deal was about it.

"Early-warning protection is the primary function of the familiars," Hunter said matter-of-factly. "It's their job to recall the pack in the event of a double-back settlement attack . . . that, and being excellent advance lookout scouts." He then turned away from Woods and Fisher and spoke in a low, calm murmur to Sasha. "As you know, my mother wasn't so lucky to have living familiars available during her pregnancy."

Sasha continued to stare at Hunter without blinking, still feeling total outrage slowly simmering within Woods and Fisher. Maybe it was also simmering within her. Could that past history have been enough to make two old men collude to this degree? If she was going to keep her head on straight, she had to jettison the insane thought for now. *Just let it go, Sasha,* she mentally told herself. *You just have to let it go.*

"Close your eyes," Hunter said and then turned to Woods and Fisher. "You, too."

Hunter waited for the anxious threesome to comply before he closed his eyes and slowed down his breaths while Crow Shadow and Bear Shadow stood beside the truck, watching.

"Envision who you want them to track and locate . . . remember what the others on your squad look like, the sounds of their voices, their scents." Hunter waited until he heard Sasha's breaths quiet and slow to steady inhales and exhales. Soon Woods's and Fisher's matched hers, and he continued to wait until they were all completely in sync before he spoke again.

"Can you see them?" Hunter asked, waiting for Sasha's disgruntled squad members to stop resisting. Little by little he could feel the tense vibrations around them ease.

"Whoa . . ." Fisher murmured with his eyes closed. "I can literally smell Clarissa's perfume. She wears that stuff . . . Angel, right?"

"Right," Sasha said quietly.

"Yeah, she does," Woods finally said. "There's a lotta garbage on the street where they are, though."

Hunter smiled and opened his eyes. "Sasha . . . they'll be able to find the others now."

She opened her eyes with Woods and Fisher. "Now *that* was cool."

"Yeah, but what do we tell Clarissa, Bradley, and Winters when we get there?" Woods asked Sasha, still clearly concerned.

Sasha gave him and Fisher a big hug. "Tell them that

for reasons you can't disclose, your death had to be staged so you could be more effective. Also tell them that I'm hunting something crazy with my, uhmmm, indigenous guide and that a call to the brass about you right now could be intercepted and thus compromise the operation at this point. You take the image of me hugging you guys directly to Clarissa, understood? As resident psychic, she'll be able to interpret from it. That's your calling card to get you allowed in and not shot at the door when you find the hidden team. They're living like a sleeper cell on our side right now and could be a little edgy, so take standard entry precautions. Wear silver, a blessed religious symbol, you know the drill, so they don't think you're an entity using a bogus body image. Let 'em know that I'll be there within forty-eight to seventy-two hours—and in the meantime, start looking for clues but be careful. Don't ever split up. You guys move as a unit."

Anxiety shadowed relief, no matter which way she turned the plan in her mind. Sure, she'd literally helped Hunter dodge a silver bullet at the interpack clan meeting, but was it the right thing to do? Only time would tell.

But she'd thought she'd pass out when Bear Shadow had gotten the broken silver chains on their amulets repaired and tried to give them to Hunter, who stepped back from his own man as though Bear were holding a rattlesnake. The only saving grace had been that Bear had misinterpreted Hunter's response as a forceful command to give the amulets to her, of course to doubly protect his mate who was in heat. The mental replay made Sasha inwardly cringe.

At least her guys, as well as Hunter's, were out of harm's way for a moment. Crow could get Woods and

Fisher to a small, regional chopper service by truck; then before nightfall the chopper could get them to the regional airport that would have much lower security than a huge international airport. Even if they had to take a crop duster out of the area, the pack had influence that would ensure her men got in the air before the moon was up.

Crow would then recognizance with Bear and the two would merge into the larger clan where there was safety in numbers—just like Woods and Fisher would soon be with a small squad again.

She had to stop worrying. If her guys had precariously made it all the way from the Afghan border, across Russia, and into Alaska, and then down into Canada with relatively no help, they could damn well make it from the Rockies down to Louisiana . . . she hoped.

Sasha released a quiet rush of air as Hunter drove in silence. She kept her gaze on the late-afternoon sun, as though staring at it long enough would keep it from setting. For the first time in a long while she found herself dreading the unknown that would come with nightfall.

Their regional exit plan was slightly modified from that of Woods's and Fisher's. Unlike her men, they'd drive to a remote pack-owned guest lodge that the pack had conveniently closed for the winter when the outbreaks began. That would be their temporary base of operation. Everyone involved believed it was a part of their data-gathering strategy . . . they'd hunt by moonlight, pick up on the trail that had a trajectory toward New Orleans, and in the morning push onward to a ranger station that had pack ties and a chopper to get to a regional airport and ultimately out. She would call Doc on the road and meet up with him in a remote location in Colorado before heading south.

It sounded logical, practical even. But in her heart she

knew that her reasons went far deeper than just protecting Woods and Fisher. There was no way she could have Hunter in a populated area if his condition was unstable. That would be like walking through a mall or a small airport with no safety on a gun and firing at random, hoping not to hit anyone or anything. Just plain irresponsible.

And they couldn't go to any of the other nine area lodges that were open. Those human vistas that boasted of no TV or Internet connections were magnets for families, honeymooning couples, and elderly retirees who were seeing the broad brush beauty of the country for the first time. Innocents. On the flip side, if anything was tracking its own kind and Hunter turned out to be a magnet, better to be in a location that was vacant but had been set up like a small artillery bunker.

"You finished gnawing on that bone?" Hunter said casually, no malice in his voice.

Sasha briefly closed her eyes and rubbed the tension away from her neck. "Is it that obvious?"

"Pretty much," he said, but kept his eyes forward as his huge hand enveloped hers. He brought her knuckles to his mouth and hesitated, before slowly releasing it. "I'm sorry . . . about everything."

She took up his hand again, squeezed it, and brought the wide expanse of knuckles to her lips. "So am I."

"They'll be all right," Hunter said quietly, his eyes on the desolate road.

"I want *you* to be all right," she confessed, saying it out loud for the first time.

"I can't promise that." He gave her hand a short squeeze before gently extracting it from her hold.

"I know." She stroked his jaw with her knuckles and then sent her blurry gaze out the window.

"You did real good back there with the clan. Earned respect. The clan needed a strong alpha she-Shadow to build cohesion . . . one with true professional training. None of the others have a weapons background, none are as adept as you with technology, or have been in tense diplomatic negotiations with other species . . . I daresay none have ever blown up bridges or set C-4 detonators. I think you chipped Barbara's front tooth, and a lot of the she-Shadows will follow you for that one gracious act alone. As you may have guessed by now, she's been a pain in everyone's ass for a long time. Her tribal name was Shadow Hawk, elder sister of Shadow Falcon, but when she moved to Florida she became Barbara—go figure."

"Yeah." Sasha's voice was flat and monotone. His compliment and his attempt at small talk to make her smile fell on deaf ears.

What could she say? She didn't care about pack or clan politics. None of that mattered to her in the least right now. It was a hollow win if she had to drop the one person in the world that'd clued her in to who she really was. Didn't he get it? If it weren't for him, she would have still been shooting up with antiviral meds that suppressed her Shadow Wolf ability, because even Doc didn't know how to refine the formula for different strains of the species.

And then there was the not-so-small matter of what his grandfather and Doc may have done to create her, as well as Woods and Fisher, in some very crazy plan . . . old men playing God. She just prayed this was all coincidence, a confluence of unnatural events that looked suspicious but weren't orchestrated. However, years of being a realist told her such was probably not the case.

Sasha swallowed hard, unable to even look in Hunter's direction. This was the same man who'd shown her how to

Shadow dance, had released her spirit to the complete freedom of merging with nature in all its wondrous forms . . . of being able to catch the edge of the shadows that passing birds cast and literally fly to the next shadow, only to emerge from a tree line or side of a building, temporarily retaining the properties of the shadow she'd borrowed.

Watching the shadows loom long in the late-afternoon sun, she remembered it all, everything good and honorable that he'd done. He'd brought her back to herself, had even taken her on a spirit walk back to her dead mother . . . had made her Shadow quiver from a Shadow caress until her body had no longer been her own. They'd gone through demon doors together to emerge champions of the hunt. Now she was supposed to just snuff out the man who had transformed the taste of fear into a righteous howl of the Shadow Wolf?

It would be like pulling the trigger on Rod all over again, but so much worse. Rod was her friend, a comrade in arms, a mentor, a crush . . . but she'd never fallen in love with him. This was something wholly different, something so rooted to her core that its very existence frightened her. She froze. Did she just quietly admit that this thing with Hunter was possibly deeper than the physical? Oh, shit . . .

Still, she was a soldier. She'd never argue that soldier versus warrior point again. Hunter had even been right about that. Warriors had choices; she didn't. If Hunter turned into the unimaginable, she'd simply have to kill him. She had no other option.

"Laissez les bon temps rouler!" the MC called out from the stage, making his smooth tenor voice carry above the Zydeco music. He was glad to see Fae peacekeeping forces in the house. They raised their glasses from the bar

to salute him in thanks for the free drinks, their opalescent auras flowing over their clothes like northern lights.

"I agree, let the good times roll, Ethan," a burly Elf shouted, lifting his ale.

Ethan jumped down from the stage and smoothed out his navy blue suit and red silk shirt before attempting to wade through the crowd to get to Dugan's side. He was proud of his French Quarter establishment, had worked hard to build it and then rebuild it to its original historic luster after the flood. The Fair Lady, named for his pretty Gaelic wife, Margaret, had a solid reputation in the supernatural community for being a safe, fun place. No human tragedies were allowed on the premises, either, and it had taken quite a bit of bargaining to get the Vampires to agree to that house rule.

Keeping his ear to the ground and plying customers for information helped ensure that everything remained peaceful. His mole would know what was about on Bourbon Street and beyond. This was the primo hour, dusk. Happy hour in more ways than one. It was still too early for the Vampires to arrive and have their pick of the most attractive clientele, but the other entities that patronized his establishment had begun to filter in.

As he pushed through to the far side of the bar, he was careful not to collide with lithe Phoenixes that were delivering succulent crawfish, Cajun-spiced meats, red beans and rice, and aromatic bouillabaisses to diners. He only employed the best magical chefs that could literally put an ecstasy charm over the food his patrons consumed.

Shamefully, though, his secret crush was Suzette, a redheaded, alabaster-skinned belle that teased him mercilessly. As he brushed past her his stomach did a little flip-flop of excitement just from the sensual near miss.

But he was thoroughly, irrevocably married and didn't mess around. For that, Suzette tortured him every chance she got. Theirs was a sexy private game of look but don't touch. She gave him a slight pout and let him see the fire burning in her eyes before turning away to set down plates on the customers' table. One day maybe she'd allow him to hold her while she went up in flames. For now, he was happy when she'd caramelize the crème brûlée in the kitchen while he watched.

"To Ethan," several archers said as he passed and slapped their backs.

"Stay as long as you like, ladies and gentlemen. Soon, the dancers will be on."

"From the Order of the Dragon?" A bright smile crested on a handsome Fae's face, causing dimples to form small divots in his ruddy cheeks. He knocked his glass of ale against his friend's, swept his long, auburn hair over his shoulder, and then turned up his glass to his mouth. "And before the Vamps come with their ungodly charm—we might get lucky tonight, old boy."

"Just for you, Monte," Ethan said, forcing a smile and picking up his pace. What had Dugan learned?

Peace. That's all he wanted was peace. Ethan patted shoulders and ordered more free rounds on the house as he passed clusters of Fae infantrymen. If everyone just stayed calm, then his newly rebuilt establishment wouldn't receive any additional damage. How many insurance claims could one man turn in without drawing unwarranted attention?

Ethan blotted the perspiration from his forehead and then away from the balding horseshoe on his scalp, and continued to appraise the crowd as he made his way over to Dugan. Tall, lean, athletically built Fae had arrived with silver-tipped arrows in their quivers. That was a good thing. No matter what hue of skin they owned, from the bluest black to the most porcelain white, if their opalescent auras flowed like a multicolored, easy stream and their hue-changing eyes continued their slow, kaleidoscope color prisms, then all was well.

He reached Dugan just as the sound of motorcycles roared outside. A general cheer went up from the bar, and Dugan pulled him against his barrel chest in a friendly bear hug.

"A sight for sore eyes, you are!" Dugan said, laughing, lifting Ethan off his feet and crushing him against his Fae fatigues.

Ethan twisted in his friend's grip, trying to get out of the way of his itchy beard. "You, too, but put me down."

They laughed as Dugan dropped him gently, and all eyes went to the door. Long-legged, buxom beauties sashayed in to cheers and hoots, each donning brilliant-colored leather outfits that seemed like various stages of undress. Red, yellow, electric blue, black. The guys at the bar were practically foaming at the mouth, and even Ethan had to admit to himself that it had been a coup to get them to agree to arrive before dark.

"I love how ya work, Ethan," Dugan said, shaking his head. "You know those big bruisers they generally travel with are surely on their way, yes?"

"Absolutely," Ethan said with a smile. "But they said they'd attend once the sun set. They're being paid for the fireworks displays."

"Fantastic . . . that should be hours, and they left these ladies all alone for so long?"

"They're only worried about Vampires and Werewolves. Sorry to say, the Dragon brothers aren't really that concerned about us."

"Ah, but they should be," Dugan murmured, leaning forward with a leer as he stroked his beard. "We and the Dragons, like the Order of the Unicorns and other Mythics, have long forest histories, yes? A little elfin magic . . . a brownie spell or a gnome curse could coax one of these flippin' gorgeous—"

"Could have my establishment burned to the ground by a fire-breather," Ethan warned with a tense smile. "The ladies are professional entertainers and just for show. You know I don't dabble in the flesh-peddling trade. I want no parts of owing the Vampire Cartel. I don't even allow succubae or incubi on the premises without a Vampire escort."

"Don't be so touchy," Dugan said, still watching the Dragons line up to ascend the stage. "I know, I know—no spells or charms."

"Well, good, as long as we have that clear." Ethan sat back and ordered a Scotch on the rocks. Now he'd have to wait. Dugan always wanted a little extra courtesy for sharing information. "After the Dragons dance the poles, the Phoenixes will be doing a little strip and burn," he said in a soft voice, trying to mollify his friend.

Dugan said nothing but simply sipped his ale with a lopsided smile tugging at his thick cheek as he watched the dancers line up. Gorgeous ladies from the Order of the Dragon flanked the restaurant still wearing their helmets that had black shields, and as one, they removed them, allowing red, blond, black, platinum, auburn, and every hue of hair one could imagine to spill out in varying textured tresses. Silken hair, long dreadlocks, curls, each Dragon was as different as her tight leather outfit, and their variety drew loud applause as they blew fire kisses and mounted the stage.

"I can see why those big bastards with the spiked leather jackets usually escort them," Dugan said with appreciation, watching intently as the music changed and the dancers took to poles that lowered from the ceiling. "But it is so unfair that you have to fight a damned male Dragon to get one to even look your way."

"Ah, leave it for the Vamps who deal in sleight of hand and mind raptures . . . or the Weres who can simply muscle their way through." Seeing an in to the conversation he really wanted to have, Ethan landed a supportive hand on his buddy's shoulder. "I might have some influence with a very pretty Serpentine who works at a friend's bar . . . where the rules are a little more relaxed, though . . . I wouldn't know by personal testimony, but I have seen them work the poles better than the Dragons."

Dugan almost spit out his beer, laughing. "Your attempt at a bribe is so subtle, Ethan. That is what I love about you—you're as innocent as a newborn lamb. So, what has you worried?"

Ethan looked around and leaned in. "There are rumors that some bad blood—demon-infected Werewolf—got out into the human population. Not like one escaped as they do from time to time, but this was human-made toxin in vials. Shadow Wolves are involved somehow, they say. Could be Werewolves . . . I don't know. The other Wereclans, like the Big Cat Federation and others, aren't in it because it's wolf-based DNA this time . . . but . . . I was wondering if you'd heard?"

"Talking to Vampires again, or did they whisper this in your ear?"

Ethan looked away and then looked down into his Scotch. "I take no sides, especially at UCE Conference time. I try to stay neutral and out of things . . . but when I hear things that could affect my livelihood, thus my family . . ."

Dugan looked at Ethan over the rim of his glass and set his ale down carefully. "I guess in the bar business you hear a lot."

Ethan nodded, his eyes nervously darting around as Dugan smoothed the lapels of his suit jacket for him.

"Dugan, don't think ill of me for remaining neutral. I have a wife who's working over in the hospital to consider—you know Margaret is a healer, and we've both tried to blend into the human population without incident. Our children . . . they're not even in kindergarten yet. If a war starts, my family could be at risk, my establishment trashed again after I just rebuilt . . . and I would so worry about Margaret contracting any contagion as bodies started coming into Emergency. I just want—"

"Peace," Dugan said, landing a reassuring hand on Ethan's shoulder. "Don't worry, my friend, that's why we're all here. But, you know, sometimes peace has a price and you have to take a stand."

"There've been so many rumors, how do you know who to trust, or if they're even real?" Ethan's gaze searched Dugan's for an answer.

"The rumors are true, insofar as something that shouldn't have gotten out of human hands did. We were all sent down here by the Fae Parliament and we got down here well in advance of the big meeting to scout out potential problems. Before we take sides, we have to unfurl the truth—and that is a nasty, wicked knot, from what I can tell. But," Dugan added with a wide grin, "how could I allow a man's establishment to go up in flames . . .

especially when he has the number for a sexy Serpentine for me?"

Any minute now, the sun would go down, and his contact could meet him. Between what he'd sold, what had been destroyed by Hunter and his bitch, and what he'd used, the product was almost gone.

Even at a premium price, there wasn't enough left to be sold to individuals to produce the necessary profit to pay black market scientists to try to duplicate the formula. There was only one way to get more of it, assuming that the U.S. military had gone back into the labs to refine or stockpile it.

Getting into NORAD had initially seemed impossible, but he'd been the one to come up with the genius plan to get into the maximum security facility that was two thousand feet beneath a mountain of granite and behind twenty-five-ton steel doors. It was about having the right tools for the job—Vampires that could assume any human form or travel as mist. They just had to be convinced it was in their best interest. Then, retina scans notwithstanding, and every other conceivable security precaution be damned, he'd done it.

A strange alliance had been formed once between his kind and theirs. As long as the Vampires thought their human blood supplies were in jeopardy from a vaccine against the Werewolf virus, they had agreed to a partnership. It had helped his ruthless but useful allies decide to assassinate the general who'd suddenly grown a conscience, shifted gears, and then mandated the rushed vaccine development. Fool. Wilkerson didn't have to worry about Werewolves as much as he needed to worry about

Vampires that hated the vaccine-tainted blood almost as badly as the actual Werewolf virus that they detested. Vampires were such purists—and duplicitous mother-fuckers.

But that was the thing that was making his hands tremble as he waited in the graveyard for them to show themselves. There could be no way to know what a Vampire might do just for sport.

He needed another hit.

"Look at him." Francois sniffed behind a lace handkerchief with disgust. He tossed his long flaxen hair over his broad shoulders and stared at the broken Shadow Wolf that had just put a needle in his arm. "Positively pathetic. They can't even control their shifts after it begins to deteriorate their systems. Sometimes they try and only a part of them transforms, leaving a half-human, half-naked growling, slobbering mess."

"And they're eating bear meat and derivations of their own species . . . timber wolves?" the elder Vampire said with a cool sneer.

"It is unbelievable, Etienne. They do it for the adrenaline rush to help the drug last longer. Next they'll be eating their own kind."

"And this poor bastard wants to form another alliance, after betraying us once already?" Etienne smiled, his dark eyes alight with excitement within his agelessly handsome face. "He *must* be high."

The two male Vampires laughed quietly, sending their voices on the wind as mere vapors.

"How quaint," a seductive blonde murmured, giving Francois a light peck on his cheek as she materialized. Her catlike green eyes dilated as she stared at the oblivious Shadow Wolf that had slumped against the mausoleums.

"*Desperate*," Francois said seductively with a chuckle, stroking Etienne's lush onyx curls.

"Ah . . . desperation. How completely delicious," the young woman said on a sultry breath, twirling her golden tresses around one delicate porcelain finger as her fangs crested.

"Shall we indulge this fool, Etienne?" Francois waited, anticipation dancing in his dreamy hazel eyes. "What say you?"

Etienne pursed his lips for a moment, placing a graceful index finger against them. "It presents a bit of a conundrum," he said after a moment, watching the fallen Shadow Wolf from his hiding place amid the broken tombs. "For the longest, the Shadow Wolves hunted our worst enemy, the Werewolves. But there was always a visceral love-hate relationship with the Shadow species, which would just as well hunt our kind when we feed, too. The Shadows are more insidious, I believe, because they are not directed by the phases of the moon . . . and to see one like this, so completely devastated, gives me pause. If they begin eating their own, hmmm . . . might they begin to actually also hunt and eat Werewolves?"

Francois drew back from Etienne with his palm flattened to his chest, feigning shock. "Appalling," he whispered, making the female Vampire giggle. "*Mon Dieu*. I am aghast at the insinuation of outright cannibalism. Even among Werewolves, they draw the line at that bestial behavior."

Etienne tugged on his lace shirtsleeves and offered Francois a droll smile. "Let us think this through and remain open-minded, *mon frère*. If the Shadows lose their minds due to a virus gone berserk and begin to eat their own kind, especially demon-infected Werewolves—"

"Which should pack quite an interesting wallop to their adrenaline-starved systems," Francois said with a sly smile, finishing Etienne's sentence.

"*Oui*, rather than competing with us and preying on humans," Etienne observed with a casual flip of his wrist.

"Ah, I hate it when the Werewolves pollute virgin bloodstreams all over this planet," Francois said with a sniff of disdain. "They are like huge vermin. Weasels."

"But if the wolves are eating each other, perhaps they might be way too *consumed* to bother with pestering us?" Etienne released a coy chuckle at his own joke, drawing the lithe blonde closer to him.

Francois smiled with a grand sweeping bow, his fangs lengthening as he sent his amused gaze across the graveyard. "Anything, as always, in the name of détente, Your Grace. Then let the good times roll."

Chapter 8

Vibrations were tense inside the vehicle as they drove, so thick that it felt like something oppressive and invisible was strangling him. Try as he might to diffuse Sasha's worry, that was impossible as the sun set.

He couldn't blame her. The best he could do as he watched the last of the light wink at him before it fell behind the mountains was to grip the steering wheel tighter and step on the gas. This was a dangerous time for the wolf twilight, when the blue-gray shadows blanketed everything and the moon was waiting her turn to promenade the sky.

Then there was the other insistent problem that had gone dormant within him while the packs met . . . Sasha's *fantastic* scent. Although he'd never say it to her unless he was looking for a black eye, it had everything to do with the big alphas' acquiescence to the plan. Arguing with a gorgeous she-Shadow in heat was antithetical to male wolf DNA, but had everything to do with what probably made Barbara crazy enough to challenge Sasha on a moot point.

The wolf within him was winning, the darker it got outside. The air inside the vehicle cabin was stifling. He could feel beads of sweat forming on his brow. His T-shirt was wringing wet beneath his parka. Hunter glimpsed the thermostat. The heat wasn't even on. He clenched his jaw for a moment, feeling his canines about to rip through his gums, and inhaled deeply through his nose, then hit the window button.

A blast of icy fresh air felt like a sharp slap across his face—one he desperately needed. It had never been this hard to control the wolf before the moon was up. Hundreds of insane thoughts tore at his mind like savage teeth and claws. The woods were calling him on either side of the vehicle. Only five more miles and they'd be at the abandoned lodge. He had to breathe through his mouth. *Damn, she smelled fantastic*. Wolf burn had started as a molten, stabbing pain in his gut that now radiated through his chest, lungs, limbs, and groin. A repressed howl was making him shudder. Tears of agony blurred the darkening stretch of road before them.

Unable to stand it any longer, he stomped on the brake, burning rubber in a skidding, careening stop, threw the gears into park in the middle of the road, and then jerked his attention to Sasha.

The barrel of a gun and a very level gaze met his anguished stare.

His hand hit the door handle. "You have to drive the rest of the way alone. . . . I'll meet you at the lodge."

"As what?" she said through her teeth. "You'll meet me at the lodge *as what*, Hunter?"

Their gazes locked for a moment.

"I honestly don't know."

He was gone before her trigger finger could twitch, merging into the all-pervasive twilight. Her mind on autopilot with a survival imperative, she was in the driver's seat, had slammed the door shut, and gunned the engine within the next blink, not even sure where she was going.

The only thing that was clear was she had to get out of the open ASAP. The lodge had rifles, pump shotguns, automatics, and the monster shells that went with them. There'd be a sat-phone there, shortwave radio, and probably enough crap lying around, like a nasty bleach and ammonia combo or alcohol and fertilizer, to do Mac-Gyver proud.

Any way she viewed it, out here, a huge predator playing chicken with an F-150 traveling at ninety-five miles per hour on a single-lane stretch of road flanked by trees wider than the truck—anybody could do the math. It wouldn't be pretty for the non-seat-belt-wearing human being behind the wheel. But she wasn't prepared to set down her gun and wasn't in a position to turn loose the wheel in order to fasten a seat belt.

Call it a premonition or pure fucked-up fate, but a herd of spooked deer rushed the road like an impenetrable brown sea that might as well have been a concrete wall. Body after leaping, fleeing body became an instant horizontal barrier. When seconds mattered, there was only one option if she didn't want to become road pizza—and that was to bail.

She landed on all fours, all wolf, tattered clothing floating down around her and boots dropping with a thud as the unmanned vehicle plowed into deer bodies, flipped twice nose over rear bumper, and finally stopped somersaulting with a shattering crash on its roof, then exploded. So much for seat belts.

But the panicked animals kept coming, jumping over flames, into flames, hurdling metal and glass strewn in the road, some breaking their legs on their fallen, dead sisters. Panicked, they didn't even stay in formation but widened and narrowed the thick wave of bodies as confusion sent sections of the massive herd in different directions.

Common sense told her to push forward, try to jump over them, somehow head toward the lodge they'd blocked. Only, there was no way to get on the other side of them until the last one crossed. It was as though the entire forest was emptying itself out on one side. Sasha instantly took cover as rounds began to go off inside the crushed vehicle.

Precious seconds passed, and then she saw her opening. Unfortunately, so did the thing that had spooked the herds.

It came out of the woods on massive hind legs standing ten feet upright, a bloodied, twelve-point buck's head in one humanlike fist with claws. An outrageously huge, bald, human male erection bounced and glistened as the thing inhaled and exhaled. Sasha briefly closed her eyes. Yeah, she was gonna have to kill him. But to do that, she had to get to the ammo at the lodge. Right now, even in wolf form, she was no match for what he'd turned into. She kept her gaze steady and moved only as he moved, staying downwind from him.

Thick, yellowing saliva leaked from between distended, gnarled canines, and the beast's broad, barrel chest was only partially covered by a ragged coat of matted fur. She could still see skin and nipples beneath the sparse hair on its chest, and its thick, tree-trunk-like limbs were sculpted with visible ropes of endless muscles. A great howl set her teeth on edge as she hid in the shadows, and then cringed as a pair of yellow glowing eyes swept the terrain.

Seeming agitated by her concealed presence, the beast flung away the buck head, dropped to all fours, sniffed low on the ground, and then stood again, howling with rage. It rushed the overturned vehicle and, seeing that she wasn't in it, roared with fury as it picked the truck up by the axle, lifting it overhead, and flung it against a line of trees so hard that two of them snapped from the force, not the weight. If it hadn't been winter, with enough snow to stop and absorb the heat, a national treasure would have been set ablaze. It then grabbed the remaining sections of the wreck, flinging them in a monstrous tantrum that felled trees from whirring car doors and broke limbs from flying bumpers.

Glass made the road glisten as though coated with a layer of newly formed ice. A bit of fabric suddenly drew the beast's attention. Sasha remained as still as stone as the huge predator tracking her lowered its snout to the crotch of her jeans, inhaled, moaned, and then went into another furious tirade, sending shards of glass into the snow-covered foliage on either side of the road.

Fallen deer bodies took the brunt of the abuse as the irrational beast spent his frustration on them. Each carcass got dismembered as it tore them limb from limb, gutted them, and then finally hurled them away. It was solely an act of violence; the beast ate nothing but had destroyed everything in its wake. She was just glad that its temper tantrum had cleared the road of most of the hazardous debris so that hopefully no lone trucker or family of tourists would collide with it and die.

While the predator's gaze continued to sweep the terrain, his nose snuffling the air as though unconvinced no one else was near, Sasha didn't move a muscle. She'd hunted this particular demon before and knew enough to know that there were only two effective ways to come out of demon-infected Werewolf hunts alive—blindside it in a human form to attack it with powerful ammo, or go after it in a wolf pack and be prepared to get good and bloody for the trouble.

Since neither dicey option was available, she stayed in a low, hidden crouch among the shadows during the entire twenty-minute ordeal. Then the beast looked straight at her and began moving in a blur like a locomotive, heading right for her. Reaction time vaporized. She didn't even have time to roll out of the way, much less meet the brute in a jaw-locking hold that would have probably ended badly with her face ripped off. Two seconds from direct impact, he leaped and sailed over her shadow-hidden frame and then disappeared into a shadow of his own.

She was out. Sasha ran the shadows as though the devil himself was on her trail. Seconds mattered, minutes were a gift. Every insistent thud of her heart meant she'd cheated death yet again. But the grim scene before her that brought her skidding to a halt meant someone else hadn't.

A huge flatbed timber hauler was jackknifed off the road. Long skid marks showed where the trucker had tried to avoid something. He'd been traveling in the opposite direction as she'd been, headed east, while she'd been headed west. Sasha sniffed the air that was still laden with diesel fuel, brake fluid, battery acid, smoke, and blood. She needed to know how soon before or after her collision with the brute this accident and slaughter had happened.

The trucker's load of logs told the story of something incredibly strong converting trees into fireplace tinder. One huge log had been horizontally rammed through the driver's-side window and door. The CB radio had been ripped out of the cab and pitched twenty-five yards away, left hanging by cables from the trees. Sasha glimpsed what had been a section of a red plaid lumberjack shirt and coat, knowing there was no use in looking for a survivor. The gore on the shirt was testimony enough.

Same deal with the ranger's squad car. The front window was smashed in and the cruiser's metal roof peeled back with wide claw marks dug deeply in it. From the looks of things, she could only imagine that the beast had probably landed right on the hood as the poor man was driving, and that was when the ranger had veered off the road and hit a tree. Fifty yards out she saw his arm still clutching his gun with his sheepskin jacket and uniform sleeve still covering it.

Judging from the radio's trajectory, part of the truck driver might have also followed it in the air. No doubt the trucker's panicked call is what lured the ranger to the site. Helicopters would be on the scene in the morning and probably crawling all over the lodge, since they'd find a third supremely wrecked vehicle, hers.

If she lived through the night, she'd be gone by dawn. All she'd need would be to have some rightfully panicked Oakies haul her ass in for possible vehicular homicide and fingerprint her, and then run her prints. Sasha kept moving, warily selecting shadows to enter, not sure which ones were safe, and then she froze.

Her and Hunter's amulets had been in her jeans pockets. Her ripped jeans and abandoned clothes and boots were several miles back in the direction of sure danger. Whatever was looking for her had obviously cut a swath from the lodge back to her, and it was clearly very pissed off that she was somewhere naked, in heat, and unavailable.

It took a moment for her to force her mind to accept it—Hunter had fled the vehicle, headed at top Shadow Wolf speed toward the lodge. He was laboring not to transition. Turned on, turned out, and straight flipping. If the beast within finally emerged, he would have doubled back for her to head her off at the pass. Whatever got between them would have become an instant casualty. He was too far gone, had actually killed two innocent humans. There was no wait-and-see, fall-back position left.

Tears stung Sasha's eyes as she turned away from the carnage and headed back toward the wreck farther up the road. A little piece of silver and amber was all she had left of him . . . and until she got to an automatic with real silver shells, that was unfortunately also the only weapon she had.

He stared at Crow Shadow's truck through wary wolf eyes. What the hell was Crow Shadow doing here, when he was supposed to be shepherding the two familiars to a pack chopper station? Hunter looked at the hastily parked truck in the lodge entrance that still had the door slightly ajar and the motor running. Skid marks said the driver had been in a hurry. Where was Sasha's truck? She should have been here by now.

Breathless and senses keened she arrived at the lodge and allowed her gaze to tear across the main courtyard entrance. Crow Shadow's truck was parked at a haphazard angle, motor still running, with blood on the seats, the steering wheel, the dashboard, and the ground. Nausea roiled within her so strong that she almost dry heaved.

How could he attack and eat his own pack brother? Horror permeated every cell in her: *Woods, Fisher.*

Hunter's scent was unmistakably thick in the air—along with the undeniable pungent blend of infected Werewolf trail. What if her squad hadn't gotten out by chopper?

Sasha narrowed her gaze as she slipped into shadows along the side of the building, hunkering down as she crept past the pine veranda. The front door was open. Understatement; it was hanging off its hinges. Whatever was looking for her was most likely still inside. Unfortunately, that's where the weapons she needed were, too. Plus, Hunter knew this lodge; this was his home court advantage. No doubt he knew every nook and cranny of the building, where the pack would have stashed ammo, and he'd be waiting laying for her to stumble foolishly into an ambush. Same dealio with the demon doors. He'd been the one to show her how to track a predator to and through them. Now that he was a full-blown demon-infected lycanthrope, he could probably pass in and out of them at will, no ward needed.

Scouring the terrain for anything she could use, her line of vision went back to the truck. To her mind, it was a bomb on four wheels. All she needed was something to detonate the fuel tank as she sent it crashing into the lodge. After that, was anybody's guess. But if Crow Shadow had been dragged from the vehicle as quickly as he obviously had, then chances were there was something left in his truck to work with. The entire pack traveled with weapons, ammo. Sasha sniffed the air; there was no residue in it from unspent rounds.

Now the only problem was transitioning to the weaker human body she needed in order to make use of the dexterity of hands.

It only took an instant for her lithe female form to step out of the shadows and begin ransacking the truck. To her horror the glove compartment, flatbed, even under the seat were vacant. Not even a tire iron remained.

Shit. Okay, new plan. Send the truck crashing into the front as a diversion to draw the beast outside, enter the building from behind, use walls and furniture to block its counterattack until blinding chemicals like bleach or ammonia could be located, and then get the hell out, turn, and fire.

Admittedly, it was a fool's errand and a really bad plan. However, given the circumstances of two to three slaughtered men, her being naked in freezing temps in the wilderness, and not a damned weapon on her that would work, it was the best shot she had.

Sasha slid into the truck's driver's seat, shuddering from the contact of ice-cold leather against her skin. In a strange way, she now wished she'd claimed the ranger's gun from his severed arm—just for the sake of being able to blow the gas tank from afar—not that the regular bullets would have done anything to the creature. Even the pump shotgun or rifle she was sure the ranger had in his trunk would be useless against a raging Werewolf.

She quickly jumped back out of the truck feeling claustrophobic and assumed her wolf form. It was beyond obvious now that to fortify herself against this predator, she had to go back to the second crash site, transform to human, get whatever weapons and blankets she could scavenge from the ranger's cruiser, and run naked, concealed by the shadows, back to set up a perimeter outside the lodge to kill the beast. There'd be no way to carry all the supplies while in wolf form. It was always a decision between using the power-body of the wolf for an attack or speed, versus the agility of the human form.

The shadows, however, had betrayed her. Preoccupied, her mind racing, she'd slipped into a sliver of darkness that contained a familiar scent and a low, warning growl.

Lunging toward the sound, blind, she made her objective a swift first strike. A whoosh of air passed over her, causing enough of a back draft to tell her that what had avoided her had been huge. Her worst fear realized, it smelled like Hunter.

Time didn't permit her to look back. Seconds granted her a head start. Propelled forward by a raging will to live, Sasha bolted toward the second crash site, her focus laser. Danger was on her heels; she couldn't hear it but knew it had to be close. Flash-fight hormone made the quick transformation back into human form so painful she cried out. An echoing howl reverberated through the glen, but it told her he wasn't as close to her as she'd thought. She didn't have two seconds to question why not. It was a gift. Period.

A frozen, blood-coated gun was in her hand, and she didn't have time to be squeamish about breaking dead fingers to get it in her grip. A single shot opened the trunk. A pump shotgun, a blanket, a tire iron, a bright yellow rain poncho, flashlight for the battery—she scavenged whatever she could find like a pack rat, rolled everything but the tire iron and shotgun in the blanket, and leaped into a shadow to disappear.

The thing she circled was wild in the eyes, knocking down trees with its massive fists, just punching them out of his way as he barreled through the forest hunting for her. She had to get back to the lodge, had to double back before the beast sensed her location.

Sasha brought both amulets that she wore to her lips and kissed them and then ran toward the truck that was her only hope of escape. With the shotgun she could detonate the tank. A tire iron could take out an eye.

Out of breath by the time she reached the truck, she jumped in, backed the vehicle up in a screeching roar, bounced onto the asphalt, and burned rubber down the road.

At a hundred twenty miles per hour, the F-150 would pack a punch when it blew. The moment a huge black wolf figure leaped onto the road on all fours, she opened the door and threw out the shotgun and tire iron as the beast charged with glowing gold eyes. Two seconds later, her wolf fled the cab, but by the time she'd drop-rolled to the ground she was all woman; naked, ornery, and then up again, going for the gun.

Anticipating her move, the beast sailed over the truck. Sasha went down on one knee, held the shot steady, and fired.

The blast from the truck caught the beast midair and in the gut. Entrails splattered the road, the line of trees, and stunk to high heaven. Her target might have been down, but she wasn't leaving that to chance. Tire iron in one fist, pump shotgun in the other, she ran to where the beast lay beneath the burning flipped-over vehicle.

There was no time for emotion. She had to do what she had to do. The Max Hunter she'd known had died within the shell of his inner beast. Casting away the shotgun, she used both hands to raise the tire iron above her head. One of the beast's eyes eerily rolled open to blankly stare at her. She used that as her cue to ram the tire iron through its huge skull.

Only then did she walk away, pick up her cast-off weapon, and puke. This was so much worse than Rod's death on so many levels. There weren't enough shadows to hide her tears as she watched the Werewolf carcass burn with a shotgun in her grip.

Another pair of golden eyes fifty yards away and a low snarl jerked her attention from the charred remains that were crumbling to ash. On her mark it was a race to the lodge. There was another one, a smaller one! It was charging straight for her. She had to get inside before it did to find the artillery stash. But she could feel it flanking her, its wolf in the shadows easily outrunning her human form. If she dropped the shotgun, she could change to she-Shadow—but she was no match for one of the beasts as a wolf.

A sudden invisible collision knocked her out of her shadow run and to the ground hard. The shotgun clattered to the road. A huge black wolf with the beginning of a Werewolf transformation and a very familiar scent signature snatched her by the leg with a human fist and yanked her toward him. Her she-Shadow came up fighting, canines bared, snapping at his groin when he went up on hind legs, but he backed up from her feral onslaught. Then a *whoosh* sound made them glimpse a figure that had entered the battle—it all happened in milliseconds.

The beast that was on her stumbled backward, wailing as something like an arrowhead dug into its shoulder. It clutched the wound site with its left hand and began scrabbling at it, then dropped to its knees. Seeing an opening, she circled him, prepared to lunge, until she saw what it had yanked out of its shoulder and who had put it there with a bow and arrow.

Another hypodermic needle hit the creature in the neck at the jugular. That last shot was delivered by an elderly man with tears in his eyes. The bewildered expression on the beast's face gave Sasha pause . . . as did the warm brown eyes that normalized as he fell forward spread-eagle in the middle of the dark road.

Chapter 9

"Some full moon, hmmm? Lovely shade of aquamarine tinting it," Francois remarked with a toothy grin. He walked around the half-dazed creature before him and then covered his nose with his hanky. "You really must do something about your hygiene when you transform, Dexter. This is just awful."

Dexter lunged at the Vampire. "Do we have a deal or not?" he growled.

Francois easily sidestepped the aggressive move. His gaze then narrowed to a withering stare and his voice dropped to a lethal, hissing whisper. "Do not let the velvet and lace fool you, *mon ami*. In your condition and at my age as an undead royal, I could snatch your heart out before you could toss back your wretched head to howl."

"Do . . . we . . . have . . . a deal?" Dexter snarled, panting out the question as his jaw began to elongate.

"Since you cannot even control your shape-shifts, perhaps we could have this conversation another evening?" Francois retorted with disdain.

"Or another *day*," Dexter growled, unfurling his growing form to block Francois's leave.

"You *dare* threaten me with a daylight tomb invasion?" Francois reared back, instantly materialized a kidskin glove in his hand, and struck Dexter across the face before tossing it on the ground.

The two entities squared off and Dexter smiled.

"You might want to pick up your glove. You don't want to throw down the gauntlet too soon."

With a sneer, Dexter swept the buttery soft glove from the graveyard floor and flung it at Francois, who caught it with one hand.

"My Vampire friend, need I remind you that, unlike any other species that walks the planet, *our noses* can find you. That's why full moons make you boys so nervous and why you hate the Werewolves so. *Because that's when we come alive.* That's when we're on the prowl. Hybrids like me can wipe out your biggest food competitor . . . and at the end, doesn't it always come down to the most primal aspects of life—food, territory, mating privileges, hierarchy on the food chain?" Dexter chuckled and a low, rough sound exited his deformed snout. "Don't look so put off. Surely an entity as old as you remembers the fundamentals. Civilization hasn't washed that primal directive out of your cold, dead DNA yet, I'm sure."

Francois's lip curled. "What is running through my DNA is revulsion for—"

"Careful, careful," Dexter said, baiting his opponent. "I might become offended. I'm not your problem. This isn't between mutated Shadow Wolves and Vampires, the original battle has always been between you and your oldest arch rivals in the underworld—purebred Werewolves."

Dexter began walking in a slow, threatening circle. "Shadow Wolves have never polluted the human blood stream. Our bites and scratches do not enter the human system and turn them into infected Werewolves. The demon-infected members of the wolf breed attack and eat humans and cause public alarm, further poaching on what you perceive as the inalienable right to human blood. So, be clear on who your true enemy is . . . and now, in this state, your enemy has become our delicacy."

"Then don't you forget," Francois sneered, "that we, *Vampiri*, are blood *specialists*. And don't *ever* forget your place. We are the only ones who can possibly slip past the security of a human paranormal military installation, or mind-daze a weak sentry. Only we can duplicate a human's body with such exactness that we can pass their retina scans or any other technology. Even with that, now that they've been breeched once, the humans will have put precautions in place that give us pause."

"We had a deal!"

Francois looked at Dexter and snarled. "We had *a discussion*. Previously, we had a deal—which you rogue Shadows reneged on."

"You know that we still have enough toxin to sell to the highest human bidder on the military black market— enough that could make us extremely wealthy with resource perks that we'd be sure involved daylight tomb raids." Dexter smirked. "What human doesn't want immortality without the daylight and blood hunger handicap?" He leaned against a grave marker and raked Francois with his gaze. "What if Werewolves became more plentiful from the toxic military experiments in foreign nations, while they employed a small army of very strong Shadows to daylight hunt and capture Vampires to experiment on?"

"I would be very, very concerned if this unsubtle threat were not coming from a junky," Francois said evenly, carefully folding his glove into his breast pocket. "Before you cry wolf under this flawless, moonlit sky, I will advise you to remember that we're your only hope of getting to whatever stash of the toxin you need to shoot up with, and we're the only ones that know how to . . . shall we say, drain a body while keeping it alive to produce more blood so that you can get your sweet Shadow Wolf blood antidote. *Don't threaten me.*"

Dexter's gnarled canines glistened in the bright moonlight as the Vampire stared at him with venom in his eyes. "My infected Shadow brothers are single-minded. They want more of the product in exchange for our thinning the ranks of Werewolves . . . but we won't forget the disrespect delivered by a Vampire if things don't work out the way we'd discussed. So *don't* fuck with me. Before I left the Shadow country, as future security dictated, I infected enough brothers to have a pack of my own. And do you think I just came down here for Mardi Gras?"

Dexter leaned close to Francois's face and snarled again with a low chuckle. "There's enough infected Shadows down here to overturn whatever graves Hurricane Katrina didn't wash away and open to the sun. New Orleans has more hidden Shadows than you can know."

Francois nodded with a blank expression and watched the deformed creature lope away from him. Etienne silently materialized beside Francois and both Vampires kept their gaze on Dexter's retreating form.

"So, my performance was *bon*?" Francois's mouth turned up at the corners, giving Etienne a wicked smile without looking at him.

Etienne's gaze stayed with the retreating wolf but his sinister smile was for Francois. "*Très bon . . . merci. Très, très bon.*"

Sasha stood, numbly gaping, adrenaline and disbelief battling within her, as she watched Silver Hawk calmly approach the wolf on the ground. He cloaked his grandson with his bearskin coat and then tossed her his doeskin shirt without looking at her. Sasha caught it with one hand. Then he calmly drew an Indian blanket over his shoulders, staring at the fallen with ancient eyes. Watching the elderly Ute Indian work was nearly an out-of-body experience. His dignified carriage seemed weary but not broken.

Despite his incalculable age, he fearlessly rolled the wounded creature into the coat and, still stooping beside it, took in a deep but measured breath, hoisted over two hundred pounds of dead weight onto his shoulder, stood slowly with a grunt, and then lifted his chin and began walking toward the lodge.

She extracted the gore-stained tire iron from the ashes by the wreck, then followed Silver Hawk's steady, plodding gait, witnessing what seemed to be the old man's former muscular structure come alive under his burden. A deep V of sweat made his blue and gray plaid flannel shirt that he'd worn beneath the doe-skin cling to him and she could almost envision his power and strength when he'd been in the full bloom of his youth, knowing now where Hunter had inherited his.

Silently they entered the gravel road courtyard of the lodge, yet her eyes remained transfixed on the body Silver Hawk hauled. She stayed close to him, understanding without words that he didn't want her help in carrying his burden, but would accept her defense if attacked by another beast. It was an odd understanding, indeed.

Remorse filled her as they slowly made their way up the front steps of the main building, knowing full well that she might have to break the old man's heart and exterminate his grandson right before his eyes. No parent should have to bury their child; no grandparent their grandchild—and neither should have to witness their execution. This was so far-flung from the natural order of things that all she could do was keep her gaze steady on the body Silver Hawk carried and pray that it didn't twitch. Her nerves were so wire taut that the slightest move would have possibly been enough to make her drive the tire iron through Hunter's skull on sheer reflex.

Although total darkness engulfed them once inside, save the blue-white shards of moonlight, Silver Hawk navigated past the destroyed registration desk, turned-over lobby furniture and splintered pine floorboards, through a massive dining room that was now a wreck. Cold air unnaturally whipped through what should have been a warm, cozy space. She peered at the shattered glass and wood sections that had obviously once been large French doors that led out to a pine deck for summer breezes and al fresco dining.

It had taken only a few seconds while passing through for her gaze to absorb enough impressions to reconstruct the scene. A beast had entered the building through the side deck doors, run amok through the dining room, turning over tables and chairs, searching for something or someone, and then had barreled through the establishment heading for the front doors where maybe it heard the sound of Crow Shadow's truck . . . then it had exploded the front doors off the hinges as it came out to attack.

Sasha kept walking, following the resolute old man before her who carried an immeasurable burden. She watched him go to the chef's center-island butcher's block in the middle of the huge, industrial-size kitchen and bend one knee. Very carefully he slid the weight he'd been carrying off his shoulder, allowing the body wrapped in the coat to hit the table surface with a gentle thud. Then, with the coat at the fallen wolf's back, Silver Hawk quickly covered the body with the blanket that had been on his shoulders, almost as though performing a silent ritual in his mind. The care the old man took put tears in her eyes and as she looked away she saw the arsenal he'd amassed in the kitchen.

Pump shotguns, semiautomatics; the distinctive scent of silver hung in the air so thickly that it put a metallic taste on the back of her tongue. The heavy silver saturation had to be caused by an airborne or liquid version of it . . . silver nitrate, colloidal silver, silver shrapnel in fine dust flakes, something. No wonder the beast hadn't come back here.

Her attention was divided between scouring the environment and watching Silver Hawk slowly check Hunter for injuries beneath the blanket. Finally, he pulled the blanket back by degrees. The muscles in her arms, back, and legs tensed in readiness to spring forward with the tire iron, lest Hunter wake up not himself.

But rather than witnessing a half-transformed beast, Hunter was in his human form, eyelids rapidly fluttering as though his mind were trapped in some horrible dream.

Again Sasha glimpsed the weapons that were collected on the stainless-steel drain board. "How bad is he?" she finally asked, moving closer as Silver Hawk inspected both arrowhead wound sites.

"There are fatigues and long johns . . . socks, boots in the cabinet," Silver Hawk said in a quiet voice, motioning to the far wall without looking at her. "The worst of it has passed. Dress. You will not need your wolf again tonight."

Although she obliged his request, she kept her eyes on Hunter as she quickly crossed the room, selected warm clothes from the stash that was available, and dressed in a flash. Until she pulled on the heavy wool socks, she hadn't completely realized just how cold she'd been. A hard shiver shook her until her teeth chattered, and she gratefully slipped on a pair of hiking boots.

There was no need for her to say a word as she passed the elderly man who'd extracted an ancient medicine rattle from his jacket pocket when she'd offered it back to him. He declined the jacket and simply covered Hunter's nudity with it, and then began a low hymn in a language she didn't understand. She gathered a nine millimeter and several clips to stash in her waistband with equal purpose. No matter what Silver Hawk hoped, or whatever she prayed, she wasn't convinced that the danger had passed.

"Give me his amulet," Silver Hawk commanded, reaching backward for it, still keeping his focus on Hunter.

Sasha complied, but sensing what the old man was about to do, she also held Hunter in her gun sight.

Ever so slowly, with his voice escalating in the chant, Silver Hawk lowered the amulet to Hunter's chest. The moment it made contact with Hunter's skin, he arched hard and his eyes rolled back in his skull, exposing only the whites. Undaunted, Silver Hawk dropped the talisman and increased the rattling chant, and then put a hand in his pants pocket to quickly extract a fistful of shimmering dust.

Sasha watched in horror as the elderly man rimmed Hunter's body with the silvery concoction. If that didn't sit him up and turn him straight insane Werewolf, she couldn't imagine what else would.

Weapons at the ready, she kept a clear shot aimed at Hunter's skull. But the second Hunter went into a hard convulsion, Silver Hawk threw his head back, howled, and then looped the silver chain of the amulet over Hunter's head. The most difficult part of it was watching the suffering.

Unintelligible roars of a wolf in pain to the very human cries of a man dying a thousand deaths made her sip in shallow breaths and barely release them. Tears leaked down Silver Hawk's weathered cheeks, his pain no less profound than the necessary torture he inflicted upon his grandson. Yet witnessing Hunter's purging made her bones hurt as unnatural joints popped and cracked, twisting his limbs in and out of the wretched Werewolf half-transition, broke his jaw, and then realigned it—the wails of agony he released sounded like he was burning alive in a molten pit of silver.

Torn between going to him and putting him out of his misery, she was rooted to the floor where she stood, completely obedient to the old man's nonverbal cues. But when Hunter began calling her by name, if it weren't for the old man's steady hand signal to back off, she would have honored Hunter's request. She knew what he wanted, she would have begged for that, too.

Soon blood began leaking from his skin and her gaze became a feral question in her eyes as it ricocheted between Hunter and Silver Hawk.

"The demons will reclaim that which is theirs, bite by bite," the old man said in a gravelly voice. "Part of him is beyond the demon doors and he must survive it alone."

"Sasha!" Hunter arched again, his nails elongating to rake the table. "Shoot me!" His voice broke on an anguished sob, his eyes not his own. "If you love me, shoot me!"

"Don't," Silver Hawk commanded, stepping in front of her leveled weapon. "Or you doom him to be trapped betwixt and between forever. Let them eat away that which is theirs to reclaim."

She was blinded by tears as Hunter's wails escalated, and her throat was so tight that for a moment only her mind could sob. "Oh my God, they're eating him alive in the Shadow realms? That's why he's bleeding? Can't we do something?"

Instinct propelled her forward; two strong hands caught her by her upper arms as Hunter yelled her name again.

"I'm his alpha enforcer . . . he even asked me to be his mate," she whispered thickly.

"I know. But if you love him, you will let him come through the doors a free man."

She stared into a pair of aged eyes, focusing on the depths of knowledge within them, trying to blot out the sounds of agony that echoed off the kitchen walls and stainless-steel fixtures. A shudder of nausea racked her, and Silver Hawk's hard squeeze into her bunched biceps helped her remain steadfast. His body blocked her vision to the center island. But the awful sound of Hunter retching finally made her have to turn and dry heave.

When she looked up, Hunter was leaning over the side of the butcher block vomiting a brackish mixture of blood and meat that she didn't even want to consider the source of. His spine had risen under his skin into huge, thick humps, each vertebra evident through skin stretched so tautly over it that the flesh had become white. Then just as quickly as his spine had distended, the sound of cracking, snapping bones echoed through the room.

Helpless to do anything but hold on to Silver Hawk's arms, she saw Hunter throw his head back, screaming as his spine realigned itself. The moment the last disc in his back normalized, he dropped to the table, panting, sweat and tears running down his face.

Silver Hawk slowly released his viselike grip on her upper arms and nodded, then turned to walk back to stand by Hunter's side.

"The worst is over," the old man announced. "This was a very bad moon."

"Trudeau wasn't lying when she said we could find all we'd need stashed in this joint," Winters said, gaping as they entered the steel cage reinforced attic. "When did she haul all this up here?"

"Better question is how?" Bradley said, clearly impressed.

"Probably had a deployment team drop-ship it to specs or, knowing Trudeau, had some layers of unnamed contacts that even the brass doesn't wanna know about broker it in and set it up. This is all pro," Clarissa said, marveling as she unlocked the cage and touched the bars. She leaned her face forward and sniffed and then ran her fingertips across the shiny surface. "Silver paint job, but I'd lay odds that there's actually silver in the bars."

Bradley nodded and looked overhead. "Sprinkler system, in case they try to burn us out, first and second floors with panic rooms and steel walls. She had to have this designed with some serious shit in mind."

"Yeah, but, like, how'd she get this done in a month?" Winters walked over to military crates that lined the far side of the room within the cage. "Sweet Jesus . . . she's got a MLRS up here."

"Whoa, whoa, whoa," Clarissa said, her voice bottoming

out on a horrified murmur. "I thought we were monitoring, not going to war . . . what the hell do we need a multiple launch rocket system for?"

"It's a steel rain, for sure," Bradley said, going over to the crates, his expression now ashen. "Not precise, but can hit a target in a hundred and twenty seconds that would take a car forty-five minutes to drive to . . . so, uh, maybe she's thinking of a preemptive strike? Hell, what's your take on it, Rissa? You're the resident psychic."

"I'm telling you, whatever she's got us monitoring is bigger than HQ knows, gotta be," Winters argued, pulling back tarps. "She's even got a metal storm up here."

"Oh, shit," Clarissa murmured, going over to the weapon that looked like a small pipe organ set in a box.

"You tell me what we need with something that can fire a million rounds a second, huh?" Winters said, his voice becoming shrill. "Like, I do computers, Bradley does radar, you do the blood and bio thing, we might be military but we're really not what you call front line personnel." He looked at the group, pure terror in his eyes. "Like, I've read up on this stuff, but do you really know how to load forty-millimeter rounds in this sucker, or grenades—yeah, it launches grenades from each one of these pipes, plus it can kick a quarter million rounds a minute and the explosion alone will collapse your ear drums and sinus cavities if you're anywhere near the blast."

"I sure hope they're sending in the Green Berets," Bradley said in a tight mutter. "We've gotta set up the systems ASAP to connect the infrared security cameras and night-vision monitors. After seeing this, I've got a really bad feeling that it's gonna get worse before it gets better."

"Ya think?" Winters fussed, walking around checking out gear. "At NORAD I felt safe. We were in the middle of an entire base, not a strategic tactical unit in the field with no real walls or fortification. There, we were dug in deep. But she's got all sorts of IEDs—and what do we need with Improvised Explosive Devices? *Us?*"

"To booby-trap the perimeter, in case something moves on us," Clarissa said, her voice far off and her gaze wandering. "Now I better understand the dirt on the first floor and in the yard. It was brick dust and hallowed earth. Floors one and two are buffer areas and where we can eat and sleep by day, but as soon as the sun goes down, this is command central." Clarissa motioned toward the crates of medical supplies, food, and water rations, and shook her head as she stared at an inflatable raft and orange life jackets. "She thought of every eventuality. I'd also lay odds that every round in here is silver-laced one way or another."

Bradley nodded and picked up a large gun that had multiple barrels. "She's even got handheld metal storms." He tossed one to Winters. "Takes nine millimeter shells, fires sixteen thousand rounds a second, with an electronic firing system—which means it can't jam and the only moving part is the bullet. Guess if we're down in Werewolf and Vampire country, along with zombies and whatever else, we gotta give it to her—at least she didn't send us down here ass out."

Chapter 10

His body hurt so badly that the mere act of breathing was agony. Each breath that required his diaphragm to lift, and rib muscles to expand and contract, sent stabbing, blinding pain into the offended area. The only reason he'd rolled over onto his side to puke was so that he didn't choke to death—but he now cursed his own foolishness, because that might have been a legitimate way out. To just fucking die was all he wanted.

Slowly he opened one eyelid by a slit to stare at Sasha. He'd never forgive her for having so little mercy. It would have been so easy; she had dead aim. The silver residue hanging in the air was making his skin crawl like mites were feasting on him. He'd hollered his vocal cords raw. Scratching at the millions of mites infesting his skin would mean he'd have to move an arm, crane fingers, and lift a limb to rip at the itch when every muscle already felt like it had been filleted from his bones.

He heard his grandfather moving about and running water. So many tears had already slipped from the corners of his eyes that they were parched like his throat. He only cracked open one eye again when he heard a huge sloshing sound. Sasha and his grandfather had wet the blanket and were bringing it toward him. He shook his head no, too weak to do more, and then cried out when they lowered the warm heat onto his skin. They were the monsters, not him.

But slowly as he calmed, he realized their intent had worked. The viral itching had soothed. A soft hand caressed his cheek and slid carefully beneath the nape of his neck to slightly incline his head. The press of plastic against his bottom lip made him open his mouth, and he was rewarded with cool, room-temperature wetness that he greedily drank.

Water spilled down the sides of his mouth and his neck, and he kept guzzling until the bottle had been drained. Panting, he fell back against the table, feeling his insides begin to cool and settle for the first time since the moon had come up. Somewhere in the distance he heard the rattles again. . . . It was complimented by his grandfather's soft shuffle and low, resonant chant. He just prayed with all his heart that the old man wouldn't touch him with anything else that would begin the agony all over again. Then he remembered how Sasha had let him suffer. He opened his eyes and pulled away from her, furious.

"You'll live, I guess," she said flatly. "You came through the—"

"You didn't pull the trigger," he said through his teeth, paying dearly in degrees of agony for his pride and the slight movement.

"No. I didn't. You're right," she said, no apology in her tone. "Want me to do it now, though?"

He closed his eyes.

She walked away from the table and holstered a gun in her waistband.

He opened an eye and stared at her, not sure if she'd decided to oblige him or not.

His grandfather had stopped chanting and put down his shakers very slowly as Sasha picked up a pump shotgun and checked to see that it was loaded. The way she broke down the barrel, snapped it back in place, and trained it on him told him it was.

"Where are Woods's and Fisher's remains?"

"I don't know," Hunter said carefully, watching her expression fade from worry to cold fury.

"You don't remember where you ate them? Then where's Crow Shadow, since familiars don't warrant memory?"

"Are you insane?" Incredulous, Hunter tried to sit up.

"The evidence is damning, but not necessarily as it may seem," Silver Hawk interceded. "I may be his blood, but I am also a clan elder. My knowledge of his soul is not clouded by my love for him." Silver Hawk looked at the foul mess on the floor where Hunter had upchucked. "He did no abomination, this I know."

"No disrespect, Silver Hawk . . . and my deepest sympathies for even having to take this position in your sight, but—"

"There are no human pieces in that refuse," the old man said calmly. "That is all undigested moose from an earlier time, maybe as much as twenty-four hours ago. Use your nose." He looked at Sasha with an unblinking gaze. "When they cannibalize their own, there are whole parts—they eat so ravenously. The smell of human flesh is also different when it comes back up."

She pulled back the weapon and walked away, suddenly needing air. "Jesus." The nape of her neck was damp with perspiration and she briefly lifted her hair up off her shoulders as a nervous habit. There were obviously two beasts out there—one had clearly savaged the trucker and ranger, was probably what had spooked the deer, too. The other one had to be Hunter. Why that only made her feel slightly better, she wasn't sure.

"I need to know what happened out there," she said, leaning against the wall on one hand, mentally fatigued. The shotgun was by her side but pointed toward the floor. Sasha rested her head on her arm for a moment before turning to look at Hunter. "I have to know how severe the transformation was . . . and if it's going to happen again."

"We all do," Hunter replied, his voice raw and his tone flat. He pushed himself up with effort and eased himself off the table with a wince.

Two pairs of eyes followed him over to the sink as he turned on the water and adjusted the temperature to as warm as he could stand it, then put his head under the faucet. If Sasha was going to blow him away, he really didn't care. Maybe she'd be doing him a great service, albeit late in the pain game. Right now he felt filthy and was focused on remedying that, since it seemed he had to live for the next few moments, anyway. To be dirty, matted, and flea-infested in whatever transformation had bested his Shadow-self was a pure violation of the meticulous wolf within. This was not the way of the Shadow Wolf. A dignified end was in order. He'd earned at least that over the years of protecting the clan.

Grabbing the industrial-size, antibacterial soap, he squeezed a huge amount into his hair and began scrubbing, then yanked the sprayer hose out from the sink as far as it would reach and rinsed off in the middle of the floor.

Blood, dirt, sweat, and grime cascaded down and off his hair and body as he continued to take a makeshift shower, furiously lathering every inch of himself. Thick globs of brownish-gray soap splashed onto the floor and then raced toward the concave drain at the center of the room. He continued the process until the suds were pristine and the water clear; he didn't even want to glance in the direction of the butcher block table. It looked like someone had performed an autopsy on it. Maybe they had.

Between slamming open cabinets and yanking open drawers, he found enough towels to reasonably dry himself, and then found the supplies stash to get dressed. Baking soda offered a toothpaste alternative to chase the horrible taste out of his mouth. The entire process had taken less than five minutes, but it was time he'd needed to think, to remember, to piece back together his own sequence of events while Sasha and his grandfather remained mercifully silent.

"I got back here in Shadow Wolf form," Hunter finally said, firmly planting his foot against the wall to tie a hiking boot. He looked up from the task and held Sasha's gaze. "The moon had risen and so had I—you were in heat and whatever else was in my system was not to be denied. I needed air." A tremor of satisfaction threaded through him when she looked away, although he wasn't sure why.

"When I got here, though, something was wrong." Hunter put his other foot against the wall and tightly tied his boot laces. "Crow Shadow's vehicle was just as you'd found it—"

"I smelled you all over it, Hunter."

He put his foot down hard on the floor and stared at her. "I'm sure you did. I went right to it, scented it out to try to figure out what happened. All his weapons were gone. His blood was everywhere like there'd either been a struggle or a slaughter. I don't know which it was."

"Then what happened, son?" Silver Hawk asked, his

eyes unreadable and his voice the balm of wisdom in the room.

"I ran the perimeter searching for a Werewolf signature, but got nothing . . . it was really bizarre. The lodge hadn't been entered, that much I could tell on the first round. So, I went in and began collecting ammo." Hunter tipped his chin in the direction of the weapons pile. "But then I heard a huge crash, and I knew what it was before I saw it." He looked away toward the window, shame singeing him so deeply that his face felt warm. "I couldn't control my shape-shift. It was male, had invaded my space, my mate was en route—it was war."

Sasha raked her fingers through her lush thicket of velvety hair and hearing her do that made him glance at her.

"The kitchen has two doors—one way in, one way out, so the wait staff doesn't bump into each other. I came out on the far side," Hunter added, again using a curt nod and the direction of his chin to indicate which door. "The demon had crashed in through the dining room deck . . . but it was bigger than I'd expected." He looked away again, not even sure how to articulate the level of insanity that had coursed through him at that moment. "I should have shot the damned thing, but was already fully committed to my wolf. The fight took us through the lobby and then the front door."

What he didn't say was that the cinder-block punch the beast had lobbed sent him in a sliding sprawl into the lobby, where it had been everything he could do to avoid the massive jaws and claws that came at him—that's how things had gotten so torn up in there. It was sheer momentum that had kept the beast hurtling forward and through the front doors as it lunged at him and he'd ducked. This hadn't been like a typical barroom brawl of evenly matched opponents. No. This was more like one entity trying to avoid being massacred while the other uprooted tables and chairs and anything the other had used as a shield. He wasn't ready to admit that part to Sasha, much less his grandfather.

"How many times did it bite you?" his grandfather asked, his voice tight and his expression haunted with clearly visible concern.

"None," Hunter muttered. "He just damned near broke my jaw."

"When he punched you, did he break the skin?" Sasha's intense gaze captured his.

"Yeah." Hunter finally looked away toward the moon beyond the windows. She had no idea how much he hated admitting that the demon had split his lip clean open with a bloody fist, and in the course of trying to stay alive by avoiding another massive blow, he'd licked away his own blood.

"Your system was already compromised from birth. Plus, given the circumstances you were already battling, it's no wonder that introducing new infection into your bloodstream completely impacted your immune system." Sasha's body hit the wall with a weary thud as she ruffled her hair up off her neck again. Then she looked at his grandfather and spoke to Silver Hawk as though he wasn't in the room. "But Hunter was struggling with this since last night. That's what worries me. He'd been going through symptomatic spikes before he got sucker-punched."

He hated being clinically spoken of in the third person and he growled his displeasure. Both Sasha and Silver Hawk jerked their attention toward him.

"I'm sorry, but it's true. Your grandfather needs to

know the full scope of what we're dealing with here. If Silver Hawk hadn't shot you with antitoxin, who knows what would have happened."

"The flux will pass," Hunter muttered in a surly tone. "It has before, will this time—"

"No," Silver Hawk said very carefully. "This time even the demons are not themselves."

Both Sasha and Hunter stared at the elderly warrior.

"I felt the demon-infected Werewolves on the move, their presence. I knew one was hunting in our territories. I saw what it did to the grizzly and the other bears; their kills were very strange. Then I came upon a carcass of one of their own that had not just been destroyed in battle, but the carcass was eaten. No living scavenger would dare approach the half-human, half-wolf form, not even one that had been left dead for days in the snow."

Silver Hawk looked away, but his voice remained steady and his chin tipped up a little higher with ancient dignity. "I did not know if this predator had become you, because I could feel you struggling with an inner beast. I could only pray to the Great Spirit that your Shadow Wolf would prevail." He looked at Hunter with intensely sad eyes that leaked compassion. "Tonight your Shadow won. But there are many more moons to come. Then there is also the UCE Conference. That is my deepest concern."

"After all these years, what set it off, Pop?" Frustration scored Hunter's mind, causing him to punch the wall as he began to pace. "All right, I admit it—I was starting to come unglued before more toxin got into my bloodstream, but I don't want to believe that . . ." He looked away from Sasha and spoke to the window. "Something significant had to set it off."

"I agree," Silver Hawk said after a long pause, both

men now speaking in a diplomatic dance around the subject of Sasha's heat.

"Okay—can we just stop talking in riddles, gentlemen?" Sasha walked forward and folded her arms over her chest. "First of all, yeah, all right, night one was pretty intense. However, I'm not buying that Hunter's entire physiology just blew a gasket over me. Would be highly flattering, but highly unlikely. And trust me, after all *this*, I am *so* not in the frame of mind for that, you have *no idea*. I know Hunter has to feel the same way, with pack brothers missing, attacks at random, and the physical trauma he just experienced . . . so what's spiking the old virus in his system?"

Humiliation wound another layer of tension around his spine when his grandfather looked away, trying to swallow a half-smile. Sasha had no concept how much focus and control it required to be in the same room with her, even now.

"Sasha's got a point, Pop," Hunter finally conceded. "It felt like something just hit me out of nowhere."

"When I tracked you to here," Silver Hawk said, his expression growing serious, "I thought there was only one beast. You. Then I found evidence of more than one . . . which gave me the hope that I had not arrived too late. I had wanted my own answers, therefore I did not go to the calling of the packs. But I did follow the trail they were supposed to take after I collected more medicine from my friend. It seems as though the beasts are also following the packs that are left in the region. That is what I do not understand. Infected Werewolves have traditionally tried to hunt as far away from our packs as possible. Only once in my lifetime did they double back in retribution."

Silver Hawk looked out the window. "That was how your mother was lost, but since then, our retaliation had been so thorough that they'd been practically made extinct in North America. Now they have cast a shadow on the northern-most Shadow Wolves."

Sasha stared at Hunter for a moment and then turned her gaze on Silver Hawk. "You saw how Hunter acted once infected Werewolf toxin entered his system. He already had the strain in him, so maybe a dirty blood hit so close to healing from a previous battle just made what was latent in him go full blown. Maybe his system just couldn't tolerate another infection so close to the last one he'd thrown off?"

She began to pace, scratching her head, and watching her was beginning to produce vertigo. Instant recall of her glistening, café au lait skin coming out of the bath she'd taken outside the pack house shoved its way to the forefront of Hunter's brain. Even though he tried his best to ignore the visual stimulation as he watched her lithe form move beneath layers of fabric, that was next to impossible. She was in heat. She was his mate. Regardless of her claims that they weren't that serious yet, or the trauma she'd spoken of, some things were basic and embedded in millennia of evolution. The scent she trailed superseded anything else in the room and awakened his libido with a ferocious yawn.

"That had to be it. I was with him after we fought in the Uncompahgre . . . he was fine for a month," she said, her gaze distant. She sent her line of vision beyond them as though seeking the moon for relief. "I wanna get him to Doc for some off-the-record lab analysis."

His grandfather nodded as the room fell silent. Hunter folded his arms over his chest, needing to think long and hard about submitting to lab tests. Sasha's eyes held a silent plea that was hard to ignore and it was his turn to allow his gaze to seek the dark horizon.

It wasn't that he disagreed with her approach or had a problem with the pack's long-time, secret family friend; it had more to do with his very real apprehension about what Doc Holland might ultimately find. Words were not sufficient, even though he knew she was waiting for some verbal response that he couldn't freely give.

Silence echoed in the kitchen while the faucet dripped and refrigerator motors quietly hummed. He wished he could draw her into his arms right now and express how much he loved the way her razor-sharp mind aggressively attacked the problem. More than that, show her just how much he loved her . . . and how her hesitation to take his life, even after what she'd thought he'd become, had forever affected him. She'd even gone back for their amulets.

Saying nothing but feeling everything, he allowed his gaze to land where the large, etched piece of amber framed in silver hung between her unrestrained breasts. Perhaps it was the insistent, cool stream of air that flowed through the kitchen, or the heat of his gaze, not that it mattered, but after a moment he could see her nipples tightening under the quilted thermal undershirt fabric.

With effort he dragged his gaze to meet hers, wishing for a fleeting moment that they were alone. The conflict she wrestled with burned deeply in her intense, wolf-gray eyes. Anguish, hope, questions, fury—he'd seen the entire spectrum of emotion wrench her . . . even down to the gentle caress she'd offered with a sip of water, a last act of compassion before she might have to destroy a beast that had done the unthinkable. Her eyes had said, *Hunter, forgive me, I love you.* In that brief ellipsis of time he knew she would have done what was necessary as a strong warrior, but it would have destroyed a piece of her soul. For her, now, more than himself, he prayed that he'd purged this latent beast within him.

"Hunter," she said softly, "just consider it once we get to New Orleans. I know there's no time to stop in Denver like we'd talked about, but let Doc look into this . . . see if there's anything he can do. You had been all right . . . it was a month of . . ." She turned away and wrapped her free arm around her waist. "You'd been okay for a long time."

Hunter nodded. "All right. I trust Doc with my life. But the tests can't interfere with the UCE Conference. There can be no signs of weakness at those talks."

He leaned on a set of stainless-steel cabinets, absorbing Sasha's voice on more levels than his grandfather could fathom. Why did she have to remind him of the nights they'd spent together for a month after the battle in the Uncompahgre? Just a brief reminder sent hot images flooding through his mind. The way her cheeks flushed as she avoided his eyes, he could tell the memory had awakened something within her, too.

"I didn't have the toxin in my system to the degree that you did after we came out of that firefight," she said as though choosing each word with great care, and then finally looked at him. "The more I think about it, I bet a lot of other Shadows from the various packs didn't, either . . . but what about those that had?"

"What are you talking about?" Hunter pushed off the cabinets. "I was the only one in the clan shunned for having the latent disease. I'm the only one with the birth defect because my mother had been attacked while carrying me."

Silver Hawk nodded and then briefly closed his eyes as though jettisoning the painful memory. "What my grandson says is true. He was the only one across all packs and clans of this era to have two wolves within him. We have been feeding the honorable one for many years, hoping to starve the dark wolf to death."

"Do we know how many beta males actually tried the illegal substance, though?" Sasha's frank question made Hunter and Silver Hawk simply stare at her.

"Sure," she said, pressing her point, "maybe the real hard-core toxin junkies died that night trying to take a stand in the Uncompahgre with Fox Shadow, but what about the ones that tried shooting up with the stuff a couple of times and then swore off it? They would have been compromised, just like you—and easy to re-infect . . . and they would home to a pack. *That is the way of the wolf.*"

"That is the way of the wolf," Silver Hawk murmured as though his thoughts were a million miles away. "They are, indeed, moving like a pack, not lone rogues the way demon-infected Werewolves normally hunt—and their eating habits are even more deadly; they will eat their own kind."

"And are driven ravenous by a she-Shadow in heat . . . not necessarily a top consideration for the run-of-the-mill Werewolf. True, male Weres appreciate she-Shadows in that condition . . . just like a male Shadow can appreciate a female Werewolf in said condition, too—but it's not our general preference. What was out there looking for Sasha was on a mission, like one of us. It was a corrupted male Shadow Wolf, had to be, raging for Sasha like that." Hunter stared at Sasha, nodding slowly. "But how? How did the toxin in that man get to me? There's been no incidents since we put Fox Shadow down hard."

"Now you're talking about issues in my territory—the

military's concern with weapons of mass destruction. This one I went to school for, fellas." Sasha gave them both a look and then began to pace. "Biohazards and biogenetic weapons that have a hundred different effective delivery systems are one of the things I'm deployed to track, isolate, and destroy."

Hunter found the edge of the sink to lean against; watching her mind hunt and wrestle the issue with a strategic defense against the danger to the pack was making it really hard to focus. It was so damned sexy to witness that he could barely breathe.

"This particular virus is insidious, gentlemen." Sasha's gaze swept past his grandfather's and pinned him against the sink. "It's worse than the Vampire strain, which has control factors. As I'm sure you're aware, Vampires can actually determine when they want a victim to turn into one of their kind; Werewolves can't. Demon-infected Werewolves can't. It's an equal opportunity agent of cellular destruction that can get into the bloodstream if ingested, through a cut, a direct blood exchange, or a saliva swap. That's why this one is considered the most formidable because it could easily morph into a pandemic outbreak, if not contained. Even I could be a carrier."

"Even though we were both battling the beasts, Sasha, you didn't have the toxin that heavily in your system, so there's no way you could have given it to me. Besides, I haven't picked up any Werewolf tracer in the pack. If our supplies had been poisoned, I would have assuredly picked up the toxin scent," Hunter countered.

"Maybe," his grandfather said carefully. "Under normal circumstances, yes. And those that had been infected could have easily hidden themselves from their pack alphas until they felt the scent had sufficiently diminished."

Sasha's gaze found the drain in the center of the floor at the same time Hunter's sought the window.

"Yeah, well, like I said," Sasha finally added, "somebody figured out how to get it into your system."

"Son, you were bitten and scratched during the last battles behind demon doors and in the Uncompahgre. You then healed quickly as our kind can do, but it was a new and fragile balance inside you. A concealed viral attack on your system, at a time when your defenses were down and you were least disposed to be aware of even the most extreme changes . . ."

Hunter looked away and then walked to the far side of the room.

"Think back," Sasha said, imploring him with her voice as she neared him from behind. "What did we eat, what did we drink? You had been all right for damned near a month after going through freaking demon doors, now this?"

"We gathered supplies, like always, from a safe pack outpost." He turned and looked at her, seeing it step-by-step in his mind, unable to stop staring into her wide, gray eyes. "We ate at one of our diners—then we set out to head up into the mountains."

"And the later it got, the thirstier you got," she said, placing a hand on his arm. "You drained an entire canteen . . ."

Hunter closed his eyes. "My plate at the diner had to be spiked, and then the water . . . you never ate, just watched me . . . because . . ."

"Of my condition," she said quietly, nodding. "I was too wound up to stomach anything—I just wanted to keep moving and reach where we had to go."

He nodded. "Yeah. I remember. And after I left the tent, I polished off the other canteen and packed them with fresh snow, then melted it over a small fire that I built into a larger one for the morning, so you'd have water when you woke up."

Hunter opened his eyes, his gaze seeking Sasha's and holding it. His body ached for her in the worst way now; the throb that being close to her produced was almost unbearable. They both shared a silent understanding and danced a quiet shadow dance of souls, leaving out the most intimate details of their interaction, skipping over sections of what had transpired. There was no need to elaborate before the wise old man, who could most likely read between the lines, anyway. But as a matter of courtesy and a matter of privacy, Silver Hawk just nodded with a grunt.

"It was in the water; it always is," the elderly man announced. "The body is made up of this element, and to poison a people and drive them from their lands, take their water—or pollute it."

They didn't ask what he'd meant. Hunter knew from experience that there were just some old wounds, which current-day events sometimes touched and disturbed, that took his grandfather further back in time than he wanted to go. He was just grateful that Sasha seemed to understand that and had let it go with a simple nod.

Chapter 11

Clarissa dropped her steaming cup of coffee in the middle of the attic floor. It slid from her hand so effortlessly that it seemed like it fell in slow motion as her eyelids began to flutter. The multiple computer screens and surrounding technology had felt like it was closing in on her as her vision blurred. Bradley caught her before she also fell and shattered on the floor like her cup. Winters was right there with a chair on wheels for her to slump into.

"What is it, Rissa?" Bradley said, rubbing her hand and then stroking her bangs back from her damp forehead. He stooped beside her, panicking, and turned his attention toward Winters. "Get a cold, wet paper towel and some water."

He continued to squeeze Clarissa's hand and stroke her hair as she began to loll her head from side to side. Then for several seconds, she stopped breathing and opened her eyes in a glassy, unfocused stare.

"Clarissa! Talk to us!"

Winters rushed over with the cold compress and placed it on her forehead. Her once-normal, creamy complexion was waxen and flushed. Bradley began shaking her more roughly, his voice tight, sharp bursts of commands.

"Breathe, Rissa. Talk to us—what do you see?"

Seconds passed and then she suddenly took a huge inhale and her eyes focused.

"They're alive and headed this way." She searched Bradley's and Winters's faces for an explanation.

"Who's alive?" Bradley pressed, wiping back her bangs and bringing the water Winters handed over to her lips.

"Second Lieutenant James Fisher and First Lieutenant Darien Woods," she gasped.

Bradley was on his feet. "That's a Vampire ploy if ever I heard one."

"I went through that body-double shit with Vampires before, and almost got a slug put in my head from the brass for allowing one into the labs by accident. I'm not proud to admit it, but that's how they got their hands on the toxin in the first place. Never again. Don't let 'em play you, Clarissa." Winters's gaze hardened, adding years to his normally youthful face. "Those men died in Afghanistan. Reinforce the perimeter with—"

"No," Clarissa said, gasping. "I need to tell you about the other images they're sending me. They'll rendezvous with us during *the day* tomorrow, wearing silver, garlic, or whatever else we require as proof positive."

"You sure?" Bradley said, his tone strained.

Clarissa nodded with a weak smile. "They pass muster."

"A coupla hours ago you guys wanted to know if Sasha was sending the Green Berets. Well, from what I understand, they're it—with a cavalry coming a day or two behind them."

Winters wiped his palms down his face. "Leave it to Trudeau to resurrect two supposedly dead guys for the mission."

Bradley found the edge of a desk and sat down with a thud. "I swear this job is gonna give me a heart attack one day."

"We need to move. This place is no longer safe," Silver Hawk said quietly, breaking Sasha's trance.

Sasha quickly dragged her attention away from Hunter and nodded. She'd been so wrapped up in the sound of his voice and the earnest intensity of his eyes that her responses fell a beat behind what made good common sense. Damned right they needed to move. What was wrong with her?

"I know there are several grounds trucks in the garage area," Hunter said and then sent his gaze toward the door.

She briefly studied Hunter's rigid posture, monitoring the tension that ran through his body and wafted from his aura, then glimpsed Silver Hawk who had discreetly averted his eyes. "Okay, let's mount up, then."

It was time to click into her military mind. There was nothing like the immediate threat of danger to put things in perspective. Sasha began loading her arms with weapons and that definitely helped her focus. But seeing Hunter do that nearly unraveled whatever newfound focus she'd claimed. Call it twisted, but there was just something about watching him set his jaw hard . . . and watching the steel cable network of muscles he owned move beneath his tight thermal shirt and fatigues.

Oh, yeah, her system was compromised by a very definite *condition*. This was ludicrous. Ten minutes prior, she'd been ready to deliver a silver slug to his skull, and now after some rhetorical conversation she was ready to jump his bones?

Horrified, she followed Silver Hawk out of the kitchen loaded down with artillery, trying hard not to look at

Hunter's impressive back . . . or that delicious dip in his spine, or his very tight, absolutely gorgeous ass that one could bounce a quarter off of.

A cold slap of air and the real dangers of an ambush, however, stopped her mind from vacillating. The three-some moved like the wind itself, sliding from shadow to shadow in stealth silence until they reached the garage.

Entering a building in a hostile environment was always dangerous. Hunter eased his weapons stash to the ground and took two nine millimeters, motioning with gun barrels for her and Silver Hawk to round the building. Now every-body needed to be on point until the all clear was given.

Silver Hawk's expert tracking was something pro-found to witness. Sasha watched the old man get down low on the ground on all fours, close his eyes, and tilt his head, and she saw the edges of his nostrils slightly flare as he deeply inhaled. Pointing, he indicated fresh tire tracks that led away from the exit, and she squinted, noticing that there weren't any footprints or paw prints to compli-ment the tire tracks.

In a lithe push-up that should have belonged to a man one-third his age, Silver Hawk rose with a bewildered ex-pression on his face and then placed an open hand against the side of the building. Sasha remained very still as she waited for his assessment. He then held up two fingers in a V shape. It was her turn to tilt her head.

Vampires?

Hunter rounded the building and gave them a thumbs-up. Nothing had barreled in there in Werewolf form, but Silver Hawk held up a hand and gave Hunter his gun be-fore slipping into the smoothest wolf transition she'd ever seen. His clothes simply melted off his body and were left in a small pool on the ground with his doeskin moccasins.

From that silent transformation the most majestic creature she'd ever seen emerged. As the cold wind blew she could see that the huge wolf's coat was snowy white beneath silver gray edging, and his wise, aged eyes seemed to hold the depths of many lifetimes. Silver Hawk, now transitioned to Silver Shadow, glimpsed back once and then leaped through a shadow into the unknown.

Sasha started forward, worry for the old man's safety rising in her like a sudden tide. Hunter placed a hand on her shoulder. But he'd gone through a Shadow door alone!

Frantic, she gave Hunter the signal that had freaked her out. The second she opened her forefinger and middle finger in a V she could see his expression harden. Silver shells would only slow that particular entity down, not kill it. They'd have to expand their arsenal on the fly, if that was what was in the garage.

The double doors creaked open eerily. Two barrels pointed at it, Hunter on one side of the doors, Sasha on the other. A low howl snapped their forearms back. Hunter swept up his grandfather's clothes and tossed them to him as he and Sasha quickly entered the building.

"I have checked the trucks they left behind and they haven't been tampered with," Silver Hawk said, dressing quickly with his back toward them. He indicated with a quick nod to an empty mechanic's bay where a truck had probably once been housed. "They siphoned the blue one for gasoline and took the fuel can," he added, pointing at drips on the floor and then toward the tool rack on the wall, "plus took some chains and tools, but everything else is as it should be."

"If Vampires were here in a garage and took those items, then it would have to have been lower-level ones, like henchmen, who couldn't materialize what they needed out of thin air." Sasha's gaze tore around the well-equipped garage. "Doesn't make sense."

"Maybe they got chased here by whatever were-pack was on the loose," Hunter offered, going to collect the stash outside that they'd set down. "Or maybe they're in on this bull again?"

"Yeah, but what's their angle this time?" Sasha folded her arms over her chest, thinking. "I thought once burned, twice learned was the way Vampires viewed the world?"

"Do not forget," Silver Hawk said, his gaze holding hers, "that particular entity never lets a grudge pass unaddressed. Perhaps all of this is a part of a much larger game being played."

That thought had definitely crossed her mind more than once. Sasha nodded but didn't comment further as she found the keys to a Dodge RAM1500, climbed in with Silver Hawk, and backed the red vehicle out into the driveway. Within moments they'd all loaded as much artillery as they could fit into the cab and still ride in relative safety, and the rest went under a tarp in the flatbed.

"Where to?" Sasha turned in the driver's seat and looked at Silver Hawk, then Hunter.

"This thing is following the packs' normal route from north to south, tracking over familiar ground. If it was made from one of us, an infected Shadow Wolf, then it clearly knows our safe houses."

"That's what had to have happened here at the lodge," Hunter said. "It knew the building as well as I did, and every move I made, he was right on me."

"Maybe that's why the Vamps came here—they could be tracking the infected Shadow too." Sasha stared at Hunter for a moment and then sent a seeking gaze toward his grandfather.

"Which could be disastrous down in New Orleans at the Conference. All they need is evidence to present and they can open a Shadow Wolf hunt, it's in the bylaws." Hunter rubbed his palms down his face. "Damn!"

Silver Hawk nodded and looked at Sasha. "You yourself said you had picked up on unusual Were-demon energy and a trail that seemed to be on the move headed toward New Orleans—this was why you were sending your team there to investigate. That is why I think we should move outside of our normal bands as we make our way south."

"Pop is right," Hunter said, opening the window and resting his elbow on the metal door frame. "If we've got infected Shadows on the move, and don't know how many—the last place we need to go is along the old route."

Sasha backed the truck out farther and turned it around to head out of the lodge grounds. "Yeah, but the only problem there is we'd have to take this payload to a civvy motel, and then pray to God that we don't have to get into a firefight."

Hunter looked at his grandfather, who was wedged between him and Sasha. "You're the best candidate for offering oblations to the universe. I don't think they listen to me up there too much."

Evidence of lower-ranking Vampires at the scene of an infected wolf attack was completely baffling. The two species were archenemies, and except for one very spurious, independent, rogue alliance that had ended disastrously with the Vampires being double-crossed, there was never an occasion where they'd peacefully cooperated with each other before. Under normal circumstances the two species abhorred each other. Therefore none of this made sense.

But they had tried to do an alliance once, and the new pressure that human technology and awareness was placing on the supernatural world was perhaps no different than what was happening to the ecosystem. Humans tended to flush things out of their natural habitats.

Sasha kept her eyes on the dark road, senses keened for another ambush with Hunter and Silver Hawk riding shotgun. Just like overzealous real estate development ate into the natural wilderness, which then had bears eating out of backyard garbage cans, or wolves eating farmers' domesticated chickens and cows, maybe something was going on like that with the supernatural wilderness?

Too bad Vampires were experts at blocking psychic invasions and were pretty good at giving as well as they got in that department. So it wasn't going to be easy to do a vision quest or a divination to get the full story. Those approaches worked better on the preternatural wolf phyla. Sasha let out a weary breath. New Orleans was going to get ugly. For now, she had to focus on one issue at a time, namely getting them all to a place where they could rest, eat, and recuperate for a hard travel day in the morning.

Silence filled the cab on the monotonous, three-hour drive to a truck stop motel. As sleazy as the joint was, she still prayed for a vacancy.

It was almost midnight and her mind was so weary from flipping the variables over and over in her brain that she was punchy. The only thing keeping her upright was adrenaline and frustration. She didn't even want to think about the latter of the two issues. It would pass; it had to pass. She and Hunter had to remain on point for danger at all times . . . but damn the moon was a sexy beast tonight.

Hunter was out of the vehicle before she had rolled to a stop. She just looked away from him through the windshield for a moment and then slammed the gears into park with an attitude. The door to the vehicle was still wide open and she couldn't even look at Silver Hawk. Unfazed, the old man slid over and closed the passenger-side door.

"They have a diner. We should eat," he said simply.

Sasha nodded but kept her gaze straight ahead. "As soon as Hunter comes back."

"I should patrol . . . you both should rest. This would be best."

She kept her gaze forward and could feel the muscle pulsing in her jaw as she ground her teeth. "We can take shifts so you can rest. You've been tracking all day and have to be exhausted. You did an amazing healing and that had to take a lot out of you . . . no disrespect intended, sir." She glimpsed him from the corner of her eye. "You've been our ace in the hole . . . if you hadn't shown up with meds . . . I don't know what would have happened."

A strong, age-weathered hand cupped her cheek and made her look at its owner.

"Daughter-Shadow, listen to not my words but my eyes and my heart. I will patrol; you rest with your mate. The trauma that you have both endured is profound, just as the battles you have fought and are fighting at this moment. Lay down your burden to heal your spirits. In the morning, I will sleep as you two drive, will do as old men do and sleep on planes, trains, buses, whatever conveyance we select. No one will be the wiser, for I am just an elderly old man." He smiled a toothy grin and nodded; moonlight glinted off his long, silver braids that hung down his chest. "But come nightfall, know that I am wide awake and still all wolf."

She was left mute and mildly embarrassed by Silver Hawk's deep insight as he withdrew from her and slipped from the truck. The old saying that Doc had once told her, *every shut eye ain't sleep*, came immediately to mind as she watched the old man's straight, proud back.

Still, Silver Hawk hadn't left her much choice. She had to wait in the vehicle until Hunter returned, given the hefty load of weapons under a tarp in the back. Sure, one could claim they were going hunting, but some of the stuff they were toting with automatic rounds would give any ranger serious pause.

Before long, she saw Hunter exit the small registration building and lope in her direction. Although his return staved off the nervous energy that had her bouncing off the walls of the truck interior while she waited, watching him take those long, fluid strides of his was truly messing with her mind. His body moved with such commanding grace . . . his eyes had found hers, had locked in on her gaze and held it as though a focal point to guide him through the night.

Maybe that had something to do with her eroding mental state; she couldn't quite articulate it even to herself. But one thing was for sure: she was going to have to explain where Silver Hawk had disappeared to and didn't have a clue.

Hunter opened the passenger's-side door and slid into the seat. He hadn't broken eye contact and the hunger in his stare was so blatant that it finally made her look away.

"I got three rooms," he said in a quiet rumble and then pushed a stray wisp of her hair behind her ear.

She nodded without looking at him, knowing that was best. Instead she stared at the dashboard for a moment while trying to stave off the burn his touch left. As it was, she could barely breathe, feeling his energy wash over her in a thick blanket of desire.

"Two are adjoining . . . have a door in between. The other is down the row a bit."

Hunter's gaze hadn't wavered. It wasn't necessary to look at him to know that. She swallowed hard, her mouth suddenly dry.

"Where's Silver Hawk?" he finally asked just above a murmur.

"I don't know," she said quietly. The moment she looked at him his gaze trapped hers. "He said we should eat, he would take first watch and he'd sleep as we drove in the morning."

"God bless him," Hunter whispered.

For a moment neither of them spoke and then she pulled out of the daze and rubbed her palms down her face.

"Wait, wait, listen. This is crazy," she said.

He nodded slowly and licked his newly healed bottom lip, causing it to glisten in the moonlight. "Insane."

"No," she said, not as strongly as intended. "What I mean is—it's dangerous, we all have to stay alert and on point, and you've got some madness spiking through your system that . . ."

Her words trailed off as he looked away and lifted his chin. She hadn't meant to offend him or call him a virus carrier, but damn, for all she knew he was. The moment blown, his next statements became a crisp series of logistics.

"You're right. Bad lapse in judgment—blame it on the moon. So we get this artillery stashed in the rooms, I'll call Silver Hawk and work out a patrol schedule with him so he can get a few hours of shut-eye tonight. We all eat at the diner together."

Sadness threaded through the ache within her. *Damn*,

she hadn't meant what she'd said to come off the way it did. She wanted to reach out and touch him as he turned and opened the door, giving her his fantastically ripped back to consider.

"We'll keep the door bolted between the rooms." He tossed her a room key and jumped down from the truck. "I'll walk, meet you over there."

For a moment she didn't move, couldn't. The man had turned her on so badly she had to grip the steering wheel to keep her hands from shaking. When he threw his head back and howled for Silver Hawk, she closed her eyes and allowed a private shudder to claim her. Drive. She had to get out of Hunter's magnetic tow for a minute to be able to function.

He watched her pull off, needing distance and a cold slap of air to help steady him. The long ride in close confines, the look on her face just now when her breathing had hitched—damn, he was so hard he could barely walk across the driveway.

"All is well?" Silver Hawk appeared and stepped beside him silently.

"Yeah, Pop. We're all going to the diner to eat after we unload the truck, should do it as family . . . stay together. I can take the first shift after—"

"Son, look at the moon." Silver Hawk smiled. "The imminent danger has passed." He motioned with his chin across the driveway. "Look at *her*. Let me take the first shift."

Hunter shook his head no and set his jaw hard. It took three failed attempts at opening his mouth for words to form. He thrust a key into his grandfather's thick hand and let out a hard breath. "I still might have virus in my system—it's best if I take the first shift." Humiliation stabbed his pride and propelled him forward, but his grandfather caught his arm.

"You purged enough to almost stop your heart. Torture yourself if you must do penance—I'm going to the diner. She is a fully matured she-Shadow and her system is very strong. Your nose is ruined for the night to anything but her. I would feel safer to take the first shift, given your distraction . . . and I left a few more shots of antitoxin in the glove compartment if things get completely out of hand." Silver Hawk added with a sly half-smile. "You are no longer a carrier."

Thoroughly frustrated, Hunter watched the old man take three long Shadow leaps and disappear. "Yeah, tell *her* that," he muttered under his breath, crossing the driveway in pain.

Chapter 12

Too many conflicting thoughts fought for dominance in his mind: Protection. Danger. Sasha. Sex. The virus. Carriers. Sasha. Sex. The future. The pack. Sasha. Sex. The clan. The predators. Sasha. Sex . . . and that lovely, gorgeous ass of hers. Honor! Food . . . Sasha—sex.

His hands were trembling by the time he'd reached the truck. She probably saw it and that's why she'd tossed him a shotgun with an attitude. He caught it with one hand, not even looking at it, still studying her rear view.

Admonishing himself, he tried to keep his focus on the truck, but watching Sasha reach and bend and lift was carving a hole in the wrong side of his brain. Especially with a motel room so, so close.

"Okay, Hunter," she said, whirling on him. "*This* has *got* to stop." She jumped down from the flatbed of the truck and glared at him.

He nodded, never losing eye contact with her. "Just tell me how . . . and I'll gladly oblige."

She let out an exasperated breath and brushed past him with an armload of artillery. He hurried to open the motel room door for her. She stopped him at the door with a hard look.

"I, uh, guess I'll take the rest of it next door."

"Good idea," she said. "Maybe leave some heat and a coupla clips under the front seat of the truck for Silver Hawk in case he needs to re-up while out on patrol."

"Right. Roger that."

Hunter moved quickly to get the rest of the weapons into his room, nervous energy and frustration making his motions jerky. He didn't disagree with her. Sasha was right. He did need to stop drooling over what wasn't going to happen for a very long time, if ever again, just for the sake of his own sanity and pride. He'd been here most of his adult Shadow Wolf life, banished by the pack females because he had a little extra something crazy in his DNA. Now it had finally gone full blown at a very inopportune time. But he wasn't sure what was worse, never having been with a she-Shadow and not having a mate, simply quarantined to human females, or experiencing the incomparable—Sasha.

Before he could even tease himself with the thought that she'd make love to him again, first Doc had to test him and outcomes had to be proven . . . probably another full moon phase had to pass without any trace of the beast. That was the only safe and logical thing to do. Plus, they all had to live through the mission—this personal bullshit didn't have anything to do with anything at all relevant to what they were dealing with now.

But as he watched Sasha go into her room and kick the door closed, he had to remember to breathe.

The slam reverberated through him as he brought the last of the weapons into his room. It was symbolic. He set them down on the dresser and stared at the door that adjoined their rooms. Even though he told himself to leave it latched, he still found himself crossing the small space that hosted two twin-sized beds. He lied to himself that he was just going to ask her if she was ready to grab a bite to eat.

It was just as possible to walk out the front door, walk a few feet, and knock on her room door and wait for her to answer.

Instead, he was standing at the partition door, flipping back the latch, trying to come up with fifty plausible reasons why that was so. Then he really held his breath, because the secondary door on her side was already wide open. *She'd* opened *her side?*

He couldn't move for a moment as he saw her standing in the middle of the floor hugging herself, trying to steady her breaths with her eyes closed. Just seeing her like that paralyzed him; then her incredible she-scent dragged him across the inside threshold between the rooms.

Sasha held up one shaky hand, her voice wavering as she squeezed her eyes shut tighter. "Don't." She placed a hand over her heart. "I shouldn't have opened the door, Hunter, I'm dangerous."

He tilted his head, not completely sure of her meaning but very sure of his own. "So am I."

She let out a breath that was a cross between a gasp and a sigh. The sound of her voice contracted his groin and made him begin to breathe through his mouth.

"Hunter," she said in a low, quiet tone, so sensual that he stepped closer out of sheer reflex. She opened her big, beautiful eyes and her gaze searched his face in the darkened room. "It's not you or that I don't want you. I'm so horny right now that I can't think straight . . . but we can't risk being attacked while in the throes, or worse, risk me getting the contagion here in a civilian installation. It's bad enough that we have all this artillery in here. But the later it gets, the worse it gets." Tears suddenly rose and glittered in her eyes as her voice dropped to a husky whisper. "I never knew that it could be so bad that it actually hurt."

With that she closed her eyes and hugged herself tighter and put distance between them by walking across the room to stare out the window at the moon.

"Baby . . . I'm right there with you." Pain was making him stupid.

He had only processed selected segments of what she'd said: the first and last two sentences. Hell yeah, it could get that bad. Agony was his middle name right now. Need had morphed into acute ache that transformed into heavy, loaded, hard-pant pain. After that his brain had shut down, even though she'd also made sense about the civilians and the virus. Notwithstanding what logic dictated, it felt like all the blood in his skull had fled there to reside in a pounding erection.

Watching her battle herself in the darkness, with a silver-blue swath of moonlight draping her, almost made him howl out loud. Gooseflesh had risen on her forearms and had made her nipples harden beneath her thermal shirt. Every shaky inhale made her breasts lift, and the slow sweep of her hands up and down her waist made him so jealous of them that he had to briefly look away.

Common sense told him to get them out of the room. They couldn't just keep standing there, silent, breathing heavy, about to pin each other to the nearest surface within the next blink. Maybe if they went to get something to eat, got away from the privacy of a space with a bed . . . but the only thing he was ravenous for at the moment was standing by the window bathed in moonlight.

He wanted to touch her so badly he almost moaned. Just to feel her velvety hair slipping through his fingers, or her creamy, café au lait skin against his palms. Her lush mouth was a study in absolute perfection; just thinking about tangling his tongue with hers parted his lips.

Remembering her satiny, graceful hands sliding across his hard surfaces clenched his stomach. Agony? *This* was agony—standing only a few feet away from her, watching her practically writhing in pain, but unable to draw her into an embrace because his kiss might be lethal, could carry a dreaded germ.

A gentle caress sent a hard shudder through him. Her Shadow had reached out and touched his in the darkness. The sensation was so intense that he put one hand against the wall to hold himself upright and dropped his head forward, spilling his hair over his shoulders and face. If she didn't stop, she was going to call out his wolf. If they were ever going to leave the room and meet up with his grandfather to eat, her Shadow had to back off, had to stop playing in his hair . . . oh, damn, had to stop running up his back and sliding down his chest . . . if she went any lower . . . all bets were off.

Though neither of them moved, his Shadow pulled hers into a hard embrace. She released a deep, ardent moan that nearly buckled his body. His mind dissolved on a single thought: *If she wanted it half as much as he did, she'd be weeping by now*. Sasha turned and looked at him without blinking, tears streaming down her face.

"Oh, shit . . ." he whispered, and started toward her, practically panting.

She closed her eyes tightly and shook her head no. He understood; it just wasn't safe. He stopped in his tracks and placed his hands on top of his head for a moment to keep from touching her.

"Then just let me Shadow dance with you," he said in a tight voice, not believing he'd gotten to the place of nearly begging. Hell, who was he fooling, *he was begging*. "In the lobby . . . I can get condoms—I know it's not the way of the wolf, but we're not going to make it through the night."

Compelled, he crossed the small space that separated them and cradled her cheek; she turned into the caress and kissed his palm deeply as she released a soft moan. Unable to resist, he pulled her into a tight embrace, her body burning against his. Her mouth rained hot kisses on his neck and shoulder, her pelvis mating his as his hands traversed her back.

"I want to kiss you so badly," she gasped against his neck. "My body's on fire."

He held the sides of her head for a moment, his fingers thrust deeply into her lush thicket of dark hair, and stared into her eyes. He bit his lip to not take her mouth and plunder it, but the agony shimmering in her eyes made that so hard not to do. Rather than risk infecting her he kissed her forehead slowly, then drew her chin into his mouth and found the cleft in her throat until she cried out while grasping his shoulders.

"Sasha . . . baby, I want to kiss your mouth so much, too. . . . I never fully understood what just that one thing did to me until I couldn't do it."

Burning up, he briefly released his hold on her but never released her pained gaze, then ripped his shirt over his head. He needed to feel her skin, even if they couldn't swap spit, couldn't kiss—it didn't matter. As long as her hands stroked his bare chest and shoulders and back he might be able to catch his breath. But as her fingertips played across his torso and her mouth French kissed his nipples, his breathing and heart went into mild arrhythmia. Suckles against his abdomen pulled a trapped moan up and out of his chest. The sensation made him pump slowly against air; her tongue promised so much just before she stood to strip her shirt off over her head.

For a second he briefly closed his eyes and turned his head as though she'd slapped him. Her pendulous breasts bounced free and the erotic sight was pure sensory overload. He opened his pants to release some of the pressure and then found her hips, pulling her closer. Fabric voiced its complaint in audible friction. Kisses that her mouth denied he lavished on her breasts. Her gasping moan encouraged him to make each sweep of his lips deeper, wetter, longer until her fingers tangled in his hair and she was practically climbing up his body.

Losing his mind, he dropped his kisses in a wild smattering against her rib cage, her waist, her belly, and forgetting, he unzipped her pants—only her fist in his hair reminded him to stop.

He looked up, breathing hard. The wince on her face made him stand and kiss her temple. "I'm sorry . . . got carried away, won't happen again."

She didn't answer; her flat palm against his back slowly became a fist. Damn . . . he knew exactly where she was at. Knowing made him nuzzle her temple hard, find the side of her neck to spill kisses down it as his hands slid down the front of her pants.

The sound she released was such a low, subsonic moan that it sent a stabbing throb along his shaft with a rush of leaking seed. He needed to kiss her so badly, be inside her so badly, yet all he could do was torture her bud, torture himself, his fingers sliding against her slippery glaze while wishing so badly that they were him.

Soon erratic, frustrated thrusts tried to capture his fingers inside her, but he couldn't risk scratching her where they might not even know that she'd been nicked. He petted her hair and held the nape of her neck while caressing the swollen part of her that demanded what she couldn't have. She kept her hands in tight fists at his back, but he could almost feel her fighting not to rake him. When her jaw filled, he pulled back to stare at her eyes that had gone wolf, and when she threw her head back and gasped, she'd lost the battle to her canines.

Frenzy was in her eyes as she slid his hand out of her pants and shimmied them down, then unlaced her boots and shucked everything off. "It's not working," she said, gasping out the words. "I need more than that while in heat."

Even though he wanted her beyond all comprehension, and knew from all he'd ever heard in the clan that *this* was what made rival males battle to the death, how could he call himself a man—her mate—if he'd risk her to becoming something his entire species abhorred? No matter what his grandfather had said, Silver Hawk didn't really know for sure. Sasha's life deserved more than playing a hunch.

"Sasha . . . baby . . ." he murmured as she slowly stalked him. "We can't . . . not like this—you were right."

"Forget what I said earlier—I'll take my chances," she said in a low, sexy growl, beginning to circle him.

"You'll draw blood like this," he said, his voice bottoming out as he backed up, shaft throbbing. "I can't even mount you with a condom."

"Why not?" she whispered, holding her breasts and then dropped her head back. "Oh, God, Hunter, why not?"

He stood transfixed for a moment, trying to remember human language, trying to remember why not, canines filling his mouth, pants slung down low on his hips, balls aching, desire like a silver bullet lodged in his temple. "Because . . . like this . . . *I'll* draw blood."

She shuddered hard and looked at him, panting. *"Then draw it."*

It was perhaps the hardest thing he'd ever had to do in his life, but he stepped into a Shadow to avoid her touch. She released a fury wail then sat down hard on the bed and wept softly with her arms wrapped around her body; he found the closest wall to silently bang his head against. There wasn't enough air in the room to fill his lungs. He needed to cum so badly he was hyperventilating. Six hours till sunrise; he'd never make it not touching her. Not when she'd dropped back on the bed and thrust her hand between her legs, then rolled over on her belly moaning with frustration. There was antitoxin in the truck, condoms in the lobby . . . *Great Spirit, give him strength, please know his heart, he loved her but was also flawed and male.*

The sensible thing to do would have been to quietly slip into his own room, close the door between their rooms, relieve the tension that was driving him insane by hand, and try to go to sleep. But he was so far from sensible at the moment; he was trapped by his own need.

Just watching her damp behind lifted up off the bed in a deep, inviting sway and undulating in the moonlight . . . listening to the slick, steady sound that he so badly wanted to be, hearing her breaths get tangled up with his murmured name—it was enough to drag him out of the Shadows. How could everything male in him not respond to witnessing the incredibly sensual combination of her hand clutching a breast, thumbing a taut cinnamon-hued nipple, while the other drove two fingers deep to a pounding rhythm?

"Hunter . . . Shadow dance with me . . . *anything . . ."*

The anguished request made his Shadow practically tackle hers. The wail she released doubled him over with need. She turned to stare at him over her shoulder, luminous eyes capturing moonlight, then she pushed off the bed on all fours in a power lunge that sprawled him on the floor. Try as he might to avoid her mouth, he couldn't. She swallowed his moan with a forceful kiss and anchored his skull between her palms. Reflex put his hands in her hair, sent his tongue in search of hers, and the sensation of her hot body blanketing him arched his back, exploding his lungs with her name.

It was too late to worry about drawing blood, swapping spit, or making any other hazardous contact. He slid into her with such heat-slicked force that tears were welling in his eyes. Her gasp cut the night as she fisted his hair and rode him hard. Choking out her name every hard thrust she drove against him, lifted him up off the floor in return, his palms halving her backside in a grip that threatened to split her.

The convulsion that hit him felt like a blade had been jabbed into his sac to send a current of white-hot lightning up his shaft, twitching his sphincter. Her name was embedded in the holler that morphed into a howl. It hurt so good he was pulling up carpet nap with each wail, charley horses formed in his hamstrings, his abs quick flexing, his spine snap-jerking—hell yes, he understood now what the old man had told him!

Tears wet his cheeks as she collapsed against him, shuddering. He dropped back with a thud and hit the floor.

"I'm sorry," she panted and hid her face against his neck. "Oh, God, I'm so embarrassed."

He shook his head, too winded to immediately speak, and petted her smooth, damp back. "Don't be."

"I've never . . . in front of . . . oh my God."

The erotic image clawed its way to the forefront of his mind and sizzled. It was moonlight and madness and he was all the way gone. The more it burned, the more it made him hunt for her mouth, and the more it made his hands touch her skin. Breathless as renewed heat entered his body, he turned her over, crouching above her on all fours. He took her mouth hard and then appraised the length of her beneath him, releasing deep, long exhales and inhales, a love-slicked erection bouncing to his breaths, and then he finally trapped her gaze within his.

"Turn over," he murmured in a half growl, "and do it again."

He sat in the diner with a knowing smile, sipping his coffee and waiting on another steak. The moon was most beautiful when she was full and elegant. Maybe, if the Great Spirit was merciful and the pack lands bountiful . . . maybe he'd even live long enough to see great-grandchildren.

"Yo, Woodsey, not complaining or anything, but this place sure looks real different at night."

"You're telling me? The daytime version was bad enough stuck in my mind," Woods said, glancing around through the rental car windows. "But the nighttime version gives me the creeps."

"Sure hope that's why the hair is standing up on the back of my neck," Fisher said quietly.

"This location is an ambush ready to happen," Woods muttered, taking the safety off his weapon as he pulled into the driveway, his eyes roving the unkempt bushes.

"Trudeau can sure pick 'em." Fisher checked his clip.

Woods and Fisher stared at each other for a moment.

"So what do we do now, dude? Walk up the steps and just ring the bell?"

Woods ground his teeth, making his jaw pulse. "Yeah, I guess—that and pray whatever's in the fucking house doesn't come out snarling or shooting."

Chapter 13

Being knowledgeable didn't help. Being a highly trained soldier didn't help. Being an alpha she-Shadow didn't help. Sasha simply stared at the ceiling listening to Hunter snore. This biological condition would happen once a quarter during a full moon, and she now knew it to be a hard fact. It would last three unrelenting days and nights, just like she'd been warned. The second night, the peak phase—a code name for the most intense night—would and had undoubtedly been the worst. She could therefore look forward to this humiliating reality effectively stealing twelve days a year from her life.

Knowing all of this didn't help. Nor would it keep her from going completely out of her mind in the future like she just had. That was the scary part. Being so out of control. She hated being held hostage to some gender-based biophenomena that felt like a biological defect.

There was still so much she had to learn about the Shadow life. In fact, one day she really wanted to know who Doc had gotten the sample from—which Shadow Wolf in the pack or the clan had supplied the donor cells to fuse with her mother's ova to give her the spark of life. She'd been so blown away by the whole concept that the details had escaped her, but the more she thought about

it, the more questions battered their way to the forefront
of her mind. Lying here next to Hunter made her want to
know all now. There was a genetic link to her within the
clan, but then that would also mean a familial link, too.
What was that old saying, one of Xavier Holland's many
adages . . . if it didn't kill you it would make you stronger?

Stronger, hell! Sasha blew a damp curl up off her forehead in exasperation. If she could live exclusively in a
Shadow pack or clan, then there'd be no problem. But she
had to make moonlight madness and quarterly heats work
in the context of the U.S. Military. Oh yeah, this would go
over big in a Black Ops Comm. Not!

Hunter stirred and she tensed, not trusting herself. Soon
his lazy strokes up and down her back made her wary.
Truly, his touch should have been comforting, a steady,
easy rhythm that asked for nothing more than a lover's
connection through an absently delivered caress. For chris-
sakes, the man was still asleep and his hand trailing up and
down her back was practically a blind reflex. However, reverse logic was in full effect.

The fact that his touch now felt like a hot stone mas-
sage and his warm, hard body had been heaven on earth
was freaking her out. It was as though the higher the
moon rose, the less control she'd had. She wondered if
her brain had fried in her skull or just gave up and melted,
then ran out of her ear—because none of this made any
kind of sense. Worse yet, the whole encounter made her
realize just how intensely she'd needed all of what Hunter
provided to function as a balanced unit. Everyone, even
he, had declared her his mate—and she hadn't decided.
That was like getting married, in wolf culture, and the
prospect of such permanence completey freaked her out.

To be someone's mate was a commitment. It said that he needed her; she needed him. All of her life she'd been a loner of sorts, and now there was this very big thing happening so fast that there was almost no time to even think about it. Nature and duty were one, citing the way of the wolf. Family, the pack, the clan fused with that duty. It was a duality, the way of the wolf . . . the way of natural order among this species. Maybe humans didn't have that same issue, but Shadows sure did. And in a world dominated by humans, this was a brand-new problem.

Sasha let her palms slowly trace the hard bricks in Hunter's abdomen and then let her fingertips gently glide against the dark mahogany skin that was stretched tightly over muscle and bone. Never before in her life had she *needed* someone else to function. The concept was anathema. It went against everything she'd been taught and trained to deal with. Yes, you went in as a team, you didn't leave your own . . . but if they died during the mission, there was no room for emotion until the mission was complete. And given the nature of most of her missions, she was a solo act. But now, damn . . .

"What's wrong, baby?" Hunter murmured without opening his eyes. He nuzzled her hair and pulled the comforter tighter around them both.

"Nothing," she said in a near whisper. "And everything," she added after a pause.

"I could tell by your breathing . . . then your body got tight." He kissed her temple. "What's the *everything*?"

She let her breath out hard and kissed the center of his chest long and slow, thinking. "How can I go back to the base with this weakness that will happen once a quarter? It's accepted in Shadow culture as just a norm, but in our culture . . . the human culture I was raised in, work in . . ."

"You talk as if you're not one of us," he said in a low, sleepy rumble, his tone holding no judgment.

"That's not what I meant," she said, tracing the stone ridges of his chest with her fingertips and speaking against his neck. "I'm just getting used to being a Shadow—just found out that I was . . . it's a little more than I bargained for and it's taking a while for me to switch up the lingo."

She could feel him smile as his face moved against her temple.

"I'll teach you," he murmured in a warm rush of air and pulled her closer, beginning to wake up.

"No, no, be serious," she said, squirming in his hold. "I'm trying to process what just happened here."

"I am serious," he said in a low chuckle that rumbled through his body. "I'll help you process every . . . delicious . . . data point."

"Hunter, listen to me. I never had good intel about who or what I was going in, and didn't know my body would react like this. . . . Imagine, after all the years you've been alive, suddenly finding out you had some undetonated explosive in your system like this, that only started ticking once you got around your own species." She shook her head. "Absolutely mind-blowing, and I don't know how to integrate this with what used to be my former, more orderly life."

Amazingly his grip loosened and the playfulness went out of his tone.

"I do know what it's like to have a time bomb in your system, Sasha," he said quietly, no longer seeking her mouth but seeking her gaze. "I just hope I haven't passed that to you."

"We're going to beat this thing, find a way to be sure it's totally gone or made dormant, something."

He touched her face. "Do you realize that this is the first time you've ever really incorporated the word *we* into thinking about the future us?"

They stared at each other between blue-white panels of moonlight that came through the window. She touched his face, tracing the high ridge of his Native American cheekbones, marveling at the fusion of cultures that also gave him a strong African nose and lush Haitian mouth and coloring.

"I was always a lone soldier and never knew how to do 'we,' Hunter. Not sure that I know how to now . . . but you make me want to. It's not the weakness caused by the heat. It's you."

She watched him briefly close his eyes and take in a deep breath through his nose. She'd stopped breathing, never having left her emotions so wide open and exposed before.

"Your heat is not considered a female weakness, like human males so foolishly view the human female menses," he said quietly, as he allowed the pad of his thumb to trace her bottom lip. He shook his head no, his eyes never leaving hers. "Nor is it a curse or any other ridiculous term. To think such is antithetical to our culture. That is what I cannot begin to process. What you've just experienced we consider a time when you step into the full ripeness of your female energy. If anything, the weakness that is inspired is within our gender . . . when a male Shadow is rendered completely and totally devastated."

He took her mouth slowly and deeply and then pulled away so he could stare into her eyes. "Sasha, don't you understand yet . . . that when you have finally chosen me as your mate, and have opened your heart to be vulnerable to me at your strongest time of passion, that is when you'll completely consume me? And as I wait for you to decide, what else am I now but yours?"

As he kissed her again, it was his turn to freak out. He'd gone into this union a freestanding warrior and come out of it her soldier. As her satiny heat blanketed him, her body welding to his, he knew that there was nothing he wouldn't do for her, short of death. Yes, even that—he'd take a silver bullet, risk clan retaliation if he had to eliminate infected pack members, regardless of the politics. He'd protect her from her own military, if they ever turned on her, and would protect her heart from any abuse this wicked world might try to foist upon her.

She scorched his mind as her moist heat soaked into his skin and bones like a warm rain. Keeping her heart safe meant that her family was his family, because they were embedded in her spirit. Woods, Fisher, Doc, all she had to do was tell him the names of those to protect and he'd bring the way of the wolf to shadow them. On her command he'd become like a dark, unseen angel of the night for them, for her, anything she asked.

Her heat was his weakness, didn't she know . . . but it was also more than that, so much more. It was the agony in her eyes as she'd held a weapon on him and didn't take the shot. It was the way she had a prayer burning in her irises that she wouldn't have to pull the trigger. It was the way she'd fought side by side with him, then against him, as well as the respect she gave his grandfather . . . along with the unspoken protection she'd lent to an elderly man without stealing his dignity. It was so many things about her that fused in a single baritone moan as she joined their bodies.

It was impossible to process any of it. There was just simply no sorting it out right now.

Try as he might, he couldn't break free. The chains and leather straps didn't allow for even the slightest movement. A muzzle had been placed over his mouth; bright, glaring lights chased away all shadows, thus any place safe to slip into and disappear.

Something was stinging or pinching the soft flesh in the crease of his arm; his head pounded from the blow he'd received. Crow Shadow glanced at his arms, panic making him thrash against his restraints anew.

Thick, plastic tubes filled with a crimson substance that he knew to be his own blood leaked life out of his body. Growls filled his throat, but with his mouth sealed shut there was no way to voice his complaint. Spewing curses was futile, he needed answers! Since when did Vampires begin drinking Shadow Wolf blood? He didn't understand; his eyes followed the very nonchalant entities that monitored his progress. Would they suck him dry and leave him a pale husk, or keep him alive to torture in some sick game?

Weak from significant blood loss and a concussion, for now all he could do was watch them fill small test tubes with what leaked from his veins. At least they hadn't put their foul mouths on him and bitten him.

A second-floor window opened before Woods had taken two steps away from the rental car. Fisher cocked his weapon, but a familiar female voice called out a split-second response.

"Drop it."

"Clarissa?" Woods yelled as Fisher pulled back.

"You're gonna have to do better than that," a familiar male voice shouted.

"Yo, Winters, hit us with holy water, garlic, whatever as long as it's not silver bullets, dude."

"Where's Fisher?" Bradley called out. "You know the protocol on a nighttime sanctuary request."

Fisher begrudgingly nodded and came out of hiding from behind the car. He opened both arms, weapon dangling from one finger, and walked up the front steps. Both he and Woods cringed as a bucket of water doused them from the second-floor window.

"All clear!" Clarissa yelled after thirty seconds.

The front door opened after a brief pause. Winters peeked out with a toothy grin.

"Sorry, guys. This was the best decontamination process we could rig up outside of the lab."

Lion Shadow looked around the gathering of pack alphas and the hair began to prickle on the back of his neck, although he wasn't sure why. Several of the other Shadows had the same reaction, he noticed, and he began to study their entourages with great care. The hunting party had agreed to stay close, to stay in communication, but several members were missing. All betas. Too many at the same time to not be noticed. Something was definitely wrong.

"Hey, Doc," the MP said as Xavier Holland stopped at the main guard checkpoint. "I see they have you running back and forth tonight," he added, making pleasant small talk.

"Yes, Joe, I have been running around like a chicken with my head cut off," Doc said calmly, trying to force his voice to remain upbeat. He smiled a tense smile. "But at my age I'm starting to forget where I'm supposed to be when. Just for the record, what time was it when I pulled in earlier—I know there was something else I was supposed to do, but for the life of me . . ."

"No problem, Doc," the younger man said, his eyes holding a combination of amusement and empathy. "It was around twenty-one-hundred hours, sir. I hope that helps?"

"Ah, perfect," Doc said with a forced chuckle. "Thank you, son."

He kept driving and immediately called the lab security phones in a panic. As soon as the line picked up he began reciting the Twenty-third Psalm. The MP on the line recited The Lord's Prayer, and only then did Doc slump back against his seat in relief.

"There was an attempted breach," he told the guard. "Around twenty-one-hundred an entity body-doubling as me tried to get into the lab. It may still be on the premises. Take all precautions."

Francois shook his head. "Ah, they have learned. We got past the entrance guards easily enough, but once in the tunnels we could go no farther. They'd created a holy water mist system with UV lights leading to the labs that would eviscerate one of us—not to mention, the garlic oil they'd sprayed in there was wicked enough to gag Dracula himself!"

Etienne sighed and waved his hand. "Such a nuisance, but this is perhaps what I so love about the humans. They are adaptable and keep the challenge generous."

"But it would have been so much more potent with antitoxin added to it." Francois fingered a plastic bag of

Crow Shadow's blood and released an annoyed sigh. "I would have so enjoyed seeing the expression on that arrogant bastard's face. I am not finished with Dexter, to be sure."

"Nor I." A sly smile creased the corners of Etienne's mouth. "But patience, patience . . . there is still more than enough time to redress the slight. Everything in this world is about auspicious timing, *n'est-ce pas*?"

Nausea made Clarissa hold on to the edge of a desk. "We've got to get out of here," she said, staving off the dry heaves.

"What, are you nuts?" Fisher said, glancing around at Woods, Winters, and Bradley. "It's the dead of night. Trudeau said to stay put."

"If we don't move quickly, they'll find us here. Werewolves. They're on the move from a cemetery less than a mile from here—you accidentally led them. For some reason they're seeing you. I don't know why."

Woods and Fisher looked at each other.

"I thought only Shadow Wolves could pick up familiars?" Woods said, his horrified gaze ripping to each face in the room. "Clarissa, before we risk going out in the night without cover in Vampire and Werewolf country, make real sure you're picking up Werewolf and not Shadow Wolf, all right?"

Clarissa's eyes held the same question that Bradley's and Winters's eyes held. "What the hell is a Shadow Wolf?"

Fisher slapped his forehead and began walking in a tight circle.

"You said familiars, like a witch's confidant?" Bradley

rushed over to an open table and extracted rune stones from his pocket, then quickly flung them down.

"Oh, just *screw me!*" Woods said, his voice escalating with his panic. "No! Didn't Trudeau give you intel yet about the nature of this mission, and the rest of it?"

"No, but the stones say Clarissa is right." Bradley looked up from his quick divination and began grabbing artillery.

"Hey, guys, I don't know about stones or visions, but radar is picking up something large, moving fast—many things, actually. Now would be a good time for somebody to pull that MLRS out and load that puppy up!" Winters backed away from the table and began to assist Woods and Fisher.

"Gimme coordinates, Bradley—tell me where to point it, Rissa," Woods said as he and Fisher rolled the unit that was pitched on a dolly toward the window.

Fisher whipped out a digital compass as Clarissa barked directional information, and positioned the multiple launch rocket system to target the center of the fast moving mass.

"Are you guys insane?" Bradley yelled, his eyes wild. "You can't fire that in a residential area!"

"Yo, yo, yo—not to mention it'll take off half the roof," Winters added, terror making his voice raw.

"It's gonna hit the graveyard," Woods said, not missing a beat. "May God rest in peace whatever's in there."

"Take off half the roof or let what's coming take off half your face—quick decision, folks," Fisher said.

One second went by and Woods made the decision. "I thought so," he said, and then set off silver rounds that exploded out of the northwestern section of the roof and sounded like bazooka tracers.

Clarissa, Winters, and Bradley hit the floor, covering their heads from falling cinders. Fisher grabbed a fire extinguisher and foamed anything with an ember glow.

"Good! Now we've got a hole," Fisher said, nodding toward Woods. "Your call, Lieutenant."

"Winters, what's up on radar? In about ten seconds you should be able to see nothing moving."

Winters scrambled up on his feet and checked the radar systems. But before he could speak, it sounded like the Fourth of July outside.

"Oh, shit!" Bradley yelled and was up on his feet. "Now local authorities will be—"

"No they won't," Woods said, picking up an M-16 and checking to be sure the magazine had silver shells. "Not if you guys get up on the roof and tack down a tarp over the hole. Then this building will look like any other dilapidated, half-repaired, work-in-progress structure in the ward. The locals will take days to go house-to-house to figure out the exact trajectory of that artillery." He turned to Clarissa. "You all stay armed, me and Fisher have gotta draw whatever made it out of the graveyard away from you."

"Roger that," Fisher said, adding grenades to his arsenal.

"You guys don't have to do that," Winters said, glancing from his screen to the two soldiers. "A big section of the mass stopped moving . . . then it looks like small splinters of it broke off and are going deeper into the neighborhoods away from us . . . heading for the Lake Pontchartrain swamplands, and some of them are headed southwest toward the Terrebonne bayou area."

Woods nodded but he and Fisher didn't lay down their arms. "Get a tarp up on that roof to camouflage the artillery hole while me and Fisher walk point, just to be on the safe side."

Sasha opened her eyes at the same time Hunter did. They both got up quickly, the haze of sleep instantly vanishing as they rushed into the shower, and were in and out in three minutes. Dressed, armed, they met Silver Hawk on the path to the truck.

"I did not want to intrude, but I sense there's been an incident," the older man said, looking at them without blinking.

Sasha and Hunter nodded.

"We know," Hunter said. "Yeah . . . we know."

Chapter 14

"We never really got to say how glad we were that you guys made it home okay," Clarissa said once Woods and Fisher had slipped back into the building.

"Then and now, dude," Winters said, giving Woods and Fisher a fist pound.

Bradley nodded. "We went to your memorial services on the base. Seeing you show up here freaked everybody out. . . . We didn't know what to think. But we appreciate everything you did."

Woods dragged his fingers through his disheveled hair. "Can't say we blame you." His eyes held a level of fatigue that went beyond battle weary. "You can train all your life, drill a situation a thousand times, but until you see it up close and personal, it's all brand spanking new. None of this fits into what I'd call normal."

"You got that right," Fisher said quietly. "You know how they ran us through all those simulations?" He let out a little snort and leaned against the wall. "That was all bullshit compared to the real McCoy. Let a real one of those suckers charge you and you'll piss your pants before you lift your weapon—I guarantee you."

"That's why we're thanking you," Clarissa said quietly.

"We were all freaked out just seeing incoming on the radar. We never even saw what it was." She looked around the group, her gaze landing on Fisher and then Woods. "Because you're willing to put it all on the line, you're essentially giving us the luxury of staying in the house, in the lab, doing our jobs, and living our lives out of harm's way. There aren't enough thank-yous for that."

"Never stated so eloquently or so true," Bradley said.

Winters let out a hard sigh. "Yeah . . . we owe you big time. But for now all we can say is thanks, dudes."

Fisher and Woods nodded and then studied the floor.

"We've gotta move out," Woods said slowly and quietly, bringing his gaze back up to the group. "Never seen so many of them charging at one time. They tell us that the demon-infected ones are solitary predators, and if they're moving in wolf packs, something is very, very wrong. We're sitting ducks in this house."

Fisher glanced around. "There's a lotta artillery to move, man. Can't leave this for the local-yokels to get their hands on. God forbid we let a military-issue MLRS or bazookas fall into the hands of neighborhood kids, drug dealers, and what have you."

"We've gotta call into HQ anyway and let them know we've had an artillery incident. They can send in the cleanup guys and spin doctors to feed the general public some bull about it being lightning that struck a house and nearby cemetery, ya know?" Winters's line of vision raced around the group and then he hesitated as he saw a mixture of emotions in Woods's and Fisher's expressions. "What?"

"They think we're dead," Woods said flatly.

"Who?" Again, Winters's face held confusion. "The brass?"

"Yeah, the brass," Fisher said and spat on the floor. "So, if we've gotta call in, the only person we give intel to on a secured line is Doc—Trudeau rolls like that, too."

"Whoa, whoa, whoa! I thought they knew you guys were really alive, had the phony memorial funeral services, that is, we thought all that once you guys passed muster, because it was some kinda top secret—"

"No, Winters," Woods said, staring at him. "Doc Holland saved our asses. The brass tried to exterminate us like they did the rest of the squad." He walked away, his voice tight and trembling with rage and hurt from the betrayal. "They thought we were infected, but we weren't! Only Captain Butler was!"

Fisher rubbed the back of his neck, his eyes hard. "Doc is the only one, other than Sasha and I guess you guys now, from inside that I trust. Woodsey told it to you straight. We were out there in the fucking Afghan mountains supposedly on a mission to look for a terrorist threat—when really they'd set our squad up to see what would happen with a trained team under live Werewolf situation def con. Cocksuckers watched it on satellite, is my bet, and then when Woodsey pushed me to safety and called in, they sent a conveniently close Black Hawk chopper in that napalmed our squad."

"Friendly fire," Woods said with a brittle chuckle. "Let it go, man, or it'll eat you alive like the Werewolves."

Tears filled Fisher's eyes and then spilled, causing him to turn away. "Gave my whole life to them. I believed! Then they did us like this? Even messed with our DNA? Our whole lives have been a lie, man. It was fucked up!"

"It was," Winters said with disgust. "We didn't know. None of us did. Probably not even Doc. And I *know* Trudeau didn't." His eyes wild, he looked around at

Bradley and Clarissa. "And I also know that nobody in here knows what you're talking about as far as them screwing with your DNA. All I do know is, we're not the enemy, and we have your back. We saw you guys do some real Superman shit just now and seriously appreciate it."

"If it's any consolation to you gentlemen, the general that ordered the mission, our own Donald Wilkerson, got his face literally ripped off by some supernaturals . . . and that's why they've finally given Trudeau her own budget and staff. She was the only one who seemed to know how to track down and eliminate the threat." Bradley glanced around the group.

"Yeah," Woods said with no small measure of pride in his voice. "That's our girl. Her and Hunter, Remind us to fill you in on this new category of supernaturals that's on our side that even the brass doesn't know about. You don't want to screw up and accidentally hit one of them in a firefight, because they might just save your ass. They're not Werewolves, far from it."

Fisher shook his head. "We'll tell you all about it, how to spot the differences in a Shadow Wolf on the move versus a Werewolf. You only have a split second to know, hold your fire, or blow its head off when it comes from outta nowhere, so you've gotta learn it cold while we wait for Trudeau and Hunter to rendezvous with us."

"This intel has gotta stay here, though," Woods said, his gaze steady like his voice. "You slip up and notify the brass before Trudeau is ready to reveal what she needs to, and you'll have us all strapped to a fucking lab table with mad scientists running tests."

"As far as I'm concerned, I don't work for the government, I work for Trudeau, Doc, and my conscience— which is this band of brothers and a sister right here,"

Bradley said, his eyes on Woods and Fisher. "After what I've heard, and from what I figured out before, I know to the powers that be I'm just an insignificant cog in the wheel, thus cannon fodder as far as the big boys in Washington are concerned . . . so . . ."

"Hey, you ain't gotta tell me twice. Trudeau saved my ass," Winters said. "Long story short, I got duped by a Vampire and she let it slide, covered for me so I didn't get life for accessory to a base breach . . . that really wasn't my fault."

"I saw how they disrespected me and Doc's work," Clarissa said in a quiet, bitter tone. "Saw how they would go against his reports and his advice until they had a debacle on their hands—then they wanted to blame that man. I saw the real tears in his eyes for the ones that didn't make it at the memorial services and felt the knots in his soul. You don't have to worry about me. Ever."

Clarissa folded her meaty arms over her ample chest and lifted her chin. "Me, Winters, Bradley were all saved by Doc from the experiments they were doing in the paranormal phenomena field during the early days. I had second sight and Bradley had innate knowledge of all things magical . . . Winters, poor kid, could make anything electrical work with kinesis. None of us wants to be one of their research monkeys."

Fisher nodded and drew in a shuddering breath. "That's good to know because it's real fucked up not having a family anymore, not being a part of anything bigger than you. Like, not having a soul you can trust is real shitty. Even in prison they've got gang family, ya know? I thought the military was mine for life."

Clarissa covered her mouth with her hand slowly and went to Fisher. She touched his back with a gentle palm. "We won't turn on you, Jim. I swear, we've got your back."

He allowed her to pull him into a careful embrace, and slowly but surely relaxed enough to exhale and lower his head to her shoulder. Two big tears rolled down the bridge of Fisher's nose as he closed his eyes and simply soaked in Clarissa's compassion. For what seemed like a long while, no one said a word. It was as though they all knew that two left-for-dead soldiers needed to heal; their bodies had survived, so had their minds, but their hearts and spirits had taken near-mortal rounds.

Finally Fisher let her go and wiped his face. Woods lifted his chin from where he stood across the room and swallowed hard, but everything in his rigid posture told her not to go to him in front of the team. One hug, one gentle caress and he'd shatter—and for the sake of his dignity it was clear that he preferred not to have that happen. She agreed with her eyes, told him with a glance that when he was ready to heal, ready to weep in her hair, he could. His response was a brief nod of thanks. In this small squad he was the alpha male and couldn't afford a show of weakness while danger was still on the move. They all seemed to understand and quietly appreciate that.

Sasha took the cell phone that Silver Hawk handed her as Hunter drove. Doc, no doubt, was losing his mind if he'd caught wind of these serious vibrations. Yet in her core she felt a distress signal from her men and the team, as well as, oddly, Crow Shadow—whom she thought was dead.

Maybe it was simply residual impressions coming to the fore, but the bleating worry that pierced her mind refused to allow her to dismiss any of it. On the second ring, Doc picked up. Just hearing his voice melted her bones.

"It's me," Sasha said. "Where are you? Are you all right?"

"I am and have the same question. Are you at the contact point yet?" Doc asked quickly.

Sasha closed her eyes. "No. I got delayed."

"Good," Doc shot back quickly. "The zone is hot. I'm moving the location."

"What happened?" Sasha held her breath. "Did we lose anybody?"

"No, but I'm going to have to send in a cleanup team, media adjustments. There was an attempted attack originating in a cemetery that required an MLRS launch."

"Oh, shit . . ."

Hunter nearly drove off the road and had to refocus on the task at hand. Silver Hawk was staring down her throat.

"Precisely. I'll send new coordinates. Will have to give the brass something to go on. French Quarter," Doc said succinctly, his tone efficient and crisp. "Vampires are involved again. Tried to breach the base, so I did have to send that up the food chain. You look alive and stay alive, Trudeau—you hear me?"

"You too, Doc." She clutched the receiver. It was all she could do not to tell the old man how much she loved him.

"Debrief," Hunter said, glancing at her as he barreled the Dodge RAM down the road.

"We've got a hot situation in New Orleans. Something attacked the safe house—or was about to, when the guys fired off serious ballistics that backed it up." Sasha's gaze ping-ponged between Hunter and his grandfather. "If they fired off an MLRS in a residential zone, two things: one, it had to be demon-infected incoming; two, it had to be an insane level of threat for trained men to go there among civilians. The other issue is Vampires are involved."

Silver Hawk nodded. "Then my instincts back at the lodge were not wrong."

"No, sir," Sasha said, anger making her voice brittle. "They tried to breach the base, probably get back into the lab. Apparently there's still something there they want— and the only thing I can think of that's in any kind of supply is infected-Werewolf virus antitoxin . . . since the first break-in all but depleted any supplies of the werewolf virus itself."

"The part that makes no sense to me is why would Vampires help those who stole the toxin?" Hunter raked his fingers through his hair, now just holding the wheel with one hand. "After Dexter, Guilliaume, and Fox Shadow double-crossed them before, why would they again partner with them?"

"I don't know," Sasha said quietly, her voice trailing off in deep thought. "You're right, it just doesn't make sense."

Silver Hawk's quiet tone drew their attention and then imploded in their minds like a sonic boom. "It makes perfect sense, if you wanted to start a war."

"We've got ten betas missing, at least one from every pack," Lion Shadow said, glancing around at his alpha Shadow brothers.

Bear Shadow's eyes roved the group. "My pack brother Crow Shadow should have met up with us by now. He took the familiars to their drop-off point where they were able to get the last flight out, and then he was to drive in as far as he could before going on foot to meet us here."

"Hunter was headed toward the lodge. I think we should go there, convene as a clan—something isn't right," a voice called out from the large gathering.

A series of howls cut through the air and the group stood slowly, each member helping to douse the large campfire. Then all fell eerily silent as a whiff of an enemy scent flitted through the night air. A twig snapped. Twenty-five shotguns lifted in reaction to the sound. Just that quickly, all hell broke loose.

Out of the stand of trees fifty yards out, massive demon-wolf bodies hurtled forward. Shadow Wolves still in human form fired dead-aim shots and then took cover, but the crazed beasts anticipated their moves and dodged in and out of demon doors, avoiding direct mortal hits. Even in the darkness and mayhem, familiar pack eyes met the eyes of beasts. The psychological destruction of seeing one's father, cousin, brother, friend transformed into the unthinkable took a devastating toll during the melee.

Shots that connected with foul creatures blew off body parts to begin an agonizing death. Demon-wolf retaliation was just as swift in gruesome savaging.

Arms, legs, torsos, and skulls littered the small snow-covered clearing that had become splattered with gore. Instant family recognition often paralyzed the shooter just long enough to commit his life to another charging beast. Complete chaos took over the hunting party ranks, as Lion Shadow's voice barked out the command to hold the line. Those with spent artillery shape-shifted and charged the much larger beasts, immediately losing their throats to the struggle.

"Fall back!" Lion Shadow shouted, watching in horror as demon-infected wolves didn't just kill Shadow Wolves but began eating from the bodies left on the battlefield.

There was no way his mind could make sense of what his eyes witnessed. His Shadows needed to regroup. They had never been attacked full-scale like this with so many beasts at once. Always it was only one beast, at most two—two being legendary . . . the time when Hunter's mother was killed. But they'd never fought in a coordinated effort like a Shadow pack. They had never been of their own kind.

Winded, wounded, but still standing, a snarl filled Lion Shadow's throat as he looked around at the ragged warriors that remained. Of twenty-five good men and women with some honorable betas who'd joined the fray, he now had only fifteen that would possibly live to see sunrise. This plague had somehow come from within their own ranks. What else could explain such an abomination? Not all those that changed could have tried Dexter's drug. Many of whom had become beasts were above reproach. This had to be forced from involuntary contagion. The beasts had to come from the lodge . . . from the only one among them that had carried the disease in his very DNA for a long time. *Hunter.* Why else would he have wanted to go forward into this level of danger alone?

Dexter leaned both clawed hands on his knees, bending over and breathing hard. He looked around the shadowed bayou at his remaining pack, seething with rage. "Familiars. Only familiars would have picked us up, just like we homed to them."

Growls rumbled from the nine wolves that surrounded him.

"I thought you said there was Shadow blood in that house," a tall, matted demon with a patchy silver and black coat complained, saliva dripping from his massive jaws as he spoke.

Dexter's gaze narrowed on him. "I smelled it, we all did."

"Don Juan, you scented it like the rest of us," a dark-eyed female snarled.

The tall wolf lunged at her and she met the charge, both wolves colliding in the air, jaws locked in a death match.

"We've already lost eleven of our kind!" Dexter shouted, reaching in with a steel grip to pull the combatants apart, and flung them to the ground with a yelp. "This dissension in the ranks is what keeps original demon-wolves weak. The infected Werewolves do not work together like Shadow packs, but we have the best of both worlds. Until we find out how many of us made it to Terrebonne, we cannot have this!"

Snarls were the response, but the combatants went to neutral corners in the swamps nonetheless.

"Get back to the blood," the beast nicknamed Don Juan growled. "Being stronger is only an advantage if you can control your shifts."

All eyes were on Dexter, narrowed to glowing distrustful slits that threatened a mutiny.

"I, for one, did not sneak away from my husband to live in the godforsaken bayou like an animal," the female growled. "I thought you had an ironclad deal with the Vampires—one that would allow us an endless supply of the drug that we could sell to foolish humans to make us filthy rich. Plus, a way to come down from this . . . this . . . high, for lack of a better word."

Dexter lowered his head in pre-attack mode, his voice a threatening rumble. "Barbara . . . *you bitch*," he said between his teeth. "You left your husband for this, first, the money second, so let's not play games and get brand-new," he said, clutching his groin.

"Personally, I don't give a damn why she left," another wolf growled, stepping out from behind dense bayou foliage. "We need the Shadow blood on tap to control the infected-Werewolf shifts now that this shit is in our systems. Without that, we're no better than them . . . no smarter—each shift I can feel myself losing the ability to think, to speak while wolf." He glanced around the group, gaining subtle nods of approval. "And the money is something we definitely need to discuss."

Growing bolder, the challenger stepped closer. "I think you got your dumb ass set up, Dex. Maybe the Vamps hit the trail with Shadow blood and we got flat-blasted by running up on a paranormal military installation?" He smiled, seeming to enjoy Dexter's momentary loss of control of the group, and turned to look at the other wolves with a shrug.

In a flash Dexter was on him and had separated the much smaller wolf's head from his shoulders with the help of both jaws and claws. "Or maybe your dumb ass just lost your head for overthinking some bullshit I already thought of?" Dexter shrugged, looking down at the twitching body and mimicking the dead wolf's smug expression. He scanned the group with a deadly stare. "Who knows? Maybe that's what happened?"

"Lovely outcome, don't you think?" Francois waved his handkerchief in the direction of the demon-infected Shadow Wolf pack with disdain, hovering inches above the swamp's muddy floor. "It's so much easier to have them kill each other off and do the work themselves than for us to sully ourselves with the effort."

Etienne smiled and then peered around the dank environment with a bored scowl. "Now it is just a matter of getting the true Werewolves to stop being little bitches and to surface."

"Perhaps we could encourage them without raising Napoleon and half of the French army."

"You are so wicked, *mon ami*. Let Napoleon rest. There are ways to help encourage our frightened friends to open their demon doors."

Francois drew back and placed two pale fingers against his plump, red pout. "*Non* . . . you have not considered . . ."

"*Oui*. The play is already in motion. They will have little choice but to retaliate once they sense a breach." Etienne sighed with a chuckle. "Come, Francois, let us return to the French Quarter. This is no place for true gentlemen."

Chapter 15

The carnage that met them at the nearest pack outpost was so devastating that for a moment, as Hunter rolled the truck to a slow stop, no one moved.

What had once doubled as a Native American trail and tour service now looked like a butcher shop. Blood splattered the windows of the small cabin and gift shop. There was clearly no need to look for survivors. The guts of the chopper that would have been their way out were strewn across the ground, along with truck engine parts, metal, and glass. Hunks of flesh and claw marks in the crimson snow made Sasha want to vomit. Some poor soul had been dragged away to his or her death in a bloodied smear. The fact that there were no bodies is what she was sure caused Hunter and Silver Hawk the greatest pain; the missing gore pointed to one inescapable fact—those who'd been killed here were eaten.

"We're gonna have to split up. It's the only way," Sasha stated flatly as the threesome piled out of the truck. "I have to get ahead of this nightmare and make sure my human team in New Orleans is properly fortified. You gentlemen have to alert the pack as well as the rest of the clan. There's no way to cover that much ground, that fast."

She tried not to look at Hunter while they all surveyed

the devastation, even though she could feel his stare boring into her. Basic instinct told her that he had to be thinking the same thing that lacerated her conscience—if they'd been on point, could this massacre, like the others, have been avoided?

Survivor's guilt was eating its way through her skin like acid. The horror and the frustration of not being able to have been there to help defend a small outpost felt like it swept over her in hot, roiling waves. It was the kind of thing that ironically Doc had told her would make soldiers take unnecessary risks. Despite his words and all the psychological training she'd endured, nothing had prepared her for this feeling—even though she'd repeatedly told herself there was a fine line between heroism and suicide.

But who was she to judge Hunter? She never could seem to find that line for herself, and on the rare occasion when she had, she never knew which side of it to stand on, anyway . . . so what could she say to Hunter, in all truth? Telling him that it wasn't his fault was an act of futility. She glimpsed his profile and could see by the hard set of his eyes and jaw that he was absorbing into his consciousness every last scream that had echoed here.

She noted that Silver Hawk saw that in Hunter, too. They shared a glimpse, his aged eyes holding hers for just a few seconds before going back to the gory scene around them. There was no judgment in his glance, just deep concern and compassion. Yet, as wise as Silver Hawk was, the old man also seemed at a loss for what to say.

Sad reality was that this shit could've happened while they'd gone to make an ammo run, ate at the diner with Silver Hawk, or when they were possibly battling for their own lives at the lodge.

"There is another way and you know it," Hunter said

after a while, his comment finally making Sasha and his grandfather look at him. He folded his arms over his chest, his gaze intense, as though the decision was final just like his assessment of the area was.

"Too risky," Sasha said, shaking her head. "Not after what we've seen out here."

"I agree," Hunter said, digging in, his voice near a low growl. "There is no way in the world you can take the Shadow pathways that are just fractions of energy away from demon doors and not expect what's in there to not make a grab for you, especially in—"

"If you say in 'your condition,' man, I swear we'll do fisticuffs out here," she snapped. "You got a better plan? I was talking about it being too risky for you, not me. You can't go through those pathways without incident, either, in *your condition*, but your situation is much more volatile than mine. You going is suicide. Not now, not with a fresh purge—and the last thing we need is for you to come out the other end of a pathway as the same damned thing that ate pack members!"

Sasha paced away, thoroughly frustrated. How in the hell else were they going to get out of the mountains and to their people in time?

True, Hunter had a point, an excellent one at that. No, she didn't want to be chased, possibly trapped, and gang-banged, then killed by a slobbering pack of demon-infected Shadow Wolves or Werewolves. But she also didn't want to be trapped between dimensions with her man, unable to help him as the raw energy from the wrong side slowly transformed him, and then have to shoot him on sight as soon as they exited near family and friends. No.

"And I take it that a cell phone call is simply out of the question," she said in a sarcastic tone that she regretted.

"It is not the way of the wolf," Silver Hawk said, lifting his chin, slightly indignant.

Sasha raised one hand. "I know, I know—case of bad nerves making me say stupid things. But at some point, we're going to have to bring state of the art technology up here in these mountains." She looked at both men hard. "I'm serious. We have a new threat, one that hasn't ever been seen—therefore, some of the old ways just won't work in fighting this new type of beast. It's not either-or; rather, it's a both-and strategy. Both new technology and the old ways."

Seeming somewhat mollified by her compromise, Silver Hawk nodded. "Both-and is an acceptable meeting in the middle."

Sasha resisted blowing a curl up off her forehead in exasperation. It would have been disrespectful to the old man. Note to self: Get gear up in the mountains next mission or next chance they got, assuming they lived.

"I'm going in," Hunter announced as his gaze roved over the bloodied landscape one last time. "If they've been in a firefight, survivors will home toward the lodge for more ammunition and supplies." He turned on his heels and headed for the truck, then jumped up into the back flatbed to select a pump shotgun and some shells.

"And if you come out at the lodge a drooling demon?" Sasha yelled, unable to contain her frustration. "Then what?"

"Give me the amulet," Silver Hawk said, walking forward with an outstretched hand. "I will go. It is too uncertain for you."

"I love you, Pop," Hunter said, and took a running leap over the hood of the cab and was gone.

"I'll just be damned!" Sasha yelled. "Of all the pighcadcd, stupid, completely reckless things I've ever seen!" She was at the side of the truck in seconds, making Silver Hawk miss her when he reached out in an attempt to stop her.

"Don't repeat his mistake, daughter! It wasn't your fault. This happened earlier—look at the tracks!" Silver Hawk shouted as she grabbed a shotgun, several grenades, and a fistful of shells, his eyes holding clearly visible fear for the very first time. "Do not sacrifice yourself for a dishonor neither of you committed."

But it was too late. Hc only got to address her back as she disappeared through a Shadow path.

Again, Hunter hadn't lied. The Shadow pathway pulled her into a moonlit, hazy dimension that had the strange reek of demon-wolf scent in it that shouldn't have been there. She immediately began loading shells. Something was really, *really* wrong. Normally the demons couldn't cross into the Shadow lands. Either something had thinned the energy between demon doors and where she stood, or worse, that meant the Shadow Wolves that had been infected could stitl use the old pathways—which meant they could probably walk in both realms now. Not a good thing, to be sure.

With the Shadow lands infiltrated by cannibalistic creatures, hell, that was no better than landing smack-dab in the middle of a demon-door hot zone. But what if the other possibility panned out to be true; that the Shadow Wolves gone Were-demon had something to do with the merging of the energies between demon doors and Shadow pathways?

Sasha shook off the chilling thought. She couldn't speculate about that now. She had to pray that demon-infected

Werewolves still couldn't slip across the dimensional border. Anything abnormal that she encountered would have to be exterminated simply as a biohazard to the super-highway the Shadows used. Right now, though, she had to concentrate on remembering how to draw up her energy and jettison herself through the path to come out at where she knew Hunter would go to warn the packs—the lodge.

No sooner than she began to get her bearings a low growl drew her weapon up. It became immediately apparent that it wasn't one snarl but many. Not waiting to learn more, she pulled the pin on a grenade, lobbed it toward the sound, flung three more toward the first one, and spun on the hurling explosives to blow them midair with a shotgun shell as several dark Werewolf forms lunged.

The impact blew her onto her back, but she never dropped the shotgun. She was a sliding blur that came out at the lodge, shotgun in one hand, forearm shielding her face from debris and demon splatter, amulet swinging. Thick thuds of nasty wet flesh and twisted limbs quickly came out behind her. On her feet in seconds, her adrenaline keened, she jumped back from the appendages raining from the pathway blast. However, several recognizable weapon clicks made her slowly raise her shotgun over her head.

"Family! It's all family!" she said fast as she looked at several very wary pairs of eyes.

Guns lowered; she let out her breath.

"Oh, shit." Sasha bent over gasping air, one hand on her knee, the other clutching her gun.

"How many did you get?"

She looked up, trying to place a face with a voice, remembering slowly that it was the alpha Bob . . . the one who had the annoying wife . . . the couple that Hunter couldn't stand. . . . Where was Hunter?

"Not enough of them," she said, slowly standing, her gaze scanning the ragtag group that was severely diminished. "What happened? When were you all attacked? Where?"

The tall blond alpha named Jason, aka Lion Shadow, appraised her carefully before speaking. "We'd turned back, like Hunter had commanded, following his plan to see if we could pick up a trail from the Canadian side—because Dexter had ties there . . . we were to then be your backup in New Orleans. Before we even got close to the border we were ambushed. Fifteen, twenty, I'm not sure. But what I do know is a lot of us lost mates, family, will have to bury our own."

Silence echoed loud, becoming a blaring refrain on the wind.

"I'm sorry," Sasha said gently. It was all she could say. She'd been in combat and knew what this level of loss could do to morale. But she had never lost a mate, a lover, someone that close, and she couldn't fathom the void in one's heart. However, with a threat still present, they had to keep moving forward, at least mentally. "Did you recognize any betas in those that attacked you?"

"Yeah," a voice from the small group said. "Brothers, cousins . . . it was insane."

"I don't understand," Bear Shadow said, risking his neck by breaking rank to speak as a beta among alphas during a war council. "Those that transformed were like brothers," he said, no fear or apology in his voice. Overwhelmed with emotion, the gentle giant drew a ragged breath and pushed on, daring anyone with his eyes to make him stop saying what needed so desperately to be said. "They were strong of mind, had no issues with their rank within their pack. They weren't wannabes or cowards. Something infected them. It wasn't voluntary, this I know in my soul!"

"He's right," Lion Shadow said, glancing around. "That was my point all along and why we risked going through the Shadow lands without an amulet bearer to get here. It already felt like we'd been sucked through a demon door with the way we were attacked, so who cared if we died heroically on the pathway? We needed answers!"

"Which brings the point home," the rotund Florida alpha snarled. "Where's Hunter? My wife—I can't even find her remains! Barbara's gone and for all I know, Hunter murdered her."

"Whoa, whoa, whoa," Sasha said, holding her arms out in front of her. "He was with me. I can vouch for Hunter's whereabouts."

"You two were supposed to be the advanced team and were supposed to come to the lodge!" Lion Shadow shouted. "What the hell happened to the plan?"

"We got ambushed," Sasha yelled back. "Did you check the road coming in?"

Angry, distrustful eyes were on her, but no one spoke.

"Our truck was totaled by a huge beast that jumped into the middle of the road, and we fled to try to get to the lodge for ammo. If you haven't noticed, they're too big to fight one-on-one in a wolf fight. You need a whole pack! On the way we saw the direction the SOB came from. It had taken out an eighteen-wheeler along with the trucker and a ranger in his cruiser. By the time we got to the lodge, we saw Crow Shadow's truck and evidence he'd tried to double back to warn us, but something got him before he could do that—and there were Vampires on the scene, too."

"Bullshit!" Bob shouted.

Sasha held up her arms, a shotgun in hand. "We had Silver Hawk with us—so don't ask me how they're in it, but they are."

"Yeah, and where's he now? Mighty convenient that the two Shadows who have always had questionable motives are missing—don't you think?"

Lion Shadow's gaze narrowed on Sasha, and in a lightning-fast move she lowered her weapon and cocked back a shell in the chamber.

"If you're running for political office, motherfucker, now is not the time for a change in administration. My suggestion is that we all pull together instead of battling each other."

Bob lowered his nine millimeter at a dangerous angle toward Sasha, causing Bear Shadow to growl deep in his chest. "Back off, little lady. This is old clan history that you don't know nothin' about and don't want no part of." He looked around, gaining nods of support as Sasha kept her weapon trained on what they'd installed as the region's temporary leader in Hunter's absence.

"Back when we was all kids, his momma got her stomach tore out with him in it. We all knew he was infected then. But Silver Hawk was too broke up to do what he had to do. Had just shot his own son-in-law for being yellow and letting his daughter get savaged. Had just watched his baby girl die a horrible death. Then his grandson was going into infected Werewolf transformation convulsions right out there under a full moon. Ain't that right, fellas?" Bob said, his voice ringing like an evangelist's.

"Shoulda shot the little bastard in the head right then,

but the old medicine man wouldn't hear of it," Lion Shadow said evenly, his eyes on the barrel of Sasha's gun. "*That* was ego, pure and simple. Silver Shadow was by then really Silver Hawk. His time to rule the Shadow clans was over, and it was somebody else's son's turn. But noooo. He wanted the next generation's reign to go to Hunter—even had a human military geneticist try to give him some nuclear medicine to keep Hunter from changing. No female wanted him; no family wanted him. Nobody would fight him for fear of getting nicked and infected by him. He got to rule by default, not necessarily because he was the strongest. Now he's gone full-blown and brought the contagion to our Shadow packs! That's gotta be the only reason we're all getting sick."

"You all are out of your minds, if that's what you believe," Sasha said through her teeth. She refused to allow mob rule to murder a man who hadn't even been given a fair chance to clear his name. "What's worse is you are running on old green-eyed jealousy. Hateration to the core. And we don't have time for it."

"Put the gun down, Sasha. He might be your lay, but you don't need to get your pretty self shot in the head over a man who ain't even man enough to stay and face the music. This been brewing in the clan for a long time, but look at him—where is he? Gone? Gonna let a female take the weight?" Bob's gaze hardened and the threat in his voice tightened it. "Put down the gun."

"Yes . . ." a deep voice said from behind the group. "Put down the gun."

Instant voice recognition made her cock the shotgun up to the sky and turn just in time to see Bob pivot and release four off-balanced shots when Bear Shadow rushed him. The huge black wolf that moved in a blur scattered the group, but also froze Sasha's heart. He'd spoken while in wolf form, something only the predators could do. He was also much larger than he should have been. The only thing that gave her hope during the ensuing chaos was that Hunter hadn't actually attacked but simply backed down anyone testing his authority.

Yet before the group could settle down, she saw milliseconds happen in slow motion. Hunter's back was turned toward a swath of night shadows. A huge predator barreled through it. Hunter ducked, missing the first assault, and then stood on hind legs for a moment before vanishing into the shadows to emerge again for an attack. Several alphas raised weapons, aimed, and fired. Another wolf came through the same shadow at the wrong trajectory. . . . It wasn't as large as Hunter . . . it was silver-coated and majestic. It was hit.

Rounds fractured the night and she knew that this was the perfect excuse for Hunter and his grandfather to be removed from the pack once and for all. From the corner of her eye she saw Bear Shadow try to yank down Bob's arm to keep him from hitting Hunter, and she spun on Lion Shadow and shot his rifle out of his hand. The message was clear: She'd blow them away if they even blinked wrong. But she had to get to Hunter—the men behind her couldn't be trusted. They had to pull Silver Hawk to safety; he'd been badly wounded and his age didn't help matters.

The only way was to get pack mentality to take precedence over mob mentality. They had to work as a cohesive unit or the huge beast that was on Hunter would soon prevail and then would attack them.

"Stay in human form!" Sasha shouted. "Weapons up on the predator only! You hit our man and you lose an amulet!

There's no telling how many are already here, and that's our only way back!"

It took only a second for the information and threat to register. They'd been lucky once going through the Shadow lands with no amulet bearer to keep them from being snatched beyond demon doors—and they all seemed to know that had more to do with the beasts' probable feeding frenzy than divine intervention. If they left Hunter ass-out, or hit him with a shell, it was clear that she'd leave the lot of them without a way to safely get back to whatever larger pack they hailed from.

Positioning quickly around the fray as the beast roared, lunged, and missed Hunter again, Sasha motioned to Bear Shadow to tend to Silver Hawk. "Staunch his wounds. Take cover!" The old man was bleeding to death, her heart was in bloodied sections within her chest, ripped apart by what she knew was happening but couldn't stop.

An abandoned truck from the garage whirred past her head, made airborne by the frustrated beast. Down on her belly she flattened herself to the ground as the enraged creature followed Hunter; then she quickly rolled onto her back and fired three successive shells, catching it in the gut.

Rolling away fast, she avoided the rain of entrails and the thud of the huge monster that crashed to the ground. It was down but not dead. Shadows on the ground held their fire. She couldn't tell if they did so to keep from hitting her, or to let the mortally injured thing do what they so badly wanted to do—let it rip her face off before they went in and finished the job.

Sasha popped up at the same time the yellow-eyed beast staggered up. Out of shells, she turned to run as it smiled. But it snatched her leg so fast and with such force that it almost felt like her hip was being yanked out of the socket. Then, its grip slowly eased at the same time a sickening crunch-gush sound filled her ears. She looked up just in time to see Hunter in semiwolf form raise the truck axle over his head while standing upright, and then drive it down into the back of the beast's skull.

He jumped off the creature beneath him, threw his head back, and howled, and then transformed into his human shape.

Sasha scrambled up, limping, and headed to Silver Hawk's side with Hunter. Bear Shadow had covered the old man's body with his own to protect him from flying artillery and debris after stuffing his shirt into a chest wound and tying a tourniquet around his wounded leg.

"He's still breathing," Sasha said, trying to instill hope. "He's lost a lot of blood, but if we can get him to Doc . . ."

"How? Take him bloody and broken through demon-infested Shadow lands? And if we got him to Doc, then what? He's not human! They'll fucking dissect him in a human military base hospital!" Hunter was on his hands and knees beside the only father he'd ever known, about to cover the near-fatal injuries with his own hands and pulled back.

Sasha's hands replaced his. There was no need to say it; the infection was rampant within Hunter's system and the effect on the old man was beyond anyone's guess. The rest of the alphas saw that, too, but for the moment, no one was willing to tempt Hunter's ability to reason. Right now, and over this one dear, blessed old man, it was clear that Hunter would take a pack brother's life.

"We arrest the bleeding as much as possible, and yes, we take the whole squad here through the Shadow lands to the safe house in New Orleans—where there are medical supplies for battlefield conditions. Ammo. Food. Water. Clarissa can do the basics—she's in-field certified as a trauma medic, if you don't trust the NORAD facility— and we have communications there, so we can chopper Doc in under stat conditions. The house has a flat roof, Hunter." She looked up into his eyes. "We'll get him through the pathways whole, we're on a mission going in armed and extremely dangerous. One pack, one family."

Hunter stood and looked around the group, unconvinced. A shirt hit him in the chest. A found pair of boots dropped with a thud by his feet. He caught a pair of pants that were slung in his direction.

Lion Shadow made a fist and crossed his chest with his forearm. The rest of the Shadows present did as well.

"One pack, one family," Hunter said, and threw his head back and howled.

Chapter 16

"You have to lead in the Shadow lands," Hunter said, pulling his shirt over his head. "Only you have a vision of the safe house now. I'll bring up the rear." He looked at the group that had carefully transferred his grandfather's limp body to a door taken from the lodge. "Tight formation, Bear Shadow on point behind Sasha watching her back and Silver Hawk's front. I want a man flanking him on each side. Drop him to cut and run, and you die in the Shadow lands. I'll bring up the rear to keep anything barreling down on us off your asses. Roger that?"

"Roger that," Lion Shadow said with a curt nod and then checked his artillery.

"No matter how crazy it gets," Sasha said, "no shapeshifts in the pathways. We can't beat the enemy wolf-to-wolf. As you've noticed, they're stronger, bigger, faster. We have to rely on human evasive maneuvers and the artillery we have on hand. That's particularly important given the precious cargo we're carrying. We need human hands, and my guys on the other side need to see humans coming out, not wolves—unless it's the enemy—because they'll wig and fire at will. We need them to hit the right targets, not us. Understood?"

"Understood," Bob said, glancing at her and then Hunter before his gaze sought the ground.

"Good." Hunter rounded on the four men that attended his grandfather, reached out to touch the old man's chest, but then, as though remembering, made a fist instead.

Sasha was at his side and covered his amulet with her palm. "You'll be able to let him know you were there for him," she said quietly. "Tell him through the light."

Hunter nodded and placed a palm over her amulet and closed his eyes. In that moment she saw how exhausted the man was—weary not just from the recent battle but the one he'd fought all his life.

And even though watching that had broken her heart into a million pieces for him, she was also plagued like the others with a niggling doubt. What if his condition worsened in the demon-infested Shadow lands?

No question about it, Hunter's mild hybridization was frightening, given what they'd seen from the more advanced cases. He'd actually spoken with a human voice while in wolf form. He'd reared up on muscular hind legs to combat a threat—and for an instant his foreleg had morphed into a fur-covered forearm, his right front paw becoming a clawed fist to rip an axle from an overturned truck. Everyone saw it; there was no mistaking what had been seen. That combination wasn't normal under any circumstances and it had been an abomination to his pack brothers to witness. She saw the humiliation in Hunter's eyes once the threat had passed and he'd normalized to human.

Guilt stabbed her as they both stood facing each other, palms over amulets, coaxing the radiant silver-white light of protection from the ancient wards. They needed the light to quickly surround them and their group; it was the process by which alpha clan leaders had moved their people to safety for eons. Only that would keep weaker members from being picked off from the group at entrances and exits. There were always entities that hovered at the fragile nexus where choice could be made between taking a pathway or going through a demon door. It might also be the only thing to hold off intrapathway attacks in the Shadow lands by infected pack members. But the light wasn't coming.

"Maybe he's too far gone?" Bob said. Although his tone wasn't malicious, it grated Sasha no end.

"Maybe so," Hunter said, and began to step away from her. "Give my amulet to Lion Shadow, then. I don't care who gets us through, as long as we hurry up. The old man has been down for ten minutes—and every minute we waste could cost his life."

In that moment Sasha knew it wasn't Hunter that was the problem. Her doubts and fears that put a wedge in the partnering trust had blocked it.

"No. It's me," she admitted. "I was scared—try again."

He looked at her, his gaze intense but not angry. A strange combination of hurt, but understanding and appreciation for the truth filled his eyes. After a few seconds he nodded and stepped closer to her. She dropped her palm away from his chest and hugged him, resting her head on his shoulder.

His embrace was initially tentative and then became all encompassing. Within moments she felt the radiating heat of their amulets awakening. When they stepped back from each other a bright, blinding swath of silver light that stretched the length of their bodies and their standing-width apart was between them. As they backed up, the light continued to expand.

"Everyone between us for safety," Hunter said, never losing eye contact with her. "Stand by. We're going in."

"It's a setup," Dexter growled, lowering his nose to the Shadow pathway. Slowly the distinctive scent of gunpowder and explosive discharge singed his nose from a place deeper within the Shadow lands. He looked around at the group and then reared up on his hind legs to his full height.

"Think about it. . . . They came in here close to dawn when we'd be transforming back. They trailed Shadow Wolf blood to draw us and then blew the pathway." Enraged, he railed at the hazy mist that covered the ground's surface. "Same tactic, just like back at the cemetery! They're using military weapons retrofitted by Hunter's bitch to work against us." Dexter closed his eyes for a moment and inhaled, then slowly shook his head. "But I have to give credit where credit is due—I'd've done no less."

"The plan?" another beast asked, gazing up at Dexter, not sure of their leader's mood. "The moon has already dropped and we haven't shifted back." He glanced around at the others, unnerved.

"The Vampires were supposed to meet us in the bayou with the blood they'd promised," a voice rang out from the pack. "We did our part, as promised, and chased all Werewolves back behind their demon doors and into human habitat hiding. We showed them what we can do— there hasn't been a sighting since we've been on the hunt."

"Yeah, we shouldn't have to lay low in the swamps," another voice called out. "The Vamps reneged—used us."

"We got played; now we're eating our own," still another yelped and then released a mournful wail.

"Face it, Dexter," Barbara snarled. "This close to dawn, the Vampires aren't making a delivery . . . unless they'd send a human emissary to do the drop-off. But then, the likelihood that he'd be eaten might make them wary to send a trusted servant."

"Point well taken," Dexter growled and began to walk on his unnaturally bent hind legs. "Then I say we take us a quiet little stroll over the Lake Pontchartrain Causeway Bridge to the ritzy district. I have a hunch that since the flooding, the Vamps might still party in the French Quarter at night and have no doubt taken up residence in St. Tammany Parish. We'll do this the old-fashioned way and put our noses to the ground and find those bloodsuckers. Maybe then we can shed a little light on our dilemma to help them understand *just* where we're coming from."

"Shogun, we have to stop. The men are dropping where they stand from fatigue and dehydration." His second in command's eyes stopped glowing as his wolf form retreated to leave a naked, shivering man on the verge of collapse. "We'll die in the tunnels, and there'll be no glory for that."

Shogun paced back and forth and then shifted into his human form. Rage and frustration hardened his almond-shaped eyes, and his normal, neat, single braid was loosed as a wild mane of black silk. "How many of us have they fed on, eaten like cattle before the UCE Conference has even commenced?" He spoke through his teeth, his eyes glittering with fury as he appraised his exhausted men. Murmurs of discontent rippled through the underground Werewolf caverns, echoing off stalactites and stalagmites.

"And the Shadow packs talked about us, separated themselves from our breed because they thought only we carried the contagion," one soldier muttered.

"Bitches," another weary were-soldier said. "They pointed the finger at us because they knew that if they caught the contagion, it would be so much worse in them than ever in us."

Shogun ground his teeth, seething as he listened and re-membered years of civil wars between the Shadow Wolf clans and Werewolf clans. Torn between his own personal vendetta that caused his father's death and what was right for the Southeast Asian clan that he now headed, he spewed words from his mouth in hot, angry bursts.

"It's a matter of honor!" Shogun shouted, having heard enough conjecture from the ranks. "For forty-eight hours they've preyed on us—infected Shadow Wolves—drawing us into lairs behind demon doors where even our own infected brethren might attack us. But our own would have enough respect not to be filthy cannibals . . . and they shun our kind? Am I not to seek redress?"

"Yes . . . but at the UCE table—not here. We've done as much as we could do, have chased as many as we could as far as we could, and have enough evidence to prove that it was infected Shadow Wolves on the loose, not in-fected Werewolves this time." His second in command held his gaze with a plea in his eyes.

"I am not placating those goddamned Vampires!" Shogun bellowed, and then spit on the ground. "To hand over hard evidence at the UCE against our distant cousin wolves is to give the Vampires what they want—an open license to kill us all. Our battles are internal . . . wolf-to-wolf."

"What about the prophecy?"

Shogun stared at his enforcer. The cavern was so quiet now that only the drip from moisture echoed amid the breaths taken by weary were-warriors. After a stunned pause, he raked his fingers through his hair. The prophecy: *When the wolf would be one, brought together by one not born of them, yet made . . . strengths of both warring wolves will be sealed in one skin, with one heart.*

Strategy replaced rage. Shogun turned away to look into the pitch-black darkness in the cave before him and then turned toward the weak light filtering in from the opening. *Sasha.* She was a Shadow Wolf. He was a Were-wolf. Although he'd never admit it to his pack brothers, he'd wanted her so badly before, wanted to tell her of the prophecy, but time had run out and she'd rebuffed his advances.

His sister would be a problem. So would Sasha's current mate—the huge North American Shadow clan leader. But if anyone could be the go-between, to get word to the Shadow packs that they needed to meet and had to form a cohesive unit before the Vampires, it was her. Sasha was different . . . even her aura was different, although he wasn't sure why it didn't resonate with the thin band of silver that would normally nauseate a Were-male. She also was oddly raised by humans, not in a pack, and worked for the human military in a way he couldn't understand. But then she'd taken a male Shadow to her bed and had hunted beside him as though they were mates.

Shogun continued to focus on the gray filter of light. This gorgeous female warrior presented a conundrum. The moment he'd laid eyes on her his soul told him she was a part of the prophecy, if not the prophecy itself. His enforcer was right—there was another way.

"We gather our forces, rest, replenish . . . and then we gather information." Shogun's shoulders relaxed and true fatigue clawed at every muscle in his tall, lean frame.

"How? When they have us hiding and on the run like dogs?" one of the men called out.

"There's a little pub in the French Quarter—The Fair Lady—that has Fae peacekeeping forces. The proprietor there, Ethan, is the nervous Fae type. He wants peace at all costs and will broker information for the grant of protection."

His enforcer smiled. "We can do that."

"Francois, man . . . I thought we had a deal?" Dexter flung the lid off the pristine, mahogany coffin that was placed on a central marble stand within the master bedroom. The Vampire within it awakened with a belligerent hiss. "Thought I might find Etienne in there with you. Coulda gotten two for the price of one."

A wicked smile tugged at Barbara's misshapen snout as she flipped on the wall light.

Francois immediately went to the gold-leaf frescoed ceiling near the crystal chandelier, arched, and spit like a treed cat wearing a paisley silk robe. The crimson fabric dangled precariously from his pale, upside-down, athletic frame as he bared fangs in a rage.

"How dare you violate my mansion! Where's my manservant?" Francois's irises became coal-black orbs of gleaming fury.

Dexter chuckled and spit out a small bone and a piece of gristle that had still been lodged in his teeth. "Tasty, although a bit old for my liking. Too chewy."

"You . . . *swine* . . ." Francois glanced around nervously at the gang of infected Shadow Wolves that were amusedly fingering his timeless keepsakes and damaging the expensive upholstery on his Louis XIX furnishings. He watched, mute and furious, as Dexter rounded his four-posted bed and yanked on the satin cord that moved the velvet drape to expose four nude and very dead society women.

"I understand that you have gorgeous gardens here, Francois," Dexter said in a low, laughing growl as he stalked to the window on his bent hind legs and clasped his clawed hands behind his back. He faced the heavily draped window, the threat implicit. "Acres of antebellum grandeur, Spanish moss–laden trees . . . so pretty in the daylight."

"Don't," Francois said, his voice tight and eyes frantic.

"Then tell me what happened with my delivery." Dexter didn't turn around.

"I was delayed, as you can see," Francois said, motioning to the bed with a petulant wave of his hand. "What began as a simple feeding took multiple delicious turns. Nevertheless, before your rude intrusion, I was going to have a servant deliver it to you—I am many things, but always a man of my word."

Dexter fingered the drapery cord by the window as growls of discontent rumbled throughout the room. "So, you're telling me that we were made to wait in the swamps for a booty call and until after *you* ate? Why, I just oughta—"

"*Non, monsieur*," Francois said quickly, assessing the tension in the room. "We didn't want to kill him."

"Don't negotiate with me or try to play me, Vampire!" Dexter shouted, glaring at Francois over his shoulder poised to let in the dawn.

"What purpose would a delay serve? Use the human part of your brain, *mon ami*." Francois's eyes scanned the room for an escape route as he spoke. "We could only capture one alive, the one named Crow Shadow. Look at how many of you there are compared to the one body we have to collect blood from, *oui*? If we drained him dry, then after this full moon, what would you have for the next, and the next? We could have sucked him bone white of blood, made him a husk, and given you all that his body contained, then thrown his damnable carcass to the alligators. But again, I ask, what purpose would that have served?"

Murmurs of consideration amid discontent rumbled around the room as Dexter kept his back to the group, flexing the muscles in his wide, thick shoulder blades.

"There has been no double-cross," Francois implored. "We thought you wanted an ongoing supply, so in order to accomplish this task, you rightfully came to us . . . blood specialists. The Shadow Wolf has to replenish his red blood cells, and to do so we must feed the creature and give him plenty of liquids. He must stay hydrated and not be abused, or his white blood cell count will go up to fight any additional injuries he receives, which could then make you sick. This is a delicate business. Most times, our victims are in rapt pleasure when we extract or never see the death bite coming. Rarely do we duel or battle them in the streets. There is a way to do things that keeps the balance of chemistry within the human body in correct proportion to maximum flavors and desired effects. We have been bottling the elixir of life for a *very* long time, I assure you—we know blood. Is this not why you came to us?"

Francois used the lilting, hypnotic balm of his voice to buy himself time as he inched along the ceiling and slowly eased down the side of the wall nearing an air-conditioning vent while Dexter considered his statements. He kept his gaze on Dexter's hand, which still fingered the window drapery cords in a most threatening way, willing it not to suddenly yank.

"How much have you collected so far, then?" Dexter finally asked and turned to face Francois.

"Enough for five syringes," Francois said nervously. "In the kitchen, in the refrigerator, they were freshly packed in a white Styrofoam container that would have gone in a cooler surrounded by dry ice. But you ate my day courier, *monsieur.*"

Uneasy quiet settled in the room. There were only enough syringes for five out of fifteen infected pack members present. Tension settled over the eerie silence so thickly that it almost made the air crackle. Then in the next second, a full-scale war broke out in the bedroom.

Wolves lunged, tearing at each other, furniture smashed; the bed dumped its dead body contents, and in the fracas two wolves locked in combat hurtled toward the fragile, leaded beveled glass windows. Francois was mist, a quickly escaping vapor down the vent. Daylight poured into the room, glinting off surfaces that probably hadn't been bathed in dawn's hues in several centuries.

Sasha lurched forward from the void with the Shadow clan behind her, calling out the names of her team members. Only a morbid silence echoed back. She glanced around quickly, as did the others, looking for signs of an attack. It took only a few seconds for her to see that the

MLRS was shifted out of place and a huge hole was in the ceiling but covered by a tarp. Laptop computers and easily portable artillery were gone. Her worst fears were confirmed in an instant: The safe house was no longer safe and her team was on the move without cover . . . had most likely been forced out under heavy enemy pressure. That would have been the only reason Woods and Fisher would have relocated the group . . . assuming they'd made it as far as this situation room alive.

Turning her gaze toward the back of the group to get Hunter's read on things, she froze. He wasn't there. "Hunter!" Her voice carried through the house at a panic-laden decibel. His amulet exited a shadowy void between worlds and clattered to the attic's wooden floor. Bear Shadow caught her by the arm as she lunged, knowing her intention was to go back for him.

Bear Shadow shook his head and motioned toward Silver Hawk's worsening condition with a swift jerk of his chin. "Hunter chose. Save the old man and save what's left of the clan's leadership . . . save your team. If he didn't come through with us, and also sent back his amulet, then that can only mean that the infection he got as a child has progressed." Bear Shadow's eyes were filled with grief as his voice dropped down to a thick garbled whisper. "He cannot exit because he cannot control his shifts. He cannot trust himself with even us, his brothers, or you, his mate. He threw back the amulet because he can no longer wear it and it will not protect him. It has rejected its owner. He is more like them than us. Please, do not go back, Sasha. You will not like what you see."

She nodded and looked away, drawing in a deep, shaky breath. "This man needs medical attention," she said, making her voice take on the military authority that came from years of training. She paced away from the group and tried to find a cell phone, sat-phone, anything, even a computer land line—and then kicked over a table when there was no communication device to be found. "Damn!"

"Home to your familiars," Bear Shadow reminded her, but made it seem like he was simply providing a second opinion for the brief moment of duress any alpha would be allowed after having just lost their mate to the dread sickness.

Again she nodded, and raked her hair with her fingers. Even this time of year the humidity and dampness could be its own brand of beast. They'd lost another five minutes. Silver Hawk had been holding on to fifteen precious minutes of life. She quickly closed her eyes, saw Woods's expression go blank as he jerked his attention to something unseen—her. She tried to envision an ambulance, a hospital, and then frustration made her say it aloud. "We gotta get him to Tulane! Doc isn't here. That's a university hospital and the only one I know for sure is still standing after the flood!"

Not waiting for the group, she hustled down the steps and out into the streets, weapon drawn and sweeping the terrain for any hidden danger. It was a long shot, but if they got a military biologist with full credentials into a state of the art facility, the old man might stand a chance until Doc arrived—another good reason to head for Tulane by ambulance; it had a helicopter landing pad.

Her brain was on fire as she raced back to the house to give the all-clear. She could commandeer highly trained ER doctors on staff; having military fatigues on and a group of soldier-looking dudes also packing heavy artillery would temporarily stop most civilian questions, even those of local police. Bradley and Winters could handle PR, flashing their NORAD identification, and could make the whole who-are-you-and-where-are-you-from line of questioning go away under the guise of Homeland Security.

The sound of a siren was music to her ears. Woods was driving, Fisher riding shotgun. The elated expressions on their faces said it all. She released a rallying howl, not having time for human protocols, and could only hope the neighbors thought she was a stray baying in an alley somewhere.

Clarissa, Winters, and Bradley piled out the back of the vehicle as the Shadow pack swiftly but carefully moved Silver Hawk into position down the steps.

"Glad to see you all, but this man's been shot," Sasha said as they lifted Silver Hawk into the back of the ambulance. "He's lost a lot of blood—and his blood isn't normal."

Clarissa looked at Sasha. "What's his type? When he gets to Tulane, they'll immediately hook up an IV, and an interspecies transfer could . . ."

God bless Woods and Fisher, they'd passed on the vital intel. "Yeah, I know," Sasha said quickly, jumping into the back of the ambulance with the human team. "It could shock his system, cause a rejection, and kill him. He'll match mine—type O positive, universal donor, with the other cellular structure he needs."

"We should stay here and wait for Hunter?" Bear Shadow asked with uncertainty, as the others glanced around.

"No . . . borrow a coupla neighbors' vehicles and follow us. Military emergency we can do that, and give the assets back to the local authorities to get the cars back to their owners." She slammed the back of the ambulance and closed her eyes for a moment, leaning against the wall. "How's his vitals?" she finally asked Clarissa.

Her expression was grave.

"Not good."

Chapter 17

"Dammit," one doctor exclaimed, slamming down his fresh cup of coffee and running forward to meet the ambulance. "I thought after Fat Tuesday we'd get a break in the action, but here we go, Tony."

"Full moon aftermath, people. Guys in fatigues, let's see what we've got," another attending physician shouted as the ER came alive in the dawn hours.

"Gonna be two full moons this month, I heard," an ER nurse muttered sarcastically toward her colleague as they dashed down the corridor. "Better get your gris-gris ready—wish Administration would make it standard on the crash carts."

"Just what we need a month after Mardi Gras, a goddamned blue moon," another nurse replied, skidding to a halt as what looked like a brigade of dirty marines piled out of commandeered vehicles behind the ambulance.

"How many injured?" a doctor called out. "Do we have a situation? Let us know what we're dealing with so we can make way for heavy incoming."

"We took care of that already," Lion Shadow said in a low rumble. "The bodies are where the bodies were left— just got one old man with pretty bad gunshot wounds to the lung and thigh."

Medical personnel glanced at each other but didn't say a word as Sasha and her team lifted Silver Hawk down from the back of the ambulance on a door.

"Winters, Bradley," Sasha said quickly, glancing at them to start the PR process. She should have made it clearer to the others that only Winters and Bradley needed to speak to hospital personnel. Damn! "Rissa, with me—get a line up to NORAD to Doc. I want the rest of you guys on point." It wasn't necessary to explain why to Lion Shadow. A VIP was in the building and, come nightfall, could be at risk.

She saw the ER team give each other confused glances as they quickly helped transfer Silver Hawk to a gurney while rushing a crash cart to his side.

"On three," the doctors said, and the transfer was seamless.

True professionals, the ER team interwove all questions directed at Sasha between their barking medical commands. But the medical team kept moving as though in the midst of a war zone. Unfortunately, this hospital, like others that had recently seen large-scale civilian disasters, had plenty of practice. One dying old man riddled with nine-millimeter slugs wasn't an incident—it was the deadly show of force that came in with him that had alerted the staff.

"It's so bad they're flying 'em into us from Colorado?" one doctor asked as the gurney burst through the doors. "You said NORAD, right?"

"At least it's not raining," another one quipped sarcastically.

"His heart rate's dropping," a nurse called out. "Where's that drip? Where's my blood order? Let's move, people!" Then she stopped, looked at the patient hard, and then gave Sasha a knowing glance.

Immediately Sasha saw the woman's Fae aura, and her kind green eyes became hazel and then blue to let her know that she'd help with the ruse.

"He's got a rare blood disease, I'm an exact match donor—what you've got in the fridge will kill him." Sasha's gaze met the nurse's and then went to the lead physician's as she yanked up her sleeve and crossed the room. "Take it from me. Until our expert Dr. Xavier Holland arrives by chopper, our lead biologist, Dr. Clarissa McGill needs a phone, access to your scopes, lab equip—"

"I knew we were gonna have heavy incoming," the lead nurse said. "Get Admin in on this, might need someone to cope with media." Again, she gave Sasha a knowing glance, even though her voice sounded harsh. Everything in her eyes said *Trust me, I'm on the inside*. "I'm Margaret. Don't worry," she said quickly, working. "I've seen this before."

Sasha nodded, hoping that supernatural healers were in full force in New Orleans' hospitals, and then she began to relax. They would have to be . . . there had to be doctors and embedded personnel in all walks of life, especially if this was the site of an international conference with supernatural dignitaries coming in from all over the worlds.

"What kind of contagion did you military boys bring in here?" the lead physician snapped, oblivious to Sasha's thoughts. He looked up at Sasha as he steadily worked on shearing away Silver Hawk's clothing. "Are we all fucked?"

"No, sir. Not yet."

"What has occurred here is nothing short of a travesty! I demand recompense! Our regional council must be enlightened . . . Le Krewe of L'Grand Duke must know, at the very least," Francois wheezed.

"*Oui* . . . to be sure. This is what happens when one does business with undesirables, but we must consider the long view—a possible elevation within the Cartels. . . . Our brothels have been most profitable, as have our legitimate hotel enterprises, but if we pull off this coup to start the wolf civil wars, as we know the old guard so desperately desires, short term, there will be nothing we cannot request. They will owe us," Etienne said slowly, speaking inside the darkness of his sealed coffin to conserve energy while he rested within his light-bathed crypt.

"But we must survive to be able to enjoy the reward. The dogs of war daylight-breached my manor!"

"All of this is disconcerting, I'm sure." Etienne's mind reached out and stroked Francois's panicked psyche. "Rest within the vents. . . . I know it is difficult to breathe as the sun heats the moisture in the very air . . . but you must calm yourself. Still yourself. Die to the morn and tonight we'll awaken together to redress this unnecessary violation of your sanctuary."

Heads slowly lifted from the feeding den floor. Low snarls echoed through the cavern as glowing gold eyes fixed on an unfamiliar male. Gazes narrowed and snouts scented the air.

"Back off," a large, humpbacked male warned Hunter, protecting the carcass he'd claimed. "There isn't enough! Not even after what we pulled from the surface during Mardi Gras. Everyone's personal hunt was aborted during this moon phase."

A female laughed low in her throat and flung a section of human rib cage to land at Hunter's feet. "Darlin,' you're way too fine to allow to starve to death, but that's the best I can do." She ducked to avoid a backhanded blow from the big male in the center of the pack.

"I say when he can eat, bitch!" The offended male glared at Hunter. "Touch it and you die."

Unfazed, Hunter looked down at the remains with disgust and then kicked it back toward the group, much to the leader's obvious satisfaction. He waited until the snarling and snapping over the returned portion died down before he spoke. "I didn't come here to feed. I came to bring you information."

"Smart move," the leader said, foul saliva oozing from his massive jaws. "What have you heard or seen on the surface?"

"Two very important things to consider," Hunter said calmly, his voice so even in tone that all demon-infected Werewolves present stopped eating for a moment. "One, it's not a rival pack of infected Werewolves that have decided to hunt in unison on the surface, abandoning the age-old methods of being a solo predator." He shook his head. "No. That's not what it is."

"Then what the hell was unleashed on us?" the leader raged, now standing upright at an impressive eleven feet at the shoulders. He walked forward a bit to better study Hunter, crushing bones beneath his girth as he sniffed the air.

Ignoring the menace and the horrible stench all around him, as well as the awful nasal sound that the beast's snout produced, Hunter addressed the pack leader without blinking. "Shadow Wolves."

For a moment all the wolves in the regional den glanced at each other, and then finally the huge leader released booming laughter.

"You, my friend, must be high." He shook his head and turned away from Hunter, dismissing him. "You'll have to do better than that to whine for scraps. Shadow Wolves can't get what we have from a bite, and their females don't mate with our uninfected brethren to ever possibly produce offspring with the recessive gene—or don't you know your history? That's why we're shunned, son."

Hysterical, wild laughter surrounded Hunter as he stood, stone-faced, before the infected alpha.

"The Vampires stole a toxic serum from a U.S. Military base up in Colorado—NORAD. The humans had been playing with trying to re-create one of us without some of the side effects. Problem is, what they created bonds real nicely with the human side of Shadow Wolf DNA, whereas a normal bite or scratch from an infected Were-wolf can normally be purged by a Shadow Wolf. So, view what the humans made as a super bite or super serum."

The pack leader slowly turned. "I heard something about that. . . . They caught one of us years back. Another in North Korea, but some human chick blew the convoy."

"Same batch of blood samples came from that first capture," Hunter pressed on, his voice never wavering as he stated the facts.

"The Vampires . . . those bastards are always involved in anything that goes against us," a voice grumbled from the now riveted group.

"Originally they agreed to steal it because it would keep more Werewolves from being made through the faulty human experimentation process. The last thing they wanted was for Werewolf ranks to increase—infected or otherwise. The humans see us all the same. But a human general got nervous and ordered a vaccine to be created instead. The vaccine ultimately would have been put in human drinking water supplies as a delivery agent in Werewolf hot zones, to prevent infections within the human population."

"Seems like we need to pay this general a visit," the leader snarled.

"Too late," Hunter said calmly. "Vampires already ripped off his face."

The pack leader folded his arms over his barrel chest. "And why would one of them do that?" He glanced around at his pack members and chuckled, garnering hyenalike laughter from the group again. "Should have followed my first mind. That boy is high."

"The Vampires thwarted the effort because the residue left in human blood would taint it . . . make it taste very close to the Shadow Wolf blend that makes them sick as dogs."

All laughter died away. Vindicated, Hunter allowed his gaze to sweep the group.

"That's when the second problem occurred."

This time there was no interruption to Hunter's story or laughter.

"Speak!" the pack leader commanded, growing restless and beginning to pace.

"A group of rogue Shadow Wolves found out that if they shot up with the toxin, it worked like steroids. Then they double-crossed the Vampires and even their own pack alphas. It bulked them up, turned betas into super alphas—"

"Bullshit!"

"No, truth!" Hunter yelled back. "The toxin the humans had was not straight virus like they'd get from a bite or a scratch. It had been genetically altered to insert itself into the human DNA spiral and embed there to give a human soldier all the strongest traits of the Werewolf species. Within the Shadow Wolf, there's the human element it can cling to. The problem is that it has a nasty side effect on the inner wolf . . . that cannot control its shifts, can't resist the taste of *both* human *and* Werewolf flesh. It makes the Were-Shadows larger, more lethal, and able to walk in both the Shadow lands and soon, I'm sure, they can come through your demon doors. That's what's been hunting and eating uninfected Werewolves on the other side of the doors. So, if you see them coming beyond the demon doors—attack. If you don't go after the infected Shadows, one night you'll find yourself trapped and being slaughtered within your own feeding dens."

The pack leader dropped down on all fours and slammed his fist into the pile of gore beneath him. "The Vampires started this travesty to wipe us out—then we shall massacre them! We cannot eat in our own territories under a full moon because of them, but have to quickly steal bodies and bring them behind demon doors to gorge until the next full moon phase . . . all because of them? Not only are our uninfected brothers hunting us in the ongoing civil war, as are the normal Shadow Wolves, now you are saying you've witnessed an even stronger predator? Now our demon doors are in danger of being breached? How do you know all of this?"

"I learned what I needed to know when I went after a smaller female hybrid that was feeding in my yard. She was almost stronger than me, even at a head shorter. I had to know why and how. . . . She told all as I slowly convinced her that the torture would stop if she spoke quickly."

Hunter smiled a sinister smile, allowing the misdirected truth to take root in the pack leader's psyche. He watched him sniff the air for a lie, but Hunter had not lied, just conveniently rewoven the truth. Sasha was a hybrid of sorts, being both Shadow Wolf and human. They actually had shared critical information, and she had fed in his hunting grounds. And indeed he had pleasantly tortured her and she'd willingly told him by her actions all he'd ever wanted to know . . . that she loved him. The pack leader could read into it what he wanted.

The important thing was to get the three main threats to human existence to help cancel each other out. If the Vampires, infected Shadow Wolves, and infected Werewolves were at each others' throats, then it would make the cleanup job easier for the greatly weakened Shadow packs, and most certainly any human military forces that deemed to get involved.

"Haven't seen you around these bayou doors," the pack leader finally said, flinging a wet human leg toward Hunter, who caught it with one hand.

"I'm not from around here," Hunter replied, allowing the sickening appendage to dangle at his side. "I was made in the Midwest . . . got chased this way. Something's converging on New Orleans."

"Take care of his needs," the pack leader ordered the female that had initially tried to feed Hunter. "I could use a good field general, with what's about to go down."

She smiled and lowered her head, skulking forward. Hunter tossed the leg to her, which he knew was an ultimate act of chivalry among Werewolves. She caught it with a feral snap of her strong jaws.

The pack leader laughed. "The whole leg? When's the last time your mangy ass has been laid?"

Hunter returned a noncommittal half-smile and winked at the feeding female. "Save me some for later. My grandfather got injured in the last battle getting out of the Rockies. I hid him well and drew them off his trail, but he's old . . . was made more than a century ago, I think. I'll be back after I feed him. He's too weak to even make it through the doors now."

This time the pack leader didn't sniff the air for a lie, but simply nodded as the group went back to its shared meal and Hunter turned to leave.

"See, that's what I like," the leader mumbled between huge bites as he stuffed his mouth with human remains. "Loyalty and priorities. Without that, a man is just a beast."

The situation had clearly spun out of control. Based on the little bit of sketchy intel Clarissa had shared, New Orleans was poised for a full-scale invasion that would mean another human catastrophe of potentially biblical proportions.

Dr. Xavier Holland kept his gaze out of the military helicopter window as it began to slowly drop to the helipad. In order to get an emergency airlift, the brass had to be nominally informed. Just like he'd had to give some cursory explanation about the need to send in cleanup crews and spin damage control after the MLRS launch that hit a local cemetery. Then the team's equipment would necessarily have to be moved . . . and he'd have to bring Sasha the latest preternatural advanced weapons systems for scouting Vampire lairs and sealing shut interdimensional demon doors.

The only thing that helped his cause of not revealing the Shadow Wolf cultures, effectively keeping them off radar as a known entity, was the top brass's desire for plausible deniability. After General Donald Wilkerson's murder rocked the foundation of the upper echelons all the way to the White House, which threatened to bring on all sorts of congressional and public reviews, he and Sasha and any resources they used were considered strictly Black Ops. If they screwed up, the military would deny giving them authority; if they did well, their funding would silently increase. That was the way it worked. Operation Dog Star was now officially off the record. Actually, he preferred it that way.

Xavier Holland looked across the helipad as the chopper came to a landing. He waited for the craft to stop rocking and for the pilot to give him a thumbs-up. An armed marine got out first and then helped him down. Doctors in white coats stood by stern-looking administrators just inside the rooftop doors, their eyes expectant. He knew what they were worried about. They'd probably already called the CDC wanting to know if, by way of an elderly gunshot patient, the plague, Ebola, bird flu, or some other biohazard had been introduced into their hospital environment, thus New Orleans, in a way that could erupt into a pandemic outbreak. If they only knew.

Keeping his expression stoic as he crossed the helipad, Xavier Holland's mind raced with alternative approaches. He needed quick access to the patient, Sasha, her squad, and anyone else that might have been near the Were-Shadow contagion. He gripped his briefcase tighter, thinking of Hunter.

"Dr. Holland," said a tall, well-dressed man in a conservative pin-striped suit, extending his hand. "Pleased to make your acquaintance. I'm Joseph Pratt. We've heard of your genetics work and would have been pleased to host you under different circumstances," the hospital president hedged. "But we'll confront that later. Let me introduce you to Dr. Ira Lutz, head of epidemiology, Dr. Michael Williams, chief of surgery, Dr. Evelyn Sanders, head of our bioresearch department, and Nancy Markland, who handles all media relations and public statements."

Xavier Holland nodded. "It's my pleasure. How's the patient?"

"Stable, for now," Dr. Williams said crisply as the small, high-powered group watched the chopper lift off. "But he's far from being out of the woods. He flat-lined twice from blood-loss shock, then his heart kept going into a mild arrhythmia. We had to take half of his right lung and are praying we can save his leg. Time will tell. The bullet passed through his thigh, shattered a portion of the femur, and fragments of that then severed part of the femoral artery. Only quick thinking at the location where he was injured saved that man's life."

"The problem is that his body's white blood cell count is through the roof, as is the donor's blood, as though fighting off some sort of rare infection." Dr. Lutz paused to peer at Xavier Holland through thick, Ben Franklin–style glasses. "We don't know if the patient came in with the unknown contagion, or if it was transferred to him by the donor who has identified herself as Lieutenant Sasha Trudeau."

"Just what are we dealing with, really?" Dr. Sanders asked, her intense hazel gaze unwavering.

"If there is going to be a quarantine or something that could affect this hospital's reputation, Doctor, in all fairness, I need to be able to get ahead of the curve to make a public statement." Nancy Markland folded her arms over her chest after straightening her red linen power suit. "Frankly, we've got what looks like a small platoon of guys crawling all over our grounds in fatigues who appear as though they've just come back from Iraq with no decontamination or debrief window."

"I cannot go into the nature of the experiments being conducted at NORAD, but suffice to say that the general public, nor any of the hospital staff, is at risk or in imminent danger." Xavier Holland glanced around at the frustrated faces and then affixed his gaze to the elevator numbers. His grip tightened on the briefcase he carried that contained the last of the vaccine. "We will corral those men and get them out of plain sight, but it is imperative that I see the patient now."

She didn't care that she wasn't supposed to be in ICU. Having the capacity to blend in and out of the shadows, filch hospital garb, and go wherever she needed to be had its distinct advantages. Right now she had to be at Silver Hawk's side. Sasha slipped her hand into his, glad that anesthesia would keep away the pain for a little while longer. It all seemed so unfair that a man who'd lived his entire life avoiding the vagaries of experimental modern medicine would now be ripped away from his holistic, tried and proven, natural herbal approaches by a new millennium virus created in a lab . . . something that resulted in his getting shot by his own clan.

For a long while she didn't move, just studied the lines in his ancient face and noticed the cool, unnaturally waxy feel of his weathered hand against hers. A deep sense of mourning filled her as she looped her amulet over her head and placed it beneath her palm against his chest. *Please don't die*. It was a fervent, urgent prayer coming from a woman who wasn't used to praying. If she hadn't left him, he wouldn't have rushed into the pathways unprotected to find his grandson. They could have—should have—gone together.

"Silver Hawk, you will always be Silver Shadow to us. . . . You are so loved and revered, and the clan needs your guidance so desperately right now. It is not your time." She bent and kissed his forehead, knowing that if this old man crossed over into the permanent Shadow lands, Hunter would die a thousand deaths right behind him no matter what his mental state when she found him. It was bad enough that he blamed himself for the pack deaths, but to add his grandfather's demise into that loaded equation was more than any person could bear.

"I'll find Hunter, you just live to see him again," she whispered and gave Silver Hawk's hand a gentle squeeze.

Refusing to leave him unprotected but needing to find Doc, she looped the silver chain over his neck and hid it from the hospital staff beneath his gown and the blankets. *Woe be unto a thief*, she thought, reluctantly leaving her charge.

A man's soul for a piece of silver? Puh-lease . . . more like some asshole's face.

Chapter 18

"Long time no talk, Ethan." Shogun took a slow sip of his beer, allowing the foam to cling to his upper lip before licking it away.

Ethan sat down quickly beside him. "You're well? All is well? There's no problem, is there?"

"Can't a man have a nice lager in a safe house without there being a problem . . . or, did you hear of one?"

"Please, I just . . ."

Shogun's hard stare made Ethan's words trail off as his gaze nervously darted around his establishment.

"All right," Ethan whispered. "Only because it's so early, and at this hour the walls don't have ears."

Shogun sipped his brew, his gaze and senses scanning the environment. "Too early for the Vamps, their succubae and incubi have probably been up late *working*, since the Conference is in town. Dragon dancers don't come in till later . . ." He shrugged. "Seen any Shadow packs with an unusual femme fatale with them?"

"I haven't seen anything, I've been working."

Cradling his beer between his broad hands, Shogun leaned in to the nervous Elf, forcing direct eye contact. "Let me restate it, then. Have you *heard* of the aura-less she-Shadow that might have come into town with the North American Shadow clan leader?"

"Why?" Ethan whispered, his eyes wide. "She seems like such a nice person—they say, uhmmm . . . I didn't meet her, but my Margaret did when the she-Shadow brought in her whole pack and even her two familiars to the hospital. One was badly hurt, shot. Then military humans flew in to help."

"Thank you." Shogun downed his beer.

"Please," Ethan whispered. "I know the Werewolves and Shadows don't get along, but innocent people in the hospital, humans, babies—"

"I didn't come for a brawl, just a friendly conversation. . . . If battle erupts, that will be because the North American—"

"He didn't come," Ethan cut in anxiously, and then covered his mouth with his hand.

Shogun tilted his head, then stood. If the big male hadn't come yet, then he was on the move, hunting, chasing whatever his pack had run into—that was the way of the wolf. New Orleans was a fallback position for the injured, his female, her familiars. . . . Then what was he after? Vampires? Infected Shadows? Infected Werewolves?

"The Fae are guarding the hospital to be sure there's no retaliation against the elderly Shadow—there had to be some sort of fight." Ethan blinked wildly as he spoke and blotted his forehead with an already damp handkerchief. "Please don't be angry at me, it's their job to keep humans unaware . . . UCE edict—and big, nasty fights tend to make humans ask questions."

"Your bar has my pledge of protection." As Shogun

began walking, a familiar female scent made him stop and abruptly turn.

"Still sniffing after that Shadow bitch?" his sister snarled, and loped over to him from the far end of the bar. "I thought after the bucket of cold water to break you two up that would be enough!"

"Lei, don't start. Lower your voice. I'm not in the mood for—"

She grabbed his arm and spoke in a hissing whisper between her teeth. "She's a *Shadow*."

"And you are *way* out of line," he said, snatching his arm from her grasp but keeping his voice low.

"I raised you—so how can I *ever* be out of line?"

Pure hatred marred his sister's beautiful face, turning her normally dark, exotic eyes to pits of rage. Her pretty mouth was now a tight line and her creamy, almond hue was flushed. Narrowing her gaze, she flipped a long swath of blue-black silken hair over her shoulder and leaned in closer to keep their heated debate private.

"Our parents made the personal sacrifice to take the faction oath to become stronger through demon blood. They did that so you and I didn't have to. They did it because Vampires were hunting us to extinction while our so-called Shadow Wolf cousins watched and sometimes helped. And now you want to bed one of them? Are you insane?"

Shogun pulled away and looked at her without apology. "Their decision to take the demon infection was insane. It was a bargain made with devils. That was their choice. It was never mine, or the rest of the clan's. You can cling to the old ways if you'd like, but the world is changing, getting smaller—and there must be another way. Brute force no longer works. Negotiations, alliances are necessary. Force will one day cause our extinction."

"It is because of whom they were that you are who you've become—clan leader of Southeast Asia."

"No," he said in a low, lethal voice. "I became what I am through learning the pure way of the wolf and meeting every challenge since the time of my alpha rise. They did nothing but make me have to overcome the shame of their legacy."

His sister's glare raked him from head to toe. "I never thought I would live to see the day when my very own brother, who I'd raised like my son, would turn his back on the old ways to dishonor his parents' death. It is bad enough that you lust for a she-Shadow . . . but to select one from a North American pack—the same pack that killed them . . . *murdered them*, Shogun. I am ashamed to call you brother. Continue in this and you will be dead to me."

Sasha promised herself that she would not barrel into Doc's arms if he silently guaranteed that he wouldn't try to hug her. Theirs was an old dance all done without words, burned deep within unreadable expressions. Promises made and kept over too many returns from too many hazardous missions to count, with too many sighs of relief to even begin to describe. But this time, with a being who was a lifelong friend in critical condition and Hunter gone and in peril, it took unimaginable resolve not to follow that natural human impulse.

"Dr. Holland," Sasha said stiffly as she entered a lab area that had been made available to him and her team. Fae entities were definitely embedded in the hospital administration and ER, she noted, as she looked around at the significant facilities Doc had been given.

"Lieutenant," he said crisply, very aware of the outsiders from the hospital that gathered around them.

"We've been working with Tulane's medical team," Clarissa said carefully, her gaze scanning the other doctors before returning to Sasha. "We're trying to isolate why a transfusion from a compatible donor is erupting the patient's system almost as virulently as a classic organ rejection."

"We cannot be responsible for the wait-and-see approach the NORAD team has adopted," Dr. Lutz complained.

"It almost looks like his system is battling a widespread staph infection, and our recommendation to begin IV-delivered antibiotics was firmly rejected by Dr. Holland—and we want that on the record," Dr. Sanders informed the group.

"Pretty soon that man's kidneys and liver will fail. His heart muscle is under attack," Dr. Williams said, talking with his hands as he leaned against a lab table. "Just be straight with us. What twenty-first century plague are we dealing with here?"

Sasha pulled off her elastic-banded paper cap and shoved it in her yellow dressing gown pocket. "Might as well tell 'em because a) they'll never believe us, b) they aren't stupid enough to stake their professional reputations on leaking this to the media, c) nobody within NORAD will confirm or deny it, and last but not least, d) if half of what was chasing us is already in New Orleans, then come the next full moon, this hospital should quietly be prepared for major triage." She leaned back on a desk. "I'm just glad it's after Mardi Gras."

Nervous glances passed around her team. The Tulane staff stared at her and didn't blink.

"Are you sure, Lieutenant?" Xavier Holland waited. "The patient is dear to me, too . . . but I don't know if we're authorized to divulge that level of detail."

"I'm sure," she said, her gaze locked within his. "We need the best minds on this in the region—because after what I saw in the field, we need more antitoxin. Not to mention, I think these specific doctors were handpicked." She gave Doc a meaningful glance. "They may be unaware, but they must have checked out—there are friendly embedded cells in this facility."

"Terrorists?" Dr. Williams said in a tense whisper, aghast.

"Hardly," Sasha replied quickly. "More like folks on our side."

She watched the Tulane staff relax, knowing they hadn't a clue why they had. But she'd take cool heads over hysteria for now. "Doc, we've got a *lot* of good men down from the last siege."

"I got a head count from Woods and Fisher," Holland said. "I brought the last of what we'd developed. In order to make more, I need a live subject—which is next to impossible to locate and even more dangerous to trap. Facilities here won't allow for that."

Sasha followed Doc's careful choice of words and watched his very wary eyes, as well as the other doctors' attention that moved between them as though witnessing a tennis match.

She placed a hand on Doc's arm, for the first time since he arrived allowing that level of familiarity as her voice became gentle. "I know of a live subject that I can get close enough to . . . who is an exact DNA match with the patient . . . who's gone full blown."

Xavier Holland closed his eyes. "Is that how the patient sustained multiple gunshot wounds?"

"Yes," Sasha said quietly. "The patient was accidentally hit by friendly fire."

"I'll give him the first series and inoculate you and your team. But I'll hold one back . . . just in case." Breaking protocol, he stepped forward and hugged Sasha. "I'm so sorry we lost him."

She swallowed hard and melted into the embrace, and then after a moment stiffened and pushed away. "I'll find him. I messed up, Doc. My body was definitely compromised by a carrier, and my system was obviously fighting the infection when we did a transfusion with the patient. But I was the only universal donor in the group at the time . . . one with the same cellular structure—we didn't know if the others had been infected, either. He was bleeding to death, hemorrhaging, and needed blood. It was a crapshoot with the rest of the clan, too. They'd all been in a hot zone, each man and woman that made it through is all cut up and has open wounds and lacerations."

"What are we dealing with?" Dr. Lutz shouted. "Enough with the cryptic military speak!"

"Demon-infected Werewolf virus," Sasha said flatly. "You're looking at a Preternatural Containment team, some of whom have wolf DNA fused with their human DNA spirals to better hunt the new supernatural predator that poses a security threat. One of our men went over the wall—went full blown and disappeared in a hot zone. His grandfather was accidentally shot. The patient has a different cellular structure—part wolf in his DNA. Like me. Like a bunch of the guys. Problem is, I was carrying contagion that my system is strong enough to fight off and didn't know how seriously infected I was. But an injured elderly man whose autoimmune system and everything else is going haywire would go into shock from a transfusion from me—had I known, *trust me*, I wouldn't have put him at risk like that. What you're witnessing now is his system trying to self-repair while also trying to adapt to contain and eject a foreign viral agent. Does that clear it up?"

Stunned mute, the senior medical team from Tulane just looked at Sasha.

"You can't be serious," the chief of surgery finally said after a moment.

"Dead serious on the next full moon, or from the looks of things, before that," Clarissa said, glimpsing into a microscope.

"Doc, we can set up distortion monitors," Winters offered, glancing between Sasha and Xavier Holland. "With the new equipment, we're able to get readings off energy displacement by setting up a grid to then tell if something physical left a heat trail entering or exiting a displacement band. That way we can be on comm with Trudeau while she's hunting to tell her if something's bearing down on her, and where it's likely to emerge from the unseen before it does."

"That's right, Dr. Holland," Bradley said. "We can also devise a two-shot projectile that will first collect a tainted blood and tissue sample as it passes through the target and closes, then breaks off at the exit wound, leaving the second part of the device with heavy tranquilizers and antitoxin lodged inside the beast," he added, opening his fist to extend his fingers. "Much like a multistaged rocket. The second cylinder will detonate inside the target using a small charge and will be filled with antitoxin and a tranquilizer cocktail strong enough to drop a charging elephant . . . so Trudeau can deliver remote range antitoxin, pick up the sample cylinder, and still have a reasonable escape window."

"You *are* serious," Dr. Lutz murmured in awe.

"You've actually seen these beasts?" Dr. Sanders

asked, her gaze quickly jerking between Sasha, her team, and the three members from the Tulane staff.

"Yeah. Up close and personal," Woods said, pounding Fisher's fist. "So have the rest of those guys who came in like dirty-faced Hell's Angels toting heavy artillery. Those boys aren't overreacting; they were in the trenches with Trudeau."

"In all my career, I prayed for a chance to work on something groundbreaking, something never before seen . . ." Dr. Lutz said, pure passion brimming in his eyes. "We all have."

"That's probably why you three were selected—handpicked," Sasha said in a weary tone.

"I prayed for it, too," Dr. Sanders said quietly. "I've been on my own personal research quest to try to understand some of the mysterious events that seem to happen here like nowhere else I've lived in my life. I've written papers that I haven't been brave enough to publish . . ."

"Well, be careful what you pray for, Doctor," Xavier Holland warned. "I thought that, too, some twenty-five years or more ago. But you'll never be able to post this in professional journals. There'll be no awards or conference circuit. No peer recognition. Whatever you learn or help prevent will be one of those great accomplishments that you'll have to take to your grave, no different than the tombs of the unnamed soldiers who fought and died so that we could have better lives . . . because no one but those unnamed souls know the extent of their sacrifice. Are you still in, or do we need to pull military rank and simply ruin your careers and lives if you mention this project?"

"I'm a doctor and a scientist before all things," Dr. Lutz said. "I've waited my entire life to know if there's more to our human, frail existence. I'm in."

The chief of surgery gave a skeptical nod. "Just to know that I saw it and my eyes weren't playing tricks on me . . . curiosity prevails."

"A pair of steel gonads better prevail," Fisher said, shaking his head, "because I'ma tell you—you'd better pray that you never see one. Everything theoretical goes out the window. It's the kind of thing that will make a grown man hope that the cavalry in the form of tanks rolling down Bourbon and Canal Streets will come posthaste as backup, if you do."

"I'm in," Dr. Sanders said, lifting her chin. "I'm with Ira. We're talking heretofore undiscovered species, hybrids of new species . . . it's too fantastic to begin to comprehend."

"Good," Holland said, "because we have a very short window to follow a very old and unreliable recipe for creating antitoxin in an unsecured lab—which resulted in staff deaths before. Some of our methods will seem peculiar and even superstitious, but one of the first things we'll need to do is secure the work area against Vampire thefts."

The three doctors from the Tulane staff just stared at each other, hang-jawed.

It had been a bullshit ruse but a necessary one. Hunter dragged himself through the demon door, exhausted from the spent energy needed to propel himself to the other side of it without his amulet. He hit the floor with a thud, having jettisoned himself back to the place he'd last held the image of Sasha in his mind. Almost too weak to lift his head he listened to the sounds of daytime street activity through the wooden floorboards.

Car horns, a fat cockroach waddling between dust bunnies across the room. A family of squirrels had taken up residence between the eaves. Pigeons were cooing and screwing somewhere nearby. Voices, human—outside. Crack dealers never gave it a rest. Hunter placed his hands on the floor to push himself upright and froze, staring at a clawed fist.

Panic ripped through him as he assessed his physical condition. The sun was up, the moon long gone, he was out of the Shadow land pathways and had gotten out of the demon doors without being maimed . . . and he was still a wolf? Worse than wolf, he was something terrible in between with a man's forearm completely covered in the thick coat of a Shadow Wolf—hands, not wolf paws! He looked down his body and tried to back away from himself for a second—he had the bent hind legs of the Werecreatures but still the thick, natural tail of a Shadow Wolf.

Instantly his gaze sought a hiding place. The Shadow lands were too dangerous, but no human could see him in this state, especially not the pack, or more importantly Sasha and her team. Before there had been momentary flashes of this abomination, now he was stuck in permanent transformation? Hunter closed his eyes. The extra poisoning from Dexter's hidden rogues. His already impacted DNA. The battles where he was scratched and bitten. The energy that entered his system from beyond the demon doors. All of it met in the middle and changed his life. How long would it be until he ate like a true demon-infected Werewolf? When would his mind slide into the ultimate darkness, never to return?

Hunter released a mournful howl. He had to get to the bayou. He was doomed.

"How's the antitoxin working on his system now?" Sasha asked, standing at Xavier Holland's side as the other doctors watched Silver Hawk's vitals and Clarissa took intermittent blood samples.

"Although the first dose jolted his system into near cardiac arrest," Doc said, rereading all the vital signs from the monitors and talking as he moved about, "now he's stabilizing. But he may need more than anticipated, given he's fighting off the infection at the same time repairing massive injuries."

Sasha closed her eyes. "Give him my dose . . . and—"

"No," Doc said. "It's too soon to tell and you're—"

"Expendable. I'm a soldier," she said, staring deeply into Doc's eyes.

Xavier Holland shook his head. "Not to me," he said quietly. "Under no circumstance have you ever been expendable to me."

"Yo, Doc, me and Winters can tell you for a fact that we didn't get scratched or bitten," Woods offered. "You need more serum for the old man, you use our dose, all right?"

"Ours, too," Clarissa said, gaining nods from Winters and Bradley.

"Never laid a glove on us," Winters said with a smile, then went back to his monitors with Bradley.

"Use mine for Hunter, if he needs extra," Bradley said, and then averted his eyes to a screen.

"Assuming we can get a sample," Dr. Lutz asked, "how long does it take to manufacture new antitoxin?"

"Barring all catastrophes, several weeks," Xavier Holland said, with a weary sigh.

Sasha just stared at Doc for a second. They didn't have several weeks. Two days prior to a true full moon, the lunation was anywhere between ninety-three to ninety-seven percent illuminated . . . full to the naked human eye and enough to allow Werewolves to shift. The UCE Conference would convene heads of state first—those senior, elder entities would meet in a secret plenary session on the third night of a full moon phase, which was last night, when the moon was *exactly* at one hundred percent. It had also been the peak of her heat. From there, it could still shine brightly for a few more nights in the high nineties of illumination power. That's when the general body would meet. That's what she and Hunter couldn't miss. One day she'd have to sit down with Doc to explain it all, but right now there just wasn't time. Still, a decision had to be made about who got meds and who didn't.

"Inoculate the guys who made it back here with us from the lodge," Sasha said, causing Xavier Holland to briefly stop pacing about the machines to stare at her. She'd thought about it long enough; they had to make sure the pack was in their right minds. "They were cut up pretty badly and need their systems stunned clean. Next full moon is gonna come right on the heels of when the serum could be ready . . . and something tells me we're gonna need it way before then. We need it during this cycle, Doc, for reasons I can't get into right now."

"Where're you going?" Doc said quickly as Sasha headed toward the door.

"I'm gonna find a shower in the joint, some clean clothes, eat, and crash for a few hours." She looked at Bradley, then Clarissa, and finally Winters. "When I come back, I'm gonna need that antitoxin-tranquilizer gizmo you guys were talking about making from the new equipment Doc had shipped in."

"Trudeau, we'll—"

"Thanks, Woods," she said, cutting him off. "No. You

and Fisher stay here with Bear Shadow. You're the only men with combat training that I trust to have Silver Hawk's back and to protect the team. The rest of those guys from the clan can lodge at a safe house that HQ can find for them, but I'd honestly feel better if they weren't the ones on my six—feel me?"

"I do," Woods said, nodding.

"What happened in the field?" Doc asked, his gaze going right for Sasha's.

"An attempted coup and a friendly-fire assassination," she said without hesitation. "If any of those guys come near the patient's room, and don't look right, you drop 'em on sight."

"You know we have no problem with that," Fisher said. "But who's gonna have your back in those demon holes when you go hunting, Trudeau? No offense, but if you're going after who I think you are, last I saw him that was one big, burly, out of control motherfucker."

Sasha nodded and turned away, heading for the door. Doc tossed her a cell phone, no further discussion necessary.

"Yeah, I know," Sasha said in a weary voice. "But I'll be fine. This is just something I gotta do solo."

Hunter clutched his stomach as he slipped from shadow to shadow. Gnawing hunger was giving him the shakes and he pressed on quickly, avoiding people at all costs. The concept of human flesh was revolting, but he was unsure of himself. The fact that cooked meats, the aromas from barbecue stands, and Cajun seafood joints made his stomach rumble was a good sign. Thankfully the houses and boarded-up landscape of the still flood-wrecked

Ninth Ward provided plenty of shadows. He just needed to get to the place that was dominated by nature and draped with Spanish moss.

A stray pit bull snarled and stepped into the shadows. Hunter released a warning growl from low in his throat. The animal had no idea how insistent the attack urge was within him until he dropped down on all fours and let the poor creature glimpse him. Releasing a frightened yelp, the pit bull spun, ran into traffic, urinating, and nearly caused a collision as it dodged to safety and kept going.

"Shoulda been on a leash, anyway," Hunter grumbled, and pushed forward. But when he came to a barbecue stand he hesitated.

Fresh slabs of ribs had been thrown on hot coals outside a small fish fry place in a halved, fifty-five-gallon oil drum. He could literally smell the spices tickling his nose as the hefty cook behind the counter piled shrimp, lettuce, and tomatoes with mayo on French bread making dressed po'boys. Old men leaned forward in rickety metal chairs, talking trash and slapping down dominoes. Zydeco music blared from a crackling radio with bad reception inside, competing with the jazz the old men were enjoying with their outside game. He was drooling and hadn't even realized it.

Steady, checking shadows, he waited, knowing that he didn't have the willpower not to do the unthinkable now. His only goal, however, was to not give the elderly patrons a heart attack. But to get to the meat, he had to come out of the shadows, even if just for a second.

It was all a blur, the lunge and then the snatch of sizzling hot meat that was just the right balance between cooked and raw. It was too hot to carry and yet too succulent to leave. Something very primal had taken him over as he guarded his hunt, growling deeply, eyes glowing, and proceeded to eat all ten slabs of beef ribs from the overturned grill.

Screams, abandoned dominoes, a shotgun blast from a righteously indignant store owner didn't stop his meal. But when he heard the pump cock again, he looked up into the eyes of a very frightened man. It was clear from the chef's expression that he thought a rowdy neighborhood dog had savaged his grill. Hunter stalked through the hot coals and punched the plate glass window, giving the owner the chance to flee.

Full-length wolf entered the establishment as the chef-owner and patrons screamed, running out the back. Po'boys called his name, half-eaten plates of jambalaya, red beans and rice, prawns and fries—he ate his way through the small neighborhood joint until he was panting and sweating. Guzzling soda to wash it all down, Hunter chuckled to himself, feeling much improved as he leaped into another shadow behind the destroyed eatery.

"Bad dog . . . very bad dog."

"We've got a three-hundred-pound chef on the verge of a heart attack claiming lukegaroo, or something I can't understand attacked his store in broad daylight—hence why he was blasting a pump shotgun in a residential district." The police officer spoke quickly as the ER team whisked the raving man behind the doors. "Our boys had to pry the shotgun out of his hands and about ten neighborhood patrons and some old dudes were talking about were-wolves. Can you believe it?" The cop scratched his head. "If it were Mardi Gras, all right. But, damn."

"Do you know if he was on drugs, or better stated, what kind of hallucinogens he's ingested?" the intake nurse asked, walking quickly behind the gurney.

Dr. Michael Williams opened his mouth to speak but no sound came out. He looked up from the head nurse's clipboard. The schedule changes that would allow him, Dr. Lutz, and Dr. Sanders to work with the renowned Dr. Holland on a groundbreaking secret project for a few days could wait. He rushed into the room where the new patient was still raving and clutching his chest.

"Sir, sir, my name is Dr. Williams. We believe you!" he shouted. "Get Nurse Margaret in here. She's the only one who seems to understand these kinds of cases," the doctor said to one of the burly orderlies that had tied down the patient. He looked at the frightened man with compassion. "Sir, I need you to calm down, tell me slowly what you saw, so my colleagues can write it down. You're safe in the hospital—we have armed guards."

The other staff members seemed skeptical but played along with the doctor who was obviously humoring a deranged patient. The chef grabbed the doctor's hand and kissed it repeatedly, weeping.

"Get this man on a tranquilizer drip to calm his heart rate, and have someone escort Xavier Holland down here stat. Where is Nurse Margaret!"

Dr. Holland looked at Dr. Williams and nodded. "Tell the police that this man shot at a wolf that somehow got out of its normal habitat—but he was right to do so and is not on drugs or a lunatic. Clear that poor man's name. Tell them that the animal most likely did trash his store so at least he can get an insurance claim going."

"You do this often?"

"More than I'd like."

Dr. Williams's previously crisp white medical jacket against his tanned, athletic, news-anchor-type good looks seemed crushed and wilted now. It was as though the man had absorbed too much truth, and that had overdosed his system and shaken his once orderly world. Xavier Holland landed a hand on his shoulder as he headed back to the temporary lab with Clarissa.

"It's starting, isn't it?" Dr. Williams called out.

Xavier Holland nodded without turning around and kept stride with Clarissa. "Get Sasha on sat-phone, Clarissa, and tell her the target is still in the area . . . and not to lose hope because he's hunting po'boys and barbecue."

Chapter 19

Facedown in goose down pillows, Sasha barely heard Doc's cell phone ringing. She heard the blaring contraption from inside a dream, one that she was too disoriented to remember the second late-afternoon sun pierced her eyes. Fearing the worst, she fumbled for the device, and as soon as she flipped it open her greeting consisted of two words, "What's wrong?"

Almost in a state of disbelief, she listened to Doc's description of the restaurant wolf sighting. The information made every keened muscle in her body relax for a second; she'd thought the call was to tell her Silver Hawk had passed away. As she took her next breath, her body was rigid again; the infected wolf that was sighted could have been the only one she knew of that would pass dozens of humans to chow down on dressed po'boys and ribs. But, still, that was a good thing.

Fatigue clawed at the backs of her eyeballs and then sent mild spasms of tension down her spine as she sat up too quickly to better hear what was being said. Hunter had bum-rushed a barbecue joint? *Wha . . . ?*

"Okay, I'm on it," Sasha said, standing, rubbing the tension from the nape of her neck.

"No. I don't have time to come back to Tulane and get Bradley's device. If I have to wrestle him to the ground, I'll get a nontranquilizer-tainted sample. Yeah. Yeah. I promise. No, I won't do anything rash. Okay. I'll be careful. Bye." For a moment she just looked at the phone. Doc knew damned well what she did in the field—don't do anything dangerous? He sounded more like a worried father than an Ops mission specialist . . . but then, everybody's nerves were frayed.

Easy come, easy go, sleep was worth more than money right now, especially after practically inhaling the homemade gumbo here before hitting the sack. Now she was glad that she'd showered in the hospital, grabbed some scrubs, made a quick change in a tourist shop, and had basically dropped like a stone—already dressed. What would have taken the average person a couple of hours had only taken her half that time, which allowed her to find a small B&B in the French Quarter to temporarily crash and burn in. But even though that brief respite had given her a badly needed one-hour power nap, the little taste of sleep now felt like a tease.

On unsteady legs, she staggered to the dresser to collect the standard mission envelope Doc always provided. Cash, credit card, ID with an alias. Plus, a local badge so she could openly wear a holster packing heat. Contents went in her back jeans pocket. Xavier Holland left no stone unturned. This time he'd added in one extra element: antitoxin. She wasn't sure if Doc had meant it for her or Hunter as she stared at the premeasured hypodermic. Sasha checked the clip on her nine and then slid on a shoulder holster. What to do with the damned needle? She sighed as she slipped out of the room with it concealed in her hand. Ask the front desk for some duct tape, of course, and tape it to her shin.

There was no need to jimmy the lock when a firm shoulder applied to the door would do. Shogun stepped into the empty bedroom and swore under his breath. Her scent was still thick in the air—warm. He'd missed her by only minutes, and he would have preferred to approach Sasha in close, private quarters rather than where she might freak out and accidentally shoot him.

He stooped and touched the floor where she'd stepped, tilted his head, and briefly closed his eyes. Damn she smelled good.

Word travels fast in the Big Easy, Dominique. Etienne lay awakened in his crypt in the dark, eyes open, still as stone. His thoughts kissed the fringes of his daytime familiar's mind. *Ah . . . yes, bring me a little something extra—lagniappe, as we say . . . oui. You say the old man is a leader of the Shadows? Ah, he bears the amulet. Bon. Très bon. Yes, bring him; we may need a bargaining chip soon.*

The orderly pushed a cart of meds aimlessly down the hall with his eyes lowered and stopped outside of ICU. He glanced in and stared at the unconscious old man. Murmurs had gone around the nurse's station that one of the strange soldiers must have left the charm after the patient had come out of surgery. Although it wasn't hospital policy to allow such an obviously expensive item to be left on a patient for both health and legal reasons, no one seemed to know what to do. No one wanted to mess with it, either, not after Nurse Margaret told folks it was a religious item and then went on to scare the beejeebers out of the staff, claiming it to be a form of gris-gris.

There'd been much superstitious speculation, many whispers. No one seemed to want to take the responsibility for disturbing serious gris-gris. But the master wanted the old man, if possible, and most certainly the charm. The charm was easy enough to filch; the old man might require some assistance from the undead—however, he could give them something that would please them.

Glancing at the patient and waiting until the on-duty nurse moved to the far end of the ward, he entered the area with feline grace and slipped next to the oblivious patient. Peering down at the helpless soul, he smiled. One day he'd be so quiet, would have the stealth capacity of the undead that he so admired. He'd be able to look down into a face and determine if that person would live or die. In truth, he had that power now. His arms were so strong, this old man so weak. Taking a life would be easy . . . but for now the master just wanted something to bargain with.

Fine woven silver caught his eye. He could slip it over the patient's head without disturbing his tubing, just like the person who'd put it on had.

Dominique reached out quickly, his deft fingers making contact with the oddly warm metal. Then his face contorted and his body convulsed. A wretched scream rent the room and brought personnel running from all areas. Silver-white static charge covered his hands as he stumbled backward, then arced from his hands to his chest, covering his body in a crackling wave only to suddenly stop as he dropped to the floor.

"Get a broom handle, anything that won't conduct an electric current!" a nurse shouted. "Don't touch that equipment! Something's obviously making it arc!"

"Crash cart! We've got a man down, gotta jump-start him!" a doctor commanded.

"Check the ICU patient's vitals—make sure that faulty equipment didn't surge his heart monitor or alter his IV drips—check his respiration!" another doctor shouted as they made sure the orderly wasn't still emitting a charge.

"Vitals, equipment, monitoring as normal on the ICU patients. All of them," a bewildered nurse said, her voice awed.

"All clear," the doctor on the floor yelled, making personnel step back as he defibrillated the orderly. "One, two, three—all clear. Come on, come on, again—breathe, man! All clear! One, two, three—shit! What the hell just happened to you?"

Midstep in the street, Sasha stopped walking. In the center of her mind she saw Silver Hawk open his eyes. Her amulet warmed and then heated so quickly it almost felt like it burned. His mouth didn't move, but his message was clear: *Go get my grandson.*

She began running, screw a streetcar. Driving wouldn't help; she needed her wolf senses ground level while on the move. Shadow hopping, she could skip through fast-passing vehicle shadows, leaping one to the other like Hunter had shown her not so long ago. That would get her to the battered store, but her sense was that he was long gone from there. She could still see Silver Hawk's intense, open eyes. His presence loomed in her Shadow vision like a guide. Oh, God, he was headed for the bayou!

Images of infected Shadows hiding in the swamps invaded her psyche. "No!" She was shouting into the wind, no one could hear her, but she needed to head off Hunter before he blundered into the dens of the enemy.

Suddenly a huge silver wolf, majestic and proud, mentally slipped in front of her human form, leading the way, making severe cuts and turns down alleys, between buildings, into shadowed gardens, and behind mausoleums. Slowly she began to understand; the wolf in her mind was taking her to City Park. If she could get to Hunter there within the fifteen-hundred-acre municipal enclave, versus the bayou where anything could happen, then maybe he stood a chance.

But the silver wolf in her mind soon fled behind a tree. As she rounded it to find him, a familiar face met her. The shock almost made her jump out of her skin.

"Don't shift, it's safe," Shogun said quickly. "Please, we need to talk."

Sasha placed her hand in the center of her chest, trying to get her heart to stop racing. "I could have shot you."

He nodded and stepped closer. "There is so much going on, we need to form an alliance."

She looked up at him and nodded. "You know about the toxin on the street?"

"Some of the story. Don't know it all, but I do know this—at the UCE Conference, the Vampires will try to divide us. That cannot happen. We can't allow any open wolf hunts. We have to stand united and agree in full session to exterminate our own problems and to retain sovereignty. We don't need outsiders coming in to do that, especially ones that have an agenda."

"That's fair. Makes sense," Sasha said, remembering every facet of his kind, dignified eyes and handsome face. She smiled, remembering how the last time she'd seen him he was clean-shaven and now his hair spilled down in a cascading, blue-black silken fall to his elbows. "How do we get our packs to understand, though? Some of those guys are pretty entrenched in the old ways."

"My sister is, too," he said with a wry smile. "Many of the packs and clan adhere to the old ways because they've never seen a new way that could work."

"Your sister?" Sasha chuckled and shook her head.

"You do remember the cold bucket of water she threw on us?"

Her smile widened. "How could I forget?"

"I told you she was my sister . . . that was truth." His smile faded and became replaced with something deeper that she couldn't allow her mind to address. "Not all Werewolves lie . . . not all of us are monsters, Sasha."

At a temporary loss for words, she simply nodded.

"I can count on you?" he asked.

"Yes. And I you?"

"With my life."

Again, she was at a loss.

"I came, before, when you were in Shadow country—twenty men strong, and we waited, we watched, were prepared to join your battle if necessary."

"Thank you for that," she said quietly. "Now I guess our clan knows what it feels like to have some of our own go rogue . . . and then have every member looked at as a potential hazmat carrier." She let out a long, weary sigh. "This shouldn't be, brother against brother . . . the physical differences between Shadow Wolves and Werewolves is so minor . . . the cultures are so close, as is the history and many of the beliefs—but this hatred is bone deep. How did that happen?" She searched his gaze for something to cling to, something that would help her understand the insane politics that had to be negotiated at the UCE

But all he offered was a good-natured shrug. "The same way it happens with humans. A rivalry turns into a bitter dispute, then barriers get erected, and the next thing you know there's war and genocide. Does any of it make sense?"

"No," she said, quietly ashamed of it all and not sure why. "I've got your back, I know what you're saying is true . . . but I'm not the ultimate authority on clan politics. I'm just an enforcer—not a leader."

Shogun tilted his head. "You're still not his pledged mate?"

Sasha looked away. "I can lobby for an alliance, but I don't have the power to make warriors stand down."

He traced her cheek with a finger, holding her gaze. "But you have influence . . . and a good heart. You know what is right for the wolf families—all clans, all packs . . . but, beautiful she-Shadow, do you know yet what is right just for you?"

Much improved after feeding, he knew he had to keep moving. The farther away from civilization he got, the better. But he could sense something bearing down on him, something that just would not relent. It was there, but not there, a vapor in the shadows. Familiar, yet strange, almost steering him—that's when he stopped and turned on it for a moment, growling, before he pressed onward. Of all places, not here . . . not where there was the Carousel Gardens amusement park for *children*.

The reality seized his chest and constricted it with grief. From a place he couldn't fathom, images and information scorched his mind. Fifth-largest municipal park in the U.S. Lush botanical gardens full of strolling couples and families. More than ten million tourists visited here annually. One of only a hundred wooden merry-go-rounds left in the U.S. resided here, which meant more families and more children. He could see a Mother Goose ride and then Art Deco–inspired fountains. People, people, a place where they held weddings. No. Something awful could not step out of the shadows here. Two predators could not do mortal combat here! No! *This* place, this healing sanctuary, could not be hunting grounds for demon-infected Shadow Wolves. Never the children, never their mothers.

Hunter stopped moving, turned on the unseen presence, and lowered his head with a warning snarl. Yes, he would run from humans, now for their own good. But something in the shadows stalking him . . . never.

Spanish moss waved at him like a maiden riding a carnival float. Ancient oak trees stood like sentries. Something was there but refused to show itself. Then, just as suddenly as he'd felt it, the presence slipped away to be replaced with one he'd know anywhere. *Sasha*.

His first instinct was to flee her possible detection, but when she stepped out of the shadows with her hand over her heart, breathing hard, something stayed his leave. He told himself that it was to be sure the other ominous male wolf presence he'd just felt wouldn't attack her, but as he studied her carefully, he knew that was a lie. Sasha Trudeau was thoroughly capable of addressing a threat. Even if the threat was him.

Using a quick, jabbing lunge to disturb the air near her Shadow in a threatening way, he sent her a message in the standard Shadow body language—back off. Instead of backing up, she drew like lightning and hardened her gaze.

"Show yourself," she said in a quiet, lethal voice.

He circled her in the Shadows, letting her feel the air move around her, letting her know he was close enough to take her life if he wanted to. He watched her move as he moved, her timing impeccable, her instincts razor-sharp. But it disturbed him that it was taking her so long to scent him, to know his signature. Then he remembered; he was tainted. Nearly everything about him had changed and was unfamiliar.

Hunter moved away, the combative aggression ebbing. After he'd fed, some of his old wolf had returned. His front paws and hind legs were again the long, muscular appendages of a natural wolf, not bent abominations and clawed hands. His coat had thankfully never gotten patched and natty to show human skin through it. Instead it had remained thick and shimmering and midnight blue-black. His canines, while pronounced, were no longer a prehistoric tangle of murderous fangs, and the disgusting faucet of demon-infected Werewolf drool had ceased.

Still, he had the very unnatural combination of a human's voice trapped within a wolf's body—evidence of a half-shift, if ever there was one . . . and he could no longer shape-shift at will. Unacceptable under any circumstances. The thing that most concerned him as he watched Sasha try to find his Shadow to confront him was, what if one day the wolf mind eclipsed the human mind and he could no longer call his humanity the way he used to so easily call his wolf?

Until this moment he didn't realize just how vain he was in her presence. There were some things he never wanted her to see, and try as he might to shunt that to the back of his mind, he couldn't. What she thought of him, even if she had to eventually shoot him, mattered. He took a long sniff against his ribs, trying to gauge whether or not he reeked of demon contagion.

"Just stop this bullshit, Hunter," Sasha finally said, rushing in and out of nearby shadows, but nowhere near him at all. "Do you know how worried we've all been? What possessed you to leave Silver Hawk? Okay, wrong metaphor, but you know what I mean. I don't give a damn what you look like or that you can't shift back at the moment—what's important is that we gather our team in tight. The old man's lying in the hospital in ICU, and we need everybody's head on straight. Are you hearing me?"

He could see frustration had a chokehold on her and well understood why. But he would do this his way. He'd go see the old man under the cover of darkness . . . would say his good-byes and make his peace the way it had been done in the clan, within the pack, and even within his human tribe for generations. This was something she knew nothing of.

However, when he turned to leave, a threatening male force breached his shadow. The presence so startled him that he came out into the dappled sunlight snarling.

"Yo, yo, yo!" Sasha yelled. "Chill!"

"It's still in the shadows," he said in a low rumble, needing to communicate with her more than preserve his pride. "It's male, in my shadow, but moves like a ghost . . . it's—"

"Silver Hawk, or a friend," she said, blowing a wisp of damp hair up off her forehead as she lowered her weapon. "Shit."

"How can that be?" Hunter studied her and then trained his attention back on the shadow he'd been ousted from.

"If you still had your amulet, you'd know," Sasha said

curtly. "He led me here in a Shadow vision . . . then a friend also came out of concern."

Hunter just stared at her.

"Yeah. Remember that heroic deed that left us all standing in the safe house with our hearts ripped out?" She walked around in a tight circle. "Why . . . I oughta shoot your mangy ass just for that!"

His gaze hardened, but he checked his coat and then lifted his chin. He was many things, but mangy wasn't one of them.

"Oh, for the love of God . . ." Sasha holstered her weapon. "First order of business, I need a blood and tissue sample."

"Why?" He began backing up, wary. "And who is this *friend*?"

"Because we need more infected Werewolf toxin to make more antitoxin, for starters. Two, we're trying to isolate what it is about your system that doesn't make you go all the way demon-infected Werewolf and simply lose it so—"

"We don't know that yet," he countered, hating every moment that she made him have to use his voice while in wolf form. "And who's the goddamned friend?"

"Someone smart who wants a pack alliance. We can talk about that later. For now, let's deal with the primary problem—your state of contagion isn't as bad as it could have been. You went for the barbecue ribs on the grill, Hunter—not the fat chef. I'm no longer worried, trust me."

He looked away. A family walked by and gathered their children near. Sasha stepped close to Hunter before he could dodge into the shadows and placed her hand on his shoulders.

"Huge but harmless," she said, watching the young couple with a stroller and a toddler blanch. "Well trained. Police canine," she said, patting her Glock. She watched their bodies relax.

"Nice to know you're on our side, officer," the guy she assumed to be the husband yelled. "Never saw one that big."

Sasha chuckled. "Yeah, he's a real prize." She gripped Hunter's coat when he began a low rumbling growl. "Let these nice folks go on down the path with their sanity, would ya? And not a word," she said in a hissing whisper. "Besides, there's probably fifty or so odd Fae marksmen in the trees just waiting to drop a predator that would draw attention to the Conference—so would ya chill?"

Hunter just looked at her for a moment, but when the passersby had gone, the next volley of questions was delivered with slow, quiet rage.

"Look at me," he said through his teeth. "I have lost complete control of my wolf! Yes, I was able to employ the ruse to get three sides to fight each other—that we can discuss later. But of what use am I to you or what is left of my pack or even the clan at the UCE Conference if my mind is eroding to the wolf mind . . . if the human is receding hour by hour, even in the daylight? Take your blood sample to help others if you must, but leave me until this purges from my system. And as far as any alliances go, forget it for now—the politics down here are vicious and I don't even know who you've been talking to. I can't commit to anything until I am in my human self."

"Okay, we'll talk about the alliance proposal later, but I'm not leaving you to be jumped in the swamps and made alligator food—because that's where the infected Shadows went. But I *will* take you up on your grudging offer to help us make more antitoxin, and maybe even a vaccine, from whatever elements we can extract from your DNA."

The fact that she had bluntly stated her point without any compassion in her voice for his dilemma grated him.

"So, to save all this Shadow hopping and energy depletion, I guess you just expect to walk me on a leash to the local pharmacy and steal some hypodermics while you leave me tied to a pole? Is that the plan? Or, I guess you'll walk me at your heel into Tulane University Hospital as a two-hundred-and-twenty-five-pound military guard dog?"

Sasha shrugged. "Whatever you're most comfortable with."

Never in his life had he been so thoroughly disgusted or humiliated as he flanked Sasha with his head held high, but he did take slight satisfaction in watching people clear sidewalks and pathways as she flashed a badge and brought him into the hospital.

The guard looked like he was about to say something, and it was admittedly a twisted pleasure to stare at the man with knowing eyes—eyes that were eerily both wolf and human, and dare him to bar them entry.

"Uh, ma'am," the security guard said as delicately as possible. "Uhmmm, I don't think for health reasons, the doctors might not want a huge, uh—"

"Sir, it's all right. Military. He's a drug sniffer. We've had an incident, and the animal will be confined to that area rendering no health risk to patients."

"Uh, yes, ma'am," the guard stuttered, and then released a long whistle as she and Hunter passed.

It was reflex, he couldn't help it. The sound bristled the

hair on his back and drew a growl with a flash of canines. He watched the color drain from the offender's face.

"Sir, please don't do that," Sasha told the guard as she smoothed down bristled wolf coat. "These animals are highly sensitive."

Hunter refrained from grumbling and offering any comment. Her touch did feel good, and was oddly soothing the way she did what she did. Besides, what had been of greatest concern was getting into the hospital to see his grandfather by any means necessary. So be it if he had to hide in plain sight, a novel concept for a Shadow Wolf, but one that worked better than he'd expected. If they could also do the lab work here more efficiently, all the better.

"We've gotta make one stop," Sasha said with a wide smile as they exited the vacant stairwell.

He looked at her hard and it was a challenge not to snarl.

"That poor chef saw a Werewolf. I want to go to his room as a military cop and thank him for his trouble, and apologize for my bad dog that got on the loose."

"Oh, hell no!"

"Oh, hell yes, because it will make it easier for Doc to send in a spin team if that chef sees what scared the shit out of him, as do several witnesses, and the man's sanity can be vindicated. This way, Doc can give him a card with a number for him to call where he can get his greasy spoon all nice and remodeled and shiny, and can talk forever about the biggest damned dawg he ever saw. Are you following me here? Can you say damage control?"

He knew by not answering her he'd conceded by omission. Public relations was not his thing in the least. This was why he and his pack shunned big cities—there was always the complexity of too many eyewitnesses for things that had to go down in the wild. True, some packs lived in the margins and functioned within the shadows of the city seams. But this was not his way at all. He cursed every footfall that landed in perfect sync with Sasha's as she led him to what would probably turn into a hospital photo op.

"Just wait here, okay?" she said, watching nurses, orderlies, visitors, and patients cling to the walls. "The man already had a near heart attack and has been mildly sedated, I'm told. So let me break it to him gently."

If there weren't already people in the hallways that had seen him, he would have told her to kiss his natural Shadow ass and found a dark supply closet to hide in. Unfortunately he'd been seen and the fluorescent lights of a hospital ward didn't cast many shadows to choose from. Heel, wait, sit, come—oh, he would never, ever let her live this down.

"Mr. Roulade," Sasha said with a cheerful voice. "I'm Lieutenant Trudeau. I'm told you had quite a scare this morning?"

"Yes, ma'am," the chef slurred, fighting the medication. "They think I'm crazy, but I'm not . . . even though that one doctor tried to make me feel better. So did that pretty little pixie of a nurse, Ms. Margaret. I know they was just humoring me so they could get me to hold still long enough for them to dope me up. So, you said, officer—so you coming to lock me up for shooting?"

"Well, no, sir, and that doctor and nurse truly believed you. I'm gonna ask a nurse or two and a coupla doctors on the ward to come on in here with my, uh, military guard dog, Hunter. I'm so sorry he ate your barbecue and went after the po'boys. The U.S. Military will compensate you for your trouble, 'cause I know that the last thing folks down here need to deal with is another insurance claim and all that mess. I got family from down here, hence my last name, Trudeau. My heart goes out for all you've already been through with Katrina."

"It's been a lot, ma'am, more than folks know," the chef said, lip quivering from repressed emotion. "I used to have a real nice place, but what your dog tore up was all I had left . . . that's why I was shootin' and probably lost my mind. Maybe it wasn't a werewolf and was just a really big dog. . . . I honestly don't know my own mind now, all drugged up. But I ain't a violent man."

"We know, it's gonna be all right. That's why I came in here to show you what had gotten loose, okay?"

The chef nodded as Sasha patted his arm, and she seemed to know to wait a bit to allow the distraught man a moment to collect himself. But the more Hunter had listened to her mollify the patient, the more he eased into going along with her crazy terms. People down here had definitely been through a lot, and if he could help it, they wouldn't go through more by way of being snatched into dark Shadows and fed upon by the unholy. As he listened to Sasha's calm, friendly approach, it was another side of her that he was learning.

"Don't worry," she soothed. "We're not gonna do you like FEMA. We can get your store fixed right up without you having to go through a lot of changes. And, uh, maybe somebody in the hall might have a camera cell phone so you can get the pic and hang it in your remodeled shop?" She smiled wide and clasped the man's hand. "Sir, I'm so glad that you and nobody else were hurt. This could have been tragic."

The chef smiled up at her with tears in his eyes. "Little

lady, either you're an angel or they put some really good drugs in the IV drip."

They both laughed and she gave his hand another squeeze and held up one finger. "I'm warning you, he's a monster."

Hunter cocked his head to the side and stared up at Sasha when she reentered the hallway. Even though she was a reasonably tall woman at five foot seven, his head was almost to the top of her shoulder. She gave him a look that begged him to be on his best behavior. He wanted to offer her a dashing smile but thought better of it. Maybe he'd embarrass her and nuzzle her crotch, since she wanted to role-play this to the bone.

"Uhm, could a couple of staff members come in—and if anyone has a camera cell phone, would you be so kind? I want Mr. Roulade to not wake up in the morning thinking he dreamed this—you know how meds are."

Several staffers inched around their desks.

"Jesus, lady, they really have those things on the bases?" a male nurse said, easing around her to slip into the room.

"Some bases," Sasha said brightly, entering the room with Hunter, while everyone else but the bold nurse elected to crane their necks to see from where they were.

"Mr. Roulade, meet Hunter."

"Holy Christ!" Roulade drew himself up into the bed. "That's him! Oh, dear merciful heaven," he wheezed, crossing himself.

"Hunter . . ." Sasha said, stooping down and then nuzzling her cheek against his fur. "Please let that nice nurse take a picture of you next to Mr. Roulade, since you destroyed his store, you bad boy."

He almost slipped and said okay, but instead paid her back for the affront of talking dog-owner-baby-talk to him by slurping her face with a giant lick. Sasha laughed and stood.

"See, he's really pretty harmless." She looked at the nurse who'd made himself extra small in a corner of the room. "Sir, you can breathe now."

"He . . . he, uh, won't jump at me or bite if he hears a click, will he?" the nurse whispered.

Sasha eyed Hunter. "No, you won't, will you?"

Hunter nosed her crotch and she squeezed his neck fur. He struggled not to laugh.

"C'mon, let these men take a picture—just one."

With great trepidation, he loped toward the bed and stared at the poor chef that had almost fainted dead away from seeing him hours earlier. The chef offered a tense grin and a cell phone camera clicked. Hunter loped away. He'd never been photographed in his life, but this woman had a way of making him do all sorts of crazy things.

"Did you get it?" she asked the nurse.

The nurse nodded and reached toward her. Instinct released a low growl in Hunter's throat. Human instinct made the man draw back and cover his head and lift a knee to protect his groin.

"I'm sorry, I'm sorry, my bad," the nurse said quickly.

"No, that was *my* bad," Sasha said with disgust, rolling her eyes at Hunter. "No sudden moves, they don't like that, especially from males."

The chef's head bobbed in nervous agreement. "I can see that, understand it. You gotta train 'em to go after criminals, right?"

"Yeah, something like that," she said, checking the picture that had most of Hunter's huge head in the shot with what looked like a very small but rotund man. She stroked Hunter's back. "All right, big fella. It's back to work."

He watched how she handled the crowd, and had to admit to being quietly impressed. The woman owned diplomatic skills with humans that he'd never seen employed until now. She waved on the way out, telling the chef that someone would come by with a telephone number to change his life later today, and then waved at the impressive crowd that had gathered at a safe distance by the central floor desk to witness the huge beast that a female MP had strolled into Tulane.

It actually wasn't so bad walking at Sasha's heel for a bit. She had a very sexy stride and smelled great.

Chapter 20

"Jesus H. Christ!" Dr. Williams flattened himself against the lab wall as Sasha came in with Hunter.

Dr. Lutz dashed to the far side of the room, huffing on an inhaler. Dr. Sanders just stood behind her microscope, her hazel eyes wide with awe, terror, and wonder. Clarissa McGill held the slide she'd been studying between two fingers, not moving, not breathing as Winters tumbled over a chair and hit the floor and Bradley held on to a desk, his knuckles going white.

"Me and Doc Holland tried to warn 'em, Trudeau," Woods said calmly.

"It freaks you out the first time . . . but there's nothing like watching the transition to make you think you're having a psychotic break," Fisher commented blandly. "Right, Doc?"

"Ladies and gentlemen, I tried to mentally prepare you as best I could, but some things defy description," Doc Holland said in a weary tone. He looked at Hunter. "We're gonna fix this, son."

Hunter nodded, but declined comment for the sake of multiple cardiac arrests.

"He understood you," Dr. Sanders said just above a whisper.

"Max Hunter, meet Evelyn Sanders, Ira Lutz, and Michael Williams—Tulane's finest in bioresearch, epidemiology, and surgery. They worked on your grandfather and so far have done a really fine job. My guys—that's Clarissa—a whiz biochemist with second sight and infield trauma medic training; Winters, a madman on computers with a little kinetic thing going on; and Bradley, satellite and radar man with special insight into the dark arts. You already met Woods and Fisher—and know Doc like family." Sasha looked at Hunter with a plea in her eyes. "Please don't speak, though, baby, or they'll have to bring in a crash cart and we don't have time for that."

"I . . . I . . . don't understand?" Dr. Williams said, his eyes wild. "You've cracked the code on human to animal communications to this level? And what do you mean we worked on his *grandfather*?"

"Michael," Doc said, rubbing his palms down his face. "It will take many hours that we don't have right now and many bourbons to sort this all out. Suffice to say that he understands everything you're saying and you *did* work on his grandfather."

"You have to mean genetically his grandfather . . . That's the human gene donor, correct?" Dr. Sanders persisted.

"No, his actual grandfather," Sasha shot back, growing testy. She looked at Hunter, clearly concerned that his patience was two seconds from ebbing.

"Then is this specimen a Shadow creature wolf or a Werewolf?" Dr. Lutz wheezed.

Unable to tolerate their ignorance any longer, Hunter spun on the Tulane staff and released a quick, snarling series of angry barks.

"Okay, we need to get this process on the road," Sasha

said. "This man has been gracious enough to endure a photo op on the cardiac—"

"What!" Xavier Holland shouted.

"We gotta rebuild the store, it was part of a damage-control strategy, and they only got a piece of Hunter's face in the pic," Sasha said with a sigh. "We had to throw the public a bone."

"This is spinning way out of control, Trudeau," Doc argued, nodding with Hunter who released a low growl.

"Well, can you draw blood and take whatever samples you need so you can hit this man with antitoxin, so he can go up to ICU to see his grandfather?" Sasha looked around the group and then her gaze returned to Xavier Holland. "Hunter can feel it, I can feel it—something happened in ICU."

"There was an incident," Doc said carefully, staring at Hunter and then Sasha. "A man tried to steal the amulet you'd placed on Silver Hawk. He didn't make it. Some-how a piece of equipment the orderly touched had some sort of electrical discharge and the man went into instant cardiac arrest and could not be revived."

"And Silver Hawk?" Sasha said as Hunter began a low series of steady growls.

"We don't know how to explain it, but ever since he's had that necklace on," Dr. Williams said, glancing at his colleagues while keeping a steady eye on Hunter's dark-ening mood, "his vital signs have been improving, his white blood cell count is going in the right direction . . . there's nothing specific that we can point to as to why, but he's markedly improved."

"How 'bout you draw that blood now, Rissa?" Sasha said, trying to hurry the process.

"You, uh, sure, he'll, uh, be okay with that?" Clarissa said, her hands shaking as she began prepping a blood drawing tray. "I mean he's a gorgeous specimen. . . . I've never seen an animal so majestic."

"You don't have to blow his head up to get him to sit still for a blood draw," Sasha said, laughing. "Keep it up and he'll sniff your crotch."

Clarissa held the tray but didn't move forward when Hunter loped away from her with a disgruntled rumble. "I mean, he really is amazing, I'm not just saying that. I've never seen anything like him."

"You should see him in a pair of jeans and a thermal undershirt," Sasha said with a wink. But then she let her breath out hard and put her hands on her hips, watching Hunter pace. "Oh, come on, you big baby, and get your ass over there so she can take a sample. The sooner you—"

"I can do it," Doc said, taking the tray from Clarissa. "His experience with needles hasn't been positive over the years."

"Oh . . . wow . . . yeah . . ." Sasha said, as Hunter made a semicircle and went in the other direction. "Okay, okay, look—they're just going to draw blood, won't hit you with antitoxin until after you see Silver Hawk, all right?" She turned to face the Tulane staff. "You're chief of surgery, Dr. Williams. You're going to have to tell them whatever you need to tell them so I can bring Hunter up there in this form. Tell them the old man is in a coma and that his faithful companion might bring him out. But I can tell you this, Hunter will turn this hospital inside out if he can't go see his grandfather real soon."

The three doctors from Tulane just stared at one another for a moment, words temporarily escaping them all.

Dr. Michael Williams finally raked his fingers through the spiked mass that had once been immaculately barbered brunette hair.

"You have *got* to be kidding me."

"I don't give a shit, call Joseph Pratt," Dr. Williams argued with the head of ICU.

"You are *not* bringing some mangy, flea-ridden animal into a hospital ICU under any circumstances, Doctor! Pratt will lose his job as hospital president if one of these patients has an allergic reaction or an airborne infection impacts an immune system and kills someone. Are you insane, Williams? Not on my fucking watch, you won't! We just had an incident up here that's still under investigation—I don't give a rat's ass about whatever politics you've got going on in your climb to greatness, but this type of madness will have you practicing medicine in some small foreign country with a rain forest in the background and no government!"

"Pratt gave me express instructions that I was to cooperate with this Homeland Security operation to the utmost of my ability—and helping that elderly eyewitness recover so that he can testify is in accordance with that." He waved Sasha and Hunter forward and watched as the other doctor gasped.

"Mother of God . . . what the fuck is that?"

"The old man's companion, who's like a grandson to him, they tell me. We're experimenting with new coma revival therapies. He'll only be on the floor for a few minutes. I trust you can live with that."

Sasha hung back, watching Hunter slowly approach the bed and then lay his head gently beside Silver Hawk so as not to harm him by even a touch. It was the saddest thing she'd ever witnessed . . . a grandfather felled, a grandson trapped between two worlds, and yet a bond so strong that it had crossed miles and minds, all on the wind through a bit of silver-framed amber.

New respect for whatever the Shadow packs termed the old ways entered her. The way of the wolf. As she continued to stare at the mute reunion, she agreed more reverently with Clarissa. Hunter was majestic, just like his grandfather. The genes bore out, no matter what else had tried to take up lodging within him.

Watching them together, now physically close but in different dimensions . . . one locked in a coma and in human form, the other trapped in his wolf and achingly present, she wondered how she would face the inevitable day when Doc got sick.

It was something she tried never to dwell on; Doc was the closest thing she'd had to a father. But the truth was, the man was already up in years. The kind of work he did was stressful, not to mention had an element of danger when not protected in the NORAD bubble, like he was now. All it took was one lab catastrophe, one slip-up, or just a slip and fall in his own home—a regular occurrence for the elderly. Then what would she do when it was her time to sit shiva at that loved one's bedside, and how would she deal with the other inevitable part of that process that she didn't want to name right now?

Sasha looked at the floor and watched it get blurry. Silver Hawk loved his grandson so much that he'd come to her in a Shadow vision to find and protect him, even while in a coma. Had even led her to Hunter while a sworn enemy—a Werewolf clan leader—was present. Damn. It had to be a sign that the old man also thought it was time for peace, time for an alliance . . . either that or the pull to his grandson superseded everything, even the future of the clan. She wondered if anybody had ever loved her that much, even Doc. That was some hard loving that went beyond the biological all the way down to the spiritual . . .

Then again, she had family from here, Doc had told her long ago . . . and she'd seen her own mother and so many spirits from her family on her spirit walk with Hunter. She had to remember that, although those folks were gone, there were so many people who'd loved her— even before she was born, they'd loved her spirit. It was taking her a while to be able to comprehend that the spirit world was an extension of her current earthly reality. If only there was time to stay in New Orleans and to find those people, to learn from their stories, and to find out about where the seer gene came from. But time to learn more about her own life had never been an affordable luxury.

Her attention jerked to Hunter as she clasped the amulet she wore and jogged over to the side of the bed. Hunter lifted his head slowly, easing from the bedside so as not to jostle Silver Hawk in the least.

"Hunter," she said as quietly as possible. "You have to let me put the amulet on you so we can see who tried to take it. What if it was a familiar—a Shadow familiar from one of the infected Shadows?" She gave the arguing physicians her back. "Right now, your nose is keener than mine. Fatigue has done us both in, but your wolf is here. What do you pick up?"

She didn't wait for his answer as she carefully removed the amulet from Silver Hawk and looped the long silver chain over Hunter's head.

"I'm not picking up a trail from an infected den . . ."

Hunter whispered so low it sounded like a growl. He watched the already panicked medical staff back away. "We don't have much time before they put us out, but it's . . . very odd. The undead had lain with that man."

"Vampires sent a day familiar over here to get a Shadow amulet?" Sasha ruffled her hair up from the back of her neck. "Then that just confirms our hunches all along . . . even with regards to Crow Shadow." She leaned over Silver Hawk's body, holding her amulet with one hand and Hunter's with the other. "He came to both of us while in a coma. That says to me that he's strong, Hunter. He's gone within to heal. He's on an ultimate spirit walk where he can see things we've yet to comprehend, I bet . . . so, with the power of three, let's heal his body and bring forth his knowledge."

"Lady, you're gonna have to take the animal out of ICU," hospital security said from down the hall.

Sasha opened her eyes and opened her palm that clasped Hunter's amulet, watching it glow white for a second and then slowly normalize.

"Just be cool," she told Hunter. "I think we did a lot of good for him and we definitely learned a lot."

"But we need more time," Hunter said between his teeth.

"Lady, we're not going to tell you again . . . or . . . or . . . we're going to have to call in the police."

"Steady," she told Hunter. "The man, by rights, is just doing his job—and we can't do anything in here that would harm any of these innocent people." She waited until Hunter nodded and withdrew from the bedside. "Okay," she called out and then stood. "Thank you. We're out."

Hunter nudged his grandfather's hand with his nose

one last time, but was paralyzed in his tracks as the elderly fingertips fluttered on their own to try to caress his coat.

Sasha swallowed hard and nodded. "I saw it." She stroked Silver Hawk's hair and softly kissed his forehead. "Now we just gotta get your grandson better."

"Pull the drape," Doc told Woods. "Like I told you earlier, no matter what they hear, unless I call for a specific individual, keep the team on the other side of the curtain." His eyes held Hunter's and then he looked at Sasha. "He doesn't want you in here, either—just patient and doctor."

"But if something goes wrong with the antitoxin . . ." she said quietly, her gaze leaving Doc Holland's and fastening to Hunter's.

Hunter closed his eyes.

"The man wants and deserves his privacy, Sasha. The trip back is going to be painful . . . probably on the order of a sickle cell episode. I've already explained this to the team while you both were visiting his grandfather. The outer door will be locked, Winters is posting 'test in progress' signage on the door, as we speak, and will be out there with an M-16 in full uniform."

She covered her mouth and touched Hunter's side. "Oh shit, it's gonna be really bad, isn't it, Doc? Let me help . . . if it gets . . ."

"No, Sasha. It's his choice, and maybe you should wait outside. The other doctors are ready to help out if a limb . . . gets twisted in transformation. That's why Williams has already scrubbed."

She glanced at the scalpel tray and the IV drip of saline going into Hunter's forearm, then closed her eyes and stopped breathing for a moment. Every beep of his heart monitor felt like one of the scalpels from the tray was stabbing into her brain.

"What you have to understand is that giving him anti-toxin after this long could be fatal." Doc Holland looked at Hunter. "He knows it and wants to try, but that's the risk. His entire cellular structure—joints, and tendons, and the placement of internal organs, et cetera—have to shift within a system made sluggish by a viral infection we have yet to fully understand. Things that normally happen in a flash could morph and transition so slowly that the pain sends his body into shock, or leaves key arteries and veins blocked, starts hemorrhages. The list of what could possibly go wrong is infinite. So, please step on the other side of the curtain. The longer we delay, the harder this will be on him."

"I'm sorry. I didn't know. We could have just done this first." She kissed Hunter between his eyes and followed Doc's request. Panic-stricken gazes joined with hers as she listened to Doc tap the side of a syringe. If she had only known . . . and what if she'd hit Hunter with the shot that was duct taped to her leg out in the park? Her gaze tore to Doc's shadow, trying to see through the curtain to no avail but sensing that he was pushing the stopper down the tube at a slow, steady rate garnered from years of medical practice.

And then came the wait. All sorts of scenarios ran through her mind. Hunter could reject, go into a convulsion, and come up off the table a full-blown problem that she, for the sake of the lives in the room, might have to blow away.

Doc never said it, but it made sense why the door was locked with a Special Forces guy on the outside toting an M-16 with silver shells, one on the inside, and her. On the flip side, he might not change at all, it might be too late, and he could possibly be left as a man trapped in a wolf's body forever. Those were the two extremes. Her mind was too fried to consider the hundreds of permutations in between, like him dying on the table as a half-mangled, bloody, transitioning mass of flesh. Or maybe winding up a half-human half-wolf deformity. She closed her eyes and wrapped her arms around her waist and waited.

The first scream made her pace. Staring at the curtain, she watched the outline of Hunter's body arch and then slump. Doc's frantic shadow made her bite her lip until she bloodied it. But seeing the shadows was nothing. It was hearing the bones snap and the sound of flesh ripping as Hunter's voice rent the air in agonized wails.

"Can't they give him anesthesia?" Clarissa asked, rocking.

Sasha squeezed her eyes shut tightly and shook her head no. "It's a suppressant in Shadow systems. Screws up the cell split timing. The only thing in his arm is saline solution to keep him hydrated."

Winters dry heaved in a waste can as the outline of Hunter's body showed the head of a wolf still connected to a man's torso as his snout contorted to the sound of pleading moans and a succession of hard bone breaks.

"Oh, Jesus," Bradley whispered and dragged his fingers through his hair.

Woods just closed his eyes and took slow breaths in through his nose. Dr. Lutz walked back and forth, methodically smoothing a palm over his scalp while Dr. Williams remained poised to rush in to assist. Dr. Sanders had found a stool, and she sat under the bright beams of fluorescent lights so quietly, so wide-eyed that she seemed like a hazel-eyed gecko sunning herself on a rock.

The rapid hard breaks slowed, and Sasha turned away from the curtain. Facial structure and human jaw complete—but the realignment of his legs and hips and arms and shoulders . . . she fisted her hair to keep from crying out with him as the first hard snap rang out with his voice. Then the god-awful sound of his nails clawing at the bed, the IV crashing, and the gunking-squishing noise that came with his innards shifting made her cover her face.

Her head jerked up at the same time Woods's did.

"He's going to beg you to shoot him—don't," she said, standing and walking across the room. "Don't you move, soldier, and that's an order."

Chapter 21

A massive wolf had gone behind the drape on a gurney—now stupefied doctors were standing over an unconscious human male body that was going into shock, and despite their incredulity, their job now was to save a human life. She couldn't watch or listen anymore.

"Woods," she said quickly as Doc Holland rushed past the drape with a crash cart. "I want a man on ICU guarding Silver Hawk, one here."

"Where're you going?"

"After the scent trails that Vampire's familiar left before it gets dark."

"Lemme put a beacon on you at least, then," Winters said, his startled eyes clouded with concern.

"Take a couple of these," Bradley offered, tossing her the sample siphoning tranquilizer shells he'd been working on.

Sasha caught them and stared at Bradley, trying to ignore the sounds of the medical team working behind the curtain to revive Hunter. "Won't need more samples, and what I'm going after I'm not trying to tranquilize. I want it put down permanently."

The heart monitor had stopped its sickening, flat-line

wail, and monitor blips allowed her to start breathing again.

"Then let me do the honors," Clarissa said with hard eyes. "After truly seeing what they did to that man . . . what this virus is capable of . . . oh yeah, Sasha, put the rat bastards down hard."

Clarissa rooted through the medical supply cabinets and talked to Sasha as she grabbed small vials. "How about a homemade, lethal cocktail in part one and part two of Bradley's gizmo? Those guys with the full-blown virus should have sustained severe liver damage already—a nice overdose of Phenobarbital, which is normally used to control seizures, will drop their blood pressures and make their heartbeats go haywire—then if I add a nice lethal dose of fast-acting thiobarbital, the bastards ought to be in a drop-dead coma before the second segment explodes. Mmmmm . . . lemme see what we can mix up . . . Veronol to paralyze their breathing apparatus, with a nice healthy jigger of Oxycodone to help promote muscle flaccidity and cardiac arrest . . . and one of my personal favs for blurred vision, Librium . . . What else do we have— oh, general purpose ammonia will always do the trick, add in some formaldchyde, and—"

"Remind me to stay on your good side, McGill," Bradley muttered.

"Sounds more like the stuff of covens, rather than a lab," Winters said. "Sheesh."

"It's all chemistry," she said, mixing her lethal solutions and filling the retrofitted shells for Sasha. "And it'll only take five or six seconds once it hits their bloodstream." She looked up at Sasha. "Try to hit a jugular or something close to the heart if you need it to work faster than that. Hopefully you'll have more time than that, but ya never know."

Strangely enough, of all people, Dr. Williams had offered her the keys to his seven-series BMW in the spirit of teamwork, and it was indeed parked where he'd said she could find it in his reserved spot in the lot.

Sasha jumped in the silver, drop-top sedan and cast the automatic weapon on the passenger's seat, glad that she'd warned the man ahead of time that his vehicle might not come back the way he'd given it. No surprise that he'd waved her off—at his salary, this was his commuting vehicle, the one he slummed in. Go figure.

But it was a silver beauty with enough power under the hood to make a drive-by sweet. Yeah, she was feeling dangerous, maybe even a little reckless. Twice in twenty-four hours she'd heard Hunter's guts get ripped out—first from a purge, then for a hard transformation. They'd caused the wrongful shooting of Silver Hawk, and then tried to assassinate or abduct him in the hospital while he lay there helpless and alone. They'd even eaten members of the clan. Some things were just over the top, so she would show them the female version of crazy.

Every instinct she'd had had been correct. Regardless of the incidents in the mountains, everything they were hunting was slowly making its way here.

When she'd begun this mission to track down Dexter, she and her team had monitored unusual preternatural activity converging on New Orleans. Even before Winters and Bradley told her, she'd felt the migration in her bones way before the Conference. Technology bore out her gut hunch; the body count was higher than normal in the

Ninth Ward, but ever since Woods and Fisher's MLRS launch, that seemed to die down.

Gravitational pull had made her bed down briefly in the French Quarter, but while exhausted, it was hard to delineate sensory perceptions from the simple human desire for comforting aesthetics. Now she knew. Hunter had picked up the scent; he'd keyed her onto it over Silver Hawk's prone body. Mind of his mind, she could Shadowvision snapshots of the dead man's previous path which led her right back to the French Quarter where her first mind had already been.

She let the green streetcar pass her on St. Charles Avenue and screeched to a stop as a man leaped from it into the seat as she snatched up her weapon.

"You have got to stop rolling up on me like that!"

Shogun smiled. "I told you I had your back. Drive before they start honking at you."

Sasha pulled off, shaking her head. "How'd you—"

"Ethan's wife. She works ER—Nurse Margaret. The fairies hiding in the fluorescent lights and ducts told the rest of the Fae how they made that man suffer. Dexter had him poisoned, as well as more Shadows . . . word traveled from the forest regions, now that most of the contingents have assembled."

"You've got proof?"

Shogun shook his head no. "The Fae have proof. . . . They always have proof but they try to stay neutral for fear of reprisal. If we can show them that we'll come together to fight a common enemy, and can win, then they'll bring their evidence to the UCE. If not, we're on our own."

It didn't do any good to argue the fairness of it all. It

was what it was. You couldn't make anyone scared out of their minds testify against entities that held a grudge till the end of time. Maybe the Fae had a level of wisdom that the wolf packs had abandoned.

"You got an extra weapon—since we're hunting Vampires by day and I can't shift till the moon's up?"

"Sure," Sasha said. "Take the semi."

Shogun studied the weapon with appreciation. "Nice piece." He turned to her with a sly smile.

She refused to dignify the comment and kept driving. This alliance was going to be hard enough as it was to explain to the clan. That was all she needed—for there to be even the remotest hint of impropriety. Therefore, the tall, bronze, animal magnetism routine was a waste on her, just like it had been before . . . dazzling smile in the sunlight notwithstanding. Hunter was laid up in the hospital, possibly on his deathbed, and this guy was joyriding with an automatic in tow, beaming like a Labrador going on a hunting trip. Werewolves. It just wasn't right.

"I could have handled this home invasion myself, ya know," she finally said.

"For the alliance," Shogun replied and lifted the weapon.

"Would you keep that down? Jeez!"

Sasha turned into a sleepy, oak-lined neighborhood. Victorian, Greek, and Spanish revival mansions ensconced with overflowing gardens bedded with bougainvillea, brilliant azaleas, myrtles, and camellias—crinolines beneath the swaying skirts of tree moss—kept her eyes keened. Yeah, this was Vampire territory, their version of slumming since the 1700s. Not as ostentatious as the huge antebellum plantations they generally preferred, but definitely in-town residences for galas and feeding fetes.

Her foot eased on the accelerator as another scent mingled in with the dead orderly's. *Crow Shadow?*

Shogun's expression had gone stone serious. "Shadow Wolves have been butchered here, Sasha. I smell their blood . . . no demon contagion in it. What we see might be terrible for you."

"No worse than I've already seen in our territory," she muttered, bringing the car to a stop. "I want these bastards more than my next breath."

Parked illegally, she was over the side of the BMW, weapon in hand within seconds. Shogun flanked her seamlessly, like he was air. The trees provided a lush choice of shadows but she had to resist kicking the door off its hinges. Opting for the magnolia-shaded side of the house, she cased the wrought-iron balconies and leveraged her way in the old-fashioned way—an elbow through the glass. Shogun moved like a gymnast, his lean, toned frame flipping over balconies, grabbing hold of drainpipes, as he scaled the walls and got in without a sound.

She'd be gone before the cops came if the house was alarmed, which she doubted. Vampires had their own security measures. She had her own antisecurity measures: silver slugs, partial daylight, and a real bad attitude.

Quickly scanning the interior of the French Gothic antebellum she'd plundered, her gaze roved the centuries-old, hand-carved cypress ceilings, then the slate floors of the double parlors, paneled bookcases, and heavily draped floor-to-ceiling guillotine windows. Moving as a Shadow against the wall with her weapon cocked, she cleared each room until she found a cellar door. Bingo. In a land where the water table made its residents bury their dead aboveground, the vague scent of damp soil, stone, and blood was literally a dead giveaway that somebody wanted something hidden badly enough that they'd endure unceasing property damage. A wine cellar, yeah right.

Shogun entered the kitchen beside her without a sound, giving her the all-clear in hand signals that the second floor was unoccupied.

Lifting the latch silently, she went for the surprise attack with a boot to the door. Several red glowing eyes and hisses met her as she became the darkness, a Shadow within the shadows, firing dead aim between red glowing eyes in split second single shots. The stench of embers and charred dead flesh gagged her, but the scent of Crow Shadow's blood drove her forward. Her wolf eyes adjusted to the black, damp environment. A shard of gray sunlight from the stairwell behind her helped. Crow Shadow weakly lifted his head and looked up at her, and then passed out.

Shogun somersaulted down the stairs, laid flat on the ground for a second as a Vampire scampered from under the table and four more came from behind the stairs.

In one scissor move, he'd flipped the one that scrambled out from under the table into the first aggressor. Milliseconds mattered when battling this predator, and he dodged a claw rake that attempted to snatch out his heart by running up the wall, grabbing the Vampire's arm, and breaking it backward. Sasha was halfway down the steps and had hit two center skulls when Shogun flipped again, grabbed the automatic he'd been carrying off the floor, and unloaded hellfire. Cinders floated down everywhere with the awful sulfuric stench of the undead igniting.

No time to spare, she yanked the bloodletting tubes out of Crow Shadow's arms and hoisted his body over her shoulder with a grunt, and then precariously leaned to the side to grab her automatic by the barrel, but Shogun picked it up so she could keep moving. Getting him up the steep cellar steps was gonna be a true bitch, but she'd have to call everything wolf within her as close to the surface as she could to get them both into the BMW alive.

Much as she hated to admit it, it was good to have Shogun there sweeping the terrain. He was more agile, had a crazy Ninja thing going on. If a Vamp came out of nowhere, she knew he had it. Fragile battlefield trust just clicked like tumblers instantly falling into place within a lock. She could now mule Crow Shadow's body with less panic. Somehow, in an undefined sliver of time, they'd become pack, squad. One mission.

But after all the gunfire report, humans would arrive soon. So would Vampire familiars, possible local cops getting a call from distraught neighbors, and God only knew what else. Sweating, puffing, she kept it moving and got the injured man to the double parlors. There was no way to do the window, then down the balcony. Out the front door, under the cover of porch and tree shade would have to do. But any neighbors watching the car that had heard gunfire report would freak when she stepped out of the shadows with a prone body and dumped it into the vehicle next to a guy bearing a full set of canines and toting an M-16. Oh, well . . .

"Got another one," Sasha said into the cell phone, driving like a maniac.

Winters turned to the team monitoring her location

and then toward the curtain. "Yo, Doc, incoming! Got a bleeder."

Francois coalesced into an angry funnel cloud of vapor and exited the vent system of his home like a stung hornet the second the sun touched the horizon. Etienne was already up and dressed and waiting for him to enter the town house cellar to assess the damage.

"They came for their own as expected. *Bon*," Etienne said, walking around the piles of ash that had once been his henchmen. "Now the table is set for full-scale war."

"They killed some of ours," Francois seethed.

"No matter. Lower levels that served their purpose. The Shadows will seek retaliation, which will further lend credibility to our claim that Shadow Wolves and Werewolves that have been infected are out of control. But the she-Shadow left the blood. *Très bon*." Etienne turned to Francois and stroked his cheek. "We redress your home invasion tonight. *Oui?*"

Francois nodded. "*Oui*."

"How can we emerge from behind our doors at full strength when the moon is not due to be at exact fullness for weeks?" a Werewolf voice rang out to their leader.

"This month we expect a blue moon," their leader growled, stalking through the carnage of rotting bodies, bones, and flesh. "Supernatural conditions dictate that from the onset of the first full moon until the next one within the same lunar month, we can come out to play. It is our birthright to feed under the full moon! It will be that way for several more days."

"But under the moon bands stretching between the first and second full moon rising, we are not as strong as we normally are until that second moon rises again in her full splendor," an older, one-eyed Werewolf said from the distance. "The infected Shadows are stronger than us. They probably even ate the strong newcomer that warned us, because he never made it back through the doors to safety."

"Our numbers dwarf theirs now, I am told. Their own Shadow packs have warred with them until their numbers are significantly diminished. The time to attack is now. If we wait, they can infect more of their own and replenish their troops."

"I heard parts of their plan," Crow Shadow said weakly as the doctors revived him. "It's going down tonight before the Conference convenes the first night of the general session."

Sasha paced between the livery that held Hunter and the one that now held Crow Shadow. Shogun had refused to enter the hospital, but she needed to break it to Hunter now that a Werewolf alliance was in the offing.

"Then, I'm—we're out," Hunter said, yanking a tube from his arm.

"Whoa, whoa, whoa—whatduya mean, you're out?" Incredulous, Sasha spun on him.

"Not advisable," Doc Holland said. "You can't afford another shape-shift, a nick, or even the physical exertion of a battle. We just jump-started your heart three—"

"I'm out," Hunter repeated, stiffly throwing his legs over the side of the livery and then staggering to the curtain past the huddle of amazed physicians and yanking it back.

Clarissa's gaze slid down his body as she opened her mouth and then closed it.

"Clothes, scrubs, something I can put on to get through

the streets in—plus I need a weapon since shifting might not be an option," Hunter said, his intense stare roving the group.

"I'm out with Hunter," Crow Shadow said, sitting up slowly and almost falling. "I can get a transfusion from one of the uninfected guys that made it to the safe house. So can Hunter. If they lived through the day, they've no doubt eaten, gotten some rest—we have fresh warriors there."

"*Jesus*, Trudeau . . ." Clarissa said quietly as Woods tossed Hunter an automatic. "You said more impressive in jeans and I say jeans not necessary."

Thoroughly frustrated, and unable to process Clarissa's comment, Sasha rounded on Hunter. "You can't do battle like this, neither one of you can! That is the most bullheaded, self-destructive—"

"Silver Hawk would want it no other way," Crow Shadow said, his voice raw.

"We are warriors, and this is what we do—defend what hangs in the fragile balance." Hunter caught a pair of scrubs that Fisher brought in and flung at him.

"Okay, since there's no arguing with you, then at least wait a few to get a transfusion," Sasha said, beginning to pace. "Plus, I need to talk to you about an alliance."

"The alliance can wait. Right now—"

"No, it can't wait, Hunter!" she shouted. "The Southeast Asian Werewolf clans want a truce, want a pack bond between the Shadow Clan of North America and them. It's necessary," she said, her gaze holding his in a deadlock, "to have enough of a voting bloc to best the Vampires—whom we know are angling for a civil war between us as an additional cause of action."

"Werewolves?" Hunter raked his hands through his hair and rolled his shoulders.

"We are in no position to turn away allies and to hold on to old prejudices right through here. We'd better accept this olive branch and bond, because—"

"Werewolves? After all this—"

"Their pack leader saved my life, man. Him and Trudeau burst into the house where they had me," Crow Shadow admitted quietly.

"Shogun had my back in Vamp territory, Hunter." She stared at him hard and then looked away out the window. "If North America merges with Southeast Asia, those are two huge Federations. . . . The others will know something went awry and vote with us, at least for a show of solidarity—even if talks break down later, outside of the Conference forum. But we should go in united, especially since the Vampires obviously tried to play us."

"We're also gonna need some additional forces, Hunter," Crow Shadow said in a firm but respectful tone. "If we're going after Dexter, where he's had time to build up troops, we'll need all the available firepower we can get."

Hunter nodded and opened the window. The Tulane doctors and Sasha's monitoring squad threesome watched in abject amazement as he tilted his head back and released a long, baleful howl. Crow Shadow soon joined him in the pack-rallying call. Try as she might, Sasha couldn't resist, and soon Woods's and Fisher's voices blended in with it.

"Damn, and we thought sonar was an advanced communications system," Winters muttered when the wolf call ended.

"This hospital will never be the same," Bradley said, shaking his head. "The entire staff is gonna have to take Xanax to get over all this."

Dr. Williams looked down at his hip and grabbed his vibrating cell phone. All eyes studied him as he listened intently. He clicked off the call and stared at the group. "The ICU patient just woke up. The attending physicians on the ward said he's trying to yank out his tubes, get out of bed, and is as strong as an ox."

"You heard the call, brothers and sisters," Lion Shadow said. "Time to mount up. It's gotten so bad that Hunter's calling for an alliance with uninfected Werewolves."

"Get the fuck out of here," Anwar said, shaking his head.

"The man said not to fire on them, we're going in as one pack," Lion Shadow said, his tone a hard command.

"Damn, wonders never cease," Tomas muttered. "Just better hope that brother is in his full and right mind, feel me?"

The other members of the pack stared at Lion Shadow for answers that their leader was momentarily at a loss to provide.

"But we're using a hospital as base camp?" Bob said, a question in his voice and his eyes.

"So far, Hunter and Trudeau got us here alive—at this point, I'm not asking questions, just following orders."

"What! We're going in with Shadow Wolves?" Lei marched back and forth along the infantrymen lines of Werewolves.

Shogun pointed a nine millimeter at her. "Challenge me at home as my sister, that's one thing. Challenge me as the commander of this clan during strategic battle maneuvers and I may forget our relationship. Now step aside."

"A rallying howl from Hunter and his Shadows?" Dexter said, eyes narrowing. He kicked Francois's Queen Anne parlor chair into the fireplace.

"Thought we got that bastard?" one of his men said sleepily, rising from a white-satin-upholstered Louis XIX sofa now stained with body grime. "Only five of us made it after the tussle in here, and that can't be a good thing if they're rallying. Feel me?"

"No matter," Barbara said, glancing around Francois's mansion that they now occupied. "There aren't enough of them left to pose a real threat. We've still got some of our own in the pathways and down in Terrebonne, remember."

Nods rippled through the slowly stirring group as she began the rallying howl that caused the others to join in.

"Damn, don't they have anything to eat in here?" a large, sluggish henchman asked as the wolf call ended.

"It's a *Vampire* house we're squatting in," Barbara said flatly with disgust. "You'll find all the bottled blood you'd ever want, but real food, forgedaboutit."

Dexter smiled a toothy grin. "Then I guess we'll just have to change for dinner and go out to eat in the French Quarter."

Clarissa tugged on Sasha's elbow as the lab filled with Shadow warriors that reverently greeted Silver Shadow and Hunter.

"I now understand why you're gone for weeks at a time," Clarissa spoke in a conspiratorial whisper. "When you come back, I have questions, lady, that will *not* wait."

Sasha smiled and landed a hand on Clarissa's shoulder. "If I tell ya, I'll have to kill ya."

Clarissa stared at her, stricken. "Seriously?"

"No, I'm just playing."

She left Clarissa limp and smiling, leaning against a

lab table. The hardest thing in the world was going to be convincing Silver Hawk to stay behind, if that was possible—same deal with Woods and Fisher. Those two were soldiers, and the old man was a fierce warrior. But somebody needed to guard the lab that was working on serious antitoxins that could help their cause later. They also needed a clan elder that had been revered and respected in years past to come to the general session at midnight.

Hunter glimpsed her as though he'd already considered where she was going. He went to the livery where his grandfather lay prone, clasped his grandfather's strong grip, and leaned over to gingerly touch his chest against his grandfather's healing chest, warrior to warrior style.

"Some of us must guard the future," Silver Hawk wisely said without contest, and then looked at Crow Shadow, Woods, and Fisher, then the human teams. "Some of us must restore the present," he added, casting his gaze around the Shadow packs. He gazed up at his grandson and then at Sasha. "And some must redress the injustices of the past."

Hunter nodded. Sasha nodded. Weapons got distributed along with vehicle keys and lethal cocktail shells. And just that simply, there was balance.

"I don't understand why we're not changing?" Barbara shrieked. "Shadow blood was supposed to bring us down, stabilize us to come out of the infected Werewolf transition, not block shape-shifts!"

"What the fuck, Dexter?" a strong beta shouted, looking at his still-human hands in disbelief.

"They added something to the blood—that's the only way. If it's not pure, if anything else is in it, just like we can't take normal human meds, it slows the shifts." Dexter slammed his fist into the wall. "Double-crossing, no-good Vampire rat bastards!"

"If we can't change, and Shadow packs are breathing down our necks . . . not to mention, if our own altered packs find us not in leadership form . . ." Barbara said, panicked and allowing the obvious risk to trail off with her sentence.

"We head to the French Quarter," Dexter snarled. "That house where they took Crow Shadow. This time we don't wait for them to do some fancy blood extraction where they can mix it. We eat it right from his flesh, direct."

"They will be coming here," Francois said evenly.

"*Oui*, they will try. But the fight is much better on that rolling estate of yours, rather than on a lovely, densely populated human boulevard where a spectacle could occur to drive away future business," Etienne murmured, unfazed as the trees outside his French Quarter property became heavily loaded with bats. "And they already put out their call to their own, I take it, before they learned that they couldn't shape-shift."

"Which should bring the other infected Shadows there first," Francois stated flatly, peering at the filling trees with his hands behind his back.

"And the Werewolves, infected and uninfected—just like the uninfected Shadow Wolves—are on the move."

Francois slightly inclined his head. "Forgive me, *mon ami*, then why are our legions here?"

"To keep the infected Shadows and general nuisance infected Werewolves from leaving your mansion area to head toward this uptown house in search of untainted Shadow Wolf blood . . . or to the hospital, savaging neighbors along the way. We simply cannot have this disruption to our lifestyle," Etienne said with a wave of his arms, dispatching half of the bats in a black cloud that blotted out the moon.

Chapter 22

Glass shattering on the first floor of the mansion sent Dexter and his crew into a sliding dash across the polished floors and up the steps. They'd found a weapons stash that the Vampire's human familiars kept on hand for Werewolf invasions, but it wouldn't last forever. Taking window positions on the second floor and over the spiraling staircase rails, they tried to pick off invaders using conventional demon-hunting artillery.

Shadow pathways opened, and infected Shadow Wolves joined in the fray, significantly evening the odds for Dexter's side. Huge infected Werewolves breached the staircase, wiping it out, and pump shotgun blasts fused with rapid-fire machine-gun sprays to send the beasts back over the rails. The battle waged hard outside in the gardens, but no one dared to go near a window to witness which side was winning. Hunkered down, Dexter and the four wolves that survived with him panted through terror-induced sweat, listening.

Screeching car wheels brought Dexter's team to the other side of the house. A silver BMW careened forward over the driveway, through the manicured bushes, M-16 rounds whirring like tracers in flashes lighting the night. A Dodge RAM spun to a skid and turned what looked like a pipe organ toward the house. Multiple launched rockets spit a death rain of silver against the property, splintering wood, glass, and wrought iron. Trapped at the top, no stairs, and angry, demon-infected Werewolves at the bottom battling infected Shadow packs, the mansion burning from grenade explosions, there was only one option. He and his small retinue of rogues had to run to the other side of the house.

A huge wolf pack appeared at the tree line and Shadow warriors spun to meet the threat.

"Hold your fire! Those are alliance forces!" Sasha yelled and then released a long howl. A return howl made every warrior seek Hunter's gaze for approval.

Hunter released a long, soulful wail and then turned to his men. "Find a gas main," Hunter shouted, motioning toward the house, "and burn the mothers out!"

No sooner than he'd called the command, a shoulder-launched rocket found the kitchen window. The impact of the explosion sent wolf and human bodies tumbling. A white-orange blaze lit the blue-black night, and bats screeched in outrage as they fled from trees hit with burning debris.

"I want those little bastards, too!" Hunter yelled, pointing an automatic toward a cloud of fleeing bats and then firing, beginning the black hail of bat bodies.

The truck turned in a slow pivot as the Shadows manning the MLRS sent silver death into the cloud of bats, making it rain teeny rodent bodies across the far acreage.

"Hold your fire!" Sasha said, panicked. "Any shells that don't connect will keep going into possible civilian areas."

"Roger that!" someone yelled from the truck.

"Direction was toward the bayou with twenty acres of Vamp land in between," Hunter called out, and then lowered the automatic he clutched. "I hate Vampires! But Sasha's right—we can't let stray shells hit houses a coupla miles away."

"Keep it that way," Sasha hollered over the din. "Conventional weapons only, hold on the high-powered as a last resort! Flame throwers."

"You got it!" Hunter raced across the back lawn that had become a battlefield. One of his men reached out an arm and pulled him up to the truck and slapped a flame thrower into his grip.

Demon doors suddenly opened on all sides, allowing in wave after wave of huge, demon-infected Werewolves to encircle the Shadow Wolves in Sasha and Hunter's pack. The guys in the vehicles that rimmed the lawn would be sitting ducks if something came up beneath them from the ground. But in the tight circular formation, there was no way for their uninfected warriors to turn and fire without possibly blowing away their own men who were engaged on the ground. Before the onslaught of predators hit the vehicles, Shogun's lethal pack was on them.

In an odd turn of events, the pack he led leaped in as wolves struck deep wounds, and then rolled away as men in lightning-quick martial arts moves. From their glistening, naked bodies they ripped away long stainless-steel blades that had been taped to their spines and hunting knives that had been taped to their thick, sinewy thighs, to come up beneath a predator and gore or behead it. Sasha paused for a moment, awed by the almost balletlike display of raw force on the field. For a moment, she and Hunter's men held their fire, also not wanting to hit an ally. It was a first on many levels. A breakthrough.

The allied clan's hand-to-hand combat style had obviously been perfected over centuries, and it used as much of their mind to outwit their opponent as it did their psychic and physical agility. For a split second her eyes met Shogun's. His hair had been a swaying curtain of midnight that moved when he moved, causing a near-hypnotic trance. It parted ever so briefly as he paused, caught his breath, and the night air opened it enough that his gaze latched upon hers.

Moonlight cascaded down his hard, bronze body, illuminating the lean sinewy steel that moved like river currents beneath his skin and bunched in hard, distinct blocks down his torso. She stopped there and looked away when he moistened his mouth with his tongue and then quickly flipped out of a predator's lunge before beheading the creature. The too-intimate exchange that was too crazy took all of three seconds. Focus returned her instantly to the battle as she pulled the trigger and blew an infected Shadow Wolf's head off.

Swarms of bats took off in a zigzag pattern, but Hunter's well-aimed flame thrower sent popping, smoking cinders to the ground in a hail of gruesome rain.

Tiny, charred rodent bodies littered the rolling, manicured lawns. The stink was god-awful. Massive Werewolf bodies lay dead and twitching. Infected Shadows lay faceup, glassy-eyed, and unmoving as the trucks inched forward and Hunter's and Sasha's ground troops turned over bodies with the barrels of automatics, and pumped extra slugs in foreheads and chests just to be on the safe side. Shogun's men separated heads from bodies. The carnage was total. They took no prisoners. This was the way of the wolf. Both clan leaders stared at each other and gave each other a nod of appreciation and acknowledgment for a battle well fought.

They also came upon four human bodies and turned them over slowly.

"Barbara . . . damn," Hunter said and spit on the ground. He couldn't catch Bob as he leaped down from the truck.

"Oh shit, oh shit—she was in there and you shot her!"

Shogun's men snarled, but their leader held up his hand. This was clearly intrapack Shadow politics. His men fell back. Hunter's men circled in to better understand and keep the peace.

"Wasn't like that, Bob," Sasha said carefully. She looked at Lion Shadow for assistance.

"Use your nose, man," Lion Shadow said calmly.

"She was raped! Dexter had her in there with all those infected Shadows—no!" Bob yelled, still holding a gun on Hunter.

A single shot fired from the bushes dropped Bob to his knees. The man fell forward, eyes still haunted. Bear Shadow stepped into the truck's high beams. "Clan policy. Never draw on the alpha. That was his third time. He was mentally gone and things are better this way."

"If he were a Werewolf," Shogun remarked calmly, "the first offense would have been enough."

Shogun and Hunter stared at each other, and then crossed their forearms over their chests in respect. Sasha hung back, waiting, to see how the Shadow packs would absorb the loss, as well as the alliance.

Silent nods confirmed Bear Shadow's decision. He was an enforcer and it had been his call to protect the clan leader at all costs during battle. This was all costs. No one argued. Bob had been a problem. An even bigger problem now was Dexter wasn't in the body count on the ground.

There was no resistance to Shogun's presence, or that of his pack—if they hadn't gotten involved, Shadow Wolves would have been lost when the demon doors flooded open.

The Shadow Wolf pack surveyed the smoking, body-riddled terrain as distant sirens sounded. Nothing moved or disturbed the still tree shadows against the blood-soaked earth.

"Flame throwers on those demon wolves; local cops will never understand," Sasha said. She looked at Hunter and then Shogun. "Dexter and the others with him, the core leadership, obviously couldn't shift. The Vampires must have done something to Crow Shadow's blood, like our man said. We've gotta move out. Head back to the French Quarter where Dexter has to be headed—that and the hospital are the only places he can go to get pure Shadow Wolf blood; the bags I left hanging when me and Shogun got to Crow Shadow, and from the lab at the hospital—which Dexter will soon be able to track, given all the activity with us there."

"We stop him at the house," Hunter said, looking at the heavy artillery, "but not like this. People, families, children . . ." He shook his head as he picked up a nine from the ground and checked its half-filled clip. Then he found a full one to jam into his back pants pocket. He looked at Shogun. "I like your style. One on one, man to man, I blow his head off nice and clean—the rest of this artillery goes back into storage after the UCE Conference. I want no retaliation incidents there, so be on the ready, but fall back and wait. No preemptive strikes. Foot soldiers guard the hospital but be very careful of collateral damage. No innocents die on our watch."

Shogun smiled a sly half-smile. "You trust us Were-wolves to guard innocent humans now?"

The group paused, their gaze going between the two clan leaders.

Hunter smiled a half-smile. "Trust you more with humans than my woman."

Shogun chuckled and shifted back into his wolf form, calling his men with a rallying howl to make the run back to their hidden posts. "Good choice," he said over his shoulder with a wink, and then was gone.

Hunter walked toward the BMW; Sasha raced to catch up with him and jumped over the side of it into the driver's seat. "You need both hands on artillery, partner."

While it was nice to be hunting together again, she continually glimpsed Hunter's jawline. It pulsed with palpable frustration as though a shape-shift was so close under the surface of his skin it was all he could do to contain it. There was no way to fathom how he felt or what it must be like to have an incredible gift all one's life, then have that taken away at the time when it was needed most. Crippling was the word that came to mind, but he seemed to be dealing with his circumstance much better than she knew she would have. Then there was the Shogun thing that she knew was gnawing at the quiet recesses of his mind.

"What are we gonna do about the Vamps?" she asked, trying to keep the subject focused on the battle at hand, while trying to avoid drawing the attention of local police as the speedometer climbed. She backed off the gas a little, knowing the only thing keeping them from getting pulled over was the fact that eighty percent of the New Orleans police force had quit after Katrina, and they'd yet to be replaced. Still, there was no reason to push it.

"I don't know. My main target is Dexter," Hunter said,

his eyes straight ahead. "One day, them, too . . . we got a lot out at the mansion, but Dexter can't escape again."

Sasha kept her eyes forward and left it at that. It was better that way, if no one said what was really on their mind.

Dexter bounced a commandeered Audi over the curb and jumped out of the vehicle, rushing the French Quarter property, taking no security measures. Wild-eyed and panic-stricken, the scent of Crow Shadow's blood drew him into the house. Bats flooded through the broken window behind him. A BMW bounced to a stop behind his car.

"Now this is *très interessant*," Etienne said with cool reserve and held up his hand to tell his bats to forestall their attack.

"*Oui*," Francois murmured as the bats scuttled along the ceilings and the two Vampires watched Dexter tear through the house toward the cellar.

In hot pursuit, Hunter and Sasha were on his heels. Dexter fired up the basement steps as it slowly dawned upon him that Crow Shadow was gone and the basement had been breached. Spinning around wildly, trapped, he saw the half-filled bag of pure blood and greedily opened it, guzzling the contents, while holding off Hunter's and Sasha's return fire.

Hunter motioned with two fingers toward the floorboards. Sasha nodded, pointing her M-16 toward the wood. Before she could squeeze off a round, the floor exploded beneath them, sending Hunter flying backward out the kitchen window and her up and through the ceiling, shells flying, bats screeching and scattering. Out of the void came a ridiculous beast.

She was dazed, her legs dangling through the splintered floorboards, and for a second she couldn't move—

that is until glowing eyes peered up at her through the hole in the floor above. She moved her legs into a tight pull against her body, and in a backward somersault avoided the snatch that took half the floor with it. Glock gunfire and Hunter's footfalls distracted the monster long enough for her to rim the room firing shells down into the hole. But she had to dive out the window as the thing punched through what remained of the floor.

It moved so fucking fast that it was dodging bullets. Shadows were all over the house and it was expertly maneuvering between them and the demon doors, making it a near-impossible target to hit. She sensed a presence behind her and spun to shoot it, but the thing she couldn't see pushed her through the hole in the floor right into the path of a backhanded blow.

She ended up sprawled on the back lawn and with no gun in her hand. A strong pull yanked her out of the path of a refrigerator.

"Fucking Vampires are in there playing games!" Sasha shouted.

"I know," Hunter yelled, throwing her his nine. "Got something in the trunk for their asses, too."

She covered him as a mass of bats ejected from the house following Hunter, who rounded the building and opened the trunk. He came away from the vehicle with liter bottles of water that Bradley had packed and flung them into the swarm as high as he could. Sasha was on his flank, dropped her left hand under her right, took dead aim, and exploded the bottles in the air. Screams and bat shrieks echoed in the night as flaming rodents littered the lawn and verandas.

Neighbors closed shutters, lights went off in houses. Vampires materialized on the front porch with a snarl.

A hurdling beast wiped them out like bowling pins. Francois was in Dexter's jaws one moment, and in the next his head was missing from his body. Etienne disappeared. Sasha was over the side of the BMW, Hunter right behind her.

"We're outta ammo!" he yelled.

"Gas, almost, too!" She looked at him, then they both looked over their shoulders, forgetting the rearview mirror as something larger than a pickup truck skidded into the streets behind them, roaring.

"Cell phone?" Hunter shouted, still looking back as she drove like a maniac.

"Dropped in the firefight!"

"To the bayou to get it away from human pop or the hospital where there'll be heavy collateral damage, but where we've got our squad and more weapons?"

"You know the answer to that," he said.

"Call in allies?"

"No!" Hunter shouted. "You see what's chasing us? I don't want their blood on an I.O.U. any more than I want to bury another Shadow from our pack. Let them guard the hospital—keep anything from that blood and antitoxin Doc is working on."

"Just checking," Sasha yelled, as she spun the vehicle around, avoiding a streetcar and several cars, and headed for the bayou. "It's almost midnight—how in the hell do we get this evidence to the Conference?"

"I know what she said," Woods shouted, "but I know what I'm feeling!"

"Me, too!" Fisher said, grabbing more shells.

"It is always wise to follow one's first mind," Silver Hawk said, slowly walking around the lab, causing the doctors to follow him with their eyes. He stared out at the moon. "We are not finished here yet."

"You guys have good gut instincts," Winters said, pointing at the radar. "They were headed here, made a hard reverse, and are heading for the bayou. Look at Trudeau's beacon. It's going crazy!"

"Hell, more than her beacon, what's the big blob behind her tiny blip?" Clarissa looked around at the others and quickly handed Woods, Fisher, and Silver Hawk fistfuls of the lethal cocktail shells she'd made.

"Get the rest of the team, especially those guys in the truck with the MLRS, on sat-phone," Bradley said quickly. "If Trudeau and Hunter hard reversed away from a populated area, then that, more than the radar, tells me something crazy big is on their asses."

"Damn it," Sasha said, bouncing the vehicle to a stop. Mud sucked at their wheels, and they'd hit a point where even four-wheel drive would have been laughable.

Over the doors, it was a flat-out run. A small dock was their beacon as trees crashed down behind them. An airboat became the destination—two steps, a twenty-foot joint leap, and they were on the aluminum contraption, Hunter firing up the engine while she untied it and shoved the boat away from its moorings.

Deep water would have been helpful, rather than the night-blackened water filled with gators, tree stumps, swamp bog, and the unknown. A raging creature kept pace with them along the ragged shoreline as moss and gnats stung their faces and low tree limbs threatened to take off their heads. More than once the beast lunged into the water, making them swerve. In the distance on the wrong side of the shore they heard their squad. Trees were becoming denser, and their men couldn't get in close to assist.

If the Shadows fired to help them, they stood an equal chance of hitting them, and then what would be the point? Running couldn't work as a permanent strategy, but for now it was the only option. That is, until the trees narrowed too much ahead. Hunter had nowhere to go to maneuver the boat. It hit a stump hidden by the water, sending them airborne, the boat flipping, just as the beast plunged into the shallow water behind them.

Wedged between two centuries-old, thick trees, the aluminum bottom sheared off from the fan, sending it hurtling back toward Dexter. Everything happened in milliseconds. Hunter and Sasha hit muddy water. The fan tumbled like a flipping top to capture Dexter's snout and cut it from his face. The momentum of his body was still hurling forward, right into the flat aluminum boat bottom that took his head off like a guillotine blade. Hungry gators left the banks, not as interested in Hunter and Sasha as they would have been, going toward the bloody carnage behind them that was easier and larger pickings.

Sasha and Hunter looked at each other.

"I didn't want to become that," he said, staring at the feeding gators as they moved slowly out of the water.

She nodded and slid her hand into his. "You were never that," she murmured. "Not even close."

Silver Hawk sat quietly loading cocktail shells into an automatic and watching the window. He didn't cheer or shout as word came over the sat-phone that mission was accomplished. He just brought Clarissa's lethal cocktails to his lips, kissing each as he loaded them and then brought the gun up to his shoulder.

A single shot rang out. The team jerked their attention to the old man and then the smoldering body that appeared out of nowhere on the floor. Silver Hawk delivered another shot that began to incinerate the immaculately dressed dead man.

"Vampire that cried wolf one time too many," Silver Hawk said simply. "A very old one after Shadow blood."

Epilogue

One hour later: A minute before midnight . . .

She didn't know what to expect, but as she stepped out
of the Shadow lands beside Hunter, she had to admit
that they'd both cleaned up pretty good. He stood
proudly, eyes forward, wearing the clothing of the
indigenous peoples of North America—elaborately em-
broidered doeskin suede. His long, black braids were
immaculate and twisted with silver and eagle feathers at
the ends. He looked so fantastic that she had to find a
point in the dense foliage to stare at. The thick, white
mist lit by moonlight was a good place to affix her sight
line as they waited for the secret meeting mansion to rise
out of the bayou.

Given that this was her first UCE Conference and intro-
duction as an enforcer, she'd gone along with the protocol
of the North American clan, donning a meticulously
beaded suede gown that was encrusted with turquoise, amber, red coral, and amethyst stones, although she would
have preferred her military blues. The opulent feathered
headdress required concentration to balance, too. But curiosity and anticipation was what made her stomach
clench, not fear of losing the Vegas-like structure to the
mud just beyond the marble courtyard.

This time her medal would be the amber and silver

medallion, and she was proud to be included along with Silver Shadow and Bear Shadow on Hunter's flank.

Shogun and his retinue cleaned up extremely well, too, for that matter. He gave her a discreet, respectful nod as his clan was announced. The red silk, native robes that he wore were thoroughly regal and his very angry sister was a queenly knockout, despite her bad vibes.

Sasha silently surveyed the groupings in awe. Were-wolves from every continent, seven in all, gathered in a small section of the open, manicured courtyard that her-alded forth like something one would imagine in ancient Greece. Were-beings from the collective Big Cat fami-lies, Bear families, and other interesting phyla that she hadn't realized existed in the Were-community, separated the Werewolves from the seven Shadow Wolf clans. The Fae gathered in small, elegant clusters, their particular ethnicities and regions denoted by size, body type, and their familial use of color auras. Phantoms gracefully slid between the hedges and marble columns, never seeming to stay in any one location for very long.

But it was hard not to gape at the treetops laden with gorgeous, streaming feathered beings in iridescent hues that showed themselves as half human on top and half bird on the bottom, their eyes a fantastic, endless pit of flames. She tried hard not to stare at the Phoenixes, but they—like the opalescent unicorns—were simply marvelous.

Trying to catch a glimpse of the Yeti and some of the more exotic Mythics, she kept her face forward but strained her peripheral vision as far as she could. Even though Hunter had warned her that they absolutely hated being spotted and often didn't even show up at Conferences, she still wanted to see one just once—like she supposed everyone else did.

Her only regret was that she couldn't bring Doc. He would have been in a researcher's paradise. She couldn't even get Woods or Fisher a pass, but she'd catalogue everything in her mind to share with them over a beer when she got back.

Thundering motors made everyone turn around, even the stoic Vampires, who were dressed to the nines in black tuxedos and tails, each with two voluptuous women or more on their flanks. They turned with great disdain, their dark eyes burning black, and peered at the source of the disruption.

"Oh, the Order of the Dragon has graced us and will be on time this year," a Vampire voice crooned with contempt.

Sasha almost broke rank and smiled. It was so like them. If she'd been back home at Ronnie's Road Hawg she would have shouted out, *Haters*! But this was neither the time nor place for barroom antics. Besides, she loved the bikers. Apparently so did a lot of the Fae, who made no bones about cheering their late arrival.

It was a spectacular display, and probably what pissed off the Vampires most—being upstaged. Each gleaming chrome bike had a humongous rider on it, each with spiked chrome gloves, spikes coming out of their shoulder epaulets, boots, and helmets. They wore heavy, thick, scaled leather pants in shimmering, opalescent hues, and every helmet blocked one's sight into it with a reflective, mirror shield.

"Ohhh . . . that's what the Vamps hate," Sasha murmured to herself, watching the female Vampires hiss and look away from the helmets.

But the female riders that clung to the drivers' backs were no less spectacular. Their skintight, colorful getups ranged from barely-there minis to full catsuits, and they unfurled from the riders' bikes with liquid grace the moment each male driver kicked down his kickstand.

"Watch this," Hunter whispered. "Phenomenal."

The motors were still rumbling, anticipation wafted through the crowd with palpable tension, then in a lithe, fluid move, the motor sections of each bike fused to the drivers' chests. Chrome handlebars grew longer and entered the drivers' bodies, fusing man with his bike in exoskeletons that were each as unique as the bike he'd ridden in on. Scaled leather pants became skin to stretch over spiked Dragon armor.

"Wow!" Sasha said with utter appreciation, not caring that she sounded like a newbie. Impressed was impressed.

Hunter chuckled, despite himself.

"You got that right," a friendly, boisterous Gnome called from the Fae Parliamentary contingent. "Wait till ya see *the ladies* do it."

Huge, fire-breathing Dragons had absorbed the bikes, and then nuzzled what now seemed like very fragile human females beside them, by comparison. But in a flash, the ladies' helmets got absorbed into their skulls to show gorgeous, exotic glowing eyes, and their skins became radiantly hued, glistening versions of the leather they'd rode in on.

The crowd clapped as the serpent-bodied she-Dragons slid over the males' backs, sensually threading themselves through their wide spikes like brightly colored silk ribbons. The joining almost seemed too intimate to watch, especially when each she-Dragon's actions produced a low groan from her mate, and then the ladies anchored themselves into place with a deep, passionate fang strike that made even the most off-put Vampires shudder.

Sasha shook her head. "Just . . . damn . . ."

Hunter swallowed hard. "Yep."

She fought a smile as the ground began to vibrate. The Order of the Dragon had made it just in time for the mansion-raising by the elders. To miss that was the height of disrespect. Everyone went down on one knee as the dark, glistening black marble rose out of the misty abyss.

"Can you tell Vampires have been heavily influencing this Conference for centuries?" Hunter said sarcastically under his breath, just low enough for Sasha to hear.

She didn't dare answer him as she peeked up at the ominous structure and then quickly lowered her eyes. If the Conference hall looked like a huge black marble mausoleum, à la Vampire style, then what frickin' chance for justice did they have? Two fairly top-level Vamps had been executed tonight, and no doubt that would be brought up as a breach of supernatural conduct, since there was really no true evidence. The Fae probably wouldn't step forward, Hunter had said, and if it came to a vote, she and Hunter had to pray that there'd be no dissension in the wolf ranks.

Sasha stood when everyone else stood and, waiting for cues to be sure she didn't create some political faux pas, followed Hunter's lead to the letter when entering the building.

To her amazement, the interior was much larger than the grand mansion appeared to be on the outside and was sectioned off by dignitary groupings just like the courtyard—but in what she could only compare to large opera boxes. Each one was retrofitted with a small speaker system and earplugs so that the language could be selected by human region and supernatural species. She also noted that no natural enemies were seated near each other, and each box section only had members of the same species at each others' backs. Interesting.

Instead of finding hard, cold surfaces inside like she'd imagined, there were lushly cushioned, extremely comfortable, high-backed leather barrister's chairs facing the elders' bench.

The bench, as it was called, was actually a long, gleaming, ornately carved semicircle ebony table that was accompanied by high-backed, red velvet-ensconced chairs. Each chair held a very old being for each order, and their grim expressions alone seemed to defy anything but the utmost civility among species.

What seemed like carved confessional screens in front of almost totally closed in boxes made her crane her neck and give Hunter a puzzled glance.

"Some species are shy," he told her in a quiet murmur. "They don't like to be seen and those privacy screens are for the Yeti, Unicorns . . . Lochness . . . mostly Mythics."

What could she do but nod as though it all made sense?

Above the main nave was balconied seating that allowed for airborne species to take comfortable perches among the rafters. Sasha glanced up at the Gargoyle population that elbowed and fidgeted with each other like nervous pigeons while the Flying Dragons wound themselves around cornices designed for their bulk.

Pixies casting pixie dust and translucent fireflylike Fairies made the prettiest light displays hovering around the huge crystal chandeliers in their miniature crystal boxes. As they settled in, they caused the chandeliers to give off bursts of pastel hues that reminded her of the aurora borealis. Just below them the phantoms created a beautiful, misting miasma that caught the colors as though living clouds.

Notably absent were demons. She would have to ask Hunter about that later, and could only assume their absence had something to do with the whole bad-blood thing that had gone down eons ago with the Werewolf clans.

Sasha sat back in her box chair for a moment and simply took it all in. "Wow," she whispered.

"It is magnificent. . . . There's nothing like the first time," Hunter said in a quiet rumble.

He covered her hand with his and gave it a gentle squeeze. There was pride in his touch, but also ownership that she wasn't sure she liked. From the corner of her eye she caught Shogun's glimpse, and saw the muscle in his jaw pulse as he subtly lifted his chin and sent his gaze straight ahead. But as civil as everyone seemed, there was also tension in the air. She was monitoring it in Hunter's posture and could feel it raising the hair on her neck, not exactly sure why.

A very, very old Vampire stood slowly from his seat at the bench with seemingly great effort. The hall went still. Blue veins crisscrossed his bald scalp beneath paper-thin, death-gray skin, and he took his time adjusting the black velvet robes around his slight frame. With one finger he opened the carved box that sat at the front of the U-bend in the table, then stood back. A heavy onyx-and-marble gavel with strange markings on it flipped out of the enclosure and smashed itself against the wood. The cracking sound that echoed through the hall was like a strike of lightning, and then the enchanted gavel threw its head back and began shouting.

"Hear ye, hear ye, welcome all to the ten-thousandth, two-hundredth and eighty-eighth year of the United Council of Entities. Vlad Temps is again this year's presiding elder. Are there any challenges before the crier reads the minutes?"

Silence echoed in the great hall behind the gavel's voice. Sasha watched the old Vampire's face, noting the very subtle smirk it now held. The venom that threaded through her as she watched his arrogant confidence almost foolishly made her stand. It was hard not to wonder how long the Vamps had the UCE on lock with their ruthless power paradigms. She glimpsed their box, and they were strangely the most handsome group of entities she'd laid eyes on . . . genteel even. They were as politically correct as one could be, all nationalities represented, everyone wearing understated, very expensive designer tuxedos and gowns—women dripping hundreds of thousands of dollars in jewels or more, perhaps enough to make Hollywood's best and most beautiful gag.

Baron Geoff Montague, who'd been her informant in South Korea just before Shogun had pulled her from his mental clutches, gave her a pleasant nod and a knowing smile. Handsome rat bastard. Sasha's gaze shot around the room. Others felt like she did, she could tell. But no one was going to put their neck, literally, on the line. Maybe it didn't matter who presided over the Conference, but something about Vampires consistently winning that coveted role didn't seem right, especially when they'd just been involved in some very foul and underhanded events.

Sasha sat back, allowing momentary defeat to claim her. Hunter squeezed her hand tightly and then let it go to grip his armrests. It wasn't her place to disrupt things. The fact that the thought had even crossed her mind made her want to slap her own face—was she trippin'? Disgust filled many eyes, but clearly no one was going to challenge the old bastard.

Complete silence answered the gavel's question. A coal-black mermaid with glistening, opalescent scales, long aqua hair, and emerald eyes was brought down the center aisle in the arms of a tanned, very nude and very buff male nautilus water sprite. Her huge fan tail was the only thing that shielded his pride and his expression was utterly zombified. The siren lifted a large nautilus shell to her lips and drew in a deep breath, closing her eyes until her pale pink lashes dusted her regal cheeks.

"No!" Hunter stood so quickly he toppled his chair.

The Titan almost dropped the crier when he snapped out of his daze, seeming bewildered as to what to do. Vampires stood slowly in their boxes and leisurely took off their gloves. Hunter's retinue was on their feet, but the expressions on their faces were very unsure. Sasha stood too, completely at a loss.

One thing she did notice was Dragons had moved into place like huge bouncers, and the Fae had sent several archers up the side aisles. They'd drawn like lightning; silver arrows were in quivers. She so badly wanted to ask Hunter, *Baby, do you know what you're doing?*

"Your complaint, sir?" the old Vampire said in a patronizingly patient tone.

"Due to the duplicitous nature of the species and recent events that could have cost catastrophic losses of the wolf clans, and have—as well as caused human collateral damage, thus outings into the general human knowledge base—the North American Federation of Clans challenges the Vampire Cartel's leadership at this conference this year."

"Due to our duplicitous nature?" a smooth, lilting voice said from the Vampire box. "But, *mon ami* . . . duplicity . . . well . . . that is part of our culture."

Subdued laughter created a low, charming resonance within the Vampire box.

"Mr. Hunter . . . you are aware that you must have evidence?" The elderly Vampire smiled a tight, toothy smile, but his eyes burned black with rage from the affront. "I suggest you throw down that particular gauntlet when you have proof—or a good attorney." He looked at the Vampire box. "How many attorneys do we have present tonight—a show of hands?" Half the box responded and then laughed.

"We'll lend you one of ours," someone called out from the Vampire box.

"You could always try to get pictures of us caught in wrongdoing, however," another threw in.

The elderly Vampire sat down chuckling, drawing the other Vampires into satisfied snickers, dismissing Hunter with a wave of his hand. "But now that you mention it, there was a disturbance that could have your species brought up on—"

"Let's do this the old-fashioned way," Hunter growled.

Even Silver Hawk landed a hand on Hunter's shoulder, but he shrugged it off.

"Not fifteen minutes past midnight and you already have a death wish?" The old Vampire stood slowly, his black gaze narrowed. "We try to have these meetings after peak full moon phase so you dogs can at least maintain some of your human composure."

"He's got proof," Sasha said, not sure when her brain had fled her skull.

"Oh . . . this should be very interesting," the presiding elder said as murmurs now filled the great hall. "But I'm sorry, mates are—"

"I'm not his mate—I'm his enforcer."

The older Vampire hissed, causing silence to cloak the hall. "Same clan, therefore not allowed."

"You said pictures," Sasha spat back. "I've got 'em. U.S. Military, Special Forces, Paranormal Containment Unit, sir!" Sarcasm had a stranglehold on her and she saluted him like he was a five-star general and stepped forward. If she'd been armed, she would have shot him, just because. "That's right, even though you undead bastards don't photograph, the lack of photo image is what nails you. I can prove through military surveillance that 'nothing' opened a lab vault with infected Werewolf toxin in it and removed it from our labs."

The Fae peacekeeping forces turned their arrows toward the Vampire box now, and she also saw they had vials of liquid that she was sure had to be holy water, locked and loaded and ready to go.

"But that—"

"And," Sasha said, practically leaning over the edge of her box as she cut off the bench president, "I have the synapse tracks of a meeting of the minds with Baron Geoff Montague." She smiled a wicked smile as his fellow Vampires sneered. "Isn't that right that you can't purge a Shadow Wolf memory . . . that you boys are afraid to go in because if you get trapped there by an angry wolf, your psyches can be forever damaged?"

Sasha paced, watching the Shadow Wolves all begin to snarl. "Uh-huh . . . I thought so. But, see, my momma was from Louisiana—a seer." She spun on Geoff and blew him a kiss and made her voice dip to a syrupy Southern accent. "Didn't know that, did ya, suga? But I bet if one of these nice psychic, neutral Fae folk goes into my brain, they'll be able to read some of the nasty little things you left behind in my pretty little head . . . things I might not have even remembered."

"This is an outrage!" Geoff bellowed, flinging his white gloves down and yanking off his bow tie.

"You wanna do this Old World style?" Hunter growled, and transitioned so quickly into his wolf that he hadn't drawn a breath.

"Fliers up!" the old Vampire shouted.

"Not until the story is told." A white-coated wolf shed his purple Conference robes in a hard, furious transformation and began stalking down the center of the polished table.

"Southeast Asia will testify. We saw the results and fought with the Shadows!" Shogun had transformed and was now precariously walking the rim of his group's box.

Every Shadow Wolf in the house transformed, creating a ripple effect of howls of support from the Werewolf Federations. Only Sasha and Silver Hawk remained in their human forms. When the elderly Vampire started to raise his finger, a black electric charge crackling at the tip of it, Fae in the rafters shook their heads no and then motioned to the hundreds of already transformed wolves.

"I have a full medical team at the hospital that saw one of yours breach a human facility to get to me tonight for my Shadow blood and the antitoxin that would be made from my grandson's blood," Silver Hawk said. He removed a pouch from his suede jacket and flung it to a peacekeeper to take to the bench. "His ashes are in there. Smell them, and see if he is indeed from your own coven."

"That's right," Sasha yelled. "We know for a fact that

Vampires aided and abetted rogue Shadow Wolves, but they also poisoned Shadow Wolf food sources. Everywhere we turned, there was Vampire tracer at the sites, and the one thing that is inarguable—we're the best trackers on the planet. We *know* what we scented, and it was undead."

"You kidnapped our Crow Shadow," Silver Hawk said. "Seers of the Fae can go into his mind and give them a clear picture that cannot be altered. His silver aura requires that his mind hold the truth. Test him for a lie." Silver Hawk looked around. "Scent the air, wolf packs and clan brothers, and then unite. Do you smell a lie on us, or them?"

Angry barks and howls filled the hall. Hunter leaped onto the opposite end of the bench. Fae archers pounded each other's fists. Dragons shot fire-warning blasts to keep the wolves from instantly going to war, but they were only warning blasts. Gargoyles bickered and shook their heads, and disgruntled Fairies and Pixies began pluming gray sprinkles of rage. The phantom mist grew dark and moaned. Yeti bellowed from behind hidden screens and Unicorns kicked the benches over.

The gavel slammed the table as even elders at the bench paced, arguing among themselves.

"You are the liar," Vlad Temps shouted at Sasha. "We do not have to take indignities from a half-human aura-deformed bitch! You don't even have the protective silver band in your aura that would guard the truth—and you call yourself a she-Shadow to challenge my people? To challenge *me*? What moonlight madness is this coming from the North American Shadow Federation clan leader? Tell me it is not that you are so smitten that as a clan leader you cannot see how you've been led astray by the human military—an organization that views our kind as lab experiments."

Vlad Temps spit a greenish slime on the bench that sizzled with hundreds of years of hatred. The pandemonium in the hall went still. All eyes fell on Sasha. Hunter loped back to her side and transformed to argue for her, but she held up her hand.

She shook her head and chuckled, walking out of the box into the center aisle. "Just like a lowlife Vampire in the end. Twisting words, changing the facts as a diversion. Fact. I was made in a test tube. Fact. My DNA is Shadow Wolf, a heritage of which I am proud. Yes, fact, the military jerked with my conception, but I know who I am." She swept her arms out and threw her head back and howled. "When you have nothing to hide, no one can make you cringe from your truth!"

"She was made, not conceived. Made, not born," a low Shadow Wolf voice rumbled through the crowd.

"The prophecy, man . . ." another voice rumbled through the Werewolf ranks.

"Bringing brothers together, isn't that how it goes?" someone else said from the back.

"My wife works ER with the humans," Ethan shouted from the Fae boxes. "We are neutral, have always been that. But what we have seen at the hands of the demon-infected and the Vampires who colluded with them has been a travesty!"

And uproar of Fae voices in a rare, unified bloc rang out. The members of the Order of the Dragon began chanting, "Oust, oust, oust, oust!"

"I am Fae, a healer nurse at Tulane," Margaret said and then held her husband Ethan's arm. "We are peaceful people; we have children, and have always been terrorized by what could happen, Vampire retaliation. But to see what I saw in that hospital . . . to see how humans, too, could be hurt if this virus got out—and I saw the honor of the Shadows, the lieutenant . . . the Werewolves, all pulling together, human and supernatural forces to stop a scourge. If I do not speak up, we'll all never be safe. Take my testimony!"

"Order of the Dragon will back you up. If anything happens . . . to the nurse and the bar owner, we'll start opening up graves to daylight," a big, burly Dragon said and then sent a flaming nostril snort toward the Vampire box.

"The gavel has been passed to the Shadow and Werewolf clan elders to co-serve for the current year!" the gavel shrieked. "With a bloodless coup, will this meeting, please, people, now come to order?"

Hunter shifted and leaped onto the Vampire box rim with a snarl and began stalking toward Geoff. Shogun pinned the Vampire diplomats in from the other side. Within seconds they had all vaporized and shot to the exit as a unit, snarling. Their elder stood erect and smoothed down his robes, his eyes now raging blackness as he levitated two inches off the floor before walking on plumes of smoke to vacate his seat at the bench.

"We withdraw our attendance this year," he said in a hissing murmur. "Perhaps once clearer heads prevail and you have better evidence, we will grace you with our return. Until then, *adieu.*"

Sasha called out to the Vampires' disappearing forms, her voice loud and clear and strident with unspent fury. "We don't need your presence here, if you're going to behave like demons! Your goal has always been to make the wolf clans fight each other so that you wouldn't have a large enough voting bloc—and you almost succeeded.

You've kept the Fae and other supernaturals afraid of your power that has tentacles everywhere, strangling the life from the smallest and the weakest. But the truth will always out. Tonight is the way of the wolf!"

Sasha threw her head back and howled and a cacophony of voices joined in with hers—even from those who, technically, weren't wolves.

Three weeks later . . .

"It's not so bad having to hang out in the Big Easy until the next full moon, just to be sure nothing untoward surfaces while Doc works on more antitoxin."

"New Orleans is growing on me," Hunter said with a deep chuckle. "Wonder why that is?"

"Wonder how we got stuck right smack in the middle of Vamp country, loving it?" She smiled and kissed him. "But we do need to watch our backs."

"So what else is new?" he said with a nonplussed sigh. "The Vampires are always gonna be pissy with us, we needed to do a lot of damage control, and frankly the Shadow packs need to be still for a while to heal from the significant losses. I'm tired of being on the move."

"I hear you," she murmured. "I might even try to do some digging and look up family . . . who knows? It's good that Doc is here with the team—I know they are *loving* New Orleans food and nightlife. This ain't NORAD by a long shot."

She rolled over and laid her head on Hunter's bare chest, listening to his heartbeat and hoping he would just let time heal him, too. "You know, sometimes you just have to be still and listen to the trees."

"You sound like Silver Hawk," Hunter said with a

weary sigh, stroking her exposed back. "He needs time to get stronger physically before we move him away from the doctors that have learned his body . . . so I suppose it's all good. I just know we need to rebuild the packs, reorganize the territories, bury the dead in righteous ceremonies . . . make sure the contagion is over. Nothing can ever threaten our people like this again."

She nodded, agreeing without words with all that he'd said, but she also knew it was a matter of timing. The main thing that he'd failed to mention was his capacity to shift had yet to be tested on a consistent basis. He'd done it under duress at the Conference, but after that hadn't been as successful . . . his wolf came very, very slowly these days. She knew that was at the core of all things. In Hunter's mind, how could he lead if he couldn't become the alpha wolf on demand? She didn't know the answer for him, but knew that it lay partly in his gaining the confidence to try again, and again, until he worked the metaphysical muscle back to its original stamina.

But, how could she even begin to ask him to attempt something that could be so painful, if she was even afraid for him? There was so much adrenaline and hype happening at the Conference; sure, he'd flipped in and out as smoothly as before. But it could have been disastrous, and every attempted shape-shift since had been almost like his joints had become arthritically brittle until he just stopped trying.

"You know," Sasha said quietly after a while, talking to Hunter's massive chest before looking up into his sad gaze. "We lost a lot, but we gained a lot."

"Now you really sound like my grandfather." He tried to smile but she saw the strain in it.

"We found out who was core to the family. Those we

saved. We found out who was not. Those we lost. We found out what poison delivery systems the Vamps and rogue Shadows used. We gained some human allies in this state and even bigger allies at the UCE—avoiding a Werewolf–Shadow Wolf civil war. We routed out some nasty Vamps, pulled off a bloodless Conference coup, and got rid of a region full of infected wolves. We saved Silver Hawk . . . Crow Shadow . . . and, frankly, you. So, we'll rebuild. Not bad for a day's work."

He smiled at her and stroked her hair. "Like the commercial says, 'Marines get more done before five A.M. than most people do all day,' huh?"

"Yep." She kissed him. "But I'm PCU—we do our thing at night."

He nodded and took her mouth slowly and then pulled back from the kiss. "If I had to be stuck in one form or another, I'm glad it's this one." His voice was a low rumble that reverberated through her chest.

"Me, too," she whispered, drawing him into another slow kiss. "But something tells me that there's still a magnificent wolf inside you."

He smiled a half-smile, his irises beginning to be consumed by amber fire. "The wolf never dies, just lays back and awaits the right opportunity . . . patience, timing, stealth . . . is the only true way of the wolf."

Keep reading for a sneak peek at the next
Crimson Moon novel

𝕺𝖚𝖉𝖊𝖆𝖉 𝖔𝖓 𝕬𝖗𝖗𝖎𝖛𝖆𝖑

Available Winter 2009
from St. Martin's Paperbacks

Purpose filled each of Sasha's long strides as she walked down the hall and then jogged down the curved staircase toward the destination of fresh air. Giving the genteel house staff a quick greeting, she pushed past the ornate, Antebellum-furnished space, through the French doors, and out into the humid night. Freedom.

No longer feeling trapped inside her and Hunter's room, the contrast between the air-conditioned, upscale interior she'd just left versus the relative grunge of the bawdy tourist's district, compounded by thick, warm air, made her seek balance in the tavern across the street. Finnegan's Wake had a Corona with her name on it. She was now a woman on a mission.

But as that instant-reflex thought crossed her mind, it also gave her a moment of pause. What was different about her going on a beer-bender and what Hunter was doing? Pain was pain; painkiller was painkiller, and self-medication was exactly that, either way.

Sasha quickly thrust her body through the tavern doors and let the instant coolness of air-conditioning and the hard thrum of music flow over her senses. Thinking too hard about it all and rationalizing it too much would make her upgrade from a beer to Wild Turkey or tequila, maybe even kamikaze shots with the fellas if she didn't stop.

The local supernatural citizenry smiled at her with a respectful nod as though the sheriff had just walked into a bar in the Wild West. If only the human tourists and kids escaping school on break knew.

There were only a few Fae peacekeeping forces left in the area since most of the Conference diplomats had pulled up stakes. Sasha had to smile as a couple of very handsome archers discreetly lifted an ale in her direction with a question in their eyes after they'd quickly scouted the joint for signs of the big wolf that normally escorted her. That was a factor she hadn't expected; how things would look if she suddenly started showing up places in the supernatural community solo. She hated that it now made a difference, when all her life she'd gone wherever she'd wanted as her own woman—not *somebody's* woman. The entire concept was not only alien but Neanderthal, as far as she was concerned. However, she'd also been a diplomat long enough to know that these things mattered. Every species had a protocol.

Sasha let out a quiet sigh and looked harder through the crowd for her team. Country music and its sad-story lyrics chafed her nerves. Why couldn't it have been all-things-Irish night? Sasha glanced at the Fae soldiers again as she elbowed her way toward the tables in the rear. At least it wasn't R&B or the blues.

Two pairs of dark, intense eyes stared back at her from beneath heavy fringes of dark lashes. One of the archers wore a chocolate leather jacket, pants, and boots so finely tooled that she shoved her hands in her pockets to stem the ache to touch them.

On first glance she might have thought he was a Vampire, because the pure sensuality that oozed off him was completely hypnotic. Yet his multi-hued aura and the warmth that emanated from him told her he was anything but dead. His smile also told her that he'd appreciated her thorough assessment of him and that she'd given herself away.

Still, it was hard not to stare at him or his patrol partner. The guy was stunning; both were, actually. The first one in brown leather owned a wash of silky, milk chocolate tresses that shone like glass over his broad shoulders, and his lush mouth was set so perfectly in the flawless café au lait frame of his face, complete with deep dimples, that he was mesmerizing. A thin darkening shadow of new beard covered his jaw like velvet. Yet for all his Fae beauty, she was a wolf down deep and preferred her males with a bit more rugged attributes. Maybe a cut over the eye, an imperfect nose from a brawl . . . it was sick, but what could she say. The fact that any of this had invaded her mind was disturbing, though.

The first archer's partner leaned forward, his midnight blue irises filled with wonder, and his face no less handsome in its stark contrast to the spill of blue-black hair that draped his black-leather clad shoulders. What he lacked in dimples, he made up for in a regal aquiline nose, cleft in his chin, and dashing smile. Tall, sinewy like ballet dancers, with long graceful hands, they were absolutely breathtaking as a pair.

They lifted a brow at the same time, brought their ales up to their mouths slowly, and then set them down in unison with exact precision. It was like watching a synchronized dance. However, the very serious proposition was in the subtle eyebrow gesture and the way they glanced at each other for a moment before taking a very purposeful sip from their skeins.

Ménage à trois . . . ? *Noooo.* Sasha chuckled quietly and kept walking.

They seemed so disappointed as she tilted her head, bowed slightly, closed her eyes for a beat longer than a normal blink required, and thus declined without a word. But that seemed to be enough to keep the more bashful of the species at bay. It was clear that if she'd said no to the tall, lithe archers, who were positively gorgeous, then the gnomes and other less aesthetically gifted members of the Fae society seemed to take that as a hint that she wasn't about to cross the line. Cool.

But she was also well aware that wouldn't mean jack to any Werewolf males present. Any Shadow Wolf males would be respectful of the so-called mate bond that had been displayed at the UCE Conference, but Werewolves . . . it was all about continual presence and show of force. New awareness of just how precarious this situation had become stoked defiance within her. Screw it. She wanted a beer.

Hulking, biker-disguised males from the Order of the Dragon functioned like that, too—if your enforcer wasn't with you, then that meant you were possibly game for whatever. If they won in a brawl, to the victor went the spoils—as in, the female. The concept was so Neolithic Period it wasn't even funny . . . but then again, that's probably the time from which the Dragons hailed. It made her head hurt.

Thick-bodied male Dragons smiled at her as she shoved past them to get to the bar where she could better scout for her squad. They seemed to take her subtle refusal of the Fae as an open invitation that only meant she didn't do that species . . . and since her big Shadow Wolf was AWOL, hey. She cast them a glare with a low, warning snarl, which they cheerfully accepted as she passed them. Damn, why did it have to be all of this? She was just glad that the Vampires had been so completely offended by the events that took place at the Conference that they gleaned to their own private blood clubs for now. Tonight she wouldn't have the personal wherewithal to remain politically correct if a member of the undead propositioned her.

Sasha ruffled her hair up off her neck in frustration. Where were her guys, and when had entering a bar gotten so complicated? It was bad enough navigating all this bull as a human female, now she had to deal with this supernatural crap, too—all because of a change in rank in relationship to Hunter? Geez!

"Finally by yourself, I see," a deep voice said in a low, sensual growl behind her.

This particular voice didn't make her spin on it with anger; instead it made her stomach do flip-flops.

"Just came in for a cold one and to catch up with my squad before we move out," she said as calmly as possible, straightening her spine and turning slowly to meet the voice that had been behind her.

For a moment, neither of them spoke, but took their time openly assessing each other.

"You look good," Shogun said in a low rumble, not hiding his admiration.

"You do, too," she replied quietly, wishing she'd put more cavalier confidence in her tone. "Thanks for the support back at the UCE Conference. We needed your voting bloc—as well as the show of force . . . also deeply appreciated your willingness to go down swinging with us out in a firefight."

An intense stare met hers. A graceful mouth slowly

lifted into a lopsided smile. Dazzling white upper and lower canines caught the tavern's overhead lights before receding into a perfect human dental line. A ruggedly handsome, copper-hued face slowly grew serious as they said nothing. Serious, almond-shaped eyes appraised the shape of her mouth, and she watched an Adam's apple bounce in a throat that seemed momentarily at a loss for words.

He'd tied his dark hair back into a ponytail, leaving his once-bald impression to war with his new image in her mind. Through his light cotton, collared Polo shirt and jeans, she was well aware that his wolf wanted out. It seemed as though the tension in his body and every sculpted muscle in his toned biceps, abs and chest were trying to hold it back. It was the kind of thing that could literally start a civil war.

"I noticed that you're using the term 'we' and 'us,' but I only see you here tonight. Am I reading too much into things, or is there an opportunity present because you've finally made some hard personal decisions?"

Now it was her turn to swallow hard. Of all the individuals who could have approached her, why would it have to be this one?

"Nothing's changed," she said with false bravado. "I just came in for a beer and to hang out."

"Alone?"

"Yeah," she scoffed. "This is *America*, last I checked. Women are allowed to go to a bar alone for the sole purpose of having a beer."

His smile widened. "True," he said, stepping closer. "In the human world. It's just that, this close to a full moon, when one has openly declared a mate . . . it could send mixed signals in *our* world." He gave a swift nod in the direction of the disappointed Fae archers. "That's why they tried a bedazzling spell."

Sasha blinked twice and refused to comment. The last thing she wanted to seem ignorant of was yet another supernatural cultural fine point. Damn, she should have known that!

"There's a lot your Shadow might not have exposed you to as a permanent mate," Shogun said with a confident chuckle, ignoring how her gaze narrowed on him. "Who knows . . . maybe I could fill in the gaps as a temporary, but regular, lover?"

"Excuse me," she said calmly, beginning to leave. "But thanks for the support."

"Wait . . . I'm sorry," he said, staying her leave with a tentative caress against her forearm. "That was out of order. Blame it on the moon."

She let her breath out hard but kept her tone easy. Although she didn't understand why, she didn't want to hurt his feelings. "Look . . . I know there's been chemistry since that first time we bumped into each other in North Korea . . . but . . ."

"I'm just satisfied that you've finally admitted that," he said quietly, staring at her with an unblinking gaze. "There was chemistry when I saw you fight in the mountains . . . I just wish it would have been with me, rather than him. We fought well together in that Vamp house to free your pack brother. It was like a dance, Sasha. I haven't forgotten it or you."

She looked away for a moment, but was drawn back to his magnetic stare. "To even comment on any of that is way too volatile given the issues at hand," she said in a very private reply. "Now it's gone beyond just a matter of right and wrong—there's détente between huge clans that haven't had peace in eons. Right now, this new alliance and new peace is very fragile . . . the last thing I wanna do is tip the balance. There's a lot to consider, like *mega* Federations on your side and mine, all right?"

He swallowed hard and nodded. "The fact that you've processed all of that . . . have turned it around and around in your mind like a Rubik's Cube, trying to see if there was any way for the colors to line up . . ."

"No. That's not what I was doing," she said, scanning the crowd, now not so much looking for her team as she was monitoring the crowd for signs of Hunter.

"Then why is the hair standing up on your arms and the nape of your neck like you're on guard just from talking about it, much less thinking it? You never even mentioned his name or the fact that the way you felt about him was the primary reason you wouldn't consider—"

"I have to go."

"He's not himself, is he?"

Again she stopped and couldn't move.

"Why would you ask me something like that?" she said in a near whisper, panic making her heart slam against rib bones.

"It's in your eyes," Shogun said in a soft rumble, blocking her retreat with a quick sidestep.

Sasha looked away and stepped around his body, careful not to brush against him as she did so. "I need to catch up with my team. Hunter is fine."